Born Light

Joolz Denby

A complete catalogue record for this book can be
obtained from the British Library on request

The right of Joolz Denby to be identified as the author of this
work has been asserted by her in accordance with the Copyright,
Designs and Patents Act 1988

First published in 2006 by Serpent's Tail,
4 Blackstock Mews, London N4 2BT
website: www.serpentstail.com

Designed and typeset at Neuadd Bwll, Llanwrtyd Wells

Printed by Mackays of Chatham, plc

1 2 3 4 5 6 7 8 9 10

To Justin Sullivan and to my parents, Ron & Cherrie Mumford

Acknowledgements
My sincere personal thanks to the following for their invaluable help and support: John Williams, Michael Davis, Nick Burnett, Nic Sears RN, Mr Stephen Spencer, Dr Christine Alvin, Kate Gordon, Nina Baptiste, Ben Stone, Julia Wallis-Martin, John Connolly, Martyn Waites, Adam Dutton, James Nash; Pete Ayrton, Lisa Gooding and all at Serpent's Tail; all those readers who kept the faith; the Galleon crew and the good people of Polzeath; Spotti-Alexander and Miss Dragon Pearl; and my gratitude & respect, as ever, to the Goddess.

Book 1

To the island-valley of Avilion;
Where falls not hail, or rain, or any snow,
Nor ever wind blows loudly: but it lies
Deep-meadow'd, happy, fair with orchard lawns,
And bowery hollows crowned with summer sea.

—Alfred, Lord Tennyson

Chapter 1

My name is Astra Selene Sharp, I have great teeth and I read a lot. Jesus, I suppose that sounds a bit odd, the teeth bit, but you see it does tend to be what people notice about our family and compliment us on. They don't tend to say much about my reading, unless it's one of those 'Got your nose in a book again, a young girl like you should be out and about, not stuck in here reading' sort of comments. Which I can't help thinking is odd, because to some extent, good teeth are something you're born with but you have to work at reading; it's a skill and I do see it as one of my better attributes, a virtue if you like. Something I'm secretly a bit proud of, as opposed to my habit of eating the family's leftovers after dinner in a mindless, hoovering way, which I'm not. But there you go, either you love reading or you think it's a bit of a waste of time; for me, it's always been the way I escape, my safety valve.

But to return to teeth for a moment. Mostly of course, it's genetics – but we have had the best dental care possible, what with our dad, Roy, being not merely a dentist, but a top-class one, a real star. He's got a nice little one-man practice in Crossford with his nurse Sally and Betty the receptionist and apart from being on call for emergencies, works as much or as little as he likes – only now of course, he works all the hours God sends. He's very, very popular, as only a truly great dentist can be; I mean, look how many people are traumatised for life by childhood dental horrors. People are absolutely addicted to dad – like, there's this one wealthy guy comes down from Bristol specially because he won't have anyone else and…God, I sound like an advert, but you see what I mean. Everyone adores dad, and he's big into no-pain, holistic treatments, and aesthetics, too, none of this English 'cacky, grey, wonky teeth are character-forming' nonsense – which was great for us and for that matter, everyone else he's treated over the years. He's got a couple of slogans about it: *'healthy teeth in a healthy body'* and *'teeth are the most beautiful part of your smile'*. That last part's on his stationery and on the wall of the surgery, or 'studio' as he prefers to call it – along with a big mural of dancing molars done by his arty friend Euan from London. Eu got a holiday, dad got the painting and very nice it is too.

Euan wasn't the only one to be happy we live here, holiday-wise. At first, everyone and his auntie wanted to stay; we're near as dammit on the beach, after all. Nowadays, obviously, hardly anyone comes, just a few old faithfuls, which is still more than when we lived in Bradford. You couldn't get people to come to Bradford for love or money, they just wouldn't; any excuse not to. Sheer prejudice – if they did make it they spent the whole time going, 'I never realised it was so fascinating', as if it were Outer fucking Mongolia or something. But I suppose that sort of thing was another factor in making mum and dad so keen to move here, so they'd see more people, people they'd known when they were young. 'The Tribe,' they'd say, 'it'll be a gathering of the Tribe, like the old days…' It annoyed me then; well, I was only just fourteen and the last thing I'd wanted was to move to Cornwall of all places with a lot of oo-ah carrot-crunchers and then have all mum and dad's funky mates raving on about how totally cool it was in Polwenna, as opposed to grimy old Bradford. I loved Bradford, it was 'home'. I never felt Cornish, really. Back then, you see, I'd just got into bands, live music, the Alternative scene, the last gasps of the Original Goth movement. It was most definitely a city thing, and God knows Polwenna and surrounds isn't what you'd call urban by any stretch of the imagination. So, I hated the pretty, ditzy picturesque countryside and I longed with all my heart and soul for Decayed Ex-Industrial Inner City cool.

I wanted to be a dark, rebellious rock-chick type, you see. Consequently, beach life was *anathema*. I used to lie about on the cliff-top like a dead bat wearing black shades and perusing a copy of something Gothic like Edgar Allan Poe and hoping everyone noticed I didn't care if they noticed me or not. The first chance I had, I was off to Newquay for the bog-standard Celtic armband tattoo and the nose and multiple ear-piercing. Anything that would distinguish me from the sunny-haired *au naturel* surf-chickies. I went in for stuff like wearing long, raggy black clothes and burgundy lipstick called things like 'Vamp' and 'Black Rose', and never taking my headphones off. Metallic bottle-green nail polish on bitten nails. Crimping irons. Purple hair. Not washing my kohl off for a week until I looked like a pimply panda with a hangover. Off-white panstick in high summer. Pointy-footed Goth bootees with concho straps, spurs and kitten heels. *Anything.* The other week, Cookie told me the whole village had thought I was a Satanist. I laughed, of course, but in those days, if His Satanic Maj had offered me the price of a train ticket back home, I'd have sold my soul in a shot and thought I'd got a bargain.

It makes me smile now; but then it was deadly serious and I fought a desperate rearguard action against beach-bummery for a good long while. But in the end, I gave in. I got sick of banging my head against the brick wall of my own teen rebellion. Anyway, the Cornish are an easy-going lot on the whole; I don't think they could be bothered to go on fighting with me – however much I wanted them to.

Polwenna, though; tell the truth, I grew to love it – how could you not? I mean, I don't think I've ever loved it like I love Yorkshire, I mean, Bradford *needs* me to love it, otherwise, who would? But Polwenna, it's a siren; a pearly, green-haired mermaid singing, a windswept, opal and silver-gilt shimmer like a ghost of Avalon. It just catches in your heart – the landscape, the warmth, the soft salt air. It casts a sort of spell on you. I mean, some people come every single year without fail for their holidays, wouldn't go anywhere else despite the unreliable English weather and the cost.

I suppose it's every stressed-out, city-dweller's dream – that smooth, blond beach edged with water-fretted purple and turquoise rocks crusted with mussels, limpets and winkles; deep little tide pools studded with ruby-red sea-anemones, and home to fearless translucent shrimps, armoured, scuttling crabs and tiny darting bronze fish. Around all this treasure the wide embrace of the tumbling lichen-splashed grey cliffs protects the strand like loving arms, their tops draped in a tapestry woven of a million shades of green and patterned with brilliant stitches of wildflowers – mauvey-pink thrift, burning yellow gorse, red campion, magenta, puce or creamy Pride of Padstow, lacy white keggas and swaying purple foxgloves. In the hedgerows, garlands of heavy-scented wild honeysuckle, bindweed with its snowy trumpets and blowsy, promiscuous dog roses tumble into the lanes like discarded bridal bouquets.

And then there's the sea, always changing, always breathing, the sound of the surf with you day and night beating in time with your pulse, the tides rising and falling with the moon, the horizon stretching away to infinity. The sea: blue-green, green-grey, jade, emerald, sapphire, thick with weed or perfectly crystalline; the cruel, killing icy steel and white cascades of winter or happily sparkling in glittering little cubes of light on a sunny summer morning. The sea: Shakespeare's 'wind-obeying deep' – the vast unknowable; beatific, pacific, the Big Blue.

OK, OK, sorry – I get a bit carried away, but you get the picture. Places like this are supposed to have been wiped out by fun parks and amusement arcades and the frantic spit and gobble of modern life. But time moves slower here, like honey dripping off a spoon; heavy, liquid and golden. We have a saying in our family: 'there's real time and there's Polwenna time'. Watch the tourists – the first few days they're bustling about, faces grey and strained, then gradually, they smooth out, slow down and then one day, you can see them stroll down to the café easy and smiling and you know they're in Polwenna time.

Still, I have to say there isn't anything much in the way of 'facilities' in the village that straggles along the beach road – a post office that sells bits and bobs along with the stamps for the tourists' picture postcards, the Spar mini-supermarket and further up the hill the dairy sells ice-creams and mail-order clotted cream. Close to the beach, the Tiki surf shop does wetsuit and board hire along with an eye-popping selection of lurid surfwear, and there's the café across from it. Behind the post office there's the midget Beachside (bit of a porky, that name)

Caravans and Campsite and on the cliff, Mordros, the caravan and campsite belonging to mum and dad's mate Dylan. A couple of pubs and the nice but not too expensive Chy an Mor Hotel and a fair scatter of B&Bs – Lavender Villa, Seaview, Morwenna House, Bide-a-Wee – the usual English seaside full-fried-breakfast-and-out-by-10am-please kind of places.

Up off the Crossford road – Crossford is the nearest actual town to us – out of the village, discreetly tucked well away behind a stand of gnarled old pines, is the extremely posh Hotel Antibes. It's all sauna, swimming pool, Jacuzzi and cocktail lounge; hideously pricey and very pretentious. I've been to a few events there, we all have, but generally, it's pretty much for the boating fraternity or the genuinely wealthy. Contrary to the popular idea of rich, upper-middle-class or aristocratic people jetting off to exotic locales for their hols, many of them adore Cornwall; apparently they think it's somehow more 'authentic' and in better taste to holiday here than to rush off with the nouveau riche to the Maldives or the Seychelles.

Further along the cliff on that side of the bay are what we call the White Houses. They're the enclave of second homes built by folk who came to the Antibes and liked it so much, they bought their own permanent place; I reckon you could buy one of the cheaper, tiny ones without the direct sea view for around half a million or so, if one ever came on the market. They really only get used in summer, and I know for a fact the one with the Scandinavian-style wood trim stands empty for eleven months out of the year – but that's not so unusual with that kind of house. Oh yes, we get all sorts here, from the *crème de la crème* in their White Houses to the bucket and spade brigade in wonky tents on the campsites.

That's more or less it, really; a discreet holiday flats development is tucked away behind the church and more holiday houses – tall, narrow uneven terraced places stacked horizontally like the herringbone slate walls in the fields behind – hug the cliff-tops and meander into the little bungalow-world of New Polwenna on one side and off towards Crossford on the other. Real people – sorry, I mean actual Cornish people who were born and bred here – tend to live in places well away from the beach unless they inherited a house and haven't been tempted to sell for the huge prices now on offer for such desirable properties.

Our house is on the hill behind the beach café. Run down the cut between the high, ragged, spicy-scented escallonia bushes and you're on the sand. Mum and dad were actually trying for a house in Polzeath, but when they rather reluctantly motored over to view this one they forgot everything and took it immediately. It's pretty nice, actually. Well, very nice now, after all the improvements and DIY's finally finished – it was nearly derelict when we moved in; years of neglect due to a family feud over ownership. Now, it's a sprawling, ranch-style split-level bungalow, lots of wood and stone, with a big open-plan front room and a truly stupendous panoramic view of the whole beach and surrounding hills, from the huge slide-across picture windows that open on to the stilt-supported deck. Mum gets quite picky about saying we had a 'deck' in the true Californian style before every DIY freak in the world laid planking on their back garden: it's her little bit of oneupmanship. Apart from all that, it's just homey and untidy and full of the family, cooking smells and more stuff than a global rummage sale.

So there you are. Polwenna in all its fabulousness. Tell the truth, I was slowly sucked into the life. I got over my fear of the sea (too much *Moby Dick* too early), learned how to snorkel without drowning and even surfed sometimes – lying on a belly-board, or 'shark biscuit' as they charmingly call them. None of that standing up on a proper board business, mind you, far too athletic. I'm never out of a sarong and flip-flops in summer. Beaker is Cornish born and bred and he always used to say I'm an adopted Cornish person, and I always went yeah, OK. But I'm not, I'm not Cornish, I'm Yorkshire, Bradford. I just got to live in Polwenna by sheer chance and hippie parents wanting to have the good life. Can't complain, really.

The twins suffered more than me, I think; it sort of dislocated them mentally and they never got right again. They'd just been about to start big school with all their little mates and all the current fads and fashions in bags and trainers sorted out to soothe their anxieties when off we went and they were plunged into a totally weird new place with no friends, no idea of what was cool and everyone telling them how amazingly lucky they were. Not good. Admittedly, they did seem to get sorted much quicker than me, got the accent, lost the urban kid thing pronto, but inside – I don't know. They were neither one thing nor the other, I suppose. They grew up uncomfortable in their skins; Gwen turned out straighter than an ironing board and Lance just became a great big hellion on a motorbike, barely speaking and a stranger to soap. Of course it didn't help that mum had them during her big Arthurian phase, when she drifted round dressed up like Helen Mirren in *Excalibur*, muttering the Charm of Making – *anall nathrach, uthras bethud, dociel dienve,* I've still got it by heart – and being Celtic. When I was born, it was astrology, with the twins, it was being Celtic – Lancelot Merlin and Guinevere Morgaine. Lance and Gwen. They won't thank you for reminding them of their true names, believe me. By the time Git came along, it was Eastern mysticism, hence Gita Devi. But she'll always be Git to us, and everyone else, poor little bugger. She's the real Cornish Sharp, born and bred. Never been home, and doesn't want to – well, Polwenna *is* home to her. She thinks Northerners are all grim and grey and *Bradford*, God – like *Coronation Street* on steroids or something.

Well, there you are, that's life, just the way it goes, eh? It divided us kids right down the middle, the move. Me to the north, Git to the south and the twins right down the middle of their poor little heads.

Chapter 2

I did go home, as it goes. I went to Bradford to do university; it seemed the natural thing. I'd done well at school and everything else was going fine. Dad was getting more and more successful, mum seemed blissfully happy, the twins were – well, they weren't doing anything noticeable. Git was the cutest baby you ever saw, all spicy auburn curls and clotted cream skin dusted with a spray of freckles over her little nose. Just chubby and healthy and into everything; sandcastles, shells and seaweed necklaces – how did Sylvia Plath describe it? Little hands like starfish? That was Git, a real beach babe and like a mer-child in the water, no stopping her. Everyone adored her when she was little, even Lance who used to sit her on his old red Ducati and go 'Brum, brum – 'ere, look Aa-straa, Hell's Kiddies…' Sweet.

So off I went, to do modular humanities, a liberal arts course, at the Ridings University. English, sociology, philosophy and psychology, all mixed up together. I enjoyed it, I really did, especially the lit bit. I lodged with Auntie Patsie and Uncle Kev, mum's sister and her husband, who were dead easy-going, kind and had plenty of room on account of not having any kids. Everything was hunky-dory, not a cloud in the sky – metaphorically, that is, it being Bradford after all. I took to town again like I'd never been away; oh sure, I missed the sea and the countryside, but I just felt like Bradford was roots, was more real to me than the seductive lure of Polwenna. My life was sorted, I had it all planned; in the second year I'd move in with a couple of other lasses off the course and you know, live it up a bit more. Then after I got my degree, travel the world for a while, get a career, marriage maybe, kids definitely. Now, it makes me smile at how naïve I was; but then, it's not a crime at that age, is it? It's the way it's supposed to be.

Anyhow, that's how I met Con – Connie Starbuck. I got a job working in her café. She'd just bought the arty-trendy place, Cha-Cha's, up near the uni and had done it up during the summer before I arrived. She'd turned it into something a bit cool and classy: stripped wood floors, cast-iron spiral staircase, big leather sofas, bookcases full of real books, excellent coffee and food. Before, according to Auntie Patsie, it had been all wonky, splatter-painted tables, day-glo fake fur-framed mirrors and that truly awful, mud-coloured crap veggie food made by people who don't like eating. It never smelled quite clean, she said, either; just a hint of old washcloth and a whiff of garbage in warm weather.

Con turned it round, made it pay, made it where everyone wanted to go. She did jazz and chill evenings, poetry readings, art exhibitions; she worked her skinny butt off. God, no one worked like Con, she was a train, no joke; she made us want to work, too, like we were all in it together, a team. Although she was quite a lot older than me, we got on straight away, and became friends. I'd always got on better with people older than myself; mum says I'm an old soul. Con and I talked for hours about books and films, and just stuff in general. It was one of those friendships where you can talk or say nothing, it doesn't matter; and if you don't see each other for a while, years even, you just seem to pick up where you left off without a hitch. Like, with some folk you always struggle slightly to get on; as Edith Wharton said, their minds are all elbows. Con's mind was like a smooth, fast-flowing river, cool and straight, very honest. I always felt we had no secrets, I could tell her anything safely: she was very loyal, like that. One thing did tickle her though, she thought it was a hoot I was up from Polwenna – she'd been going there since she was a kid and loved it. She used to take fits laughing when I told her about how I used to drift around like the Black Widow; she used to swear she'd seen me, but I don't know, she was always joking in her dry, sideways Bradford way. Still, it was a something we shared, Polwenna, it knitted us together.

She wanted to move there, eventually, you see. It was her ambition. She used to say she didn't want to live her whole life in one place, never be anywhere else. She wanted to live by the sea. It was the only time her big, rather prominent navy-blue eyes got dreamy and distant; it was her romance, her soft spot. A lot of people said Con looked hard, a real businesswoman, and I suppose she could come across like that. In the wrong light, she could look a bit angular in the face and her figure – well, a bit of a plank, to be honest. But there you are, she looked great in suits and boy's jeans, like a western cowgirl, I used to think. Her eyes seemed to see further than anyone else's, too. Like someone born on the prairie instead of up Allerton.

Anyway, she had this dream of buying the old Bluebird Café on the beach and doing it up and living in the flat upstairs. She said she wanted to walk barefoot on the sands in the early morning sea-fret and hear the gulls calling and the surf whispering before getting down to the business of the day. Not like Bradford, where fond as we were of it, you got up in the icy pitch dark and listened to the traffic roaring and the pigeons coughing their guts up. I think it gave her hope when I'd tell her old man Trevisa was always going on about selling the Bluebird and moving out to Australia to live with his daughter. And I think she thought if mum and dad had done it – well, she could too. It was only her fiancé, Dave, who wasn't up for it, but then, he wasn't up for anything much, in my opinion. It was all football, incipient beer-belly and his job at the insurance office with him; I didn't know how Con stuck it. She said they'd talked seriously about getting engaged, going so far as to look at rings in shop windows, but I couldn't hear even a tiny tinkle of wedding bells. They just trotted along in a big old rut, as far as I was concerned. At eighteen, I thought Con was crackers – she wasn't bad-looking, for an older chick, she had style, she was full of life. She should just dump boring old Dave and go for it. Things like habit, and security, and better-the-devil-you-know had no meaning for me then.

So that was me at uni, free as a bird and loving it. I had Con and my job at the Big Bean, I had a great social life, lots of fellas and loads of mates and my studies were easy enough; it should have all been fantastic. It *was* fantastic.

Then mum was diagnosed with multiple sclerosis and the world turned pear-shaped.

Chapter 3

Mum had always been frail, I suppose. She was one of those too-thin people who live on their nerves. She looked like she was being blown about in a stiff breeze, her crinkly, sandy hair hennaed to a metallic auburn, floating in unmanageable wisps around her long, pale face with its faintly unfinished-looking features. I used to think her face looked like it had been pinched out of Play-Doh, not in a nasty way, but that's what it reminded me of. Her shapeless ethnic print cotton frocks hung on her like old curtains and her poor old lumpy hippie's feet were always stuffed into multi-coloured socks she knitted herself and hideous handmade shoes or sandals like leather pasties one of the Tribe had conned her into buying. Her nose-end was always pink and her soft grey eyes always a bit watery.

Mum, yeah – her favourite perfume was something brown and glutinous in a tiny bottle with a picture of Shiva on it called 'Astral Love'. It reeked of ylang-ylang and cheap sandalwood, but I can never smell it without being catapulted back to childhood. It was mum, like the undrinkable herb teas and shelves full of small-press books with titles like *Free The Inner Child*, *The Celtic Woman's Wisdom Resource* and *Beyond God*. Mum, who although wired to the moon in many ways, was always fiercely determined we should have the best life she could wrestle from an unyielding straight, corporate world for us. It was organic, soya milk, home-made muesli like grated bricks and her own brand of myopic, passionate love that almost shook her insubstantial body as she fought to keep us from the clutches of MacDonald's, food additives and the road to Hell.

But healthy, no. Mum was never healthy despite the whole-earth thing. If there was a cold going round, mum got it; if there was a virus she had it for twice as long as anyone else. I know dad was always clucking round after her, his huge hands, so deft and gentle when it came to sick wives, little kids or dentistry, wrapping her in her favourite mulberry-coloured shawl and stroking her bright, unnatural hair. He's a great big, brown bear of a man, is dad; really huge. He always has his thick, curly black hair in a pony-tail and his beard trimmed neatly to satisfy the dreaded dental inspector, but body-hair sprouts from his cuffs and the neck of his whites as if he was wearing black mohair coms. We always joke that if you go into the shower after dad, you'll find the soap's turned into a hedgehog. Lance and I have got his colouring, his sherry-coloured eyes and that black hair that comes from his Andalucian grandmother. He's a gentle giant, like so many guys his size, with that rather cumbrous good humour they adopt so you won't find them threatening. He and mum were like two adolescent sweethearts, always holding hands and saying 'miss you already' if one of them left the room for more than two minutes. We all used to go 'yuk' and make sick noises, but we loved it really; it was so different from the niggly, sniping atmospheres at so many of our friends' houses, everyone trying to get used to their new mum or new dad or struggling along with just one parent.

But dad fretted about mum. When they met, mum was an arts-and-crafts teacher and dad worried then that she was doing too much, cared too much about the hopeless, snot-glazed inner-city kids who ate the orange crayons and drank the black paint in the bog-stinky run-down schools where she worked for sod all. Dad said in the early days of their relationship, when they lived in an unheated stone-built flat for a fiver a week, his heart used to break watching mum struggling home in the icy winter evenings toting a vast unmanageable portfolio, a six-foot stripy scarf wrapped round her thin neck and the wind whistling past her beige crochet tights and homemade green corduroy mini-suit. So after she had me, she packed in work. Then when I was toddling, she tried going back part-time. But it was no use, she'd sort of missed the boat, work-wise. After the twins arrived, she gave up. Just filled the house with arty projects, half-finished collages, unravelling macramé, wonky découpaged boxes filled with bead bracelets and earrings in bizarre colour combos and the odd drawing of a sleepy child – the only way she could get us to pose for her.

She'd always wanted to be a professional illustrator but as she herself readily admitted, she really wasn't good enough. Oh, it's nice having your friends and family ooh and aah over a pretty pencil sketch, but mum wasn't wholly daft. She knew the difference between good and excellent. Still, if you wanted to please her, you just had to get her yet another art book full of pictures – then she'd sit for hours dreaming over Degas or Arthur Rackham or Caravaggio, whoever. And if she heard 'Vincent' by Don McLean – blimey, break out the hankies, *floods* of tears.

But dad never lost the habit of worrying about mum. If anything, his concern increased with the years. After we moved to Polwenna, I used to catch him frowning, his big paw wrapped round his hairy jaw as he watched her sleeping on the sofa, dead beat for no real reason, her breath snuffling and her narrow hands with their wavering, pointy-ended fingers twitching slightly as she dreamed. He used to struggle to get us his one and only tea – organic beans on brown toast followed by carob bars all round. Bletch. I used to see him rein in his irritation with Lance so as not to upset mum, as Lance slormed about the house refusing to wash, or help or do anything except bait dad by letting his teeth go green and trailing motor oil everywhere like a big biker slug. It drove Gwen nuts; she did nothing but rag on Lance about how 'awful' he was and how ashamed of him she was. That didn't help, believe me. Dad tried everything with Lance, his only son and his physical mirror image, but it was no use. Lance, monosyllabic, resentful and hostile, just stuck his square jaw out and glowered at dad's attempts to get him to do the washing-up so as to spare mum a job. It was like two lions, the old and the young, circling each other, both too wary and unsure of victory to really start a proper fight, thank God.

But though we realised mum wasn't right, not he nor any of us imagined just how ill she was getting.

It was a locum doctor who figured it out. Our own doctor, Doctor

Lanyon, had mum down as a neurotic hypochondriac for months and months. Just another hippie crank into brown rice and acupuncture. He'd try to give her tranquillisers or a 'tonic' and send her away. I think she sometimes wondered if she was going mental, imagining it all. It sapped her confidence. Still, give him his due, he apologised after the tests came back, but the result of his former attitude was to drive mum into the arms of alternative therapies like a sinner in search of redemption. No theory too bonkers, no treatment too mad. Didn't matter. Conventional medicine had let her down as she saw it, and in a way, I think she almost blamed the doctors for her condition, as if they'd given it to her in some way, as if they'd let something and nothing turn serious by not believing her fears and worries. We could barely get her to swallow her tablets some days, she was so set against them, and of course, any emotional upset made her worse if she was having a flare-up. Drove dad crackers; he was burnt up with worry as you can imagine, but he'd sit with her and hold her hand and gentle her down – 'There, there, my little flower,' he'd go, 'There, there – just take this lot and tomorrow we'll see...' And grumbling she'd swallow the pills, her hands shaking so much he'd have to hold the cup to her lips while Git clung to her and cried as if her little heart was breaking.

Then, of course, it was me doing the meds, and on her bad days, changing her linen and washing her and feeding the family and – and – everything. It was me and all thoughts of travelling and clubbing it till dawn and being a career girl, gone. University over. My life turned upside down in one summer.

I mean, when we found out, naturally, I'd been devastated. I'd only just finished my first year and had gone back down south for the summer and my old job at the Chy an Mor Hotel, chambermaiding. I was looking forward to it: the Chy was a good place, with a fun crowd working it. It promised to be a hot season, the sky was a round bowl of brilliant blue and nearly every day the wind blew right for some cracking surf. You could feel the bright, buzzing air right down in your lungs and I fairly ran up the path to work, butterflies skittering on the wind as I disturbed them from the bramble and gorse flowers. From the cliff-top, the view was pure picture-postcard. I used to breathe deep and drink it in, then feel slightly guilty about Bradford and try and remember how nice the town hall was. Poor old Bradford.

Two weeks into the vacations, we got the news. Mum had been very poorly, trembling with fatigue, complaining of being dizzy and having terrible pins and needles then numbness in her right arm – but we though she'd just slept on it awkwardly, like you do sometimes. She was always taking her specs off, too, and wiping them as if they were dirty, then saying she must need a new prescription, these were giving her a pounding headache. Of course, I helped as best I could, but although I was worried like dad, I thought it was a virus or something and probably her eyes did need testing properly. Even when we found out, I still didn't realise what it meant. I didn't know what MS was; I thought, you know, some pills and she'll be right as rain. I didn't know it was a life sentence, until the doc at the hospital explained it. She said mum didn't have the worst sort of the disease, either, and we should be grateful for that at least. I can't say as I felt that bloody grateful at the time – now I am, when I see the bad cases. I hardly took it in when she went on about mum relapsing and remitting, how for long periods she'd be practically normal then bingo. And each relapse would do more damage to her nervous system, more permanent damage until…But hey, loads of research going on, loads of new treatments – only, sadly we weren't lucky enough to live in a health authority that let their docs prescribe the MS wonder drug beta interferon. Apparently, the cost of it was too prohibitive in the UK. If we'd lived in America now, they handed it out like sweeties; the doc went on and on, but I could hardly hear her.

I know I felt like a brick had hit me between the eyes, and Gwen – she just got up and walked out. Just left without a word and got the bus home alone. Lance wasn't there, of course, but I told him later. He didn't say much, just kept on polishing his bike. You'd have had to strain quite hard to hear him chanting 'Fuck no, fuck no, fuck no, fuck, fuck' under his breath, like a mantra.

I remember the day in late August when it finally came to me that nothing would ever be the same again. I'd been up at five, because mum had wet herself in the night and was desperate with shame and humiliation, weeping like a child. I'd changed the bed, while dad comforted her and then loaded the washer, his face grey and strained. I hardly caught my breath when it was time to do breakfast and dress Git, who roared and held her arms and legs out stiff so I had to wrestle her into her shorts and T-shirt. Then I had to reassure and say goodbye to dad, who hadn't wanted to go to work, wash up, clean the house, get mum settled on the sofa which dad had pushed up by the picture window so she could look out at the view of the beach and the sea because she couldn't read or watch TV. Even listening to the radio gave her a headache on her bad days. Then I ran down to the shop with Git stumbling along on her chubby little legs, crying because she was so unsettled, got the dinner things and ran back up, only pausing when I got nabbed by the world's biggest gossip, Mrs Liddicoate, and her insane yappy terrier. I only managed to get away after rushing out that mum was doing better, thank you, sorry, sorry, got to dash, bye.

Then I realised I was going to do it all again tomorrow. I mean, I realised that not just intellectually, more like it stuck its claws into my heart, squeezing and ripping. It would be the same tomorrow and so would the day after. And the day after that. Because there was no one else to do it; there just wasn't. I sat on the deck while mum and Git had a siesta and stared at the melting horizon, sea and sky merging in a wash of tender blue. Out there was the world, all I'd dreamed of, all I'd wanted. I could just run away, I could, people did it all the time; you read about it in *The Big Issue*, in the papers. I could just leave, because it wasn't fair, it just wasn't bloody fair.

But I knew I couldn't. Something stubborn in my heart wouldn't let me because much as I wanted to run, frightened as I was – and I was, believe me – I knew it was wrong. I knew the difference between right and wrong and if I legged it, I'd never be able to live with myself, so the freedom I'd given everything up for would be a waste of time. The bad thing I'd done would eat me up like the disease was eating mum; only she couldn't help it, and I could. And I felt a sheet of white calm fall through my aching heart; it was a done deal. *It was just how it was.*

OK, well – I felt my mind ticking over, trying to work things out.

Dad must carry on working, no matter how he might feel; we'd need all the money we could get. I could manage Git and mum, I'd talk to Lance, he listened to me, I'd make him help a bit more with stuff: he could look after the garden, do decorating if we had to have any done, stuff like that. Dad would have to buy a dishwashing machine, that was all. And a new washing machine and – oh God. Jesus. No, no panicking. We were a family, we'd stick together.

I felt myself pulling the broken strands of my life back together, knotting them up in my heart. It'd be all right, we'd manage. Gwen would help me, of course she would. As soon as she got over the initial shock, she'd cope like the rest of us. I mean it might even bring me and Gwen closer together, things like this do that sometimes.

I was so young, so young. I believed I could do anything if I just set my mind to it. I always had in the past; it had always worked before. I was the reliable one, everyone said so, always had been. The calm, strong one. I never made a fuss, just got my head down and got on with things. It would be OK. I'd make it all all right.

Jeez, I was so *young*.

Chapter 4

It's a hard thing to say you hate your own sister; it leaves a nasty, ashy taste in your mouth. I know some people never get on with their sisters, I mean, it's not obligatory to like someone just because you're related. Then again, other people adore their sisters, are incredibly close – Con, for example. Absolutely worshipped her younger sister Angela, or Angel as they call her. Always showing you photos of her as a kiddie and filling you in on her latest doings. Beaker gets on a treat with his sisters. Me, I can't say as I'd ever been extra close to Gwen; I mean, she was four years younger than me and you'd be surprised what a difference that makes with girls. But still, she was my sis. The one that took after mum, in her looks, but not, as it turned out, in her heart.

At first, when we found out about mum, I was too busy to notice Gwen wasn't having any of it. When I did, I tried to get her involved, tried to get her to help me, but she just turned her sealed-up face away like in the hospital, and just left if I 'nagged' her. She was like a skinny white robot, just studying and staying with Kathy, her best friend. I thought it would wear off, this rejection of the situation, but four years went past and it just got worse. She wouldn't even babysit Git, and hardly even touched her, which I found really difficult to cope with – after all, Gwen might in some weird way blame mum, but Git was just a child, it wasn't her fault. But Gwen didn't seem to care; she was as cold to me, Git and Lance as she was to mum and dad.

She had always been quiet and rather self-contained, kept herself to herself, even as a child. In fact, she was always a bit prissy, but I put that down to having Lance as a twin. Talk about non-identical. He was a big, disgusting animal as far as Gwen was concerned, and she wouldn't even talk to him most of the time. Just did that 'Dad/Astra please ask Lance to remove his horrible socks from the bathroom, the smell – it's not exactly hygienic…' business. Lance just laughed and walked away, but you could see she hurt him, loath though he would be to admit it. Gwen just couldn't stand the thought she was related to Lance, to an ignorant dirty biker, as she put it. It put cogs on her that they'd shared the womb, I suppose. In fact, I think things like wombs put cogs on her, generally; she wasn't what you might call physical. To be honest, I was too busy to give her much thought and if I did, I suppose I just imagined it was a phase she was going through, and she'd lighten up when she got a bit older, started dating, that sort of thing. It was my fault she did what she did, in a way. I was responsible and I let her drift. But I really did think she'd see the light eventually, and if not embrace the family again, at least come to terms with what we'd had to become.

Instead she joined the Young Christian Good News Fellowship. Then she told us that mum was ill because we were all Godless sinners who had brought this upon ourselves – that mum had brought it on herself because of her lax, immoral life.

Oh, my parents aren't married, by the way. It was that she meant. We were all damned in the eyes of the church and God and she thought it her duty as a born-again Christian to tell us.

She was nineteen years old when she dropped this bombshell. I was twenty-three and I'd been mum's and the family's carer for four fucking full-tilt years and during that time, remember, she'd done nothing to help me. She'd just shut herself off from it all. I'd seen her tut and leave the room if mum cried or if nystagmus made her eye go wobbling off orbit, like it did. Once I saw her cross the road and run into the shop to avoid mum as she wobbled along the front for an airing on her sticks. She told people (Mrs Liddicoate) that there was nothing wrong with mum, she just wanted attention. Mrs L told everyone and at least four of them commiserated with me afterwards for dealing with mum's 'mental problems' so bravely and 'Ooh, ain't the liddle 'un a darlin' look at 'er precious curls, ohh, poor liddle thing, it's a shame…' I wanted to shake Gwen so hard after that one, believe me, but when I confronted her she didn't do anything, didn't apologise, just stared at me as I fumed then calmly walked out. Again.

I suppose I'd just assumed – in fact I think we'd all assumed – that given time, she'd come round. But instead, she was Born Again. Jesus came into her life and instructed her, apparently, to pray for us, which she was going to do, and also, He thought it would be better if mum and dad got married properly after having confessed their transgressions at meeting. Then everything would be all right.

Jesus, I thought, was going it some for a dead guy, and anyway, with His family, He had room to talk.

It was so crap, I wanted to laugh, you know what I mean? I'll never forget it, never forget the freckles standing out like paint splatter on her peaked, blind face as she perched on the edge of the easy chair, her hands squirming in her lap, her sandy hair – mum's hair – scraped back into a twist, her cheap, yellow 'Stand Up For Jesus' T-shirt so big it made her white arms look like bones sticking out of its flappy sleeves while she told me I was a Godless heathen but I could be saved, if I just made the effort.

I remember looking at dad, speechless. Mum started crying, slowly, painfully, and asking Gwen what she meant; did she really think she'd brought this horrible disease on herself, that it wasn't real? Dad got up stiffly and put his arms round her while Gwen just *nodded*. Dad looked gutted. He opened his mouth as if he were going to speak, but no words came out. He just shook his head and his expression was terrible to see. They'd brought us up like the good liberals they were, never trying to impose their beliefs on us, never hitting or humiliating us like some parents, always allowing and encouraging us to find our own way. And now Gwen had. She'd found the way to express her rage and resentment through a religion that would let her feel she'd found the high moral ground then built a bloody castle on it. I mean, Gwen – quiet, namby-pamby Gwen, the last person on earth you'd imagine turning into Torquemada. Or yeah, maybe not. Maybe the worm just turned. I could hardly look at her while mum sobbed and asked dad to take her into the bedroom to lie down.

As soon as they'd left, I rounded on Gwen, my face burning. I'm not a shouty person normally, that's just not me. Don't get me wrong, I get angry all right, but usually I – I sort of put it away. But I tell you, I've never felt so furious, never felt so absolutely incandescent as when my own sister sat there with that smug, self-righteous expression on her pallid little mug.

As usual when I'm furious, I could hardly get the words out. 'What – what the fuck are you on about, you silly bitch? Look what you've done – you know anything upsetting makes her worse, what d'you think you're...'

'I don't see swearing is going to help; profane language is the refuge of the Godless, Astra. You've got to get your mind right – mother isn't really ill, it's her poisoned spirit and her...'

'Oh, *bollocks*. Who's been filling your head with this crap, eh? Who? Who told you to come and upset mum this way, just when she was getting a bit better...'

'Jesus told me to tell the truth. I discussed my feelings with Pastor Elms and he...'

'Pastor Elms? Pastor fucking Elms? Who the fuck does *that* wanker think he is? The fucking Pope?'

'Pastor Elms cares very deeply about me – about all his community. I told him I felt you were pressuring me to get too involved with what I thought was an unhealthy situation. I have my own life, my own... I'm just not going to give in to our mother like you have, I'm not. It's all made up, she could be well if she wanted to, if she confessed her sins, just repeated the sinner's prayer and dedicated herself to Lord Jesus. She could get married and Our Saviour would forgive her transgressions, if she just...'

I felt my anger shrivel into a tiny, hard nugget, felt it fold itself away deep inside me. Like I said, that's what always happened; I made it go away. It was a habit, I suppose. I just didn't like being cross, there was no point to it usually; it just made things crappier and shoutier, not better. Even now, I couldn't really keep up the shouting, if you see what I mean. Anyway, I suddenly knew there was no arguing with her. There just wasn't. None whatever; you could see it in her watery oyster eyes. She'd found her safe haven and nothing was going to coax, threaten or cajole her out of it. I sighed, and pushed my hair off my hot forehead. Then I stared at her pointedly. At least she looked away.

'Are you going to go on living here, Gwen?' My voice sounded very steady and in a way, I think that got through to her better than if I'd kept on yelling at her. Yelling was what she wanted. Martyrdom. She was gagging for persecution, but I wasn't going to give her the satisfaction, this time. I could still hear mum crying and dad's murmuring voice – how could Gwen have – oh, no use going on. She had, and that was that. Thank God Git was at her little friend Marnie's for tea and Lance was out as usual. Lance – God! Wait until Lance heard this.

She looked up, surprised. Gotcha, I thought ungenerously.

'Living here?' she said, puzzled. 'Of course, I can't afford – I couldn't, you know I couldn't...'

Yes, I knew she couldn't afford to move out. I couldn't, Lance couldn't, even though he spent most of his time at his girlfriend Poppy's council flat in Bodmin, where she lived with her two-year-old son and probably at least three stripped bikes of dubious origin belonging to the Bodmin Beasts MC, if our garage was anything to go by. None of us could afford to rent or buy a place round here; the prices were like London – worse even. The high-income second-home and holiday-house owners saw to that. People like we'd been, prepared to pay the massive mortgage for our place in Shangri-La. Now us kids couldn't leave the nest. Of course Gwen would be staying. I smiled grimly.

'Well, if you're going to stay, Guinevere, there'll have to be some rules. Oh, you needn't look like that, I don't care what you think. Right, I know you're not going to help me with mum and Git – but from now on, you look after yourself, do you hear me? Watch my lips, Gwen – you cook for yourself, you wash for yourself, you clean your room and you do what housework I say you do. Yes, I'll make a rota, it'll be fair – but the most important thing of all is, you will keep your stupid God-bothering to yourself. Don't – don't say any more, please. You've done enough for one night. I know you won't apologise to mum and dad, but the least you can do is get out – go to Kathy's, you'll just make the last bus if you hurry.'

'Don't call me…You can't order me about, you're not my mo…'

'No, I'm not, that means I don't have to put up with your crap. Look, I know it's hard, what's happened with mum and everything…' She opened her mouth but I put my hand up. 'It's hard on all of us, but you haven't exactly helped, have you? I thought your lot were supposed to be kind and merciful and all that – well, I know mum will forgive you, that's her way – but not me, Gwen, not me. Not for a long time. So get your stuff and do us all a favour – go and stay with Kath. You can tell her your hard luck story, I just don't care.'

'I'll pray for you, Astra…' she said, hurriedly picking up her bag.

'You do that, missie.' I turned away, and heard the front door slam as she ran out for the bus.

I was trembling all over, my legs quivering. I sat on the sofa that had been turned to look out of the window and stared at the towering winter clouds piled in dark roiling masses of grey over the slatey sea that was ruffled with creamy breakers. Stupid, stupid – how could my own flesh and blood be so stupid? Pastor Elms; I knew him, the smarmy bastard, with his big fake smile and his dead, shark's eyes. I had heard about his precious 'community' of sappy, devoted fools who thought he could do no wrong, his summer tent revivals on Howlek Campsite out by Padstow and all that bullshit about if you pray hard enough your fillings will miraculously all turn to gold as if God was some kind of crazed cosmic dentist. The childishness of it, the downright silliness of grown people slavering and howling 'in tongues', having holy-roller orgasms and calling it religion. And now my own sister tormenting her sick mother in the name of a Christ I'd always thought was supposed to be gentle, loving and forgiving.

I sat on the sofa as the rain started to lash the window, the view obscured by the glittering drops on the glass, and for the first time since it happened, I wept. I cried like Git for her lost teddy: snottily, hackingly and quietly, so no one would hear. Then I wiped my swollen face, made myself a cup of tea, and crawled off into my room to sleep; after all, tomorrow was going to be another long, long day.

Chapter 5

Mum's illness was characterised, as the doc had said, by long periods of remission, and longer stretches of not-too-badness and occasional violent flare-ups. It wasn't a quick killer, this thing, it just simmered in her central nervous system and very slowly devoured her alive. They told us she could live for thirty years, more if new drugs were discovered, new treatments invented. What this meant to us was that we settled down into a routine; after the first dreadful years, we just got used to it, though some people think that's a terrible thing to say.

Mum dealt with it by being reiki'd, shiatsu'd, reflexologied, aroma-therapied, 'healed' with crystals, moxy-bustioned, hot-stone-massaged, acupunctured (that one did help a bit, to be fair), Hopi ear-candled and God knows what all else. At one point she was drinking her own urine, but fortunately, that didn't last. She spent as much money as she could on therapies, she was High Tor Healing Centre's best – or most gullible – customer. At home, she was vegan and for one heady period, fruitarian. All our water was filtered and if dad hadn't done it years ago, she'd have had him replace her amalgam fillings with white ones in case it was mercury poisoning. Even her soap and shampoo stuff was certified sodium laureth sulphate free, and her vest and pants combos, bedlinen and towels came from the Organic Cotton Clothing catalogue in shades of natural beige. Everything had to be washed, cleaned, spritzed or wiped in Ecover organic cleaning things which we got in bulk from another catalogue along with recycled loo roll and unbleached cotton tampons. No evil Tampax or wicked Daz whites for us, believe me.

Personally, apart from the acupuncture and the massage, I thought it was a big waste of money, but it made her happy, it made her feel like she was trying to fight MS herself. She said it made her feel like a modern day Celtic warrior-woman battling an evil demon. Oh, mum – still, different strokes, after all. It just meant dad worked all hours to foot the bills because being ecological costs a packet, so I ended up getting part-time jobs in the season to help out, or at least, make sure I wasn't a burden.

That's not as altruistic as it might sound, really. I hadn't meant to, hadn't given the idea a second thought; I had so much to do bringing up Git, caring for mum and the family. For years, all I did was that; barely even managed to read a short story, never mind a novel. I gave up all hopes of attempting Henry James – not that I'm alone in that, truth be told. I did everything for Git; apart from mum, she was the centre of my exhausted, scurrying world. I mean, obviously there aren't proper words to say how much I love my family, especially Git, and OK, I'd planned on having kids myself one day – but that was the operative phrase, *one day*. Now, for all intents and purposes, I was my little sister's mother and secretly, naggingly, it scared me silly. What if I totally fucked her up? What if I was doing everything so wrong that it ruined her life, but I didn't realise? I'd started hovering over her, analysing her every squeak and burble, worrying myself sick if she looked even a tiny bit out of sorts. Let's face it, I started suffocating the poor mite, but I couldn't help it. One night, she ran a bit of a fever, nothing really, just a childhood thing, but you'd have thought the world was coming to an end the way I went on. I wanted to take her to Casualty, I was sure it was meningitis at the least, I paced up and down the living room like a caged tiger, snapping at everyone, until mum stumbled off to bed and dad brought a pot of tea in and put it on the low, carved Afghani table in front of the sofa.

'Sit down here, honey,' he said, settling down amongst the mirror-work cushions one of the Tribe had brought us from Nepal. I kept pacing and he picked up mum's pretty millefleur pattern dope pipe from the table, where it lay with her baggie of grass and her silver and turquoise Navajo-style lighter. I have to say mum smoked a bit, she and dad always had, it was a hippie culture thing with them. Also, it was one of the things that actually did seem to help mum's MS. She always waited until Git had gone to bed, though, and tried to be as discreet as possible – not that her discretion cut any ice with Gwen; as far as she was concerned mum and dad were 'drug fiends'. I lived in secret dread she'd inform the police about it in a fit of righteousness, but so far, she'd contented herself with snidey comments and an expression of sour disgust on her face when she smelled it.

Dad turned the little pipe over and over in his big hands. He didn't use a pipe normally, preferring his weed in a skinny spliff, but he packed the pipe and lit it, the aromatic fumes filling the air as he puffed.

After a moment, he repeated 'Come and sit down a moment, hon.'

'What? I can't dad – God, how can you be so calm, I mean, what if…'

'What if what, kitten? Sit down now, I want to talk to you.' The smoke twirled in a fine wreath round towards the big window, and outside, the sun was falling slowly into the gleaming mercury sea. He patted the sofa again.

I perched, unwillingly, twisting the silver wave-pattern ring Beaker had bought me round and round my finger, like I was trying to unscrew it at the joint.

Dad sat back and looked at me, his broad, Henry the Eighth-type face set and concerned. His soft brown eyes – so unlike the real Henry's glittering slits of selfishness – troubled.

'Astra, your mum and I are really up with what you're doing for the family, you know that, don't you? We know it's no fun for you, and we both feel very unhappy about your university course – no, we do, we do. And, we're hanging in there, as a family, because of you. You're a tower of strength, we're very proud of you. Now I could lay some trip on you about gratitude and all that, but I don't think I need to, because you know how we feel already. But I will say, and don't get this wrong, your mum and I think it's time you loosened up a little, cut yourself a bit of slack. Had some you-time. Your mum – both of us are worried you're getting seriously freaked, especially with Gita.

You're young, honey, we can manage if you want to – well, put a little distance. We understand, your mum understands. We can't change fate, but we can flow with it, can't we? Gita will be fine, but we want you to be fine, too. Yeah?'

He tugged at his pony-tail and gazed at me seriously, then sat back against the balding claret chenille throw and laced his big paws over his belly. Have some *you-time* – who spoke like that anymore? Well, dad and mum, for starters. Unaccountably, I found it very funny. You-time – I felt giggles bubbling in my breath and I pressed my lips together, but it was no use. I was hysterical, between tears and laughter. Laughter won.

'Oh, dad – *you-time*, honestly…'

'OK, laughing is good, that's cool. You-time is good too, hon.'

By this time, I was rolling about helplessly, tears streaming from my eyes. Dad nodded calmly, puffing on the tiny pipe like a huge dope-smoking Buddha.

'Yeah, laugh it out, that's good medicine, the best in fact.'

'Ah, God – no, you're the best medicine, dad; God, you really are. OK, you-time it is.'

He was right, I knew it, but it wasn't easy. I started by dragging Beaker away from his keyboards and computer to go to the pictures in Crossford, having day trips to Newquay for no particular reason, that sort of stuff. Not every night or anything, just every now and again, when I needed, um, you-time. Me-time. I even started an Open University course at one point, but I didn't keep it up, I couldn't work the video. And of course, I read. Everything I could get my hands on. I exhausted the mobile library in a matter of weeks – there were some Barbara Cartlands left I hadn't tried, but you can only sink so low, frankly. I even read all dad's stash of *Fabulous Furry Freak Brothers* comics and his tattered collection of fifties and sixties detective stories with names like *Beware The Curves* and either a picture of a Mansfieldesque blonde in fishnets, or a square-jawed geezer in a trench-and-trilby combo on the front. In a way, it didn't matter what I read, as long as it put me in another place; it was my drug, my narcotic.

Some afternoons, if it was nice and I was able to, I'd take a book and just sit on the beach or the cliff and read. But more often than not, my eyes would slip over the text as if the pages were glass, because I'd start watching the surfers. No, I'm lying – oh, it's so stupid, it's so – OK, the fact of the matter is, I'd sit there, book in hand like a picture of innocence, and I'd watch Luke.

Luke. God, what to say about Luke? I suppose, officially, he was one of what we called the Yahs. 'Oh yah, Tobes, do pick up a nice Chardonnay; um, yah, I know, pukemaking, India.' Yahs. And Baby-Yahs. Rich kids, rich parents, London and the home counties. Their families had those holiday houses on the cliffs and since Cornwall was undergoing a revival, mostly due to surfing, it was too, too cool to be a surfer or a surf chick. The Baby-Yahs simply *yearned* to rush down to 'Wenny', as they called Polwenna, as soon as their public schools broke up. Mummy and daddy could always do a little boating or go to the posh fish restaurant in Padstow while the children amused themselves with their expensive Malibus and top-of-the-line wetsuits, so everyone was happy. In summer, the village was awash with pashminas and the Spar sold shitake mushrooms and squid-ink pasta alongside the baked beans and sliced white bread.

In the season, the Yahs flocked down in their Volvos and Audis *en famille*, to the disgust of the Baby-Yahs, 'Too horrible, Jade, the parents – God, I could just die', settling noisily in their summer houses like migrating birds. If ecstatically parentless, the Babies roughed it up at Dylan's Mordros caravans and camping site, in a 'van, or in a tent. The tent ones didn't last long, I can tell you, they soon got sick of slumming it and got a 'van. The all-summer Glastonbury, they called Mordros. More hip even than ultra-hip Polzeath apparently – there was even an article in the *Independent* about it one year. Dylan was livid, or as livid as an über-hippie could be. That sort of publicity he didn't want, thank you. The Baby-Yahs, having settled down to a drink-and-drug fuelled life of shagging and partying that would have horrified their doting parents had they known, got part-time seasonal jobs in the Chy or in the Tiki to fund their dealers and the off-licence in the Spar. That's the girls, of course. The boys begged Joe for a job on the wetsuit-and-board hire for the same reasons.

They all either wanted to be Luke, or have him. None of them succeeded, either way.

Luke Scylur, aka Luke Skywalker, aka God. Our own summer Spirit of the Beach, rising from the waves in form-fitting neoprene with a diamond sparkle of surf on him. The best surfer in Britain, the one who never entered competitions because 'that would spoil it'. The brown, salt-blond, perfect sea-eyed King of the Break, with his big, watermelon grin and those eyes, those eyes that looked far beyond you and way off into the Big Blue. Even his tattoo was the best I'd ever seen – an armband taken from Hokusai's *Great Wave of Kanagawa* by some top-of-the-line guy in the Midlands called Van Burgess. No wonky local tats like Lance had all over himself for the Skywalker, *oh* no.

His family had owned Lanterns, the big detached Victorian house perched like a great stone heron on the far edge of the cliff road, for three generations. Now, because the second Mrs Scylur, an American, hated Cornish holidays, they rented the house out most summers, but they'd done up the flat over the garage especially for Luke, and from May to September, that's where he lived. I'd known him, in a vague 'Hi Luke' kind of way, for ever; and I'd never let it get beyond that impersonal salute, because I was so scared that if he turned me down, I'd never find all the pieces of my shattered pride.

But oh, man – all the pictures of Luke in my head; snapshots neatly filed away in the smooth cellophane of my love for him, my unrequited passion. Luke in one of Joe's handmade wetsuits unzipped and pulled off to his waist, a custom Malibu under his arm, his hair almost white from sun and brine, his rash-vest fitting like a Lycra second skin, the shocking-lime collar pointing up his brown face. Luke eating a chip buttie like it was dinner at the Ritz, or his smile and the soft tone of his voice the night he bought me a drink at the Chy when I was barmaiding and we were virtually alone at the end of the season. Luke playing volleyball, Luke riding a wave like Neptune kissing Mother Thalassa. Luke skateboarding down the hill and falling off laughing on the grass by the benches. Luke, Luke, Luke – sometimes I wished he'd never come back, just go off and play at rich surfer kids somewhere posh, like Hawaii or Australia. But every May I started counting at the first of the month, waiting for him to come back from snowboarding in Chamonix, waited to see him on the beach, or in the Bluebird, waited to hear him say 'Oh, hi there…er…yeah…' and see him smile, even though it was just his everyone-smile, not special, not specially for me or anything. He was like nobody else, was Luke, like a creature from another dimension where handsome, cheekboney blokes with major talent are nice, unpretentious and modestly good-natured.

Because he was; he was nice. Nice to me, nice to Mrs Liddicoate, nice to the teeny-kids who followed him around like lost puppies, nice to the Saffies and Sophies and Giseles who mooned over him and stuffed their bikini tops with Kleenex for him, nice to their hero-worshipping brothers who swaggered in his wake after he murmured 'Good surf, eh?' to them in his gentle, offhand way. He was even nice to Gwen and the YCGNF when they did their evening beach patrols, leafleting and looking for immorality in the form of beer-drinking and snogging. Gwen was convinced she'd converted him at one point because he smiled at her and took her comic book-style gospel pamphlet; she was sure he wanted to be saved. She couldn't have been further from the truth.

Oh, they all thought they knew him, all thought they understood what made him tick; but they didn't. I did. I'd seen that look in his eyes before, in the faraway gazes of men – and it usually was men – who came back from Peru, Borneo, Thailand or the slopes of Chomolungma. Members of the Tribe who'd returned home to England but who ran from the thick, heated scramble of the cities and stayed with us, wandering across the beach like burnt-out phantoms dressed in tattered kurtas and baggy salwar, their smiles slow and sweet, their eyes fixed on something so far away from our homely life that they seemed to be talking to angels in their heads. They'd stay awhile; sometimes their left-behind women would visit them and we'd hear the pleading and the sobs and the low, calm replies followed by dawn departures and squealing tyres. But eventually, sooner rather than later, they'd cut their moorings again and drift off back to their beloved distances, to places so far from their past they could close

those terrible eyes and submit to the embrace they craved so much.
I knew what Luke was; like those wandering men, he wanted to kiss
God. He wanted more, more than this life could ever give him. He
was head-over-heels for the Infinite.

And I loved him so much it made my jaw ache not saying it.
Because I never, ever could say it; I had Beaker. Dear, loveable, faithful,
absent-minded Beaker, who'd stood by me no matter what, driven
me and mum to the hospital on his day off, made me comp tapes
of his favourite bands, cuddled me night after night on my lumpy
futon in the granny studio I lived in at home; cuddled me because I
was too exhausted to have sex with him. And he never minded, never
complained. My Beaks, my good, good boy. Not a rich kid like Luke,
not blessed, and favoured and perfect, like Luke Skywalker. Just lanky,
bony Beaker who'd never quite grown into his nose.

I'd known Beaker vaguely at school, he was the only other
Alternative kid in my year, but he'd left and got a job in Bice's the
music shop in Crossford, selling guitars and electronic organs to
sulky children whose parents wanted them to be 'musical'. He really
had looked like the muppet Beaker back then, his natural light brown
hair a severe, dyed-black spiky-topped short-back-and-sides, his
thick black plastic-framed specs falling down his big, sticky-out nose.
We'd been sort-of mates then, but four or five years ago, we'd met up
again at one of the Chy's famous New Year's Eve dos that everyone
went to and we'd drifted into 'going steady' as mum put it. Now he had
a neat crop and cooler, black wire-framed arty-type specs. This was
because of his band, Element. Style, he said, was an important part
of the music industry. He liked calling it that – the music industry.
Serious you know, real-life, not just mucking around. He was the
keyboard player and like all keyboard players, thought he was terribly
underrated and not valued enough by the brainless poseurs he was
forced to work with. He was right, too, they were awful morons, the
others in the band. Terry Hale the singer had been a tosser at school
and now he was allowed to show off on-stage at their infrequent gigs,
was a right little pop star *and* a tosser. But Element and their future
mega-stardom was what Beaks lived for, night and day. Every shitty

little gig in some grotty backroom of a pub was just practice for the NEC, or two nights at Wembley Arena. Element was gonna be huge.

But only in Beaker's mind. In real life, they were a third-rate copy of Coldplay and Terry as a frontman had all the charisma of a trout. I used to watch Beaks, his forehead glistening with sweat as he wrestled with his keyboard and the biscuit-tin PA, a mob of scarlet-faced piss-drunk Young Farmers gallumphing round the dance floor bellowing 'Do Tubthumping, you barsterds' and my insides would go all sore with pity and love.

I know there are people who'd say that pity isn't exactly a good basis for a relationship and I was mothering him; that I should dump him (how I hate that expression) and go for it with Luke. But Beaker was sweet, loyal, kind and doomed never to realise his ambitions in life. How could I break his heart? How? And don't give me that 'you've got to live your own life' crap. Look what all that did for Gwen. No, if I couldn't get Luke out of my mind, so be it. He'd stay just in my mind. A dull ache, a sweet, bruised pain I would pick at in private. Nothing else. Anyhow, to be real, he'd never look at me in that way. Apart from my nice shiny mass of black curly hair – my best feature – I was all bust and bottom; hourglass, mum called it. Like a Russell Flint gypsy painting, she said, and she'd show me one of them in her art book. Yeah, like, I wish; no one's tits did that in real life. But still, however gypsyfied and brown I might be, I wasn't one of the whip-thin, floppy-haired, bee-stung-lipped slinky girls with impeccable accents who were Luke's equals. He was never any nicer to me than he was to, say, Dot Ince who worked at the Bluebird and had all her back teeth missing and put her orange lipstick on without a mirror. There was no point in hurting Beaker for a *fantasy*. I might be misguided, but I wasn't bloody cruel.

Apart from Beaks, it was Con kept me sane through the years. We'd never stopped being friends, and she didn't drop me like so many others did when my life changed; that just wasn't Con. Every year she came for her holidays and though she never stayed with us, not wanting to impose even when mum was in remission, she became like one of the family. Some years she came at Christmas, too. She rented one of the holiday flats in the Gweltek apartment house, same as she always had. For a while, she came with Dave, then he ran off with a girl from his office and she came alone. She said in some ways she was glad he'd gone; he'd been having it off with the other woman for months, apparently, in the office and in his car. Pathetic. Con said she was well rid, but some slow anger and hurt slid and coiled behind the fierce dark blue of her eyes. She'd never brooked disloyalty, it was the worst crime possible, in her book. Once or twice she brought her mum, another whipcord-and-steel Bradfordian woman, tiny and stiffly determined to enjoy herself. One time Con appeared with a big, bluff blond fella called Jimbo who looked like he'd been carved out of tinned ham and did nothing but play golf. That didn't last, I can tell you.

But she was always Con. Always easy and sensible and clear-sighted. In between visits, we wrote and sometimes phoned. Not about anything earth-shaking, just about what we were doing, how my mum was, how her mum was, our private jokes and stories – stuff.

When her mum died quite suddenly of a stroke, I sent flowers from us all; we felt as if a distant but loved relative of ours had passed over.

Then one bright, crisp October day as I was strolling on the beach for an airing before starting the laundry, with the wind quite nippy and the sand scouring grit in little whirlwinds round my bare ankles, old man Trevisa signalled me over.

'I'm sellin'.' He never was one for talking. Sometimes he greeted customers with 'What you be wantin'?' The Yahs didn't like it at all; one of them once told him he lacked the proper deference. He told her to bugger off. It was a scandal – naturally, it had us in stitches. He was a 'character', i.e. a surly old sod and no mistake.

'Are you?' God, I was as bad as him.

'Yus. Your friend, that one from up your way, she still want it?' He jerked his head at the run-down beach café that was the focus of Con's dreamworld.

'Yus – yes. Yes she does. She does. I'll get her to ring you. Tonight.'

'Right enough. Don't want no bloody toffs gettin' it. Buggers.

She'll 'ave ter coom up with the cash, mind you, I ain't selling cheap fer no one.'

'She will, I mean, I'm sure she…' But he'd gone back inside, like a wrinkly, irritable turtle pulling its head back into its shell.

Con got it all right. She sold everything. Sold the Big Bean to a brewery wanting to make it into a fun-bar, sold her very desirable barn conversion out Hebden Bridge way, moved down to a short-let flat up on the cliff until the café flat was habitable and put me on the insurance of her beloved silver GTI 'just in case'. It was always 'just in case' with Con. Or 'you never know'. She liked to be prepared. She paid Mr Trevisa with a personal cheque and it was all done and dusted by the following January.

By the first of June, the Bluebird was officially the Spindrift Café. Dad, in a moment of wild good humour suggested Con call it 'Starbucks'. We all just looked at him and Con, keeping a straight face, asked him if he wanted to help her with the legal bills if she did. He paused for a moment, not sure if she was in earnest, then hugged her with a big, hairy arm and wandered off chuckling to himself, while we fell about. He thought Con was a desperately sharp career woman, and was slightly in awe of her 'business brain'. The only hiccup was when mum got upset that Con wasn't going to run an organic wholefood place; she was having a bit of a bad spell and got caught up in things, couldn't let them go. But Con spent a long time talking to her, discussing the issues seriously in the way mum liked, until she settled again. Con was good like that, with people who genuinely needed a bit of extra time. She was more patient than me with mum sometimes. I admit I got a bit – you know, I just couldn't hack it sometimes. I got – well – snappy, short with her. I'm not proud of it, but there you are, no point pretending to be what I'm not. I used to be crushed with guilt, I felt really awful when it happened, but sometimes…

Con, though – she'd spend any amount of time talking with mum about her latest 'cure', clipping bits out of the papers about alternative therapies, bringing her little treats like special organic apple juice and fancy carob bars. The only time you saw Con's temper was with rude people, customers who were nasty to her staff, that sort of thing; or anyone who was underhanded or told lies. She was very protective of her friends, and her sister. You could feel Con's loyalty like the sun warm on your face, it – it was – well, it was comforting to know she was on your side.

In an unstoppable fever of belief, Con had all the work on the café finished by the start of the season. She was like a whirling dervish; the contractors had never seen anything like it, I swear. In what seemed like moments, instead of the grubby, peeling, flat-fronted chip-and-pasty hole, that stepped back off the beach on two levels, there was a perfect surfers' café with a 'driftwood' veranda and distressed wooden tables and chairs made by some mad bloke from Brighton. Con got a great big Gaggia Italian coffee machine, oversized pastel crockery and put up some beautiful paintings of the sea she'd had sent over from America. It was a lime-washed, faded turquoise and pebble-strewn wonder. Even the kitchen was nice. The only problem was, we needed a cook.

Just when we were beginning to get just a lick desperate, you know, trying to be cheerful about it and not mentioning the C-word, fate intervened in the tiny, determined form of Cookie Quintrell. She came one morning as we were at our wits end, dragging a pushchair over the sand, her evilly synthetic navy blue Adidas zip-leg tracksuit crackling with static, her long, permed brown hair screwed tightly into a high topknot bang on top of her head and the sun glinting off her huge square gold creole earrings.

'Jesus, that's Cookie Quintrell,' I said, my mouth agape.

'Who?' muttered Con as she frantically tacked up a menu – despite our lack of chef.

Cookie's pale, pointy face was set in determined lines as she heaved the pushchair ever nearer.

'Cookie, she's one of the bloody Quintrells from out Whennek way – out on the Crossford road, that turn-off by the Daffodil Tea Rooms. It goes up and then it's the Quintrell's smallholding, or scrapyard, more like. God, she's got the babby with her by the looks on't.' We always got more Bradford when we were alone, it was one of our things.

Con stopped, and put the rest of the menus down to look. She scratched her scalp thoughtfully through her coppery-coloured bob, which she'd screwed into a shaving-brush pony-tail with an old elastic band. 'Whose is the babby?'

'Oh, hers – it's hers all right. There was a hell of a scandal, it's mixed-race see, half-caste. Some of 'em round here don't like that sort of thing, not one bit; that's something you'll have to get used to, I'm afraid.'

Con's face set into hard lines at that, her long, thin-lipped mouth compressed. Con never 'got used' to anything she didn't want to. She tapped the tack-hammer against her other palm thoughtfully.

'She looks about twelve – far too young to have a child. How old is she?'

'Oh, about twenty-odd, I should…Oh, hello, Cookie, hello…'

I was looking at the baby – well, toddler really. He was absolutely gorgeous, with a halo of tea-brown curls and bright, dancing grey eyes. His cheeks were round and pink with health and someone had dressed him in a Manchester United away strip.

'Smoky, I call 'im, on account of 'is eyes. But 'e's really Adam after my Granda. Adam Quintrell. They says in the village how as you need a cook.' Cookie never minced her words and her olive-coloured eyes were knife-sharp.

Con stepped forward. 'Hello, Cookie, I'm Connie Starbuck, the owner – yes, we do need a cook. Do you know someone?'

Cookie stuck her jaw out, speculatively. 'Me, missus. I'm the best bloody cook in this area. Cooked fer everyone at home since I was eleven year old, that's why they call me Cookie. Then I done my schoolin' an' got to caterin' college. I got distinctions fer my cookin', they said I was 'eaded fer great things, said I had a feel fer food, understood it. I'd a finished the course an' all if it hadn't been fer Smoky 'ere. Now see, I need a job, I can't go on livin' off me ma, it ain't right. Anyhow, she doan – she doan think as much of Smoky as what I do, see. Look, missus, you need a cook, I need a job, all I'll say is I'll have to bring the boy with me sometimes, on account of I can't leave 'im at 'ome all the time. That's my offer. I work 'ard. She knows that.' Cookie jerked her head at me, her stiff curls jumping.

'Well...' Con looked at me. I looked at her. Cookie eyed us both like she was prepared to bite if necessary.

'Cookie is a hard worker, Con. It's true – and she did go to catering college, I know that, but...'

In his stripy nylon pushchair, Smoky crowed and smacked his hands in a shaft of sunlight. Con watched him, a curious, tender frown on her angular face.

'You'll have to start tomorrow, Cookie, early, and – and you can bring Smoky when you like. Well?'

Cookie visibly relaxed, her ramrod back slumping in her horrible, shiny top. 'Tomorrow it is then. I'll be 'ere at six. You'd best get what you need from the suppliers by then, missus.'

'Con, Cookie, call me Con.'

'Er, Con. An' – both of us thank you. Me an' Smoky.'

And without another word, she stumped off with her baby back across the beach.

Con smiled, showing the slightly uneven teeth that drove dad crackers. 'Have I done the right thing, d'you think?'

'I expect so – Cookie's all right really, she's the best of the Quintrells. I know she's tried to get other jobs round here and had no takers – the baby, you see. They won't let her keep him with her, plus, it's, well, with some of them it's out and out racism, to be honest. Not, mind, that you'd ever get them to admit it, they'll just say she isn't suitable, or all the other things they cover it up with. The bastards, it drives me crackers. I mean, you know, they're not all like that, of course; God knows the real Cornish are so laid back they're fucking horizontal – but some people, Jesus...It's that bad apple thing, you know? Poor Cookie...And Mrs Quintrell, she's not fit to look after a budgie, honest.'

I felt quite flustered when I'd finished; in some obscure way I felt guilty because I'd never tackled the tiny but horrible clot of racist fuckwits in the village – but what could I have done? I'm an incomer, not Cornish, not local, no one would take any heed of me. Still, I should have done *something*. Oh, bugger it.

'Have you known Cookie and her family long, then?' Con was still smiling.

I blushed beet red and I felt my ears burning. I'm terrible for blushing when I'm embarrassed or uncomfortable, it's a bastard, I can't hide anything, I just go scarlet. Now my sordid past reared up in front of me.

'I – er, I went out with her brother Danny. Oh, not for long; he's a friend of Lance's. I mean, oh, you know. God, Mrs Quintrell was so happy, Danny was knocking off a "real lady" – I packed him in when she told me she'd had a dream we got married and Danny was in black leathers and I was in white ones. With fringing. From the catalogue. Oh, stop laughing, I was horrible to Danny. He wasn't a bad lad back then – I feel awful about it now, but I was only a kid, you know how it is. He couldn't read or write, you see, it – I – oh it just wasn't any use. Cookie's the only one of 'em that's got past first school, she's a – seriously, Cookie's a good lass, I don't know why I didn't think of her before.'

But I did know – I just didn't want to think I was the evil, snobby cow that my interlude with Danny made me sound like. I just hadn't let the Quintrells cross my mind since. How we bury the mistakes of our pasts, but karma will always get you. Always. God, Danny; he'd been so handsome in a bikery, Carver Doone sort of way, and a brilliant snog, I wonder…Oh, please, shades of the Youthie, at my age.

So there we were. The Spindrift up and running. Me, Dot and a couple of part-time girls waitressing, Con behind the counter, Cookie and Smoky out back in the kitchen. Perfect. We did that season like nutters: everything that could go wrong, did and everything that could go right, also did. We had our regulars, leftovers from the Bluebird, and Con made sure they were welcome because like she said, they'd been here longer than she had and there was no point making enemies. Anyhow, they were all right: just old Mr Eddy the car park attendant – he was a right laugh on the sly, the postie if he had time, the lifeguards Jim and Joey with their red uniforms and matching, sun-blasted faces who arrived at the end of May from their exotic winter surfing homes and departed back to them at the end of September, and Tim Norris, the local accountant who went running every morning come rain or shine and wore those indecently brief running shorts in shiny fluorescent yellow. Con thought about using him for the business at one point, but then decided the shorts put her off. You couldn't talk VAT to a man whose packet you saw every morning when he panted in like an excited Jack Russell and asked for his hot chocolate with exactly the same phrase every day: 'My usual, please Miss, and don't spare the cream, I'm a hungry man!' You could set your clock by that bloke, you really could.

Eventually we hired more part-time girls and a weekend assistant for Cookie – village girls, or local girls home from uni or college for the summer – not Yahs, I put my foot down. They got all the jobs usually and it wasn't fair. I must say, Cookie made food to die for. Of course we did the usual pasty and chips stuff, we had to, the tourists wanted it, but alongside Cookie did 'specials' – her stargazy pie was the real thing, fish heads and all. Con also had the great idea of getting the W.I. ladies to bake for us and so everyday, we had the best fruit pies and scones in the village, courtesy of Mrs Liddicoate's Cake Commandos.

Winter came, and Con, Cookie and Smoky came to ours for Christmas Day, just like old friends. Cookie was a bit nervy at first, but as soon as she saw mum playing choo-choos with Smoky on the kilim and had nodded manfully at Lance, who made out he wasn't a bit surprised to see Danny's sister and her son come for dinner, it went fine. Even Git emerged from her pubertal crisis long enough to enjoy herself, going so far as to don a paper hat and wear a tinsel boa. Gwen, of course, spent the day worshipping her God and then went to Kathy's for supper and carol-singalong.

Then we had to do all the repairs and decorate Con's flat properly, stuff we hadn't had time for in the summer. There was a little room next to the kitchen, and we – or rather, Lance, for a small fee and huge dinners – cut an archway through from the kitchen itself and did it up as a staff room. Or that's what it was supposed to be; really, it was a play-room for Smoky. Con was besotted with the child, she was always buying him toys and little bits and bobs. She got a big playpen so he could play safely while Cookie was working but more often than not, Con had him with her in the café. It certainly won Cookie over and Smoky was happy with Con. I used to watch her playing with him, cooing at him and sneaking quick kisses when she thought no one was looking. Shame she never had kids, I thought, she obviously wanted them. Yeah, there was me, a substitute mum by default, and there was Con, obviously dying for motherhood.

Life was weird. I mean, I didn't regret raising Git, I loved her as much, if not more, as if she'd been my own child. I didn't feel like it had cramped my style or anything silly, but I hadn't asked for it, I hadn't particularly wanted to be a 'mum' at nineteen. If I'd had a choice – to be straight about it – I wouldn't have done it. But there you are, we don't allus get our druthers, as Con's mum used to say. I sighed; some things just weren't fair. Con would make a great mum, but unless she met someone soon, well. Whereas me, I just busked it with Git and hoped for the best. Especially now she was in full-blown adolescence at thirteen. I was sure girls were maturing younger these days. Those magazines she got that talked about nothing but lip-gloss and shagging, it wasn't right at her age. Maybe I should have a little talk to her about stuff – God, listen to me, the voice of the older generation. *How* redundant?

It passed so quickly, time, so quickly. They say that's a sign of getting older, don't they? The days fast-forwarded like a blur. Before I knew it, it was May the first again. I was twenty-seven years old, and though life hadn't turned out how I'd expected and sometimes not how I'd wanted, with Con here, with the Spindrift, I felt tons better about things. For the first time in as long as I could remember, I was truly happy.

Then Luke came.

And so did Angel.

Book 2

In a solitude of the sea
Deep from human vanity
And Pride of Life that planned her, stilly couches she...

Over the mirrors meant
To glass the opulent,
The sea-worm crawls – grotesque, slimed, dumb, indifferent.

—Thomas Hardy

Chapter 6

I woke up feeling absolutely gross. The thing I hate the most about menstruation is I put on what feels like ten pounds in water, and my belly, along with feeling as if someone took a baseball bat to my pelvis, sticks out like I was six month gone. And I get a big spot on my chin in exactly the same place every time. I won't even dwell on the shitey, greasy mess my hair becomes and as to pre-menstrual tension – pre, during and post about covers it. I felt like total poo, as Git would say.

Fortunately, Beaker's pretty used to it by now. I won't say he's a doting New Man or anything but he knows enough to bring me a bit of toast, tea and two Nurofen as I lie raggled up in the quilt looking like a crushed owl, my pimple glowing like a laser pointer. For this service to womankind, I am grateful beyond measure, bless him. And for the fact he doesn't go on about it like some blokes do, either, telling you to pull yourself together because, like, it's not as bad as having to *shave* every day. Or trying to be 'understanding' because they read an article in their woman's *Cosmo* about caring and sharing. No, Beaker's The Man as far as I'm concerned – once a month, at least.

I managed to drag myself out of bed eventually and after half-heartedly washing and applying nuclear-strength spot lotion to the zit, I crawled into my baggiest *Prisoner Cell Block H* denim dungarees that had previously belonged to Lance when he went through a faux-rustic hayseed look and wore them with nothing but his jocks underneath, displaying acres of big pecs, leering skull and dragon tattoos and major chest hair. Now they were my hide-yer-belly gear. I wandered into the front room to survey the damage. Mum and dad had been up late smoking with Dylan. To be honest, it wasn't that bad, I mean, it wasn't like they were drug-crazed kids or anything – it was more the mature hippie equivalent of a dinner party, only instead of G&Ts and nouvelle cuisine it was blow and leftover snacks from the café. The place was swimming in discarded muffin cases.

Mum was still asleep by the looks of things and there was no special reason to wake her; she wasn't due at High Tor until the afternoon for her Reiki, so I left her. She was having a bit of a remission thing and so was able, and happy, to look after herself in small ways, including getting a taxi by herself up to the Centre. I looked in on Git, but she was long gone off to school, the kitchen bearing witness to the Human Tornado's breakfasting habits. I hoped to God she'd cleaned off the black hologram-glitter nail polish she'd put on last night and she hadn't worn her punk-fairy-queen diamanté tiara. I didn't want another run-in with Mrs Connock, who had to be a contender for scariest head teacher of the year. Dad dropped Git off every morning, and you'd think he'd put his foot down about stuff like the nail polish, but he either didn't notice or rambled on about how appearances were immaterial; Git was a creative being who should be allowed to express herself freely and it was the inner spirit that counted. I mean, of course he was right, but I noticed *he* never dealt with Iron Lady Connock.

I opened all the windows and emptied the ashtrays, ripping up the roaches as I always did – not that we'd be likely to be raided or anything, but still, I'm cautious by nature. I noticed Dylan had left his manky, knackered Palestinian scarf behind and folded it up, trying to ignore the rank whiff of aged patchouli that clung to it. How old was Dylan? At least fifty-odd, I reckoned and still dousing himself in that mouldy brew. Still, apart from his taste in perfume, he was a nice enough fella. He always made a point of bringing mum some weed and spending time with her and dad, just hanging out and chatting over old times and old music. He was part of the Tribe, really, only he was permanent, unlike the others. He was pretty much the standard old hippie in looks and outfit, with long, straggly grey hair in a slipped-off-his-bald-bit ponytail, flares, a kurta and waistcoat combo and moley little Lennon specs with misty, fingerprinted lenses he never cleaned. Most people in the village tolerated him – even thought of him as a fixture: 'our mad hippie' and all that sort of tosh. Harmless old Dylan, and never mind the blow he shipped in from Amsterdam or wherever. It was never anything stronger than a bog-standard old-style mellow weed, mind you. No skunk, he disapproved of that and the new super breeds of what he considered the Sacred Leaf. No chemicals, either, he didn't walk that road *at* all. It was just him and his trusty chillum. He gave most of his stash away – hardly the grim dealer of legend, Dylan.

Still, it wouldn't do to think he was just a silly old git, because he wasn't totally daft. He owned Mordros campsite outright. He'd inherited it from some uncle when it was a farm back in the sixties, predicted the boom in caravan holidays, invested in some nice 'vans, then some monster 'mobile homes' and bob's yer uncle. Not a poor man, Dylan, though God knows he didn't seem to spend the money on himself – or the site, which was pretty basic by modern standards. Admittedly, his wife Maudie had done the business end of things until she'd passed away some years back – cancer, awful; poor thing, and poor Dylan, he was devastated – but Mordros was a going concern, even if Dylan neglected it a bit these days. He'd had heaps of sky-high offers to sell, but he hung on – I think he'd wanted his son Bora (it means 'dawn' in Cornish, like Mordros means 'sound of surf'; Bora couldn't stand his name though, and now calls himself Bob) to inherit it but Bora/Bob had emigrated to Canada and worked in some computer company. Man, he was *never* coming back. He hated Dylan after Maudie died, blamed him for his mum's death because she'd opted for holistic cures and wouldn't have the chemo. Bora/Bob loathed the hippie thing after that, despised Cornwall as being the raggety arse-end of nowhere. He lived in Calgary or some such boom place now, about as far from the sea as he could get. Sad, really, because Dylan just loved him to bits and was always hoping he'd come back home eventually. We all hoped so, for Dylan's sake, he was so lonesome these days, up there in his big old caravan all alone with no one but herds of cawing Baby-Yahs and the sound of the surf crashing against the cliffs for company.

Brrr. I shivered despite the mild warmth of the spring day. It was beautiful out, though, even if I didn't feel especially beautiful myself. The beach stretched away like a promise of love, all smooth, gleaming sand and the flirtatious white of the wavelets smooching up on to the shore like fluttering lace on a Victorian petticoat. The sky was a tender iris blue and just delicately wisped with clouds. A gull meandered gormlessly along our deck, his beady dead yellow eye scanning for scraps. I banged on the glass and he took off mournfully – bloody rats of the air, gulls, along with pigeons and crows. I gazed out of the window in a sort of minor trance. Only a few tourists were out, plus some early surfers, their regulation surfie VW campers garlanded with wetsuits like weed-strewn rocks. Suddenly I realised the time, and also, that I'd promised to take a couple of old wicker chairs of ours that dad wanted rid of down to the café for the 'staff room'. I hollered for Beaker – no peace for that boy even on his day off – and together we struggled down the path with the unwieldy chairs.

Red-faced and puffing, we turned the corner and to my extreme gobsmackedness, the café was shut – and Dot, Cookie, Smoky and the part-timers were sitting on the veranda. Cookie and Dot had lit up and were blowing the smoke away from the baby and eyeing me speculatively.

We set the chairs down and I stood up, rubbing my back and feeling the dragging ache in my belly. Beaker pulled out his fags too, not realising the full import of the café being closed at 9.30 in the morning and the regulars wandering about the beach like lost souls. Well, Jim and Joey, anyhow.

'What's up, Cookie? Where's Con?'

'Doan ask me. I just turns up as usual an' nothin'. I banged on the flat door, but no answer. We've 'ad to turn people away – Tim was really put out, you know how 'e is, Mr Fuckin' Routine. You go try, see what's what.'

Dot nodded in agreement, her cadaverous face with its wonky, black-pencilled eyebrows and wild dash of Orangina lippie wriggling with gossip-fever.

Worried, I went round the back to the flat door and knocked hard.

Nothing, not a sausage. I banged again, then had an inspiration and checked the road for Con's motor. There it was, sitting pretty as per usual. She must be in. I felt a ragged little flutter of panic – was she ill in there? Passed out? How would we get in to help her, should I call someone? I banged on the door even harder.

I was just about to actually pound on the wood, when the door opened a crack and Con's bloodshot eye peered at me through the gap. She looked like she'd been dragged through a hedge backwards, then forwards, then back again.

'Oh, it's you, love – look, be a pet and open up for me – here's the keys, I'll be along in a bit…'

She seemed distracted, unlike herself, clutching her blue fleece dressing gown at the neck. She looked stringy and old. Not like Con, not like the Con I knew at any rate.

'Con, are you all right, are you poorly? Shall I get…'

'No, no, it's not that it's – oh, Astra, Angel's here! She called me from the airport in Plymouth this morning – she'd got an early bird flight, got in at 6.30 – I went to pick her up, she's sleeping, worn out, poor little scrap, and I…Do you mind – about opening up? I'd like to – to have breakfast and a bit of a chat with her. I think she's had a bit of trouble, I…' She pleaded with me, her face taut.

'No – God, no, I don't mind, not a bit. I'm – well, I'm glad she's come to visit, you take your…'

But the door had already shut.

Confused, I wandered round to the front and began opening up, telling Cookie the news. She wasn't impressed.

'That's all very well, but you can't be neglectin' stuff on account of yer relatives – know what I mean, Dot?' She jerked her fag in Dot's direction, for support. 'We gotta business ter run, an…'

'Yeah, I know, Cookie, but she dotes on that lass and…'

But Cookie had already grumbled into the kitchen and set things going. What was it with today? Was it Let's Ignore Astra Day or something? Bollocks to it.

Crossly, I heaved the chairs into the staff room and, wrapping myself in a clean apron, went out and started to wipe the veranda tables off. I felt full of a formless resentment – why should Con's sister arriving mean everything getting totally disrupted and why was it always me who had to get things together? It didn't help that I could hear Cookie and Beaker laughing at something, counterpointed by Dot's high, wavering giggle. Well, glad *someone's* having a good fucking day, I muttered to myself as Jim and Joey stumped up the stairs, their red lifeguard tracksuits glowing like their noses.

'Mornin' Aas, lovely day,' they carolled brightly. 'Aas'? *'Aas'?* Dear God.

As I stood there, spaced out and narky, a voice behind me said 'Hi, are you open now?' I whipped round in a spin of irritation.

I snapped. 'Yes, yes, we are – we are – just go in and…'

It was Luke. He smiled at me pleasantly, his dark blond hair grown out from last year's get-rid-of-your-dreads crop into a shaggy pageboy, his triangular, cat's face smooth and tanned, with just a touch of snowburn on his high cheekbones. He hunched inside his old blue Quicksilver jumper and stuck his hands in the pockets of his faded jeans, looking up at me through his fringe, shuffling his sheepskin surfie boots and smiling that damned smile that stabbed in my heart like a blade.

'It's Annie, isn't it?'

My pulse thumped in my ears and I was acutely aware of my apron, baggy dungarees and greasy hair/big zit combo. For God's sake, I scolded myself, grow *up*.

'Er, no – it's Astra – you know, like the car? Vauxhall Astra?' *How* stupid? What possessed me to blurt out that old joke like a great fool to someone who wouldn't have a blind clue what I was burbling on about and just think I was stark mad.

'"Astra" – star – that's a pretty name…oh, we did Latin at school, useless, I suppose but some of it sticks. Have you had a good winter?'

I couldn't believe we were having a proper conversation. The only time I'd exchanged more than two words with him before was that New Year's Eve. He spoke as if we were old acquaintances, and weirdly, I wondered if he'd sort of forgotten we didn't actually know one another, on account of him seeing me around for so many years.

'Oh, thanks. My parents are into funky names...' Don't go there, for God's sake, girl. 'Yeah, winter was OK – you?' Miss Cool-and-Breezy – not.

'Yeah – fine. Well, good really. Went to South Africa for a bit then Cham – Chamonix – for the snowboarding – ever done that? It's cool.'

'Er – no, no I haven't. I stay here, you see, we – I live here, you know an' my mum's ill, so I look after her and the family.'

His sea-coloured eyes scanned the shoreline. I mean, he was listening to me, but at the same time, he wasn't.

'Right. It must be nice here in the winter. I guess you guys get pretty sick of us summer types – I bet you're glad to see the back of us come autumn. I must say the café's looking good, much better than the old one, very nice. The new owner must be pleased with it.' He smiled again, and ran his long, blunt-ended fingers through his shaggy hair.

You guys? Oh, like – you natives. The ones who don't leave at first leaf drop. I felt a prickle of irritation, then puzzlement. This wasn't going the way I'd always planned our first proper talk to go, the one where I dazzled him with both my glorious beauty and my stunning intellect in one fell swoop. The one where he told me I was his heart's desire and begged me to run away with him to a life of sin in Tahiti. He was talking like a Summer Person. Well, I suppose he was a Summer Person. Not a full blown Yah, but...He was Luke; Luke wouldn't have those patronising attitudes, Luke wouldn't be all...'You guys'. OK.

'Yes, she is, definitely – and her sister Angel's down for a visit so she's extra happy. We're all from up North, you know, the same town – Bradford.' I sounded snappy. If I was in Bradford, I'd be bridling. Actually, I was bridling and stopped myself, but it didn't matter, he hadn't noticed.

'Oh, the North, yeah.' You could see he didn't have the faintest clue where Bradford was. I should have said Leeds, or worse, Manchester. Southerners always knew where *they* were. Harvey Nicks and Cheetham Hill. Up North somewhere. That place where the M1 turns into setts and women in shawls and clogs shout at blokes in flat caps with ferrets down their keks.

I couldn't believe he was annoying me so much, that I felt so disappointed by him. All the years of – of worship, and our first conversation was just *crap*. I felt strange; upset. All right, it was my period, PMT and all that, but Luke...Yes, he was still gorgeous, still my own personal secret love, but actually talking to him – I don't know. Maybe it was simply that no one could live up to being someone's dream. But he was Luke, and my heart scrambled just looking at him. Suddenly, I felt like crying and a thick lump came into my throat. I swallowed hard and took a deep breath. It wasn't his fault, it wasn't. It was my fault; I expected too much, it wasn't him, it was me. He was trying to be nice and I was just being a stroppy cow. Poor Luke.

'Angel, eh? It's a good day for pretty names. Still – I like Astra, yeah.' He smiled again. 'Well, I'll go get a chip buttie, then – I missed them in France...Nice talking to you.'

And he patted my arm and sauntered into the café. *He patted my arm.* I sat down heavily on one of the chairs, damp rag in hand and stared out at the sea. Why was nothing in life like you think it is? Why was no one like you think they are? What on earth had I expected? A discussion on the finer points of Virginia fucking Woolf? Jeez-*us*.

Beaker sat beside me and I looked at him, unaccountably annoyed. Then I felt guilty again.

'Bloody surfies.' He scowled at the beach, taking off his specs and polishing them on the hem of his black Element T-shirt.

'What?'

'Bloody surfies. They make me ill. They got no fuckin' idea about the real world. Bloody wasters, the lot of 'em.'

I stared at him, amazed. He'd never said a word about surfers before, never mentioned them. Admittedly, he never went near the sea or for that matter, the beach generally, but that wasn't uncommon round here, Lance never did either. Still, I'd never heard him say anything like that before.

'Ooh, I've just got back from Cha-mon-ix, I have missed my chip sand-wiches...' His voice had the sing-song of the playground as he imitated Luke's voice. 'Bloody rich kids, is all they are. Mummy's boys, spoiled brats. Bloody Yahs.'

'God, Beaks, I didn't know you felt like that…'

'Well, I do. I can't stand watchin' 'em swannin' around like the whole fuckin' world was their fuckin' playground an' everythin' an' everyone's just 'ere to fuckin' entertain 'em, kow-tow to 'em. I have to work like a fuckin' bastard just to get along, can't buy a house, can't get a new keyboard, still livin' at home with me mum and dad at my age, while the likes of 'im, ' he jerked his thumb in the direction of the café, 'fuck off round the world on mummy and daddy's money and I ain't never been out the bloody country even to bloody Jersey or somewhere. An' I never will, I doan suppose, neither.'

I didn't know what to say. I felt awful. Poor Beaks, he was right in some ways, it was hard to see the rich kids arseing around all summer while Beaker and the other local lads worked at crap jobs and earned fuck-all. I took hold of his hand, so white and bony with bitten nails and a scattering of coarse black hairs on the backs of his fingers. He sighed and squeezed my hand.

'Oh, I know they're not all like that – some of 'em are OK. It's just 'is sort – they piss me off sometimes.' He let go of my hand and stood up, stretching and pulling at his neck as though it was tense and sore. 'You like 'im, doan you?'

I went puce. 'Well, he's – he's all right. Polite, you know, not like some. They say he's the best there is, the lads do – I don't know him, really, I…' Did Beaker suspect? Did he *know*? What? I held my breath.

'Yeah, King Surfie. I know. Luke Skywalker. Walks on fuckin' water. Oh, never mind, I doan mean it really, just got outta bed the wrong side I s'pose. Look, I think I'll go back up the house for a bit, do some programmin', I gotta get on, we've got that gig at that Jangles place comin' up. Should be a big do, I want everythin' to be right. You know.'

I stood up and hugged him, desperately relieved he didn't appear to be aware of my sordid little secret. I held him a moment and I could feel the bony cage of his ribs and under my hands, the knobs of his spine. He was very thin.

'Love you,' I whispered in his ear.

'Yeah – you too, see y'later.' He pecked me on the cheek and sloped off, stooped, his hands thrust deep into the pockets of his black Levis. Luke had done that too, stuck his hands in his pockets, but he made it seem cute, cool. Beaker just looked depressed. Defeated. The fact was, lately he had seemed a bit – and then it hit me.

I stood quite still, the damp rag clutched in my hand. All that about 'a house of my own' – did Beaks want to get married, or have us live together? We had been together for years, just kind of drifting along. Like kids really, seeing each other after work, him staying at ours, using dad's computer, eating dinner with us. He'd never said anything about marriage – but then, he never said much about anything. That's why his outburst against the surfies had been a surprise. Beaks never lost his rag, ever. It just wasn't Beakery. Then, for the first time it really hit me that I wasn't – my situation wasn't exactly a going prospect relationship-wise. Did Beaks think him and me weren't going anywhere either? Not like his mates, like Terry the singer for instance, and his fiancée, Janice. Her flashing the diamond and sapphire chip 'gagement ring and jogging towards the big white wedding; the meringue dress, the reception at the St Petrock Hotel, the vast mortgage on the tiny 'starter home' out at the Larchgrove Homes estate down Lancollas? Was Beaks sick of me and my family – and mum? No, he loved us, he did, he wouldn't be so nice to us if he didn't; but if he was fed up with me, with us, Christ, I couldn't blame him.

I thought of all those carers you only hear about when the papers do an exposé on their lonely lives and how the Social has let them down. Jane Austen-type spinsters. Spinster of this parish. *'She looked after her parents all her life, never married, you know; poor thing.'* That was me, if Beaks left. Well, sort of. And I couldn't – wouldn't stop him. That would be crap; he was a decent, kind-hearted bloke, he'd make a great husband. And father. Father – God, yeah. Kids. Did he want kids of his own? I mean, that sounds like I had kids, single mum sort of thing, which of course I don't. But I do, in a way. I've got Git; and she loves Beaks, rags him around chronic, practises flirting on him, makes him get her the sort of CDs he hates. He's dead fond of her, too, you can tell. But she's not his blood, not his child.

She's mine.

If Beaks left me, I'd be heading towards the big Three-Oh with nothing to show for it, no partner, no lover even, no nothing. Increasingly near my sell-by date. Spinster, *spinster*. All dried up and scratchy; unloved and therefore, unlovable. I could see it all, stretching away like one of those dreadful Scandinavian films where it all drags on drearily until someone eventually chucks themselves down a well. Jesus. *Jesus*.

I felt a twinge of anxious panic and guilt; God, why did everything have to be so stressed out today? I fixed my eyes on the glittering horizon and did the breathing thing. Calm, think calm thoughts. Then I scrubbed the tables very clean, and then the chair seats. Then I did the handrail of the veranda. It didn't make me feel less shit. I thought of Beaker, and his poor, defeated-looking back. Never mind about being so selfish, I'd sit Beaks down, alone, and really talk to him, I would. Really thrash it out, show him how much I appreciated him, how much I loved him. I did love him; you couldn't not after all he'd done for us. We'd get ourselves sorted, proper.

I stretched; shoving my fists into the small of my back and wriggling them round to ease the ache. There was a girl walking up the rise towards the café – right, welcome ye tourists one an' all. Emmets, the Cornish called them – ants. Swarming everywhere. Well, good. We needed their lovely, lovely cash. The girl stopped and looked at the café, then she bounced up the step.

She was beautiful. More than that – she looked perfect. I'd never seen anyone so incredibly well turned out. From her long, smooth tanned legs emphasised by silvery trainers, soft expensive little sweater and faded denim short-shorts, to the platinum blonde elfin crop and neat blue topaz earrings and pendant set, she was completely flawless. A billion-dollar babe. Her figure was fantastic, like a model in a magazine; not the crap, anorexic heroin-chic wasted type, but the gorgeous Brazilian supermodel variety. Tallish, healthy-looking, with a tiny waist, slim but rounded hips and a good-sized, up-and-at-'em bosom.

I gawped, I'm afraid to say. She smiled. I noticed her eyes were the most astonishing shade of misty violet; real eyes, not contacts. Violet eyes, like Liz Taylor's supposed to have. I'd never seen them in real life before. They looked almost unearthly.

OK, maybe she wasn't flawless, but you simply didn't notice any wonky bits, the rest knocked you for six. Her wonderful, silky complexion and magnificent bone structure, the sort that gets better and better with age. The full curve of her rose-coloured lips. That body and the way she had of managing to show nearly all of it without seeming tacky or cheap. Always the nicest, the best clothes; always the discreet 'natural' make-up that lads never noticed, always beautifully groomed and that strange quality she had of drawing all the light to her, of being somehow bathed in it; she glowed as if she were made of wonderful, white spun-gold, gleaming, as if all the light in the world was her personal spotlight. Like God said 'Let there be Light' and there was and it was all hers.

Finally, I managed to smile back. Her smile broadened.

'Hello, you'll be Astra, then. I'm Angel, Con's sister.'

Her voice was a shock; a low, breathy, slightly broken-up husky voice with the broad, flat accent that could only be Bradford. It was nice, attractive, after you got over it coming out of this Golden Girl. It made a contrast, made her more real and not so much of a walking lad-mag pin-up.

I dropped the rag on the table and wiped my hand on my apron, forgetting I was supposed to be annoyed by her and her disruption of everything. She was so friendly and open I seemed to lose my resentment of her in the warmth of her greeting.

'Oh, right, pleased ter meet yer.' I slipped back into Bradford myself, without realising it. We shook hands. Her grip was firm, her hand dry. She shook nicely, not like some lasses who just sort of lay their hand in yours like a dead plaice. I noticed her nails were lovely, filed to a sort of squarish oval and lacquered a shimmering blue to match her jewellery. I tried not to be jealous.

'I like your jewellery, it's lovely – topaz, right?' I said, to cover my sad envy.

'Yeah – I were working in a jeweller's up London for a bit. I like that blue colour, don't you? Makes me think of holidays – the seaside an' such.'

She laughed, and pulled the pendant back and forth on the chain. 'I've got some earrings like these I never wear – you can have 'em if you want, no good to me, I'll dig 'em out for you.'

'No, I couldn't – I mean, they must have cost a...'

'Oh yes, yer can, I dint pay for 'em. The bloke who owned the shop used to give me loads of stuff, honest. They're nearly the exact same ones as these, I don't need two pair. Anyhow, they'll suit yer. You look just like Con said, like a gypsy, Spanish. Lovely, I love that look. I wish I 'ad your hair, I do – that curly hair, smashin'.'

I felt unreasonably pleased at her compliments. Typical English woman, starved of flattery, I suppose. But she seemed so genuine, artless. She smiled again and turned towards the door.

'I'm gonna have a coffee – d'you want one? Con's in there, I just run round to look at the beach – int it gorgeous? I should 'ave come here before, I really should. Oh, come on, Con says you opened up an' everythin' for her, you deserve a break.'

She glimmered in the dimness of the doorway like a – well, like an angel from a picture book. For a second, she looked almost uncanny; I shook myself. Periods, who needs 'em. Fuck up everything. Put your brain out of gear. I lectured myself firmly; Angel seemed nice, really nice. Just as Con had described her – only much better-looking than Con had said. And very generous and kind, too. All in all, a very nice lass indeed. Just as Con's sister should be.

'Coming,' I said, and followed her into the dark of the café.

Chapter 7

Con was standing at the counter talking to Dot when we came in and Angel ran up to her and enveloped her in a big hug, then swung her round with an arm around her waist, kissing her pale cheek. Con looked somewhat better than earlier, her hair neatly pulled back into its thick tuft of pony-tail and an ecru cotton-knit sloppy joe over her usual jeans. She flushed with pleasure at Angel's hugging and then pushed her away, mock-cross, wiping her face where the faint, rosy imprint of Angel's lipstick lingered.

'Get off, you great lummox, honestly, what *are* you like?' She beamed at Angel who kissed her cheek again unrepentantly and sat on the table next to her, swinging her legs like a five-year-old.

I caught a glimpse of Cookie, who rolled her khaki eyes and shook chips into a big bowl for Jim and Joey. I almost laughed out loud at the sight of them. They were staring at Angel like men dying of thirst in the desert would stare at a bottle of Evian. I felt like walking over and shutting their mouths with my finger under their silly chins. I looked back at Angel and saw she was totally unaware of the men's stares. I mean, really unaware, not putting it on like most girls would. She just didn't seem to notice even though the two fools were lollygagging fit to burst. Maybe she's just used to that sort of thing, I thought, lucky cow. I'd never provoked that kind of reaction in the male sex, mostly they slapped me on the back and told me what a good lass I was, just like a sister to them – or worse, just like one of the boys. Even the ones I'd shagged said that, and I mean, what did that say about them? *Blokes*, I thought, half-seriously, *I despair*.

Then I saw Luke, over in the corner, a mug of tea in his hand, a surfer mag open in front of him, the remains of his buttie pushed to one side.

He was staring at Angel too. Not like Jim and Joey, who were just tripped up by their hormones, but really staring, his face pale and his knuckles white on his mug of tea. I felt my breath catch, he looked – bereft. He wasn't ogling her body, or anything like that, he was locked on her as if he was drowning and she was the only thing that would save him. She noticed that all right – she'd followed my gaze and she caught him at it. She smiled ever so slightly at his white face, fractionally curving her full, pink lips and hooked his stare, reeling him in, giving him the full benefit of those huge amethyst eyes; then instantly, she looked away.

He dropped the mug. It smashed into two pieces on the floor, the thick china rolling and sloshing tea everywhere. He jumped up, tea soaking his trousers, his face painfully red now, and flustered around trying to pick up the bits of mug while Dot trotted over with a cloth.

Flustered? Luke Skywalker, flustered? He was apologising to Dot like an idiot, trying not to look at Angel, who was quite oblivious, laughing at something with Con. Cookie shot me another look, and I went over and took the pieces of broken mug from him. He didn't even see me. I could have been stark naked and he still wouldn't have seen me. Something hot ripped in my heart – the Lukes of this world don't drop mugs because some girl flirted with them; dreams didn't stand there all red and white and sweaty with sodden keks because a pretty woman smiled in their direction. My Luke didn't, not Luke who'd been importuned by every nubile chickie in Polwenna since he was fourteen and apart from the odd fling had never let anything come between him and the Big Blue.

But there he was, stammering like an adolescent and, I swear to God, his hands shaking.

'Your keks are soaked, you'd best get off home and change them.' In my shock and crossness, I spoke to him as if he was five years old. 'Go on, you'll need to get changed – Luke, you'll need to change.'

He came round a bit when I said his name. He looked at me, bewildered.

'Uh – yes. Yes. Oh, yeah. Sorry, sorry about the…Who's that…'

I felt my stomach shift and something in me wanted to slap his face; at the same time, a terrible kind of sorrow drenched through me, as if I'd seen something awful happen, a death or something, not just a bloke drop his tea mug.

'It's Angel, Con's – the owner's – sister. I told you about her…'

He looked at me sharply and I realised that until then, he hadn't twigged who I was, that we'd talked earlier. Then I went out of his mind again.

'Angel…' he said, like a breath. Then he just walked out. Without another word.

Livid, I jounced past Jim and Joey, the Besotted Brothers. 'Put yer tongues away, lads, yer catchin' flies.'

They started, embarrassed, then laughed in that 'huh-huh-huh' lad kind of way, elbowing each other. I put my head on one side and tutted at them. No effect: they were off in some Boy's Own Shagfest World. I went into the kitchen and chucked the broken mug in the bin. Cookie was sucking her teeth and infinitesimally wobbling her head, her metallic conker-brown curls shivering stiffly.

'Cookie…' I hissed.

'Well.' She said. 'Honestly. I doan know. She doan look all that to me – look at 'er. All legs an' eyes, like a bloody spider. Fellas, though, honestly. Even that Luke, an' 'im so nice an' all. Mind you, it's them sort of fella as falls 'ardest. I doan worry about them great fools.' She nodded at the lifeguards. 'It doan mean anythin' 'cept dick to *them*. I mean look at 'em, practically droolin'. No, it's yer sensitive types like that Luke – did yer see 'is face? Pathetic, like 'e'd been knocked out or somethin'. It swipes 'em sideways when it comes to 'em, poor barsterd. I always wondered why 'e didn' 'ave no steady, lookin' like that an' being so posh. Still, 'e's fallen now, you can see that a mile off. There'll be trouble there, you mark my words.' She sucked her teeth and looked sage.

'Oh, come on, Cooks, you don't know that. I mean, how come you're the expert all of a sudden?'

She pointed with her spoon at Smoky, sleeping in his lobster-pot playpen. 'His daddy. 'E were like that Luke. I says to 'im, "It can't come to nothin', not you an' I." But 'e didn' care. 'E was crazy about me, like I was someone special or somethin', not just a waitress in a caff. He wore 'imself out chasin' me. What else could I do but – you know. 'E used to read poetry to me – that's the sort 'e were. Just said nothin' mattered to 'im but me an' – but it were no good. 'E were from London, posh, on 'is 'olidays. Lovely fella, like kissin' chocolate, 'e were that sweet – oh, I did love 'im. But t'were no use, 'is family took 'im 'ome, off to university. 'E were crying when they took 'im off, like a kid, breakin' 'is poor liddle heart. 'E doan know 'e's a daddy, an' it doan matter, I doan want 'im to, doan want 'im obliged, see. Let 'im have 'is memories like I got mine. That's all I can give 'im, the poor bugger.'

'Oh, Cookie, I'm sorry, I…'

'It's OK. I got 'im. I got my Smoky. That's all that matters to me these days.' She wiped her face with her apron and looked straight at me, her dark green eyes level and cool.

'You can't live on dreams an' wannabes, Astra. No, you can't. You gotta be practical in this life, see what I mean? That Luke, 'e's not practical, 'e's dreamy. It's all very well, but it doan get nothin' done, do it? 'E's fallen bang hard for Little Miss Trouble, an' it'll bring 'im no joy, that I do know. Chalk an' cheese, ain't that what they says? Opposites attract. Bound to 'appen sooner or later, with that type of fella.'

Yes, but Cookie, I wanted to say as I watched her narrow little face so full of passionate love for her child – Cookie, why couldn't he have fallen for me, not *her*? But I knew she'd think I was soft, and soft to Cookie wasn't an option in life.

I turned back towards the café and saw that the lifeguards had managed to get into conversation with Con about sod all, by the look on her face. Angel had taken her jumper off. Underneath, was a tiny little aqua strappy vest. You could see her bra straps – turquoise lace with glitter threaded in it. I just knew, in that psychic-jealous-woman way, that unlike me, her knickers matched her bra. Thong knickers, probably. I sighed. On anyone else the outfit would have looked common but she somehow made it look hip, ironic, not tarty. She was still swinging her feet, her arms straight by her sides, hands gripping the table edge. This had the effect of pushing her bust out even further than normal, her cleavage smooth and tan with no visible bikini marks. Jim and Joey couldn't keep their eyes off that gleaming exposure. They looked like they'd drop at her feet and worship her as a goddess for tuppence; you could see them pumping up their beautiful swimmers' bodies under their unflattering uniform tracksuits and posing like peacocks. Angel paid no mind. Did she do these things on purpose, or didn't she realise the effect she had? I looked at her face. She was gazing into the middle distance, no expression in her eyes, as if she were just daydreaming. It was strange; she must have been aware of the fuss she'd caused by – well, by *being*. But she looked blank, not in a deliberate, purposely bored way like a clever flirt – no, just blank. Like a sheet of paper with nothing written on it. Like, weird.

'She's weird, 'er.' I started as Cookie delivered this judgement – it had been just what I was thinking.

'Oh, Cook-*ee*, she's Con's sister – we've gotta be nice to her, she seems OK when…'

'When there ain't no fellas around, is what you mean. Well, yeah. Well, we'll see.'

And she went on sticking things in the microwave and frying sausages like a woman possessed.

Chapter 8

As the weeks went past, Angel came to fascinate me. And not just me, either. I don't mean lads – you can imagine the havoc she wreaked amid the male population of the beach – it was Git, too.

Git adored Angel. From that first day when she bounced furiously into the café after school, sparkly tiara in hand and a burst of chatter about the bloody-mindedness of La Connock, it was love at first sight. A major crush. Git hung on her idol's every word and whim, running errands for her, repeating her aphorisms, deserting her mates, who phoned pathetically and got the big brush-off.

'No, I can't – God – *swimming*? In the *pool*? Get a *life*, Marnie. Do you know what chlorine does to your *'air*? Angel says you may as well wash it in *Domestos* and 'ave done. No, Angel's gonna show me how to do proper make-up tonight – yeah, *well* – Angel says you can't learn too soon. She says if you doan take advantage of yer looks yer crackers an' – no, she is not. She is *not* – I doan care *what* yer mum says, what does *she* know? Well, I doan *care*, Angel says...'

Hmmm.

Marnie and Jo and Ally hung around the café like little lost ghosts, or draggled up the hill like a clutch of orphans – for a while. Then the backlash set in and they took to loudly rubbishing Git at every opportunity. But Git didn't care. Angel said women always turned on you if you were successful and pretty; it was dog eat dog. Do or die. And Git nodded in agreement, her shining eyes filled with faith. You can imagine what Gwen thought of 'that woman', as she termed Angel. 'I saw that woman yesterday – practically naked. Pastor Elms says she's a living lesson in immorality and sin.' I did notice that the stout-hearted boys of the YCGNF made a special effort to bring Angel to God. Never stopped plying her with pamphlets, bless 'em. Nice to see so much good, Christian devotion to the sinners amongst us.

I didn't count the YCGNF, though; no one did but themselves. They disapproved of bikinis, for – well, for God's sake. They were having a bit of a thing about the evils of espressos, too; all that filthy Italian-style coffee leading to Satanic goings-on – tight trousers, scooters, loose morals. I'm not kidding, actually, they gave us an illustrated leaflet about it. We pinned it up, and sales of espresso doubled.

As the time raced by, it became pretty obvious that not everyone – everyone normal that is – liked Angel. Cookie didn't, but then, she wouldn't, Angel really wasn't her type. Beaker refused to comment on her and Lance thought she was buff but he never took her seriously. Apparently, and to Gwen's disgust, he said he'd 'give her one' – but hey, that was our Lance for you. He'd give a melon one if he could find someone to cut a hole in it. Which he had, if legend were true. Dad, I have to say, seemed a bit nervous round her; she was too groomed for his taste, and though he never said anything critical, his body-language was decidedly tense. Mum, though, really took against her.

'I don't care, Astra, it's not right what she's saying to Gita, all this nonsense about clothes and boys and make-up – *make-up*! I don't mean a bit of lip-salve and nail polish, there's no harm in that, it's fun, but foundation and blusher and eyeshadow and that horrible thick mascara and – and – Gita's only a child, it's just not right. Gita told me the other day if I "let myself go" any more than I had, I'd be sorry! What does *that* mean? She offered to "do my face" for me – as if I was some sort of glamour girl. What happened to feminism, Astra? Where did we go wrong? I thought all that rubbish about painting your face and being some sort of silly beauty queen was over. We fought against all that nonsense, we…In my day…'

'Mum, Git – Gita's thirteen, nearly fourteen – they grow up quicker these days. It's only a phase, she'll get bored of it soon and…'

'No, it's wrong – turning my baby into some sort of male plaything, a traitor to her gender – I didn't bring her up for this…'

You didn't bring her up, mum, I thought. But I soothed her as best I could and vowed to keep a closer eye on Git. How could I explain – how could I *ever* get it across to my parents about the way things were now. They'd be horrified. Their tentative engagement with the world had ceased utterly when they moved to Cornwall and the good life. The ironic, retro, lad-mag, clubland, porno-culture and worst of all, disco-revival mess Britain had become passed them by unscathed.

Angel was from an alien place they knew little or nothing of, and what they did know, they despised. She was the living avatar of all they thought of as citified and worse, patriarchal, materialistic, unreconstructed, corrupt and a threat to the counter-culture they thought they belonged to. Angel wasn't a post-feminist; in their terms, she was a quisling. She wasn't the *Cosmo* stereotype of a confident, powerful young woman comfortable in her own body and at home with her sexuality to them; she was a traitorous Vamp in pythonette stilettos. All those protests they reminisced about, mum's happy days at Greenham Common, would be gone for nothing if they woke up to the ugly truth of Cool Britannia. They'd think they'd failed because it hadn't turned out all lentils and tie-dye. Things had just drifted. Back down to the lowest common denominator. That's what they'd think, and in their terms, I couldn't blame them. But I comforted myself with the thought that it would be OK in the end because Angel was only on holiday, just visiting. Soon she'd be gone and Git's crush would fade.

And mum and dad would be safe again in their Whole Earth, organic macramé cocoon – which is what I wanted for them. They were too frail, too unworldly to beat themselves up over something they couldn't change. It would be cruel to rip their cosy illusions to bits at this point in their lives, with mum ill and dad struggling to cope, for no other reason than a silly girl in a Wonderbra happened to sashay into our village for a seaside treat. Even if she was my best friend's sister. No. I'd just shut up and put up until she left.

But mum fretted and worried over Git. It wasn't good for her and she spent more and more time up at High Tor having therapies. In her defence, I will say Angel tried her best with mum – and dad. You could see her trying. But it was hopeless. The more she shimmied around in her mini-slips and hipster short-shorts, her ice-white hair sparkling with diamanté hair clips, her high wedge sandals clacking on the wooden floors, a palpable aura of perfume ('chemical stuff' as mum put it) floating in her wake, the more uncertain and in mum's case, downright disapproving, they became. For once, mum, dad and Gwen seemed to have something in common – and it was that Angel was unsuitable.

They never actually said anything to Con, of course, but she sensed it and it upset her.

'Why don't they like Angel, Astra? She thinks the world of your family – especially Git – she thinks they're lovely and she really feels for your mum, she does. What's she done wrong?'

I sighed. How could I explain Angel hadn't done anything wrong, as such – she just came from another planet as far as my parents were concerned. And God, was I sick of *explaining*.

'Oh, Con, it's not that they don't like her, they do, of course they do, it's just, they're worried about Git, the teenage years, the awkward phase, you know. They just get a bit antsy about Angel's, well, her influence; it's just the clothes and the make-up, it's not – look, give them time, they'll get used to her and they'll see just what a lovely person she is. And she is lovely, Con, we all think so, we do. It's just that mum and dad, well, come on, Con, they're terrible hippies, be fair. If she reeked of Dewberry and wore something ethnic, they'd adore her. I know it's not fair, but please, be a bit patient. Please?'

Con sighed and shook her head, lips pursed. 'I suppose she is a bit trendy, but she always loved fashion. I thought she'd be a designer. When she was little, I was forever making outfits for her Barbie doll, and...'

And we'd be off on another nostalgic journey through Angel's past. It was plain Con more than just loved Angel as a sister, she adored her. Nothing was too good for her 'baby sister', and Angel anecdotes were recited as if they were holy creed. How Angel had bested the teachers at school with her cleverness and wit, how she'd left at sixteen (naturally, with her talents she didn't want to be stifled by academia) and got a job at a fashionable boutique in Leeds, leaving when the manageress had shown how jealous she was by accusing Angel of some trumped-up thing in an attempt to get rid of her. Con had wanted to sue over that, defamation of character, but Angel refused and just got another job, this time in an art gallery as a receptionist. How Angel had been the toast of Leeds and Bradford society when she was eighteen, clubbing it until dawn in fabulous outfits and always keeping her cool, never giving the time of day to the wealthy boys who fawned over her. How she'd moved down south and graduated to the very cream of the London scene, working with top designers and rock bands, living the high life to the full. Naturally, she didn't get the chance to visit home very often, but what could you expect? Anyway, Con was happy to get her the little things she needed like paying for a flat in Islington; I mean, what are sisters for? It's a family thing. And when the jealousy that always followed a girl as exceptional as Angel reared its ugly head, and she lost the job, or fell out with the friends, or had to put up with hurtful gossip – Con was always there for her because she knew her Angel was solid gold, all the way through. It was the others, the envious, mean-minded ones who were eaten up with spite because they couldn't stand to see a girl like Angel succeed. They were jealous. Just plain old jealous.

'You see, Astra, I know you'll understand. It's like you and Git. You have to take that extra bit of care over them, don't you? They're precious. And…look, I'd rather you kept this to yourself, but you see, when she was – when she was born, there was a bit of a problem. She was quite – poorly. I mean, she's as sound as a bell *now*, hardly a day's illness since and you can see how healthy she is, just radiates it, doesn't she? But I still worry, y'see, I can't help it. The thought of anything happening to her just makes me – oh…'

She shivered and her gaze drifted off in the soppy, misty, adoring way that was so bloody annoying.

I couldn't help it, I thought Angel was a spoilt brat. It unsettled me to see Con, usually so down to earth, behaving like she'd lost all reason.

And yeah – I was jealous, just like Con had said. Not of Angel's effect on men – OK, well, I was – but it was more than that. It was the envy you feel when you're at school working your butt off, really struggling, and the kid that never tries, but for some reason all the teachers like, gets straight As. That was Angel. She never *tried*. She never begged or pleaded for anything. If Con, Luke, Jim, Joey or whoever wanted to do things for her, fine. If not, hey, there'd be others. She swam through her life easily and gracefully like a sleek, silvery fish.

Still, despite my misgivings, I liked Angel well enough. God knows she was easy to get on with if you didn't want anything more than a chat about clothes and such, or her exploits. I couldn't have lived with her or anything; she'd have driven me mad with boredom because she never read a book, or saw anything except popcorn movies, or took any interest whatsoever in the news, politics or culture of any sort. Nothing. Nada. Rien. Still, give her her due, she was generous to a fault and kind to people if it didn't actually cost her any effort. To be honest, I don't think there was a malicious bone in her body; she never bitched about anyone or put anyone down – but you can't be the object of such unquestioning worship all your life and be *right*, can you?

It wasn't only Con who thought the sun shone out of Angel's pert little butt, either. Apart from Git, as the season started to get under way, a flock of Baby Boy Yahs and just about every male regular in the café fell under her cool, distant spell. Luke hung around like a whipped puppy, I couldn't bear to look at him, and Jim n' Joey were pathetic. Even Tim Norris got the bug after she took him his 'usual' one morning, dressed in a scoop-neck aqua cashmere skinny-rib jumper and faded lo-rise boot-cut jeans that fitted like they'd been tailored for her and exposed her firm brown tummy with its blue topaz set belly-button bar piercing her perfect innie navel. As soon as she fixed him with those great, violet eyes and murmured, 'Here you are, love,' he was a goner. Mere running couldn't account for the sweat that broke out on his lumpy forehead. But she didn't notice him or the rest of her 'fan club', as Cookie called it disgustedly. She just drifted around like a vision of unattainable gorgeousness. La belle dame sans merci. What was that silly Flanders and Swann track dad used to play? Oh yeah, 'The beautiful lady who never says thank you'. That was Angel. A bloody phenomenon. A sort of mirage, a ghost you couldn't fight.

But Luke, Luke; it wasn't fair, it wasn't. She could have had anyone, anyone in the whole world. Why did she have to pick my Luke to play with, like a cat plays with a mouse? It doesn't mean to kill, it just wants a toy, a distraction but, oh dear, look: the mouse is dead, what a shame.

It broke my heart and I couldn't say a bloody word, not to *anyone*.

Chapter 9

'Astra? Astra? Have you seen those glittery scarves Sam brought back from Goa? I know I put them in my things drawer, but I just can't…'

'I'll get them, mum, I put them in the big chest – going out clubbing, are we?'

'Honestly, Astra – sometimes…I'm going to do a new class that's starting at High Tor. 'Oriental Dance: Reveal the Goddess Within'. Belly-dancing, you know. It's very exciting – it's about reclaiming our inner womanhood. Lots of us have signed up – Wanda and Janet and Sue are doing it, so I won't be alone. It's an old, old technique, from Pharaonic times. Ancient Egypt. I mean, Western people have totally misunderstood the whole nature of Oriental dance, all that stuff about being sexy for men when in fact, it's about women, for women. No, it is, really – look, read this leaflet, it's fascinating stuff. A *brilliant* woman called Nefertare Salop is teaching. She came the other day for a quick introduction, she was so centred, so calm and yet, wonderful energy just *radiated* from her. She's come all the way from Hampstead just for this course.' Mum's eyes widened and she looked quite pink. 'She's danced in Cairo, too. Cairo! In a real Egyptian place called the Palmyra! She showed us photographs, it looked amazing, really authentic. I mean Astra, can you imagine! Egypt! She's a proper belly-dancer, the real thing. So mystic, so spiritual!'

'And lovely frocks, too, I suppose?'

Mum's blush deepened. I couldn't help teasing her, and she didn't mind, really. Belly-dancing – my God, whatever next? Still, I rather fancied the idea myself; it did seem glamorous and all that wiggling had to be good exercise. Maybe Con would go with me – or Cookie. Now that, I'd pay good money to see.

'Oh, it's not – well, the outfits are – it's not about that. Well, not just that. It's a dance therapy for women, a healing thing. The clothes...'

Mum suddenly sat down on the bed, her hands full of gleaming sari fabric in shades of sapphire, fuchsia and imperial purple, the sequins and gold thread winking like a courtesan's eye.

'Astra – I – I do look rather washed out, don't I? Pale, I mean, you know. And my body – it's the muscle wastage. I know they said to expect it but...I was thinking about what Gita said, what Angel – I don't want your dad to, well, to – I thought this class, the pretty clothes, the exercise, the meaning in it...It might buck me up a bit, as a woman. It's not silly of me, is it?'

I knelt down and hugged her, her poor little shoulder-blades sticking out like bony wings through her saggy green jumper.

'Oh, bless, mum, of course it isn't. It isn't. It's a great idea, it really is. It'll do you the world of good, and all your pals are going. I fancy it myself – I do, honestly. As long as you feel well enough...'

'Yes, yes, I do, and Nefertare says we all go at our own pace and we just sort of *sway* if we can't keep up, or even sit quietly and watch – it's just as good as long as you concentrate properly on developing a true sense of the inner goddess...I want to do something, Astra, what Gita said worried me, I mean, I know it shouldn't matter, it doesn't matter, but...I can't help thinking that in a way, she's right. I shouldn't neglect my womanhood, my physical self, and this...'

'Sounds perfect, mum. I'm sure you'll – you'll benefit no end.' I should have said 'you'll have a fabulous time' but that would have rubbed her up the wrong way, even if it was true. It was therapy, OK?

It didn't stop me wanting to shake some sense into Git though – worrying mum with trivialities. Or were they? I had to concede a bit of fun like this would be good for mum, and – oh, you know. Every cloud has a nice, glittery sari-silk lining.

I wandered down to the café humming an Eastern-type tune (well, OK, the Fry's Turkish Delight theme) and imagining myself as a mysterious veiled houri dripping with jewels and swathed in diaphanous silks; I could get into it, I really could. Make a change from the baggies and old 'Surfers Against Sewage' T-shirt I was sporting. I practised smouldering.

'You got somethin' in yer eye?' asked Cookie as I slinked in.

'No, I'm thinking of taking up belly-dancing, actually. What d'you think, eh, Cooks, wanna come to a class with me?'

'Get away with yer.' Cookie bridled wonderfully and glared at me in outrage. 'All that foreign going on – half naked, wrigglin' yer arse about and showin' yer – yer – showin' all yer buzum! No thank you, I doan think so. What yer thinkin' of, at your age?'

'Oh, thanks a lot, I'm not *that* old, and you don't show yer buz – bosom, you can wear a long dress if you like, I saw the leaflet. Mum's going to do it, up at High Tor.'

'Your mum? Goin' dancin' – I doan believe it, I doan!' This really did stump Cookie, who viewed dancing with considerable suspicion and had never been seen to actually take the floor. 'What's possessed 'er? Poor liddle thing, it ain't right, she ain't strong – did you put it in 'er head?'

It took me five whole minutes to explain and I knew she didn't quite believe I wasn't forcing mum to go mad and fling herself around naked and unashamed.

'Anyhow, Cookie, being half naked's not a crime. You don't say anything about the girls on the beach, and…'

'Or in 'ere.' She gestured with a wooden spoon dripping chowder. 'Look at that. I dunno, Astra, it ain't right – she's hotter 'n' a bitch mackerel that 'un, as me gran used to say. Doan laugh! She's no better than a…'

'Cooks, don't.'

But I could see what she meant all right. Angel was draped over a chair, wearing denim micro shorts, a barely-there halter neck and a teeny beaded tie-front pink cardi. A rose-coloured sequinned mule swung from one immaculate toe and she was pouting as Tim Norris fiddled with a smart little lap-top computer and ran a finger round his collar. Tim – Jesus, I couldn't believe it. During the *afternoon*. Unheard of, like, totally. Dot was staring like a googly-eyed fool and

Ellie, one of the part-timers, nearly bumped into her with table four's pastie and chips.

I sauntered closer in a casual manner and started collecting plates. I couldn't stop staring at Tim in his ill-fitting polyester summer wash'n'wear suit and nasty cod-regimental tie. It was bizarre. He *never* varied his routine, ever, come rain or shine. He came in the morning after his run, delivered his little speech, had his hot chocolate, and that was it. Clockwork. Now here he was, blushing like a virgin bride and obviously demonstrating the ins and outs of computing to Angel. But why? I had to know, my finely developed gossip-radar demanded it.

'So you see, Miss Starbuck...'

'Oh, Timmy, call me Angel, please. I mean, there's no need to be formal – especially after you've been so kind – Astra! Come an' see what Timmy's brought me – int he kind! It's a little computer an' I can do the Internet on it – it's fantastic!'

She turned her mega-watt smile on poor, hapless Tim and a tide of red crept inexorably up from his damp collar.

'Oh, no – it's – really, it's nothing, I – it was – I've had it hanging around for – for months, it's no use to me. It was a – an unwanted gift. Yes. From a client. When I heard you mention the trouble you'd been having with your mobile – I mean, round here – it's...'

I thought he was going to choke. He didn't see me at all, he was like a doomed moth, all his being fixated on the flame beside him. Angel increased the wattage and gestured to her cute flip-open phone lying discarded by the computer.

'See, it don't work, Astra – they don't round here, do they, love? It were drivin' me crackers an' Tim heard me tellin' Con this mornin' that if it went on, I'd have to think about goin' on account of I couldn't get hold of anyone an' suchlike. You know, I mean, anyone in London, about a job – I mean, I've got ter get another job sometime, can't be on me holidays for ever, can I, Timmy?'

'Couldn't you just use the normal phone upstairs?' I sounded ungracious but it was awful watching 'Timmy' sweat at the thought of Angel leaving – which I was pretty sure she had no intention of doing until she was good and ready.

She laughed, throwing her head back and showing off the long smooth column of her throat. Then she put her head down and looked up at me amusedly through her lashes. 'Ooh, but I wouldn't want to interfere with Con's business stuff, now would I?'

Before I could think up a witty retort, or just a retort, actually, Tim was in like a shot.

'No – no – that wouldn't be at all wise. I mean, your sister's business, the phone, it's an essential – you're very thoughtful, Miss – er, Angel…'

'Oh, it's nowt, honestly, Timmy, I just don't like to get in Con's way. After all, she took me in when – when it – when I 'ad nowhere else to go an' that man 'ad been so awful…'

Tim knotted up like an enraged terrier. 'When I think of…'

'What?' I said, fascinated. 'What man? What happened?'

'Oh,' she tutted in that hissy Bradford way that always seemed so odd coming from her perfectly painted mouth. 'I were just tellin' Timmy – it were the bloke I were workin' for. At that jewellers in Kensington. "Bijoux" – that's French, like, for "jewels". 'Ave you heard of it? It's in *Vogue* all the time…Oh well, never mind. The owner, my boss, like, he got a bit – well, you know. A bit funny. I told 'im I weren't interested – I mean, he were *ancient*, nearly forty! An' not exactly a looker, if you know what I mean. Oh, loaded, sure, filthy rich, but what a creep! Anyway, I come home from a club one night, an' there he is! Only waitin' for me in his bloody Merc parked up outside my flat! Says he's left his wife an' kids, an' we're to go off together somewhere – to France or somethin'! I couldn't believe it – I never give him a bit of encouragement, never! But he got all mental, I 'ad to call the coppers, it were just awful, him cryin' an' carryin' on about me ruinin' his life – I were *so* embarrassed! After the copper come, he takes off, an' next thing I hear is – he's only gone an' took an overdose! *Honestly*. He didn't die or anything – it were a cry for help, they said in the hospital, a mid-life crisis. Not that I went to see him or anything, Zoë did that, the other assistant. I were grateful to be out of it, I can tell yer. But he had his lawyer send me all these nasty letters about giving back the jewellery he'd give me? Not that I particularly wanted it, or owt, but a lawyer! I put me foot down then, I mean, it's not like I'd *asked* for it or anything. So I come down here – to visit Con, like. I mean, I were that upset…'

I realised it was useless to comment. Tim had joined the Misty Gaze club and Angel's face was a mask of self-righteousness. *Wait till Cookie hears this*, I thought, then it occurred to me the earrings she'd given me were ill-gotten gains from this bloke. Jesus. I promised myself I'd give her them back tomorrow. Definitely.

As I mechanically collected dirty dishes and took out bowls of soup and hot rolls, plates of pasties and chips, Surfer's Specials, ice-creams and cappuccinos, I thought about what Angel had said. It bugged me. I mean, if you sort of analysed it, she sounded incredibly selfish – but then again, what could she have done? I suppose I did tend to blame Angel straightaway – you know, *I bet she led him on*. It may not be nice but that's what my first reaction was – her clothes, her looks, that curiously distant flirtiness as if she went through the motions of seduction because, well, because that's what a girl who looked like her should do. In a mad moment, I wondered if she'd have been happier as a rocket scientist or something, if she'd stayed at school, been academic. Then she wouldn't have had to bother with all this pretty-woman stuff; and it did seem sometimes as if her mind wasn't really on the pouting and eyelash-fluttering. But what was it on then? She certainly didn't give the impression she was interested in anything else, so, what was ticking away in that blonde head? Was she a heartless gold-digger, or merely a rather naïve, slightly dippy girl? What *was* Angel?

Well, whatever she was, it didn't seem to matter to Timmy-baby. At one point as I slormed past balancing plates and mugs he was telling Angel how to set up an Internet account – something I was dead jealous about, as I wanted one but so far, I hadn't got round to setting one up. I hovered, discreetly; fortunately, we weren't busy.

'So, this is a modem, in this case, it's a portable one, you just slip it in the side of the computer – here – and you then take this end and put it in the telephone…Look, I – perhaps we could go upstairs and I could set up the whole thing for you, if you don't mind that is – if you don't think your sister would…'

I butted in. 'Oh, the Internet – I really want to...'

Tim glared at me and I stepped back involuntarily. *Easy, tiger*, I thought, *steady on*. I wouldn't dream of coming between you and your putative totty, Timster, old mate. Tosser. I picked up their cups and pretended I hadn't spoken – Angel smiled lazily, her attention drifting to the beach. I looked too, and saw she was watching Luke, who was coming towards the café. He saw her and waved, his face lit up like a beacon. He was carrying something, but I couldn't make out what it was. I looked away quickly; his expression was too naked to bear.

'Hmm,' Angel said, stretching like a golden panther, Tim's muddy blue eyes riveted to her arched back and consequently, to her pointy *buzum*. 'Let's go, Timmy. I really need to get in touch with people and since you're here...Oh, you don't 'ave any work, or anythin', do yer? I wouldn't want to be a *nuisance*...'

Tim managed to tear his gaze away from her chest and burbled something about how totally, totally free he was, tripping over himself like a circus clown. Angel wandered off with El Timmo in tow in time for Luke to see the door to upstairs shut behind them. His smile collapsed like a sandcastle at high tide. I stood in front of him while he craned to see round me. There was a small, persistent hurty place in my chest when I looked at him, but increasingly, it was mingled with a faint but unmistakable twinge of exasperation. He looked like a sucking foal who'd lost his mother.

'Want a coffee, Luke? *Luke* – coffee?' I couldn't believe how I talked to him these days, but if I didn't go at him like his mum, he didn't hear me.

'What? Oh, er – yeah. Sure. Er, do you think Angel will be long? Only, I – I wanted to ask her if I could take some shots of her for – for...'

I didn't say what came rudely into my mind. 'I didn't know you were a photographer? Is that your camera – looks posh.'

He looked at the camera in his hand as if it were something peculiar he'd picked up on the shoreline. 'I – yeah, I like to take pictures. This one's digital, so I can put stuff straight on my computer, fiddle with it, you know. I've been thinking of taking it up, professionally. My father's company have some magazines – I could...I took loads of shots this winter, I was thinking, perhaps, sports pics – my sort of sports that is, surfing, snowboarding – I mean, with the weather as it is, there's no surf and not likely to be for ages, so I – I – look, about Angel...' He was flustered again, strained and flustered, his face white except for two splotches of red on his cheekbones. It was so unlike the Luke I'd – well, not that I'd known, but who we'd all thought of as unflappable, serene, distant, that it made me angry. I don't know who at: him, me – or Angel?

'Sorry, I'm not her personal secretary. Perhaps you'd better book an appointment.' I sounded snotty. I was snotty. I was about to get snottier when he took the wind right out of my sails.

'I'm sorry. I'm sorry. I really am. God, I sound like a real idiot, pathetic. I'm sorry, Astra – Star. See, I remember, I'm not completely fucked up. Star. You are a star, too. You'd have every right to tell me to fuck off and – I – she doesn't even notice me, does she?'

He looked so crushed I didn't have the heart to tell him it was all part of the game to her. Nothing personal. Treat 'em mean, keep 'em keen. Just a reflex on her behalf.

'Oh, Luke. Look, she's – she won't be long, I'm sure. That Tim Norris, you know, the running bloke, the accountant, he's sorting her out with the Internet, lending her a computer. They won't be long – here, have a coffee, on the house. I'll bring it you, just you sit down, love.' Poor sod, he looked gutted.

He waited an hour and a half. He looked so doggy even Cookie felt sorry for him and gave him a plate of chips. Eventually, Tim, Angel and Con came downstairs and with much inept, twittering gosh-it-was-nothings and just-call-me-anytimes Tim managed to force himself to leave. Angel put her arm round Con's waist and kissed her cheek, like she always did.

'Think I'll go fer a walk, love. You comin', Luke ? Ohh, is that yer camera? Nice...'

I watched them walk away, Angel pausing to take off her mules on the sand and stroll on, swinging them like a Fifties film star. Luke was obviously talking to her excitedly, but even at a distance, you could see she wasn't listening.

Con smiled thoughtfully. 'He's a nice boy. Good family. His dad's worth a packet and there's no one but him to inherit. She could do worse, definitely. Mind you, he hasn't got a proper job, so I don't know...'

'Co-*on*! You sound like a bloody *matchmaker* – listen to yerself, honestly!'

She bridled and made a face. 'Well, I've got to see her right, I can't have her runnin' off with any Tom, Dick or Harry. She needs security. A decent income. Look at her, just gorgeous, int she? I can't believe she come from our lot, we're all such skinny sticks, but her! Well, there you go.'

I sighed. This was not the Con I'd known, not at all. She was so totally caught up in her sister she seemed to have lost her sense of humour, everything. I shrugged, feeling left out and to be honest, a bit miffed. Still, I suppose Angel was her only living relative now; maybe she felt she had to be extra responsible for her and it was weighing her down. I caught sight of Cookie, who was rolling her eyes. I sighed again. I seemed to be doing that a lot recently. *Wow, heav-vee sigh time*, as Dylan used to say to me when I was a depressed Goth.

Yeah, too right. Wow.

Chapter 10

'Shoo! Shoo! Git off, you raggy barsterds! Git, off, go!' Cookie flapped her stumpy, work-reddened hand at the black smattering of crows picking at the bins out back, waving her broom at them, her face squinched in distaste. 'Ugh, I 'ate birds, I really do, nasty bony, beaky barsterds, yuk.'

'Oh, so I won't get that canary I was thinking of for you this Christmas, then?'

'Thank you, clever clogs. But look, there's loads of 'em, loads more 'n usual this time of year.' She squinted up at the cloud-flat sky and pointed. There were lots of crows, it was true, circling and splattering away into the grey like drops of ink from a pen and the eaves of the house further up the hill was a mass of gulls.

'Well, never mind, they can't hurt you. Do you really not like them, birds, I mean, like a phobia?'

'I saw that bloody film, didn' I, when I were liddle. Urgh, never liked 'em since. Sneaky things, nasty, pecky buggers. Gulls, too, dirty things. But specially crows. Always know more'n they tell, crows, my nan says. They're the devil's eyes, she says, spying on us, waitin'. It ain't funny! I doan like 'em one bit. An' something else, too. If the weather doan clear up soon, we're stuffed. Mrs Liddicoate says the B&Bs are gettin' cancellations already an' we've 'ardly started the season. It ain't good. Bloody crows. '

She grumbled off and I started to follow her, then I paused. She was right, the weather was lousy. It wasn't rain, so much as cloud and no wind; not a breeze stirred the marram grass or the black silhouettes of the tall pines on the hill that were engraved sharply against the dull, lowering sky. It was sticky and warmish, but somehow chilly at the same time – like fever. Not comfortable at all, and a creeping whiff of rotting seaweed from the cove round the headland that always filled up with weed and debris seemed to hang like a horrid sort of incense in the flat air. The tourists we had were getting grumpy, and yesterday someone had complained indignantly to Jim that there was no surf, so he'd told them the council had turned off the wave machine due to economic cuts. We'd thought that was hilarious, but no surf meant no tourists. The beach that stretched away in a rippled arc of soft, beautiful sand, the little sheltered nooks in the cliff where grannies could doze undisturbed while mums read their beach books and dads beat their kids at cricket weren't enough these days. Surfing was cool, it was the body-board and Malibu hire that drew them; no rolled trousers and knotted hankies anymore, it was all ill-fitting neoprene and cheap-jack eye-popping surfie wear. I remembered what Luke had said too – no surf and no sign of any to come. If anyone knew the weather and the sea, it was him, so if he thought it was going to stay calm, it probably was.

A crow fluttered down on to the wall beside me, its shiny black wings folded behind its back like an old-fashioned lawyer in a tail coat, a knowing gleam in its wicked jet eyes. I stared back at it defiantly. It cocked its head and opened its beak, the liverish hump of its tongue visible. I don't think it thought a lot of me. I shivered involuntarily; someone walking on my grave. God, I must be getting cranky if a bloody bird could make me feel – what? Guilty, nervy? Neurotic, more like. I stared back at the raggety brute. It stared back, unabashed, then skittered sideways in that curious, mechanical-doll way they have. Bloody thing. I stood up abruptly and pinched my bra down at the sides, getting myself settled. I could smell my body, warm and lemoney from my deodorant. At least I was flesh and blood, not a bony bundle of feathers and lice like Mr Soot here, the old git. I turned on the crow, suddenly cross for no reason.

'Gerr, get off, go on, fuck off! Cookie's right, you're all beaky barsterds!'

If a crow could laugh, it would have done. I went back into the café.

It was a good thing I did, too.

As I opened the door and stepped through, there was a Godalmighty row coming from the front and I ran in, but as I started for the seating area, Cookie grabbed my arm and hissed at me.

'Easy, doan go gettin' mixed up in this – it's bloody madam again, only this time, Con's in it.'

'Wha – what?'

Cookie nodded, her face set. 'Angel. She were – "helpin" you know. Wrigglin' about, pickin' up a couple o' dishes then prancin' back with 'em like she were doin' us all a favour. Anyways, some of them Yah boys from up Dylan's said somethin' – you know, about shaggin' her, I didn' hear properly, but you can guess, an' Con heard. She's gone ballistic, chucked 'em out. I dunno, what's it comin' to when this sorta stuff happens? I 'ad all sorts said to me when *I* were a waitress, but you doan pay no mind, do yer? It ain't right, Con bein' this way with that girl, it ain't right at all.'

Cookie looked furious, her lips pale and her eyes sparking. I began to speak when I realised something. She was jealous – oh, not of Angel's looks like the rest of us, but of her special treatment. The way everyone protected her, looked out for her. I suspected the only person who had thought Cookie worth protecting was Smoky's dada – no wonder she loved him so much. But Cookie would never admit jealousy, she'd just say it 'weren't fair'. I was about to say something conciliatory, on a reflex, like I always did at home, but I stopped. She was right, it wasn't fair. In fact, it was bloody unfair the way people treated non-Angel type girls – women, oh, whatever. You know, fat girls, even plump girls. Plain girls. Spotty girls, girls with buck teeth, great big legs or ditchwater no-hope hair. Nervy, shy girls; over-compensating, insecure, loud girls. Girls who cried into their pillows at night and slept with lads no one else would because that was all they could expect to get. Girls about whom those lads said 'You don't look at the fireplace when yer stokin' the fire'. Or girls like Cookie who seem so capable, or 'hard', as stupid people say; Cookie with her feckless alcoholic ma and surly dad – the kind of fella who'd rather fight than eat meat, as they say round here. Cookie with her narrow, white face and slanty khaki eyes. Cookie of the jangly gold creole earrings, crunchy perm and nylon tracksuits. Cookie the survivor who'd die rather than be pitied or play the googly-eyed girlie card. Who had loved so loyally and lost so proudly and was the fiercest little mother in the world, bursting with love for her kid at every seam. No, it wasn't fair and no one gave those lasses a second look – or chance, in Cookie's case, while the Angels of this world…There was nothing sensible I could say. I made a worried face at Cooks, who snorted disgustedly. With a heavy heart, I walked over to where Con was standing, hands on hips, shouting out of the door like a fishwife.

I couldn't believe it, I really couldn't. Con acting like this, it just wasn't her. I mean, sure, she had a temper and she could be pretty damn steely about stuff, but red in the face, bawling, *messy*? No, not Con. My knees felt shaky with adrenalin as I touched her rigid shoulder.

'An' don't you come back, neither! Your sort aren't welcome 'ere – yer dirty-minded little…! Filthy – what would your mother think of yer? Go on, get off, get off wi' yer!' Her accent was pure *Brat-furd*. She was trembling, her chest heaving, her cheeks mottled.

'Con – Con – come on, love, come on. Leave it, it ain't worth it, leave it now. Come an' 'ave a cuppa, come on. Sit down now, please.' I spoke gently but she turned in my hold like a stick of wood grinding in an iron socket.

'Oh, it's you – I – I – oh Astra, honestly, the disgustin' – the way they talk, these lads, it's not right. What he said! I'll not – I'll not 'ave 'em in here goin' on like that! It's my place, I can do as I please, I…' She swayed a little and I put my arm around her waist, like Angel always did. I could feel her heart thudding. I guided her towards the back room, away from the fascinated gazes of the few customers remaining, who sat gawping at the side-show, chips falling from their open mouths. I made the one-handed tea-sign at Cooks, who nodded and poured a mug out, handing it to me as I settled Con on the creaky wicker chair next to Smoky's lobster-pot. He looked very subdued, his perfect rosy lower lip stuck out, his beautiful eyes the size of saucers, a string-leg cow toy grasped in his dimpled hands.

Con glanced down at him and gave a deep, wobbly sigh. 'Oh, Smoky, little love, Auntie's sorry, darlin', sorry for shoutin'. It's all all

right now, all all right. Look, look at Mrs Cow, look at her leggies
– show Astra Mrs Cow, sweetheart…' She turned her head away, tears
glittering on her sandy lashes. I played with Smoky for a while until
he was settled then made Con drink her tea. Dot looked in, her face
a question mark, her skinny crescent-moon eyebrows disappearing
into her matte orange curls. I nodded at her and she sucked her back
teeth (what was left of them) and went out again.

Con blew her nose and sat up straight in the frayed chair. 'Sorry.
Sorry. I am – I'm sorry. I don't know what come over me, I really don't.
It's just…'

'It doesn't matter, love, honestly. Those lads can be…'

'No – I were wrong to go off the deep end like that. It's just – oh, I
can't bear to hear someone like that talk about her in that way. Do you
know what he said?'

'It doesn't…'

'It does. It does matter. She doesn't have anyone to – to defend her.
I mean our dad's gone, she's got no husband, not even a steady. If she'd
had a boyfriend even – but she doesn't and I just don't understand it.
That lad said' – she leaned forward, away from Smoky, as if he could
understand – 'he said he'd like to – to do it to her – up the bum. Only
not in them words, you know what I mean. That's what he said, plain
as day, and all his dirty little mates sniggering. Oh Astra, it made me
so mad, so mad that someone like that would insult her an' get away
with it. I don't know, I just – I just sort of lost control.'

'It's OK, Con, it really is, it's only natural. I'd go loopy if anyone
said something like that about Git, I would. Anyone would, Angel's
your only family now, your little sis. Don't worry, it's the weather too,
it's so stuffy, it's drivin' us all crackers. Look, you go have a lie-down,
then later, you could…'

But she wasn't listening. Her face was turned back to Smoky, who
was bouncing Mrs Cow around and humming to himself. Con leaned
over the edge of the playpen and stretched out her hand to him. He
looked up and smiled. She chucked his round cheek and ruffled his
curls, then she got up and smiled shakily. You could almost see the
fibres of herself twitching as she got them under control again.

'I – er, I think I'll go and look at the accounts, maybe go up to Mrs Liddicoate's and see about more scones. Will you be…?'

'Oh yeah – we'll be fine, you go.'

'Thank you, love. Astra – I – you're a good lass, one of the best. A good friend – I – there's stuff you should know, I ought to tell you – it's just – oh, thank you for puttin' up with my nonsense. I think I'm a bit over-tired or summat. I haven't been sleeping so well, you're right, this muggy weather…'

I looked at her strained face as she left and wondered, not for the first time, if she was starting the menopause. I drifted back to Cookie.

'D'you think it's the Change?'

Cookie stopped frying and considered. 'Might be. Comes to us all in time. Course, it might just be stress, like normal. Must be a stress, 'avin' that un round all the time, just hanging round, doin' nothing but upset folks.' Nothing would make Cookie give an inch about Angel. I still felt somehow it wasn't exactly her fault, though. It was just that – well, things happened round Angel, that was all.

The rest of the day passed pretty uneventfully, apart from two kiddies being brought in with weaver fish stings. The first one belonged to a nice family who were very grateful for our help – we make the victim put the stung bit in very hot, then very cold water; it usually does the trick. Bloody painful though, the weaver fish business. The second lot just moaned about how little Jonty was making a big fuss over nothing and spoiling their picnic. Idiots, the poor kid was as white as a sheet and crying his eyes up. Still, there's no accounting for people. Two kids in one day was a bit odd and I sincerely hoped there wasn't going to be a weaver fish plague, that was all we needed.

There was no sign of Angel all day, then just before we shut up for the night, she floated in, stretching and yawning like a cat.

'Any scran left?'

I brought her a plate of chips and a tea-cake.

'Where you been all day? Con was very upset, you know.'

I tried to sound stern, but it was useless, it rolled off her like water off a duck's back.

'I know, sorry. I just can't stand scenes, though.' She toyed with a chip, as if it were a Tiffany bangle or something. 'I went to Crossford, to do some shopping, then I went to the pictures. Tim took me, in his new car – it's a Saab. He says it's a top-quality car, nothing flashy, not like some folk would go for. I must say it's very comfortable.'

'You went with Tim? But it's a weekday – what about his work, he...'

'His – oh, he says that's the joy of self-employment, you can do as you like, pretty much. Don't look like that, Astra, honestly, he's just that sort of bloke, likes to be useful – a handbag-holder, we say in London.' She giggled.

'But he'll think – you going round with him – I thought you and Luke...'

'Well, you thought wrong, then. Oh anyhow, please! Tim? I don't think so. He looks like Ma Liddicoate's terrier. No, he's just a bit of a lonesome fella, you know. Just him and his old mum in that bungalow. There's no need for me to be nasty to him just because he wants to get out a bit more.'

And spend his money, I thought. A new car, Tim? Whatever next, a micro-scooter? Rollerblades? Plastic surgery? I was barely listening as Angel prattled on about the film and how gorgeous Brad Pitt was, as if no other woman had ever made that startling discovery, when I jerked back like a hooked fish.

'...so I said of course I can't move in with you, don't be daft, I hardly know yer! But that's Luke, such a kid! What a dreamer! Oh don't get me wrong, he's great, but I want someone a bit older in himself like, a bit more mature...'

I felt a dull thud in my heart. Luke must really be serious if he'd wanted her to live with him; he was always so solitary, so self-contained. Oh, fuck it...

'Are you OK? You look all weird.'

I sat down heavily. 'Yeah, yeah – it's just – well, round here, Luke...'

'Oh, I know. Mr Surfie God. Well, not much for him ter do these days, is there. Flat as a pancake out there. God, don't look like that, it weren't serious. I couldn't be wi' a bloke like that permanent or anythin', he hasn't even got a proper job, a career, nothing. Still lives offa his mam and dad – well, his dad really, seeing as his mam's only a step. Here, have a sip of my tea, you look terrible. You're not really upset about Luke, are you? You're too sensitive, that's your trouble. Look at how you go on wi' your family – I mean, you're a saint, really. Everyone thinks so – no, it's true. Givin' up your life to look after yer mam like that. It's like one of them historical dramas on the telly. I don't know what I'd do, I really don't. Con says you give up uni and everything...' She sighed, and gazed at me thoughtfully. 'Yer know what? When I go back up London. You should come an' stay. It'd do yer good, get out a bit, meet people. I mean, you're ever so pretty – no, you are, really. I love your hair, like I said. Lose a bit of weight, get a proper cut, some new kit – you'd be a stunna! Luke loves you to bits, he does! Says yer name means "star" – does it? Now, int that lovely. He thinks the world of you, says you're so friendly and kind. Well, you *are*! I could talk to you all day, I could.'

'But – isn't he upset – that you won't...'

'Nah – well, a bit, I suppose. But you know lads, they just hang around lookin' doggy and think it'll all come out how they want it to if they go on about it enough. I don't mind goin' round with him an' – you know...' She giggled again. 'But that's as far as it goes. He's not really my type. No more'n Timmy is...' This time she laughed out loud. I winced, as if Tim could hear what she thought of him all the way up in New Polwenna, as he sat in front of the telly with his mam knitting him yet another Fair Isle tank top or whatever they did of an evening.

Angel suddenly squealed, nearly giving me a cardiac. 'Oo! Yer know what, I nearly forgot! I were e-mailing them mates of mine in London, an' tellin' 'em how lovely it were down here and some of 'em are gonna come for a week to a house near Newquay that a mate of Richie Lomas has lent them! And Richie himself's comin' too, it's perfect! Come on, Astra, Richie Lomas – you know!'

I looked blankly at her and she sighed theatrically and rolled her eyes. 'Rich-*ie* Lo-*mas*! Him as *owns* Imago Records! An' he's gonna come to your Beaker's gig – I told him to, said I 'ad a mate down 'ere whose fella's band were fantastic, really cool – I did. Him and the crowd are just dying to hang out down here, ever since *Esquire* did that Cool Cornwall thing and Madonna and Guy had that holiday here they did pics of for *Vogue* – so I says, "here I am, come on down!" So they are – int that great? Now, Richie, there's the sort of fella you could go for – if only his wife would divorce him and have done wi' it…It'd be so fantastic if he signed Beaker. He's such a *nice* lad, Beaker, so quiet…' She beamed happily.

Imago Records, Jesus H. Christ. Wait, oh *wait* till I told the Beaks!

The next morning, we got the first rose.

Book 3

The dragon-green, the luminous, the dark, the serpent-haunted sea.

—James Elroy Flecker

Chapter 11

It was on the counter when I got into work; a glowing scarlet rose, thickly crimson and velvety like a splotch of blood on a long thornless stem, stuck in an empty mineral water bottle for want of a vase. I sighed as I saw it because guess what? Somehow I just knew it wasn't for me. Ho hum.

I could have done with cheering up, too. It had been a hideous rush at home that morning. Mum was off to her belly-dance class and had got a dither on, couldn't find her favourite scarf and then Git had walked past, wearing it raggled up in her hair, so there was a row about 'personal possessions' and Lance, who for once had slept at home, had come storming out of his dank hole of a room swearing because Gwen had pinned one of her tracts to his pillow so he had a right go at her for being a silly cow in general and…Me and Dad sat out on the deck and tried to have a civilised breakfast but the sight of yet another still, steaming, hazy day made my organic cornflakes stick in my craw.

'Coleridge,' Dad said, munching on a bit of toast. He chucked a crust at one of the hordes of ravenous gulls that were clotting up every available perching place that wasn't taken by the sodding crows. Behind him in the sitting-room, Git was flouncing and mum was stuffing glittery things into an eco-baggie. Fortunately, with the French windows shut, we couldn't hear them.

'What?' I said, puzzled.

'Coleridge:

> *All in a hot and copper sky,*
> *The bloody Sun, at noon;*
> *Right up above the mast did stand,*
> *No bigger than the Moon.*

Day after day, day after day,
We stuck, nor breath nor motion;
As idle as a painted ship
Upon a painted ocean.

Ta dum ta da, ta dee ta dum – I forget most of it. Had it by heart at school. *The Ancient Mariner.* Wow, those were the days, I *don't* think – still, it's pretty much that sort of scene out there again today, isn't it? Cool guy, Mr C. Trouble with his teeth, though, by all accounts, took opium for the pain. Now, when I took it in India that time, it was some weird trip, let me tell you...'

And he wandered happily off into hippie drug nostalgia until I kissed his big old head and ran down the path to the café.

The rose – in all its expensive, perfect glory – was waiting, a tag hanging from it limply.

'Ooo, for moi? You shouldn't have!' I trilled sweetly at Con, who smiled and chucked a cloth at me. She seemed her old self again today and I felt a little wave of relief.

I looked at the tag; it was from Posy's Posies, the smart new florist's in Crossford and the dedication read '*To my Angel*'; no sender's name. Well, yeah, I hadn't *really* thought it was for me.

'Lovely, isn't it?' Con said, still smiling. 'A secret admirer, eh? It was outside the door when I got here, all wrapped in cellophane and that curly ribbon stuff. She's seen it, I took it up to her – but she said to put it here to give the place a nice splash of colour.'

Show it off, more like. Oh, grouchy cow award – OK, OK, I'd like everyone to know if I had a besotted swain. Still after the news about Imago Records and the Future Of Rock And Roll as I now secretly called Element's up-coming gig, I practically did. Beaker was making like it was all my doing and last night we'd – well, I won't kiss and tell. I felt pretty sparky meself, though.

A rose arrived every day. The same thing, the same tag. No name, just '*To my Angel*'. Every morning dead early, the delivery fella dropped it off. Con stopped him one morning and asked who was sending them, but he said it was more'n his job was worth to tell as the person had wished to remain anonymous. But he would say how as it were a standing order so we could expect 'em ter keep comin', and what's more, they weren't cheap, neither, and he winked. Oo-er. It was the talk of the café – well, there wasn't much doing apart from more weaver fish stings, and then on Thursday the morning tide brought in a dead sheep that lay like a stinking, matted bone rack oozing into the flat, rippled sand and was the fascination of the tourist kids until the council came and removed it.

Oh, and the fact Angel bought a dog. A puppy, actually. A fat, squirming yellow Labrador Andrex pup called Piglit. As in Pooh. Apparently, she'd been out with Timmykins in the Saab for a drive and there'd been a sign saying 'Puppies' , and – oh, Piglit was just too, too cute to *leave*.

He was immensely cute, it was true. We all fell deeply in love, especially Smoky, but there were just a few teensy problem-ettes. The no-dogs-allowed beach for one, and who was going to train him, walk him, feed him? Who would have him when Angel went back to London because her flat was a definite no-pet zone; Con, of course. She nearly put her foot down but then she saw Smoky and Piglit sleeping in a tangle of silly yellow pup and brown baby curls and she crashed in flames. Piglit was home and free.

Actually, he was a bit of a draw in the café. All the tourists adored him and small children fed him ice-cream until he puked and we had to put up a 'Please don't feed Piglit the Pup between meals' sign that no one paid any heed to, naturally. Con said walking him would do her good and she got a book out of the mobile library van about dog-training. Cookie made Angel take him to be injected and wormed on the grounds of Smoky's health and I wasted hours fuzzing him up and generally worshipping his tiny paws. I love animals, totally soppy, and we hadn't been able to have pets after mum got ill in case of allergies, or just the hassle of looking after one more sentient creature while she was at her worst. Now she was more steady, we'd talked about a cat, but never got round to it. Now there was a ready-made pet-share scheme. I bought in, good style. Piglit *ruled*. At last Angel had done something everyone could approve of – despite the impracticality of it. And she made such a pretty picture, hugging her puppy dog and pouting.

It didn't take long for us to discover who'd actually shelled out for Piglit. I mean, Piggie was a pedigree Lab and not cheap, not a rescue mongrel by any means. Tim made sure everyone knew exactly who'd paid for Piglit; he'd dwell long and hard on the price, the pedigree and the generosity of his gift in that indirect way some people have. Bringing it up every time he spoke, but always pretending it was in reference to something else. Like, oh, a bloke he'd met who'd said Labs were inbred, but in Tim's opinion, a dog with Piglit's pedigree, who cost that much, was definitely a bargain because, etcetera, etcetera. Every time he came in. And he came in all the time now, not just in the morning – when Angel wasn't usually up anyway – dressed in strange, brand-new Marks and Sparks bloke's leisure wear. Not the trendy M&S stuff, but the older-chap polo shirt and pleat-fronted chino kit in shades of sludge. He obviously thought it was rippingly dashing gear and his tufty moustache bristled with pride as he sipped his hot chocolate or tea and stared fixedly at Angel, following her every movement like one of those robot car workers. Click, click, click – you could practically hear the joints in his neck moving.

Tim was one of those men who are fifty from the age of sixteen. Like those awful brats who speak at the Tory Party conferences. I don't think he was much over thirty-five but you'd think he was a pensioner, the way he talked; living with his mum made him like that, I suppose. It gave me a bit of a shudder, listening to him. I mean, what if I got like that, all picky and stiff, full of stock phrases and automatic judgements? Like Angel said, a character from a historical costume drama. 'Dear, dear Miss Sharp, such a devoted daughter, an example to us all, don't you think, Vicar...' Bleugh. No, not me, please; and the hair would prickle on my neck.

But that wasn't the only thing that made me shudder – well, cringe, to be accurate. It was the way Tim treated Piglit. He obviously hadn't had much to do with animals and he kept trying to impress Angel with his manliness. He'd pick Piggie up by the scruff and let him dangle pathetically, then shake him a bit and say something about what a fine dog. But Piglit was too old to be picked up like that and when Tim set him down, he'd cower with his silly little tail between his legs and then try and scarper when Tim's eye was off him. Then Tim would try coaxing him, rubbing his fingers in that come-along-doggie way and making kissy noises. But Piglit would have none of it and a flare of anger would mottle Tim's flat cheeks.

One day, he grabbed Piglit and must have nipped him somehow, because Piglit squealed like his namesake and the whole café turned to stare. Tim went puce and dropped the pup sharpish. Angel whipped round and picked up the dog, kissing and soothing him as if he were a baby.

'What d'you think yer doin', eh? You hurt 'im, you clumsy bugger… There, there, Pigsie, mummy's got yer now. Jesus, Tim, he's shiverin'.'

'I, er – it was an accident – I…'

'Oh, right. Fine. You hurt *my dog* again, Tim, an' you'll be sorry. I won't 'ave it, I won't.'

The whole place was fascinated by this exchange and you could see all the blokes admiring Angel in that what-a-spitfire, you're-so-beautiful-when-you're-cross way. Not that they'd have cared to have that anger directed at them in public, oh no.

And neither did Tim. He went white, then magenta, then white again like a bloody traffic light and he worked his hands together convulsively until the knuckles cracked. You could almost see something squirming in his mind, then it jumped out of his mouth like a frog out of a hole.

'It's my dog too. I paid…'

Clutching the now wriggling Piglit, Angel took a step towards Tim and he blanched whiter still and stepped back. Suddenly, all that was square and angular in her jaw, and ugly in the pulled-down corners of her pouty mouth leaped into sharp relief. She shifted Piglit under one arm and stabbed at Tim with her index finger.

'My dog, Tim. *Mine*. Just you remember that. A gift's a gift, matey. Well, it is where I come from, anyways. If you want the *money* for him, if it's the *money* you want, *Tim*, just ask. Well, d'yer? Eh, do yer?' Tim was speechless. 'No? Well then, that's an end of it – oh, get outta my sight, you useless – go on, get out. Blokes like you, yer all the same, everythin' wi a price tag. Yer mek me poorly, you do, *poorly*.'

Tim stumbled out and Angel stalked out the back and defiantly lit a fag, dropping Piglit, who skittered off, his claws scrabbling on the wooden floor, to his beloved Smoky.

She sat on the low wall that ran round the yard, smoking furiously, kicking her silvery trainers against the concrete, the crows that had been lurking hopefully round the bins scattering in a splatter of blackness. I sat next to her.

'Stop it, you'll spoil your shoes.' I sounded mumsy, even to myself; it was a habit I couldn't break, it seemed.

She cast a sidelong glance at me, mutinously. I folded my arms and waited.

''Spose you think I shouldn't 'ave gone at him like that, don't yer?'

'Well, to be honest, I think it were a bit much. You know what he's like, and since he did pay for Piglit apparently – if you...'

She sighed and cast the half-smoked fag away. All the anger had gone out of her, just like that. It was as if she just couldn't be bothered to sustain it for any length of time. Too much hassle, and Angel hated hassle. 'Yeah, yeah, yeah – I know. I shouldn't let him buy me stuff, Con's always on at me about it. But I can't hardly stop him, can I? Not if he's dead set on it – how can I? He'd just do it anyways, he's that sort. Like them bloody roses. I never asked for them, now did I?'

Oh, so it *was* Tim. I'd sort of thought as much. It was either him or Luke and I didn't think it was Luke's style. He'd be more likely to bring his beloved a pretty shell he found while he was snorkelling or something. No, on reflection, it was very Tim. Conventional. Straight. A dozen long-stemmed red roses for the girl you loved.

'...it's just an Internet thing, them flowers. All he has to do is order 'em and bingo! I can't stop him if he does that, can I? God, Astra, you're so – so *good*. Oh, I don't mean it nasty, I don't, honest. But you know what I mean. Look, I know I'm not the brightest button in the box but I'm not thick, either. Blokes look at me – they look and they think they're in love – you know, *in luh-ve*. But they int. It's just shaggin'. It is, don't look like that. It's just they think, a lass like me is – expensive. Not a bit of totty they can knock off an' no questions asked. I look classy, I know I do. I've made mesel look that way because, when blokes think like that about yer, that you won't give it up easy, they mek more effort. They like the chase, that's all. Astra, love, see, if I want a nice house, nice clothes, a nice life, then I have to find the right bloke. That's how it is for me. I'm not like Con. I don't want to work my bollocks off in a caff fer sod all an' end up an old maid who...'

She stopped, and stretched out her hand to me. 'I'm sorry, oh, I'm sorry, Astra love, I didn't mean...You're not like that, you're not. It's Con I meant, just Con – I mean I love her to bits but you know how she is, all work, no play. You're young an' pretty, you've got Beaker an' everything. God, me an' my big mouth, honestly.'

I swallowed hard, the lump in my throat wedged tight. 'It's all right. I didn't – don't worry. I know what you mean. But Angel, please – Tim's not in your league, he's just a – well, he's a geek, be honest. He's not – well, he's not *right*, is he? Not the full ticket, even. Don't laugh, you know it's true, everyone says it. Just let him down easy, that's all. I mean, he's not exactly fair game, now is he?'

She giggled lazily. 'Yeah, yer right. Poor sap. I shouldn't mess about wi' the likes of him, but I just get so bored, you know? But tell yer what, Richie e-mailed me last night sayin' how much he was lookin' forward to seein' me, so...'

'What about Luke?' I couldn't help it, I just couldn't.

'What about...? Oh, I see what yer mean. My little holiday romance. Shame about 'im really. I mean, he's dead nice-lookin' an' that, an' he int poor, that's the truth – but...Nah. No get-up-an'-go, that one.' She tapped the nail of her index finger against her front tooth and fixed her eyes on me thoughtfully. 'Yeah, I'll let him down easy, too, I promise. You've got a right little crush on him, ent yer?' She smiled and stubbed out her cigarette.

I went so red, so suddenly, I thought I'd explode. Sweat sprang out under my hair and I felt my insides go quivery with embarrassment. Jesus! 'What – no, don't be daft! Me? No – it's just – well, he's got a lot of respect round here and...'

'Get off wi' yer. You fancy 'im rotten, I can allus tell. Nowt wrong wi' that, nowt at all. Only natural. Just because you're goin' steady an' all don't mean yer can't *look*, does it? Yer only human, girl. He likes you too, an' all. Well, when I'm gone, why don't yer go for it? Who's ter know, if yer careful. Get it while yer young is my advice.' She must have seen the look on my face because she laughed again and got up.

'Oh, you! What *are* you like! I'm only kiddin'! Don't mind me, just 'avin' a bit of fun. Anyways, talkin' of Mr Lukey Luke, I'm off up to see his pics, if you know what I mean. Wouldn't want to disappoint him after I promised, like. See yer – an' don't worry! You worry about stuff too much, it'll give yer lines.'

She bent down and kissed the top of my head. 'I like you, Astra. Star. You're a good 'un. Not like me. Still, it teks all sorts, eh? See yer.'

And off she tripped, to shag the man I loved. Oh, *bollocks*.

Chapter 12

The day of The Future Of Rock And Roll dawned deliciously bright and sunny, really – it was gorgeous. This was a considerable relief, because the crap weather, combined with Beaker's appalling nerves about the gig and consequent loopy, erratic, leave-me-alone-to-programme-my-keyboards-for-God's-sake behaviour, interspersed with periods of his being convinced he had flu/food poisoning/a brain tumour/leprosy, when in fact, he just had stage fright, had been driving me crackers. But the day was as bright and fresh as a soap powder ad, I felt my spirits lift just breathing in the salty, brilliant air. What a day! Perfect.

The Saturday trippers swelled the ranks of the holiday-makers and a rash of stripy windbreaks and nylon mini-tents sprang up on the beach, peopled by wriggling grub-white kids and their equally pallid parents, who looked like they hadn't exposed a particle of flesh to direct light for months. Which, this being England, they probably hadn't. The exception to this heaving expanse of blanched lumpiness was a gorgeous black lad who had us swooning until his equally beautiful girlfriend appeared and whisked him off beachcombing.

We were all in a really good mood; I don't think we'd realised how the muggy weather had been getting us all down. Cookie was humming as she fried, microwaved and toasted; her weekend girl Lisa, who usually moved with the alacrity of a stunned sloth, trotted about positively enthusiastically. Dot was in good form, too, and had slapped on so much peach foundation, coral blusher and orange lippie she looked like she'd been enamelled. Con bustled about happily in a nice pink T-shirt that gave some colour to her usually pale face and I was bursting with good will to all men.

Everything was fine until around midday. Then the clouds started appearing and the beautiful blue sky we'd enjoyed so much began to thicken, thunderheads boiling up out to sea. A chilly wind sprang up, making the trippers retire back into their lurid cocoons of fleeces and trackie bottoms. I went out on to the veranda and looked at the sky, then snuffed the air – even over the café smells you could pick up that faint, electric tang of a storm coming. Still, the surfers were happy as the swell started to rise – it was almost decent surf. I wondered if Luke would go out. There was a new boy who'd come down this season; everyone said he was magic. Luke would have to work hard to keep his crown this year – not, of course, that I cared. Not a bit.

I think we all felt deflated; it had been such a promising morning... I wondered about rain keeping people away from the gig, but then sometimes, you could have a blinding storm here and just a bit of wind and rain further south. Maybe it would be like that. God, I hoped it would be like that.

Angel drifted down around one, plopped yet another rose into the vase we'd borrowed specially from Dot's mum and came out on to the veranda just in time to see the handsome black bloke leaving. Her eyes followed him and his girl as they sauntered out. She went back in and leaned on the serving hatch, then asked Cooks for a coffee. It was a mark of Cookie's good temper she signalled Lisa to get Angel what she wanted instead of telling her to get her own.

Angel sipped her latte thoughtfully. 'Cookie, why dint you marry Smoky's dad?'

Cookie paused, spatula raised, her eyes narrowing. I winced and started to say something to head Angel off, but she went on before I could – I don't know, scream or hit her with something, I suppose.

'Because, I mean, it's dead brave of you, havin' a half-caste kid all on yer tod an' that, because it's not Bradford round 'ere, now is it? You know what I mean, Astra, don't yer?'

I gulped and my mouth dropped open. Angel took this as agreement and wandered on, oblivious to the sharp drop in temperature.

'Up home, like, it's nowt special, there's all sorts up there, all colours of the rainbow – but 'ere... They must have given you some stick, mustn't they? An' you all on yer own. Shame. You shoulda made him wed yer, it's not right him skippin' off. No sense of responsibility, some blokes. I mean, I told Ma Liddicoate the other day – it's no good goin' on about stuff like that to me, I'm from Bradford, it's nowt to us. I said to her, I think Smoky's the cutest kid goin', I do, whatever colour he is, it don't make no never mind ter me. An' I told her I thought you was a right good 'un for not gettin' rid, but you know how they are, them old biddies, natter, natter, natter…Great coffee, Lise – well, I'm off ter fetch Pigsie for his walky before it rains. Shame about the weather, int it?'

And off she sauntered, smiling and oblivious.

I gave Dot and Lisa the high sign before Con saw, and dragged a practically immobile Cookie, spatula still in hand, out the back.

'Cookie, now – now look, she doesn't mean anything nasty by that – come on, you know she doesn't, it's just her way – Cookie?'

Cookie blinked several times and looked bemusedly at the spatula, while the rising breeze danced sand and a ruffle of discarded crisp packets and sweetie wrappers round her thin ankles.

'Did you…'

'Oh, Cooks, come on. No, I did not tell her anything. I know she thinks we're best mates but…I wouldn't. I wouldn't tell her anything important. It must have been Con. An' look, Cooks, I don't think she actually knows any details, not from what she said, it's all gossip and, and, wotsit, er – supposition. Don't be mad, don't, she's not…'

'I ain't mad. I ain't. I know what they say. That old bitch Madge Liddicoate. An' the rest. It doan make no difference to me no more – honest. It's just – the stuff she says! Angel I mean. Sometimes…It's like, a thought comes in 'er silly head an' bang! Out it comes, wallop. She just caught me off-guard, is all. Sometimes I think she doan even see other people, like we ain't real to 'er or somethin'. It's just 'er that matters to 'erself, if you see what I mean. You're the only one she takes to, really – lucky old you, I doan think. Oh, doan worry, I won't say anythin' to Con; Angel ain't worth losin' my job over, now, is she?'

'Cookie, Con wouldn't…' I stopped, as Cookie locked eyes with me and pulled a wind-whipped curl away from her mouth.

'Oh, really? Well, never mind, you think what you like. I'd better get back – doan worry so much, Astra, I ain't mad, not at you anyways.'

For the rest of the afternoon, on and off, I pondered on Cookie's words. Con wouldn't, would she? I didn't want to think she'd fire Cookie because of a spat with Angel, but the way she doted on her sister, anything was possible. Families, eh? Jeez.

The day crawled past. I'd arranged everything to do with the Big Night previously, because I knew I needed to be as calm as possible on account of Beaks being beyond flaky. Everyone was going – even Cookie. Con was having Smoky for the night, and frankly, Cookie had hardly got the words out before Con jumped at the chance to play mums. Well, there was a small person who was going to have a night of being spoiled rotten, all tucked up with his furry friend and a heap of chocolate in front of the wood stove, watching kiddie vids while the storm blew outside. I almost envied him. OK, I did, except for the videos part.

At my end, Git was having a sleep-over party at Marnie's and had gone over there already. Mum and dad were going to an organic wine and cheese evening at High Tor and Gwen was – I don't know. Saving fallen women, or something. Punching Satan on the nose, or whatever. I didn't care. We hardly saw her these days and it was a relief, to my mind. Lance said he might drop in to the gig, but it depended on what the other Beasts were up to and how the weather went. He did tell me to tell Beaker to 'give the barsterds hell, mate'. I don't think Lance realised what sort of music Element played. As far as he was concerned it was Metal or die. Still, it was a sweet thought.

I wasn't going over to the gig for the afternoon, I wouldn't have, even if I could. I'd made that mistake in the past. People think watching the band set up and do their sound check is fascinating; they think they're seeing a glimpse of the real rock'n'roll. Maybe if it's a big, famous band, OK, even though personally, I doubt it. But at Element's level it meant sitting around in a dark, filthy, stinky, freezing pub concert room, with nothing whatever to do except watch your beloved screw himself into a rigid knot of unspeakable tension while the band apparently tries to throw all its instruments down a flight of stone steps repeatedly. At least, that's how it sounds, and at top volume through a knackered old system created exclusively from Victorian biscuit tins and gaffa tape, manned by some dreadful old rocker with a greying mullet and a what-the-fuck-do-I-care attitude.

Or you can talk to the other girlfriends. But I couldn't, I just couldn't. Now, I realise this might sound awful to the type of lass who breezily prefers women's company and likes nothing better than a good old night out with the girls, but that's not me. Actually, I wish it was. I really, honestly do. I love movies like *Thelma and Louise* and I have this kind of empty space in myself where I think having good mates should be. It's just that what with leaving uni before I made any really lasting friends – except Con, of course – then mum, and Git, and being so long with Beaker… Sure, I knew a couple of lasses in the village and I suppose I'd thought, given time – but nothing had ever progressed beyond a drink at the Chy or the pictures once in a blue moon at Crossford and nowadays, nothing.

But to be honest, try as I might, I just couldn't hit it off with Janice and co. It *was* Janice and co., too. As the singer's fiancée, she was Queen Bee. Maybe that was it; I was used to being a bit of a Queen Bee myself and we just rubbed each other up the wrong way. Brought out the worst in each other. Janice was a formidable opponent, as well, with a good clerical job at the council, taffy-streaked blonde hair pulled into one of those big plastic nippy-clips that look so uncomfortable and an unwavering line in brainless sub-Tory knee-jerk commentary. Over a vodka and tonic (lime or orange were *so* childish) she'd pontificate about 'blacks', or asylum seekers, or benefit scroungers. She'd grind on until I wanted to punch her in her pink-lipsticked gob. I knew for a fact – because she told everyone with the air of a person who knew her worth, thank you – that she'd never touched a black person and never would. Not even a handshake. It just encouraged them, apparently. And look where fraternising had got *Bradford* for instance, *please.* This shaft was always delivered with a raised eyebrow and pursed lips as if to say we all knew where *that* was.

Naturally, at first I'd tried to retaliate. Bradford was a multi-cultural, multi-racial, energetic, cosmopolitan city, I'd stammer over my increasing fury; it was a meeting place for the whole world, a melting pot, a…Silence would fall. Oh yes, Janice would say with a mouth like a cat's arse. Quite. I soon realised my defences were not virtues to the likes of Jan, but waymarkers on the road to Hell and the destruction of the white race, Englishness and dear old roast beef and two veg. My sort of thinking led to Europe, foreign food and mixed marriages. It was hopeless. She was a terrible, ignorant little cow who would grow to be a terrible, ignorant and cruel matron.

The others just went along with her because they couldn't be bothered not to and didn't care anyway. On the whole, in a lukewarm way, they agreed with her, though Tania the bass-player's girl, who thought herself a bit of a trendy surf chick in that she worked at one of the tourist clothing boutiques in Crossford that sold Kangaroo Poo and Salt Rock holiday wear, sometimes ventured a mild opposition to Janice's hang-'em-and-flog-'em routines, bless her. At least she tried and I thought for a while we could be mates but beneath her pastel strappy vests and beige microfibre pretend combat trousers there was a deeply conservative heart and I frightened her, because I pushed too hard.

So on the whole, it was drink, ciggies and gossip. I didn't know how to join in, I didn't know the people they talked about or the soap operas they watched. They were all Crossford girls born and bred and I wasn't even really from Polwenna. As a desperate last resort, I tried books with them, but the only books they read were sex-and-shopping blockbusters, idiotic things about tedious, one-dimensional single girls obsessed with dieting, or family sagas. That is if they read at all because mostly, it was TV, the pub or sometimes a club and Element's infrequent gigs.

As a result of this social mismatching, the other girlfriends, and therefore their boyfriends, thought me stand-offish. Stuck-up. I know this because Beaker told me. It pissed him off, to be honest, that I couldn't be more 'easy-going'. Get on with people. I tried telling him about the awfulness of Janice but he thought I should ignore her 'ramblings' and just rub along with folk. I said I'd tried. He said I was being a snob. I said it wasn't that, it was the politics, the racism

– class didn't come into it. He said I was too quick to condemn people who weren't into books and stuff like me. I'd opened my mouth to reply, then shut it because he was right about that bit. I got red in the face, he went white. We'd had a bit of a tiff, then. One of our few rows, actually; we never normally fell out. But we'd argued, then we compromised. I didn't come to sound checks, and he didn't ask me to. Fair enough.

No, I was going over with Angel in Con's car. I did want to set off in good time, be fairly early, though. It was at least forty-five minutes' drive to the gig – Jangles Fun Bar, or The King's Head as was. I'd arranged to be at the flat, washed and buffed up, by six.

I was there at 5.45. Con was doing the evening shift with Lisa, Dot and Dot's mate Pat, who could cook a bit, so I popped my head in and did a twirl. They all ooh'd and said I looked nice, and for once, I agreed with them. My hair had gone right, I had on my three-quarter jeans embroidered round the hems with sequins and beads, my best cowboy bra (round 'em up and head 'em out) with a lilac scoop-neck T-shirt, my Voodoo Dolls mini backpack and fat blue suede Reef trainers. I'd nearly put on Angel's topaz earrings, but then remembered I meant to give her them back and settled on my best set of small, thick silver hoops that descended slightly in diameter down the four piercings I'd got left in each ear. I changed my normal plain silver nose stud for a nifty little diamanté one and bingo! Ooh là là, c'est moi! I thought I'd achieved a nice effect – subtle, yet not un-funky. I'd even put on mascara and some ultra-shiny lip gloss on – no holds barred tonight. I was *hot*.

Or so I thought. I waited in the flat for nearly an hour as Angel sang tunelessly in the bathroom and told me at fifteen-minute intervals she'd only be a min, honest.

Then she emerged, and I saw what hot really was.

She looked as near to an orchid as a human being could. A jewelled Fabergé orchid. Naturally, her ice-white hair was immaculate, spiky and glistening with a subtle opalescence. Her skin was flawlessly bronzed, her violet eyes enhanced by cleverly shaded gleaming dark eyeshadow. Her lips were glazed with shot-gold fuchsia; iridescent, expensive. I won't dwell on her outfit save to say I wouldn't like to think how much her fabulously perfect jeans cost, never mind the artfully ripped sequinned chiffon baby-doll top that screamed 'designer' or the gold spike-heeled jewelled sandals.

My catalogue-and-surf-shop kit couldn't even begin to compete with her gorgeous London rock-chick chic. I tried not to feel crushed, and failed.

She set down the big bucket bag she was carrying and put on a collarless, butter-soft black leather jacket.

'Oh, you look grand, love. What a cute outfit – them jeans are nice.' She smiled. Again, I had that strange sensation that she was drawing all the light in the little room to her, absorbing it somehow. I felt as if I were in the shadows.

But I smiled back. What else could I do? Sulk? How attractive would *that* be. There was nothing I could do about it, and anyway, what had I expected? Sackcloth and ashes? Jesus, she'd make that look sexy, as well I knew. Also I realised, looking at her, that it irked me how concerned about clothes and appearances generally I had become since Angel arrived. I mean, not that I'd been madly anti-fashion or anything, but it had never seemed that important before. Now it was as if my hormones had tricked me into trying to compete with her – on her terms. As if I could. This was Angel, after all. I suddenly felt over-done and a bit silly, not myself. Right, too late to do anything now, but in future – I surreptitiously licked off my shiny lip-gloss and sighed, heavily. Then smiled again. I was determined nothing would upset me – there was too much at stake for Beaker, and me being in a paddy would help no one.

As I was sighing, I noticed a thick, overly sweet perfume, rather like a sort of strong, chemical chocolate smell mixed with a sour-sweet undertow. It was too heavy and unsubtle for Angel, I thought. Not like her. I hadn't smelled it before.

'New perfume?' I asked as she picked up her bucket bag and a little gold leather backpack.

'Oh – yeah. Didn't Con – 'ere, come to that, what d'you think of *this*...' Setting her bags down again she went back into the bathroom while I looked at the clock and cursed myself for distracting her. She came out with a big glitzy blue box labelled 'Thierry Mugler – Angel'.

'Cop a load of that. Come this morning, special delivery. It's got everything in it – all the bath stuff and everythin'. Not sample sizes either, the full monty. Must 'ave cost a bomb. It's from some Internet perfume shop, see the label…It's "Angel" perfume – Angel, like me, see…An' here's the letter that – well, I think he delivered it 'imself, there's no stamp. It's mental, just read it.'

It was from Tim Norris. Begging her to forgive him. How sorry he was. Telling her he couldn't live without her, that they were destined to be together for ever. Pleading with her in strange, disjointed sentences to take him back. *Because they were engaged.*

'Angel – he – he says you're engaged, that you've planned the wedding and everything, he's booked the church and…I don't understand…'

'Hah!' She snorted triumphantly. 'Engaged. As if. See, he's mental, that one. Radged. Engaged! Honestly. Anyroad, it's all bollocks. I went out fer a drive with 'im a few times so I could go shoppin', had summat to eat, took in a couple of flicks, but honest – that's *it*. Yeah, OK, don't look like that – he bought Piglit for me. I know. But listen, right, I never even held his fuckin' hand, fer Christ's sake. End of story. But oh, no. Now he sends me stuff I don't want and he thinks we're *engaged*. You said he weren't right – and he int. I mean, look how he hurt my Pigsie fer one thing, an' now this.'

I looked at the note again – word-processed and single-spaced, it must have been six or seven pages long, but from what I could tell, it said the same things over and over. It was, literally, desperate. Poor sod, talk about getting the wrong end of the stick. Jeez, someone was heading for a broken heart, good stylee.

'Angel, you should have sent it back – the perfume. After what we said, I think…'

'Yeah, yeah, but I didn't. I meant to – but…OK, OK, if he sends owt else, I will. I promise, on me honour. Oh, don't look like that – I will, honest. Tell you what, if it'll mek you happy, I'll do the decent and send him a nice little e-mail tomorrow explainin' how he's gone an' got it all wrong. Nothin' nasty, but you know – final, like. An', I tell you what, I'll get Con to send 'im a cheque for Piglit. Now, how's that? See, I can be a good girl too, y'know…Anyhow – look at the time, we gotta fly, I said we'd pick Luke up at his and…'

Luke? *Luke*? Oh, for fuck's sake – what *else* could go pear-shaped tonight? What?

Chapter 13

'Oh, love, I'm so, so sorry, it's really crap…' I rubbed the back of Beak's neck as he sat, head in hands, in the cubbyhole the landlord called a dressing-room. The whole place stank of mildew, grease and fag smoke and hummed with the sour cold undersmell from the huge rusty fridge that took up most of the space not filled with stacked plastic chairs, boxes of paper napkins and empty beer crates. It was grim, but not as grim as Beak's face.

Luke had noticed the poster as we scrambled from the GTI after a hair-raising trip involving Angel driving (in those sandals) at breakneck speed along the narrow, rain-wet winding roads whilst listening to a Madonna compilation and doing the wiggly hand movements to 'Frozen'. I was in the front; she made Luke sit in the back and the expression on his face was more than enough to make me wonder whether Luke Skywalker, the King of the Break, was gone for ever to be replaced with a human version of Piglit. It didn't improve my mood. He paused in the porch and stared at the poster for the gig.

'I thought your boyfriend's band was called Element?'

'They are.' I snapped.

'Oh, sorry – it's just, they aren't on the poster – look.'

I looked. There was the date, so it was the right poster and there was the support band Psychedelik Starfish – *wow*, I thought, *Beaker will go ballistic, he hates them* – and there was *Elephant*. Elephant, not Element. Jesus H. Christ. Fuck, fuck, fuck; no. How totally crap was that? Element's biggest break ever and the bloody idiots at this stupid, stupid dump had got their name wrong. I felt my body contract with cringiness. Oh, poor Beaks. God, he'd be doing his tits, I had to find him fast.

I left Angel and Luke and shot into the venue at top speed, seething with impatience as the girl on the door laboriously searched for my name on the 'guest list' – which was written on a bit of lined paper in handwriting that looked as if a beetle had stepped in ink then crawled over the page. Beak's writing, I'd know it anywhere.

Finally, just as her jaw dropped at the sight of Angel doing one of her grand entrances, I ran down the corridor and in through the double doors. The noise hit me like a brick in the head. Through the hot, smoke-filled haze, I could see Psychedelik Starfish ('The Fish', maaaan) were on-stage already, beaded goatees, multi-coloured dreadlocks and piercing jewellery flailing as they bounced like a bunch of E'd up, surfie Tiggers through the merry shambles that was their set. I liked The Fish, actually, though I never dared tell Beaker; young, toned, tanned and crackers, they obviously couldn't play a note and just as obviously, they couldn't have cared less. They were having a great time and the heaving, moshing crowd in front of them were too. The whole band was bare-chested and for some reason, seemed to be covered in tons of body glitter and fluorescent paint that nearly obscured their big, bold tattoos – nearly.

I found Janice first. Cookie was with her, that's why I spotted her so easily. Cookie looked cool and collected in a sleeveless white cotton blouse, pedal pushers and her usual huge gold creoles. I waved at her gratefully and she rolled her eyes at me. I knew she knew what was going on, that she would have sussed the mood and how the band must be feeling – Cookie always knew everything; she was a born survivor, always surveilling the scene. They were sitting at a table crammed in the carpeted bit at the back of the hall with all the other Element girlfriends. Apart from Cooks, they looked absolutely livid and were smoking in that exaggerated way women do when they're pissed off and downing shorts like the future of civilisation depended on their alcohol consumption. Cookie had a Coke and I knew there was nothing else in it, because she hated drunks and with her family, who could blame her. At least I could depend on her to keep her head.

I didn't try to speak over the din, just made 'where' signs and Janice glared at me then jerked her head in the direction of a door marked 'private' next to the bar.

Mouthing 'thank you', to which she replied with that wobbly-head 'yeah, right' expression, I shoved my way to the door and into the storeroom – sorry, dressing-room.

With the door wedged shut, the racket of The Fish's demented thrashing was somewhat muffled; or maybe the noise was dampened by the atmosphere of suicidal gloom that filled the space like a thick, dark fug. Terry and the others barely registered my entrance and after a perfunctory 'hiya' I squished up next to Beaks on a spare up-turned beer crate.

I felt so sorry for him. So sorry. It made a lump in my throat and my eyes prickled with tears, hot and furious at his humiliation. OK, maybe Element weren't the next global supergroup, but they – well, they tried hard, they did their best. They played their own songs when they could have made good money doing covers. God knows they spent all their spare cash on equipment and all their spare time rehearsing and now the only chance they'd have of being signed by a proper, real record company was jinxed by a stupid mistake about their name. It might seem unimportant to an outsider, but a mistake like the name thing could ruin a gig for a bunch of nervy, temperamental musicians, even small-time ones like Element. In fact, it was probably worse for them than for a famous band; when you're struggling like bastards just to get a crappy gig in a crappy pub in the arse-end of nowhere, the idea that the people coming won't even know your proper name, just a comical error, is devastatingly humiliating.

'You seen the posters, then?' Beaker muttered miserably.

'Yeah – but look, Angel's friend won't mind that, he's bound to have seen worse and he'll just – he won't pay any mind to it, I'm sure…'

'It's not just that. It's fuckin' everything. Everything that can go wrong, 'as.' He dropped his voice and hissed in my ear. 'Even Terry's fuckin' 'air, for fuck's sake.' He cast a look at Terry, who was lurking in the shadows talking morosely to the drummer. I tried not to stare. Terry's fuzzy-looking hair was the colour of Dot's Tango lipstick, in patches. The rest was either egg-yolk yellow or mud. There was an angry rim of red round his hairline where the bleach had obviously burned him. He looked like – like an escapee from a long-term institution.

I put my arm round Beaks's shoulders and whispered so poor old Terry wouldn't hear. No point making things worse. 'Wha…'

Beaks muttered back, 'Thought 'e'd do it blond, the fuckin' idiot. Problem is, 'e did it himself with some crap 'e got from the chemists. Didn't think 'e needed a proper 'airdresser, oh no. Why today? Ain't we got enough on without havin' a singer who looks like a right fuckin' tosser? Oh Astra, it's fucked. Everythin's gone wrong since we got 'ere. All the gear's gone dicky, nothin's as it should be, the sound man's a wanker, 'e won't even fuckin' try, just sits there smokin' dope an' goin' "Cool it, maaan". Cool it? Fuckin' *cool it*? This is my – our big chance, for fuck's sake. Aw, look, I ain't mad at you, love, I know what you done, how you got that fella here, you done your best for me an' I'm grateful…'

'Well, it wasn't me exactly…' He wasn't listening.

'But it's all fucked, nothin's gone right all day. An' that fuckin' Fish lot – Jesus, bunch of fuckin' amateurs, listen to that crap…My keyboards is playin' up, too, I knew I should 'ave got the new one, Don woulda got it for me, an' – I just…Are they 'ere?'

'Who – oh, the record people? I don't know, pet. Look, I'll go see, you just – just try to be calm, all right? It's not so bad as you think, honest – and no one will notice Terry's, er, hair, when the coloured lights are on him, it'll sort of merge, I promise. I'll come right back, I'll just go look…'

He nodded unhappily and slumped back, his long angularity folded uncomfortably on the low crate. I hugged him and kissed his cheek, my heart hurting for him. In that moment, I'd have done anything, anything at all, to make it better for him. I'd find Angel's Richie-boy and somehow, make him see how dedicated Element were. He'd sign them up if he knew how much it meant to them and how hard they'd work for him, I knew he would.

Outside in the hall, I paused for a moment, trying to spot Angel. I saw Cookie again distantly, but she didn't see me; she was talking to a girl whose face I couldn't quite see; she was in the shadows but her bright hair reminded me of Git's. At least Git was having a good time, I thought grimly, toasting marshmallows and doing other adolescent stuff at her sleep-over. Briefly, I felt a big wave of longing to be thirteen again wash over me. Then I wouldn't have to be responsible, wouldn't have to run round like a bastard fixing stuff. I tried waving at Cookie, but she didn't see me and I couldn't wait. I wished I could have a word with her, though. Cookie's calm good sense would be soothing in this bloody mess.

The Fish were crashing their way to a climax and the room was packed. I saw their T-shirt stall lit up at the other side of the room and made my way across to it on the grounds that going somewhere was better than standing still. I have to say it was a great stall; draped in swathes of fluorescent tie-dye fabric and ropes of fairy lights, manned by two Fishchicks (as their girlfriends called themselves) with ragged-up luminously multi-coloured hair extensions in high bunches, multiple piercings, tattoos and teenie little luminous pink and blue tie-dye Fishshirts emblazoned with the Fish logo in blaze orange. They were also covered in glitter, and a sign on the stall read 'Free magik-dust with every T!!!!!' in wonky handwriting. It was quite a crush; people were sitting on the stall, or standing, buying the mad shirts or home-produced Fish CDs, and everyone was thick with sparkles. Before they could spray me with 'magik-dust' I ducked and nearly knocked over Element's stall.

'Lo, Astra,' mouthed Fat Gaz, Element's faithful dogsbody. He stood moodily behind a bare trestle table on which Element's black T-shirts vanished into the gloom.

I leaned across and shouted in his ear. 'Sold anything?'

He shouted back. 'Two CDs. A bloke says 'e'll 'ave a shirt if 'e's got any money left at the end. I wish them girls'd leave off with that glittery stuff, it gets everywhere. It's spoilin' my shirts.'

I looked at the said shirts; all the cheapest, thinnest, most shapeless shirts possible, all XL, printed with 'Element' in white slopy block capitals across the chest, and I sighed. We were not talking Armani. 'OK, well, good luck, then...'

He leaned back and nodded mournfully, pushed his specs back up his greasy nose and folded his meaty arms across his chest.

I stood on tiptoe and peered through the thick, roiling darkness. Nothing. Then I remembered there was another bar if you went across from the front of the stage and through an archway that led to the pub itself. I headed for it, shoving through the sweaty excited crowd. As I got near the stage, in the heaving mass of dancing nutters, I caught a glimpse of someone who seemed familiar, just for a split second before they disappeared into a boiling heap of moshers. It was that girl again, the one Cookie had been talking to who looked like...But then they were gone in the ruck. I shook my head, no time for that now. I felt as if I'd been injected with speed, there was so much adrenalin pumping through me. I was on a mission, no matter what, I was going to make it all right for Beaker.

I turned through the arch, pink and dishevelled, my ears ringing, and there they were.

It was a long, narrow room, dimly lit, and by a trick of acoustics, reasonably quiet. Angel sat at the far end, against the dingy back wall, glowing gold and dark like a smoky citrine that had fallen into the mud. She was surrounded by a little knot of people dressed in outfits of the sort they show in fashion mags and that normally, you never see in real life. Now I could see why; their clothes were wearing them. Luke sat to one side, a pint of cider in a dirty glass untouched in front of him.

'Astra! *As*-tra! Everyone, this is my best pal down 'ere, Astra – she's just the goodest lass in the world, aren't you, Astra? She's really nearly a saint! Not like, me, eh, Richie? Eh?'

Thanks for the intro, Angel. I sloped over to a chorus of languid 'hi's' from the fashionistas and a look of despair from Luke. *No good lookin' at me like that, lad, I can't help you*, I thought. Again, a wave of irritation mixed with horrible disappointment washed over me at the sight of him. Another one of Angel's handbag holders. As I thought it, sure enough, I spotted her little backpack on the seat next to him. Oh, fine. Right.

'Astra – this is Richie Lomas, of Imago Records.' Angel intoned this introduction in a serious voice as the man next to her got up, empty glass in hand, obviously on his way to the bar. He pushed his way out towards me, displacing a translucent, faintly murmuring person of indeterminate gender dressed in mauve slashed leather and lime tartan who rejoined the clot of Londoners nearest to it like a drop of mercury sliding together with its fellows.

'Very pleased to meet you, very pleased. Any friend of Angel's, y'know – she's told me all about you, haven't you, poppet?'

The man with the empty glass was Richie. He stuck his free hand out. I shook it, dazed.

Now, I know stereotyping is wrong, and judging books by their covers etc. but Richie was not what I had been expecting. I suppose I'd imagined a sort of more business-like version of Keith Richards; a gaunt, desiccated corporate devil's disciple type or something. Not Chirpy the Cheeky Chipmunk.

Because that was Richie; his round, cheerful face, little pink splodge of a mouth with slightly buck teeth that would have had dad reaching for the braces, trendy specs that kept sliding down his cute button nose, a clipped tuft of thin dark hair that wavered bravely and the warm, damp paw he extended all reminded me irresistibly of a cartoon character – maybe Penfold from Dangermouse. He was short and rotund, his podgy tum bowing his neat navy-blue designer T-shirt. But Keith Richards? No *way*.

I shook his hand warmly and felt hope blossom in my heart. He seemed nice, a nice ordinary guy, not scary at all. His brown eyes behind his yellow tinted lenses were warm – he'd understand about Element, he wasn't a cold-hearted rock executive type at all. I bet he'd come from a small town somewhere and struggled his way up from nothing, he was that sort, definitely – he'd see Element for what they really were, never mind the name thing and the hassles of a crappy gig. I smiled at him and he smiled back. What a *nice* bloke.

'So, Astra – great name, by the way! Angel's told me *all* about you! Thinks the world of you, she does – bless her!' He beamed and twinkled at me.

I risked a glance at Angel. She was chatting brightly to a long-haired, hawkish-looking Asian fella, whose whip-thin frame, blank, manic eyes and raw nostrils indicated a severe coke habit and who appeared to have been shrink-wrapped in black rubber. Richie shook his head happily.

'What a gal, eh? What a stunna! If only she'd let me give her a go in the business – she'd do a bomb with those looks – and that accent! Brilliant! I tell you, you can't buy that kind of thing, it's priceless, really. But you know Ange, too bloody modest for her own good! "Oooo, I joost couldn't, Rich, not little me…"' He stretched his smile even further as he did what he fondly thought was a Bradford accent.

I looked over to Angel again and tried to see her in her modest provincial lass role. Somehow, I *joost* couldn't. Then I heard the electronic burblings of Element's intro tape start. I turned to tell Richie they were on but he'd gone to the bar; I couldn't get to him through the mass of other people all wanting drinks at the same time. I caught Angel's eye and pointed at the gig. She smiled and nodded; she'd tell Richie Element had started. I couldn't wait, I had to go, I had to support Beaker. After the gig I'd have a proper talk to Richie. It would be all right. I felt we'd made a start, made contact. Afterwards, we could relax, have a proper chat. Making my excuses, I pushed my way back into the hall. I felt so much better now I'd actually met Richie and I only wished I could have told Beaker before he went on.

I shoved my way to the back, past the Fish stall, and gave Fat Gaz, sitting on his trestle table, the thumbs up. I saw Cookie standing off to one side of the stage and waved at her, and she waved back. I thought about going down to stand with her but I clocked Janice and the girls down the front, trying to look cool as they danced round their handbags. They were so stiff with tension and crossness you could have snapped them in half. I stayed where I was.

They were about the only ones who were dancing. The Fish stall was heaving with people laughing and messing around and the bar was four deep. Only a small huddle of three or four serious shoegazers were standing near the stage on Beaker's side, trying to groove in that non-moving way they have. I suppose it was nearly dancing, for them. Everyone else made like there was no one on the stage at all. It was horrible and I wanted to shout and make people shut up and watch. But obviously, I couldn't. All I could do was sit there as the whole thing ground on. Then halfway through 'Portland Ten Six', the fourth number in, Beaker suddenly looked frantic and the keyboards went out of the already appalling mix.

They never came back in. Beaker fumbled and prodded and I knew he was cursing but even though he eventually seemed to get things under control, the sound of his beloved keyboards never reappeared. Not that anyone apart from me and Fat Gaz, who stared at each other in increasing horror, seemed to notice. Terry, meanwhile, appeared to have suffered some kind of brain injury due to his impromptu bleach job, because he just stood and clutched the mic stand to his flabby chest whilst contorting himself like a kindergarten kid wanting the loo. I could hardly hear him, either. I also realised I'd lied big style to Beaker about his hair, too. The others played like miserable automatons, their faces grey with nerves. The guitar endlessly and excruciatingly went out of tune, the bass was a fat, blurry rumble and the drums sounded like ET being hit with the back of a wet spoon. I thought desperately about rushing over to the sound man and yelling at him to do something, but when I looked, he was sharing a joint with a leathery, hatchet-faced slapper as if the band weren't on at all. I knew he wouldn't listen to me – a mere *chick*. I gave up, there was nothing I could do except watch, paralysed. I can't pretend it was anything other than a fucking shambles – it was also bloody endless. They finished with 'Dance, Dance, Dance' and sloped off, heads down. There was no encore and Janice and Co. clapping loudly and giving the uninterested punters hard stares didn't help. I saw Cookie, her arms folded, watching. Her face was as impassive as ever. I took a deep breath and tried to decide what to do for the best.

There was no point going to see Beaker straightaway; he was always in a terrible state after a gig and tonight he'd be worse than usual. The best thing I could do, the most practical thing I could do for him, was to go back and talk to Richie. He was an experienced music business person. He'd see the potential under the cock-ups. I took another breath and fought my way back to the side bar.

Psychedelik Starfish had obviously had the same idea; someone must have told them who Richie was and the ranks of Angel's group were swelled to bursting with bouncy, glittery, body-painted Fish all giggling and bumbling around, while the fashionistas tried not to get covered in fluorescent paint and sparkly sweat and failed. Richie was talking to The Fish's singer, whose ratty locks were thick with shocking pink and orange paint. They were laughing and clinking bottles when I stumbled up.

'Ah, Astra! Now, which one of these mad bastards is yours, eh? Eh?' Richie smirked and tapped the side of his nose with his forefinger while jerking his head in a knowing way towards the singer.

'What?'

'Come on, which one's your fella, eh? Oi, watch the shirt, guys, please!'

I felt it in my body before I understood: a slow creeping tide of awful anticipation.

'No – none, I – I – my boyfriend's the keyboard player in Element. They just…'

Richie looked confused, then the Fish singer grinned and whispered something in his ear. 'Oh, *Elephant*!'

'No, Element. Element. The band Angel wanted you to see. They've just finished. They – They're really good; you did see them, didn't you? I…'

Richie got up and taking me by the elbow with surprising firmness, moved me out of earshot of the mêlée. 'I'm sorry, poppet. I understand now. Angel just said "a band", just said they were very hip, very…Just a band, you see, not which one. My mistake. I did see some of Eleph– Element. Look, I perfectly understand they had some technical problems, that was obvious – the keyboards just weren't happening and that singer…It's a shame, but unfortunately, that's not the point – they're just not what I'm looking for. They're simply not – marketable. I am sorry, you're a nice kid, but business is business…'

'And I suppose the bloody Fish are business, then?' I mumbled furiously.

How had I ever thought Richie was just a fun, cartooney guy? Now his round face was hard and his eyes behind his mad specs were black glass. I felt a rush of humiliation; how could I have been so stupid? You don't own a company like Imago Records because you're a cute little fella with a big heart who'll 'understand'. You own it because you're determined, ruthless and a fully paid-up capitalist with an eye on the main chance. No matter what you look like.

'I know you're disappointed, poppet, I do realise that and I know your band will be too,' he said briskly while I gritted my jaw so hard I thought the hinges would crack. 'But yes, The Fish are business. They're young and fresh, they're sexy. You understand? Your boys – well. Nothing wrong with that sort of stuff here in the provinces, for a hobby, but it's not…Look, I'd do a lot to oblige Angel, really I would, but…' He shrugged, and went back to the party.

I felt blind with fury, with a terrible pain for Beaker – but however unwillingly, I knew Richie was right. The Fish were sexy – they were marketable. To be honest, that was one reason why I was so mad, because I knew that and I knew Element were the opposite and always had been. It was just that – oh, just that I'd so wanted Beaker to be happy. What was I going to tell him? I turned to go and bumped into a girl staggering out of the Ladies, clutching a bright pink, bulging drawstring bag that looked very familiar.

'Sorr…Jesus fucking Christ, Git, Jesus, what – Jesus, *Git!*'

It was Git all right, now it clicked. I'd thought I'd seen her in the ruck, those spicy curls, that – and I had. She was the girl who Cookie had been talking to. I just couldn't believe she was actually here. I was quite literally flabbergasted; how – when – what about the sleep-over? I didn't know what to think, I was totally thrown.

She grinned at me blankly and giggled, swaying ominously. It was obvious she hadn't just had a few, she was mortal, weaving drunk. There was mascara and glittery blue eyeshadow all over her face, and she had on an embroidered denim micro ra-ra skirt, a teeny halter-neck barely covering her chest and a pair of huge silver platform wedgies; all stuff that I'd never, ever seen before. No wonder her bag was splitting at the seams, her bloody *clothes* were in it. She was also covered in paint and glitter and as I took her by the arm the Fish guitarist shouted out "Ey, Courtney, Courtney – come on, darlin', come back to daddy!' and made smacky kissing noises at her while the others fell about laughing. She giggled again, then turned a fascinating shade of pale, luminous green. Despite the smeared make-up and tart's kit, she suddenly looked about five. Oh, *Git*…

'As-tra, I doan 'alf feel funny…' she moaned piteously.

And dangling by one arm from my iron grip, she puked like a fountain all over the floor.

It was grim. I looked around desperately for help but it was hopeless. Who cared about a bit of jailbait sicking up? No one. They just ignored us while Git gagged helplessly. Then Luke saw me, and giving him big eye-contact, I mouthed 'help' at him, past caring about anything except getting Git out of there. More than a tad reluctantly, he tore himself away from Angel and her chums. Not that she noticed – and he knew it. I wondered if he thought she'd stop him, but hey – she was having a great time laughing like a drain at Richie's obviously hilarious repartee.

We struggled with Git while the landlord ranted and raved about his precious carpet. He only stopped when I told him she was thirteen, I was her sister and my parents would be contacting the police. Then he stopped, the fat bastard. Luke helped me get Git to the porch out the front by the car park, where she collapsed on a bench. At least it was under cover. I unpacked her bag and got her fleece on her, then told Luke I was going back in to say goodbye to Beaker and round up Angel. Git, who looked like death on a stick, begged me not to leave her. I felt a stab of pity, but with a sigh, Luke said he wouldn't budge until I got back, so off I went.

I couldn't find Beaks at first, then I went round to the dressing-room. It was empty, apart from him – and Cookie.

They didn't see me at first – oh, not that they were doing anything untoward. They were just sitting together, not even touching, on separate beer crates, half turned away from the door. I expect they thought it was one of the band coming back in – whatever. Cookie's white shirt, still miraculously crisp, gleamed in the murky light and Beaks was obviously talking. Going over the gig, like he always did, no doubt. Song by song, note by note. The red glow of Cookie's cigarette brightened and dimmed as she drew on it. The smell of her cheap, brutal tobacco and the mouldy stink of the damp room wove together like a pall. I started to walk towards them, then I paused for a moment. At first, I didn't know why, then it dawned on me.

I felt like I was intruding.

They looked so natural together, you see. Sure, I knew they'd always got along at the café, and Beaker liked playing with Smoky, but I hadn't really noticed before – they looked as if they belonged. And they did, I knew they did, I knew it. They had more in common with each other, more to talk about, or more importantly, *not* talk about than Beaks and me ever had. They were easy with each other.

It had never really been like that with me and Beaks – he'd wanted me at first because I was different, and he'd been straining to be different himself. Struggling to be more than the narrow, inward-looking society of Crossford. And I liked him, I always had. How could anyone not like him: he was a good-hearted bloke, if a bit inarticulate. But that just added to his niceness, in a funny way. But we were miles apart in so many ways. Our upbringing, our thoughts, our opinions; the marriage thing – kids, a little house. I'd come to realise how much it meant to him, but me – I wanted to get away, travel, live in the big world before I did that, if I ever did it at all.

It was like, I suddenly realised habit had smothered us with its dead hand and though I thought the world of him – and I did – it wasn't love, it was all about being safe, and that wasn't enough, anymore. I'd known it in the crammed and untidy back cupboard of my mind for months, if not years, but until seeing him and Cookie together, I hadn't wanted to face the fact. I wasn't sure I wanted to now.

I felt some tight-wound string in my heart snap, but I didn't feel hurt, I just felt – sorry. Sorry that it had to be like this, sorry and nostalgic for all the good times we'd had in the early days. But I didn't feel devastated, or jealous, or angry. That almost surprised me, but I didn't. I just felt *sorry*.

All this flashed through my head in a series of half-realised pictures, like a broken film flipping through the projector. I only half understood it all myself. It was just a *feeling* more than anything else. Still, there was nothing I could do about it all tonight – of all nights. I wasn't that bloody selfish. I turned to leave, but Cookie saw me. She touched Beaker on the arm and he stopped talking and looked at me. I could see in his poor face the news had already reached him of The Fish's triumph.

He didn't say anything, just looked, then put his head down and stared at the floor. I felt as if I should go to him – but I didn't. Cooks waited a second, then said, 'Hiya. You found 'er, then.'

I knew she meant Git. 'Er, yeah, I did. She's in a right state. I don't know, I thought she was at Marnie's.'

'Yeah. She told me. Said she got the bus to Newquay this afternoon, did some shoppin' with her bit o' savin's then come 'ere. I told 'er you'd be livid but she said she were sick of bein' treated like a kiddie. Told me Angel said she oughta be able to come if she wanted – that she'd be missin' a good do. As if Git was a grown-up or somethin'. It's like I said, that Angel just doan think before she speaks, know what I mean? Still, I bet poor liddle Git's learned a lesson, she was awful drunk, poor devil. She ain't 'alf gonna feel it tomorrow. That Fish lot been givin' 'er all kinds of drink, the bastards; mind you, it's a blessin' it only were drink – leastwise, as far as we know it were. Lucky we was all here really, if she'd been on 'er own – no tellin' what might 'ave 'appened. ' She took a last drag, then threw her ciggie on the floor and ground it out with her trainer.

I winced inwardly. Cookie was right, and Angel was going to get a good talking-to tomorrow. Fancy telling a kid Git's age stuff like that – I mean, I remembered myself at thirteen: it would have been a red rag to a bull. I'd have done just the same as Git – which didn't mean I was going to let her off with it. She was grounded, oh yeah. It wasn't so much the escapade itself, but lying like that; no. She could have got herself into some serious hassle – you read about that sort of thing in the papers. Some young 'party girl' found – ugh. It gave me the shivers even thinking about it. I didn't relish the sulks that would be the result of me ticking her off but it had to be. I wasn't her so-called buddy like Angel, I was her sister. I sighed yet again. Maybe I should have felt annoyed with Cookie for being the bearer of bad tidings, but I wasn't – Cookie wasn't a gloater, she was just stating facts, like she always did. That was just how she dealt with things, by looking them straight in the eye, without fear or favour.

'Yeah. I – she lied about the sleep-over, I guess. I'd – I'm going to take her home. She's in a right state, been puking her guts up. Beaks, I'll – I'm so sorry, love – look, see you tomorrow, yeah? Beaks?'

'It's always your family, ain't it, Astra?' He looked up at me, and Cookie looked away.

'I'm sorry, I…'

'Never mind, it doan matter, nothing bloody matters. Go on, she's only a kiddie, take 'er 'ome.'

His face was hard to read in that light, but the tone of his voice…I knew he felt like me. I knew it; it was over, finished. Our relationship, his hopes, his last chance to escape from the iron pattern of his life, lay smashed in that stinking, dirty pub back room; it was all dead, gone, ashes. My heart contracted painfully, bloodless and drained. It was awful, it wasn't – fair. Oh right – not fair. Well, nothing was bloody fair. Jesus, I was such a kid, wanting everything to be *fair*. Life wasn't ever fair, when would I get that through my thick skull?

So I left them. Left Beaks in that lightless hole with Cookie guarding him like the tough little soldier she was. I left because quite literally there was nothing I could do. Nothing I could say. I started to go over to him to give him a kiss, but I stopped again. I don't really know why. It just didn't seem right.

He looked up, the dim light carving lines and angles into his face, shadows that aged him twenty years and I saw what he'd become; I saw his future, his fate. I wasn't in it.

'Beaks…'

'It's all right, Astra, it doan matter. Go on.'

I left. I left him. I left my good and faithful boy.

Chapter 14

'Angel, come on, I've got to take Git home, she's…' I shouted over the row The Fish were making and the clunking grind of the disco that was in full swing now the DJ was in control and the what he obviously considered *annoying* live music was finally over.

She swayed over to me, looking more perfect than ever in contrast to the matted, unravelling chaos of The Fish and their hangers-on. The dense, synthetic chocolate smell of her new perfume still clung to her vaporously. It made me uncomfortable; it wasn't her, it seemed incongruous. Coarse. An imposition. I wiped my nose reflexively. Angel smiled beatifically, and handed me the car keys.

'You go, love, I'm off to party with the gang.' She winked conspiratorially. 'With Richie, know what I mean? Don't worry, I got me big bag out the boot OK. Saw your sis with Lukey, she looks done in, poor scrap – 'ere, it's a good thing I told that Fish lad she's only thirteen, he thought he was on a winner – you shoulda seen 'is face! We're all off back to Richie's. It'll be pretty wild, with this lot. Not your scene – Luke'll go with yer, I told 'im he ought ter, that you needed a fella ter look after yer what with your kid bein' in such a state – you'll be right enough…see yer!'

'But Angel, I don't want to drive, I don't…You can't…Look, I want a word with you about – Angel, wait! What'll I tell Con?'

She looked back over her shoulder and smiled again, totally unfazed. 'Tell 'er owt yer want, she int me mam…Go on, 'ave a nice drive 'ome wi' Lukey-boy.' And she gave me another wink. It was hopeless, there was no place to get a grip on that smooth, porcelain exterior. Nothing touched her, nothing. It was exasperating, I could have slapped her – not that it would have done any good. She genuinely wouldn't understand what she'd done. She never did.

I wasn't up for the drive back at all. I never liked night driving and in fact, I wasn't much of a driver generally. Oh, I could do it, sure, you had to drive round here, but I'd never been easy with it like some. I thought about asking Luke to do it but he wasn't insured for this car and somehow I didn't want him to think I was frightened. I'd manage; I just had to keep calm.

We snaked through the deep-cut roads sunk between high banks fluttering with briars and wild flowers that were black and tentacled in the blowsy wet dark. Once a great dark shape swooped terrifyingly across the road in front of us, causing me to brake hard and nearly put us in the embankment. Git moaned in the back seat and Luke went rigid, his foot straining for the brake pedal that wasn't there, like all drivers condemned to be passengers. The shape had been an owl, a big one, and superstitiously, my heart pounding, I crossed and uncrossed my fingers as I gripped the wheel. An owl, the bird who takes the spirits of the dead home, silent and inexorable, into the dawn. I stretched my eyes open wider, trying to shake off fatigue and the sense of something dark and unwholesome that dogged me. Jesus, Jesus, just let me get us all back without an accident. I mean, that owl, God.

I gritted my teeth and drove on through the lanes, vowing I'd never drive at night again.

As we neared home, the storm intensified a bit, though at this time in the morning, it was on its way out. I'd been right about it being worse by us, though, it must have been a cracker at its height. Given I didn't like driving much at the best of times, in the pitch black, on these roads, with a silent Luke staring out of the side window and Git (or Mud, as her name would be tomorrow – never mind bloody 'Courtney') blind drunk and unconscious on the back seat, stinking the car up with the sharp reek of vomit, it was all I could do not to stop the car, get out and have a right good scream. At least there wasn't much traffic, that was something.

I pulled up at the car park by the café, with a feeling of intense relief that the whole hideous night was nearly over. I'd just have to leave the car here and drag Git home on foot. I'd explain to Con tomorrow morning and give her the keys; what else could I do? It was a fucking nightmare, all of it.

As soon as I got Git out and into the fresh air, she puked again and started shivering uncontrollably. As I struggled with her, Luke came round the car and helped me – he looked as bad as I felt. After a bit of manoeuvring, we got Git dangling between us with her arms around our necks. The rain splattered our faces and we were soaked straightaway – so much for my good shoes and big hair. Luke's face was as white as a sheet, the water running down it in rivulets. I did feel a bit sorry for him, I have to say. It hadn't exactly been a great night for him, either. But I couldn't dwell on that, because I had a bigger problem on my hands with my idiot sister.

A car pulled up next to us in a spray of gravel. Its headlights were on full beam, and as we all staggered, knocked off balance by the surprise, and dazzled by the lights, a man got out, slamming his door.

'All right, where is she?' His voice was thick with anger; I think both Luke and I took an involuntary step back while Git moaned and a gust of wind threw rain over us mixed with salt spray. I had to get her home, she'd get fucking pneumonia at this rate – who was this idiot, what was going on?

'What? What the fuck…?'

'Don't pretend, I know you were with her, you all went together to that – that place. This is her car, you – you – where is she? Where's my Angel, where is she?' He was practically yelling, his whole body rigid.

He stepped forward, his fists clenched at his sides. In the watery, swaying gleam of the car-park light, his face looked blanched and gelid, like wet tissue-paper had been laid over his skull; his eyes were like burnt black holes. His tufty hair was plastered to his head.

It was Tim Norris. He was *livid*.

'Come on, come on – you know where she is, you do, I know you do. God, *why* does she persist in hanging around with types like you? I've told her and told her – warned her about people like you, just out to use her for your own filthy ends! Look at that creature, drunk, half naked – and you, *supposed* to be her friend! God, you're all disgusting, disgusting! When we're married, this will all stop, she'll be safe, away from the likes of you – my God! You've left her there, haven't you? Abandoned her! Oh, my God, I must find her before anything happens to her – my poor girl, my darling…'

He shot back to his car and with a squeal of wet tyres and another spray of gravel, belted out on to the road and back the way we'd come. Back to Jangles, no doubt. To save his fallen Angel.

Then it hit me. No, there hadn't been much traffic, just this pair of headlights behind me wavering in the rain and the wet darkness, all the way. I hadn't really registered them. But he'd followed us – he'd probably been in Jangles car park waiting, all night…Jesus, he was crazy, *really* crazy…

Luke offered to help me haul Git up the bank to our house, and I let him. Tim had put cogs on me and I was grateful for Luke's company. We staggered up the bank, then finally, I managed to get Git into her bed without waking the whole house. I ragged and squirmed her wet things off and put her winter nightshirt on her for extra warmth, got her a bucket and a bottle of water, did her face with one of those cleansing wipes and arranged her on her side propped by pillows. I was exhausted, and my back hurt from shoving Git's dead weight around. I took my soaked T off and put one of Lance's XXL jumpers on, picked up a towel and, rubbing my hair, went back into the kitchen. To my surprise, I saw Luke was still there, sitting at the table, head in hands, dripping quietly on to the floor. I was thrown for a moment; I'd assumed he'd have gone straight off to brood. This was one fucked-up night and no mistake. Reflexively, I chucked the towel at him and offered him a cup of tea.

Amazingly, he accepted straightaway, like he'd been in my kitchen often. Like we were mates or something. I watched him as he drank two cups of Darjeeling and ate three of mum's big, heavy home-made oat biscuits like an automaton. The way he ate made me think he probably hadn't eaten anything all day. Any other time, I'd have been tripping up over myself to feed him, opening tins of soup, buttering bread, being mum. Now I couldn't be bothered.

We were sitting there, in the faint glow of the single Eco-bulb overhead, in silence. My ears were still ringing from the gig and I felt as if someone had hit me all over with a baseball bat. I was just thinking I was glad I'd arranged to have tomorrow off, when he spoke.

'What did he mean – when they get married?'

'What?'

'That – Tim. That guy in the car park. What did he mean – him and Angel get married?'

'Oh, ah – he seems to think they're engaged or something. He keeps sending her stuff – flowers, presents. You know those big red roses on the counter in the café? He sends those. Well, not him personally, it's a standing order sort of thing, apparently.' I hardly knew where to look; after all, it wasn't really my business. Or was it? Everything was so blurred, people were so blurred, nothing was normal anymore.

Luke stared at me, bemused, his face tired and strained. 'But – I don't understand – I mean – we're – she and I – we're…'

I was too tired to be diplomatic. 'Look, Luke, I realise I don't really know you very well or anything, and I don't want to be out of line but – Angel isn't *with* anyone. Not you, not Tim – I'm sorry, I'm sorry, I *am*, but that's just…'

'But we – I asked her to…' He didn't look cross, or anything, just puzzled, as if he genuinely didn't get it.

'Live with you? Tim asked her to wed him and you both got the same answer. Look, I'm really sorry, but it's how she is. And yes, she told me what you'd asked her and that she wasn't up for it. It's the same with Tim if it's any comfort, and you can see how it's got to him. I don't want to sound preachy, but…'

He looked down, his salt-streaky, damp fringe hiding his face. Tired as I was, I felt angry he should have come to this. Let himself come to this. Didn't he know how it looked? Didn't he realise what it was doing to his rep? A little voice in my head whispered *'Didn't he care he used to be my hero?'* I heard that, and I heard 'used'. Used to be my hero. It was a night of endings, it seemed. Now Luke was just a good-looking, miserable lad close to tears, sitting at our kitchen table, a cold mug of tea in his hands. Mortal. Not a god anymore.

Just a lad, like any other. I felt so, so old. A real spinster, just like I'd feared.

He looked up, his expression void and empty, scoured like the beach after high tide. 'I'm sorry, sorry, Astra. You've got enough to cope with without…It's just…I'd better go.'

I saw him out, there was nothing I could do to help him. At the door he turned and reaching out, briefly touched his cold fingertips to my cheek; it felt like he'd been in the sea too long. I thought *'If I look at his fingertips, they'll be white and wrinkled from the water. Like a drowned man.'* I felt myself shiver at that touch, partly out of shock he'd touch me at all, partly out of – a kind of ragged reflex of desire. Then it was gone and so was he.

Chapter 15

I lay awake on my lumpy old futon, and gazed out at the morning. I'd meant to lie in, have a proper Sunday morning laze, but I couldn't sleep any more though it wasn't even nine. I knew I should get up and face the music, but I just couldn't. The room was warm, my bed linen was just the right mixture of washed yesterday and slept in last night that makes you want to lie in bed for ever. Outside, the sky was flat cloudy again. I wished I'd been here with the storm; I always go out and watch the sea in that sort of weather; it's so bloody vast and elemental. It's a lunging, crashing grey-green fury, then, the foam like the legendary white horses, galloping through the waves like pale demons. Sort of puts your own little problems in perspective. Something greater than yourself and all that. I've never been a one for religion, Christianity anyway, though unlike some I've actually read the Bible – it's amazing what a bookaholic will read if there's nothing else. I suppose Gwen's silly evangelism put me off the church even more – but in a storm, by the sea, that's something else altogether. What do they say? The gods arrive...

Or I wished I could go on a holiday. I hadn't ever had a holiday in the sense most people meant it. The Balearics or Crete or somewhere packagey. In an aeroplane, a hotel, lazing by the pool, going to night-clubs, pissed up, E'd up, bright red and shagging some paralytic fella from Sunderland on the beach. OK, well, I couldn't really fancy that sort of malarky. Say, something a bit more laid back. How about Hawaii, floating in a thermal mountain pool whilst being showered with tiare flowers by a gorgeous, half-naked (or fully naked, I'm not proud) tattooed Polynesian bloke who absolutely adored me. Now, that's more like it. God, I *wish*.

Foreign holidays just weren't something I'd ever done. I'd only flown once, and that was to Paris on a school trip. We always went camping in Wales when I was a kid, sometimes in tepees with a bunch of other hippie families, or we rented a big caravan down here. Now we lived here. In other people's holiday heaven. I thought of somewhere far away. As far away as possible. A picture of Ayers Rock in Australia sprang into my mind – it had been in dad's last *National Geographic*. Red and mysterious, rising out of the desert like an ancient fist. That would be the place, just about as far away from Polwenna – and Bradford – as was possible, both physically and in its very nature. Perfect. I could backpack like the Tribe always did, relying on the kindness of strangers. It worked for them, why not me? I didn't want to be safe anymore, I didn't want to be good old reliable, responsible Astra any more. I wanted to – oh, I didn't know what I wanted. Stuff. You know.

Still, it was no good. I had to get up sometime, I was dying for a wee. I struggled into my old pink candlewick dressing gown and went to the bathroom, then headed for the kitchen. I felt cranky and itchy, my scalp seeming to crawl under my screwed-into-knot unbrushed hair.

I heard mum crying before I opened the door, and dad's bass rumble comforting her as always. My heart sank even further. They must have found out about Git already, sod it.

'Mum, dad?' This was overreacting, surely. Mum was weeping and rocking while dad knelt beside her, his broad, normally florid face grey.

I pulled my dressing gown tighter across my chest, feeling like a complete heel. I couldn't believe they were so upset about Git's adolescent escapade. God, Lance had done much worse. Maybe it was because she was a girl. Feminist mum might be, but I suppose when it's your own child, unreconstructable nature takes over.

'Mum, I'm sorry about Git, but I'll talk to her and she ought to be grounded for at least a month. I mean, I have to say it's not the going to the gig I think was so wrong, but lying, putting herself at risk – you know what you've always said about lying and I agree, it's not...'

'Astra, Dylan's been arrested. He's over at Crossford, the police came for him yesterday tea-time – we didn't know, there was no warning, they just took him...' Dad looked grim.

'Oh, dad – no – oh, poor old Dylan, I don't understand – oh, is it the grass? But that's way over the top, I mean...'

'Oh, Astra...' Mum wailed, her pinched face almost blue it was so white. 'Oh, love, they say he's a child molester, a – a paedophile. They say in the village he took a little boy, a little holiday boy who was staying on the site, took him into his van, took all his clothes off and did things to him and sent him back to his parents wearing a black cloth or something covered in Satanic symbols and...I can't – it's too awful, I don't believe it, but the police...'

'No, not Dylan, oh, mum, no – I don't believe it either – dad?' I gasped; it was unthinkable, terrible. Dylan couldn't be one of those monsters, he couldn't, not *Dylan*, it wasn't possible.

'And there's more, hon, last night, the village lads went berserk, they...'

It took a while, with mum interjecting and dad going back and forth, trying to explain, trying to make sense of it. But basically this – and a lot of it we only found out properly ages later – is what happened.

It all started in the Swan, apparently, while us lot were off at the bloody gig. It seems the news that Dylan the weirdo hippie had been 'arrested for child abuse' had got around like wildfire. Tempers were high. The Swan is the village pub, not a tourist place really; what tourists do go there stay in the lounge, and the village boys have the so-called 'games room' out back. It's pretty rough in that galumphing Young Farmer/village lad way – lots of beer-spitting and drinking contests – and personally, I hadn't been there since I'd hung about with Cookie's bro.

That evening, things were a bit different from the usual drink-yourself-insensible routine. The place was seething with talk of Dylan's 'arrest'. A lot of the boys blamed the incomers for 'bringing that sort of thing to Cornwall'. Like it never happened in God's own county; yeah, right. They spouted off about the bad influence of all these people who weren't Cornish living in their village, people who bought the houses that the local youth could never afford, people like Dylan, or the ex-ad agency couple from London who lived in Bryally Cottage and never seemed to work, and I imagine, us. Hippies, weirdos, up to who knows what and now, *proven* to be filthy paedo bastards. Some of the drinkers tried to be reasonable, arguing not all incomers were bad, look at so-and-so, he's a good bloke, or that couple on the hill who helped old Mrs Truran when she was ill, and...But they were shouted down. Someone told me months afterwards, 'It was more'n yer life was worth to stick yer neck out.' I believe him. The devil was in those lads that night and they brooked no opposition while the talk boiled through the room like acid, eating up their reason.

Outside, the storm was howling like a soul in torment and the surf was up to the road. The boys were drinking even more heavily than usual and according to the head barman, Chris, who is Mrs Liddicoate's nephew, there was a lot of speed about. Not that he told Mrs Liddicoate that, mind you. Everything else, but not that. There's a big pretence in some sections of the village that our decent lads don't take drugs. Sure, they may be hard drinkers, that's manly, but drugs – oh dear me, no.

Ha bloody ha.

So, whizzed off their tits, drunk and full of piss and vinegar, they became vigilantes for the night: die-hard, death-wish, wannabe-Rambo motherfuckers out to cleanse the streets – or campsite – of filthy paedo scum. They piled into their motors and screamed through the rain to Mordros. Whipped up by the drugs, the storm, the booze, and their righteous fury, they found Dylan's big old hippie-fied, muralised caravan and, yelling like men possessed, they destroyed it.

They ripped his rainbow porch with its madly fluttering windsocks and jingling chimes down and bricked his Celtic-decaled windows in; they kicked his flower pots over and stomped them, then broke his statue of a fairy, that he'd made himself and was so proud of, into a thousand pieces. They managed to get the door off its hinges with a tire-iron quite easily. Dylan had never put extra locks on anything in his life, and the old 'van wasn't exactly designed to withstand maximum force. They got in and trashed the place, ripping, tearing, smashing, wrecking. All his records, books, clothes, posters and paintings were gleefully reduced to unrecognisable bits of trash. His higgledy-piggledy campsite accounts, his personal papers, all went fluttering like white crows into the maelstrom outside. They pissed on the photos of his dead wife and tore the pictures of his son to pieces. Then they dragged his futon out into the rain and tried to set light to it but obviously they couldn't, so they contented themselves with slashing it to pieces with Dylan's own kitchen knives, which some of them kept as souvenirs. Then they trampled his ancient sit-up-and-beg bicycle to a twisted mess.

Almost nothing escaped them. His stash of dope and cash money mysteriously disappeared; the boys didn't miss a trick. Finally, satisfied with their vengeance, screaming obscenities and high as kites on the heady cocktail of whizz, booze and adrenalin that had put so much fire in their bellies, they tried to torch the 'van, but again, the rain put paid to that – though it was fortunate they apparently forgot about the gas bottles. Well, alcohol and gear don't usually create logical thinkers, do they?

Piling back into their vehicles, soaked wet through and still full of it, they drove off into the dark, leaving the now silent devastation of Dylan's life behind them: the pages of books fluttering in the wind, the cotton stuffing from the mattress scattering over the campsite like the thick foam of the roaring sea on the beach below.

No one else on the site, the Baby-Yahs, the families, the hikers and the surfers, all locked up tight against the weather in their 'vans and tents, moved a muscle – and I don't blame them, really. Well, not much, anyway. Frankly, I dread to think what would have happened to anyone trying to interfere with the machinery of 'justice' that was in motion that night. If Dylan had been there, I have no doubt whatsoever that they'd have lynched him. None. At. All. Not a bit. They'd have killed him without a second thought, like the beasts they'd become, these nice village boys with their soft Cornish accents and blunt, sun-stained countrymen's faces. For that night, they were both horribly more, and infinitely less than themselves; they were the Mob, the many-headed beast howling for blood and destruction.

I could hardly take it in. It was like something from the Deep South of America – all it needed was a burning cross.

Dad stood up and automatically put the kettle on, just as I had last night, for Luke. He turned round and looked at me, tugging and scratching his beard as he did when he was nervous or upset. Mum's sobs redoubled. I was glad Git wasn't up, and Gwen and Lance weren't about. I dreaded to think what Gwen would say, and in a different way, Lance too. As for Git, something I couldn't explain made me want to protect her from this, to stop up her little ears and cover her eyes. I didn't want her touched by it, didn't want her tainted by it.

'Astra, they say – Mrs Liddicoate told me this morning when I went for the paper – that's how I heard – they say he was *seen* taking the child into his van, and stripping him. On Thursday, in the afternoon sometime. It was an eye-witness. I can't believe it myself, I can't. He's our friend, he's – we've known him for years. I'd know if there was anything – anything like that. I know he's had a pretty heavy time recently, and OK, he's depressed, but this? No, I can't. I just can't see Dylan doing anything like this, it's not his vibe. He loves kids, like we all do. No more than that. This is a big mistake, I know it, hon.'

Mum burst in, her voice trembling. 'What's the world coming to, Astra, what's happening when an innocent man can be…when little children are hurt by…Oh, it's awful, awful…' Mum was shaking like a leaf. Palsied. It wasn't good. Dad and I put her back to bed, where she fell into an exhausted sleep. This was just the kind of stress the docs said she should avoid. Dad and I went and sat on the deck again, like we had before all this horror had happened, when he quoted poetry at me and I'd thought there was everything to play for. We talked about it a bit, but we kept faltering, falling back on our disbelief. Dad was nearly in tears and I felt numb, to be honest. I just couldn't seem to take it in.

I ate some muesli without tasting it, my head in a whirl. I didn't want mum bothered with the Git thing, but I told dad and we agreed to ground Git for a month. It seemed so trivial in view of this stuff about Dylan. I could not believe it. Dylan, a paedo? No way. It just wasn't possible. But he'd been seen. I shivered. Dylan, God, it couldn't be true – could it? He'd played with us all since we were kids, played with Git – no, I'd have known, I'd have sensed something, definitely... But would I? Just because he'd been all right round us didn't mean he...No, that was crap. It was Dylan, *Dylan*. He wasn't like that. He wasn't.

I did some housework on auto-pilot, more for something to do than anything else, and when Git got up, still green about the gills, smelling sour and by the look of her, still slightly drunk, I made her aware of her fate in no uncertain terms. Then told her to apologise to dad. At first she looked mutinous, but I told her we had bigger trouble than her, and what it was. She went very quiet then, her eyes going saucer-big as she struggled to understand.

'But, Astra...Dylan's nice. Why would people say stuff like that?'

I couldn't answer her. Why indeed? She cried a bit and I struggled not to join her; it wouldn't help if I got in a state too. I just didn't know what to do. I felt like, if I knew what to do, if there was something I could do, I'd feel more in control. But what? What could I possibly do?

The village was seething when I went out midday. I was collared about five times by people wanting to know if we knew anything, 'seein' as he was our friend'. I didn't like that, didn't like the way they said it. I didn't like the way they looked at me, either – or was I being paranoid? I didn't know. I just walked along the front, through the tourists who moved around me, insubstantial, unreal, like ghosts. They didn't know what was going on, they were just enjoying their ice-creams and playing at surfing while someone I'd known for years and years and years was in Crossford nick accused of a terrible, evil crime. It was like the village was separated into layers, like thundered cream: the villagers and the emmets, and they moved in the same space but never touched. It suddenly seemed like a sort of grotesque carnival of the ignorant and the absurd. I couldn't stop shivering.

I went to the café to see Con and explain about last night. I wanted to do something ordinary, something practical. It was nastily ironic that last night's disaster was today's minor, trivial problem.

I found her in the flat, cleaning, Piglit having been a bad lad. She called me to come straight in when I knocked and stood with a J-cloth in her rubber-gloved hand and a reek of disinfectant and puppy piss wreathing around her spare figure. She looked even thinner than usual. I hadn't noticed before but she was very nearly gaunt. She pushed a strand of hair back from her damp forehead with the back of her red, bony wrist and shook her head.

'This is a bad do, Astra. Very bad. I can't hardly believe it of him, he seemed so harmless. Cookie told me when she collected Smoky – her mam told her. And what those buggers did to his caravan, the morons. What a mess, eh? My God, though, stuff goes round quick, here – bloody jungle telegraph.'

'Con, nothing's proved. They're just questioning him – I don't, we don't believe it. Dylan's not like that; he's just an old hippie, you know he is. It's a big mistake, you'll see.'

She grunted and stretched her neck as if it were stiff. 'Aye, well, it'll all come out in't wash, as they say. Thanks for the keys. Where is she?'

'Hasn't she phoned? OK, we left her – she stayed on at the club, then went to that friend of hers for a party.' I couldn't quite bring myself to say Richie's name.

'Oh, I know she stayed at the club. Tim Norris told me. He rang here at 6.00 a.m. Then at eight, then ten, then – in fact...' she looked at the wall clock, 'he's due now if he keeps it up. Wants to know where his *fiancée* is, why I don't take better care of her instead of letting her roam around all over the shop with surfers and – well, I won't say what else he said. He says he went to "rescue" her, but she wouldn't come with him, told him to – to eff off, I suppose. He followed her when she came out of the club but lost her and her friends in the lanes. Serves him right. What, Astra, is going on?'

I was filling her in on last night's happenings when the phone rang. Con rolled her eyes, then answered it.

'No, Tim, she's not. Yes, Astra is here, how did you...Look, it's none of her concern. No – no, she won't – look, Tim, I've had quite enough of this – no, I...'

I went over and signalled her to give me the phone. I felt curiously sharp, charged, anger beginning to twine through me, hot and jumpily electric. Con leaned close to the handset so she could hear.

'This is Astra, Tim. Look...'

I didn't get any further. His voice was tinny and compressed but you could hear the fury in it, just like last night. He cut in on me, across what I was saying as if I weren't of any account, weren't even worth being civil to.

'Listen, you – I know what you're up to, I know you're trying to split us up. Jealous, I suppose, just plain jealous of her beauty, her purity...I'll make sure you can't get your knife in anymore, you fat bitch. You and your filthy child-molesting friends – oh, yes, I know, I know all about that. You wait, you wait, you won't get away with it anymore, I'll – where is she? Where's my fiancée? Where, you know where, don't you? Don't you...'

His voice rose to a spluttering screech and Con took the phone out of my hand. I was shaking and my knees had gone to jelly, the anger drained out of me in a chilly rush. He was mad. Quite mad – certifiable, in my opinion. The hairs stood on end all over my body.

'That's enough, Tim. Don't you dare phone 'ere again, ever, d'you hear? Angel's not your bloody fiancée, not anyone's fiancée. Do you understand? No, I don't care. You've said quite enough – yes, and I expect an apology to my friend when you've pulled yourself together. Enough, Tim.'

Her voice was solid steel, her face set and furious. I wobbled to the sofa and collapsed, Piglit dashing over and jumping up so he could lick my face, lick the tears off my face because I couldn't stop crying. The tears poured out, hot and choking and I couldn't stop.

Con sat next to me, her arm around my heaving shoulders.

'There, there, you cry, you cry, you poor little thing. Bloody men. Bloody Tim bloody Norris...Get it all out, that's right. Stay there, I'll get you some tissues. Bloody buggers, blokes, all of 'em.'

Finally, I managed to snuffle to a stop and I looked at Con miserably as she sat fuming next to me, Piglit whining and squirming on her lap, his eyes huge and seal-like.

'Jesus, Con, what's his fuckin' problem – sorry, but what?' I never usually swore round Con, I don't know why.

She waved her hand in a palm-out, don't know gesture. 'Mad about her, that's what it is. It's happened before, oh aye. There were a fella from Leeds – well, least said soonest mended. I just wish she'd settle, get wed. Then she'd be safe. Still, Tim, he's the worst yet, what with the flowers and things. You wouldn't think flowers could be nasty, would you – but comin' from him, after what he just said to you – ugh. I shall throw 'em straight in the bin if any more come. Straight in the bin.'

'Oh, Con – it's not just that, it's Dylan, and mum, and Beaker and everything. I'm that fed up – I wish I could just go away, just get away somewhere and...' I felt my voice wavering and I stopped before I started blubbing again.

'I know, love, I know. You're worn out. I've seen this comin' for years, you need to get away. So do I – everyone needs holidays, don't they? Look, how about, this winter, you and me, we go somewhere nice, just for a fortnight, you can leave your mum for that long, I'm sure. Your dad won't mind. Somewhere in the sun, eh? A proper holiday – what d'you say? My shout, you can pay me back – whenever you can. That is, if you don't mind goin' with an old bat like me? I know I've been a bit – a bit preoccupied since my – since Angel came, but I haven't forgotten you, really. I'm sorry, love...Now come on, no more grizzlin', it's sorted, then. Winter sun here we come!'

We hugged, stiffly, like Bradfordians. Then we had a cuppa and the chocolate Smoky hadn't managed to eat. Cadbury's Buttons – proper chocolate, none of your Belgian nonsense. I felt the old companionship, the old closeness back, like it had been before Angel and it was a light in the dark for me, it really was. If you've got a proper friend, it's worth more than anything, isn't it?

Chapter 16

The police had kept Dylan overnight, then let him go around four in the afternoon, it seemed, and no, they'd got no idea where he was now and if he wanted to report the vandalism to his caravan, that was of course his right but they couldn't – blah, blah, yadda yadda yadda. Dad had finally decided to ring the station at seven, to see what was going on, not without some trepidation as he was worried that if the police really thought Dylan was a child-molester, he might get tarred with the same brush just because they were friends.

'I know, I know it's crap, hon, but you know how the police are with this kind of scene, it's like the old drugs thing only worse: guilt by association. Not that Dylan's – he's not. I know that, I do. It feel it...' He tapped his big chest over his heart. 'But I tell you, kitten, mud sticks. I mean, there are gonna be some who will always suspect Dylan after this, you know, no smoke without fire and all that jazz. Crap, but that's humanity. Shoot first, ask questions later.'

But he rang, and the police were reasonably cool about things. Dad explained Dylan was all alone, no family living in the UK, no blood relatives and we were his closest friends, so they told him what they knew.

They'd released him on receipt of a phone call, then a visit from the child's parents, who had returned from an early morning 'pilgrimage' to Tintagel to find all Hell let loose. Horrified, they'd immediately rung the Crossford police station with the explanation of what had happened – or rather, what hadn't. Then, with all their kids in tow, had appeared at the nick protesting Dylan's innocence, bless them.

They were another set of hand-knit hippies, the little lad in question, Rowan, being their youngest, aged six. That Thursday afternoon, he'd been playing in the beck in the woods behind the campsite, on his own because the older kids had wandered off, leaving him behind. He'd been swinging on the old car tyre attached to the tree overhanging the pool, which he'd been forbidden to do, of course, since the pool was deep, full of rocks, and considered a drowning risk by everyone's parents. I'd done it myself, often. We all had and we'd all been forbidden to, but we went ahead anyhow like kids will. He'd been swinging, then of course he'd fallen in. Dylan heard him yelling and splashing while he'd been 'in the wood', i.e. tending his dope plants. He'd run over, pulled the shaken kiddie out and taken him back to his 'van, where he'd stripped off the boy's wet clothes, rubbed him down with a towel, put arnica on his bruises and dressed him in an old Grateful Dead T-shirt – a black one with a design of dancing skeletons on it – that covered the boy from neck to ankles. Then he'd taken him straight back to his parents, who thanked Dylan profusely and scolded the kid in their 'Hey, wow, Rowan, heavy' way for disobeying them. They'd had no idea Dylan had been seen 'doing things' to the child or that the rumour mill was grinding like a bastard all that Friday. So, without a care in the world, on the Saturday, they'd wandered off in their cronky old car dead early while it was still dark, to see the dawn rise over Tintagel Castle. They didn't see Dylan's 'van, because they were in a 'van at the other end of the site and the back lane out didn't take them past it. They'd had no idea about what had happened until they'd gone to the village for ice-cream after their trip out. It had taken them a while to understand it was their kiddie that was being talked about.

As soon as they realised, about midday, they did the right thing. After a time and plenty of paperwork, as far as dad could make out, the police had let Dylan go. And they didn't know where he was. Dad said the copper on the phone had sounded faintly concerned about that, which made dad even more worried and start rumbling about 'police brutality' and 'you never know what goes on behind closed doors'. He worried that the coppers were worried that they'd gone too far in their interrogation of wobbly old Dylan. I worried about it, too. We were all plain bloody worried, frankly.

I don't mean to sound down on the police, I really don't. I don't think they're 'pigs' on the whole despite the inevitable corruption that we all know happens. They do jobs I wouldn't want to even think of doing, see things I know, I really *know*, I don't want to see. I don't think being a copper is glamorous or exciting or anything like those police thrillers on telly. I expect it's more saddening and depressing than anything else, having to clear up after the persistent stupidity and cruelty of your fellow man. No wonder they get narky sometimes, or cynical and aggressive. I know I would.

I think we all understood their feelings, why they went for Dylan like they did. I mean, I could understand it, only this time, they were wrong. OK, they had cause to be over-zealous in view of the fact that there was a big news story at the time about yet another truly hideous international paedophile ring being discovered on the Internet. The papers, the TV, the radio was full of it: the pictures the coppers had found, millions of pictures of children being brutalised, and even computer video clips with sound, the voices of those little children being…It made me sick to my stomach to think about it, and everyone else I knew felt the same. We'd discussed it in the café. How 'normal' the men they'd caught looked; family men some of them, too. The destruction rippling out from them in hot, unbreaking waves.

I mean, that's the point, in a way. Dylan looked normal, for a hippie. Just another old Sixties drop-out, but you couldn't tell the monsters from the rest of us by how they looked or behaved in public. I mean, those paedophiles had done the most vile things possible to imagine, then popped off home to fish and chips and a night in front of the box with the missus. You just couldn't tell. Awful things do go on, and I expect the coppers just overreacted to the 'number of calls regarding the situation' they got from the village. Better safe than sorry.

Dylan called us, reverse charges, at ten. Could dad do him, like, a real big favour and come fetch him from Crossford? He'd wait by the big Nat West bank on the corner, only he'd got no money on him for a taxi, sorry to be a, like, trouble. Dad shot out in the car while we all waited with baited breath.

They got back about half past eleven, Dylan half dead with

exhaustion. I made them all – mum had waited up – a cup of herb tea, then I showed Dylan to Lance's room, where I'd made up a clean bed for him. It was pitiful the way he thanked me, I could hardly bear it.

Dad sat in his old easy chair, looking terrible. He'd told us, in a low voice, how he'd driven as fast as he could to Crossford, and found Dylan where he'd said he'd be, nearly unconscious. He said Dylan looked like a dead man, all the life gone out of his eyes, his hands shaking. As if he'd been sucked dry and all that remained was a husk. Dad said he was shocked at how grey Dylan's hair was, how suddenly old he looked. I mean, it was true Dylan had never really recovered from Maudie's death and Bora's desertion, but he'd struggled along, taking bits and pieces of pleasure from a nice sunset, a pleasant stroll, an evening with his old mates, reminiscing. Dad said, looking at him leaning against the wall, waiting, that he knew the last remaining spark had gone out, and Dylan knew it, too.

On the drive from Crossford to Polwenna, he told dad about how the coppers had pulled him out of his caravan as he'd sat reading and listening to a tape of Steeleye Span, thinking about what he'd have for his tea. They'd given him no explanation, hardly even speaking to him, just manhandled him into their car and driven at breakneck speed back to Crossford nick. Terrified and shaken, he'd been hauled into an interview room with two coppers who looked at him as if he were shit. He'd had no idea what it was about and had assumed it was the dope. Until they told him. Then his world had unstitched at the seams and shrivelled away into dust like rotten silk.

He'd been seen abusing a little boy, they said. Seen by a young woman walking her dog; they shouted at him that she'd seen him drag a weeping child from the woods into his 'van, strip him naked and grope his shivering little body before slamming the 'van door shut. Other informants then stated he'd sent the distraught child back to his parents draped in a black cloth scrawled with Satanic symbols with a warning that if they told, he'd have them killed. That's what was said. Now if Dylan confessed and shopped his fellow paedophiles, they'd do their best to go easy on him. They went over it and over it, again and again, threatening him, telling him what would happen to him in prison, that they knew everything, that he was a disgusting, filthy pervert who they could hardly keep their fists off, but they were officers of the law, they had to abide by the rules; but wait, just wait until the other prisoners got him – a nonce, a sex offender. He'd be tortured and killed, they'd be surprised if he lasted a week. It went on and on. Dylan's horrified, quavering protestations of innocence were swallowed up in the swelling tide of the coppers' rage and sense of triumph; finally they had a paedo in front of them, finally they could actually *do* something about this most horrible of crimes. They weren't going to let *this* fish go. The night wore on, then they'd put him in a cell 'for his official rest-time', so he could 'think about things and be sensible'. Then in the morning it had started all over again when suddenly, the officers had been called out, leaving him terrified, with a scowling, unspeaking constable for company.

The family had phoned, then they turned up at the station with their kids, with the kid in question, who was thrilled to be in a real police station, just like *The Bill* on telly. With a juddering effort, the coppers let Dylan go. No apology, no nothing. Turfed him out as if they still couldn't bear to look at him – and maybe they couldn't. Maybe it was too crap for words to have made that kind of mistake and they couldn't handle it. He hadn't minded that, though, he said. They were just doing their job. He hated child-molesters as much as they did – why, if anything had ever happened to his Bora, he'd have gone mad, he would. But how could anyone think – how could they say he would do a thing like that? He loved kids, loved their innocence, they were the future of the world; if you hurt a child, man, you hurt all our futures. How could they say he'd done such a vile thing?

He'd wandered about, out along the river, staring at the muddy, storm-swollen water, with no sense of time or even of getting home. His head whirled and ached with the awfulness of what had happened to him, of what could have happened if the boy's family hadn't contacted the police. Exhausted, he'd realised he had no money on him and blindly found his way to a phone box. He'd half expected us to disown him and when dad had jumped out of the car and caught him up in one of his big bear hugs, he'd thought he'd collapse with relief and gratitude that someone still cared about him. Had believed in him. Dad said he'd felt horribly guilty about that, because he'd hesitated to ring the coppers and there was Dylan, thinking him a saviour. With a big effort, he'd confessed this to Dylan, who just shook his head sorrowfully and said it didn't matter, what mattered was that dad hadn't condemned him out of hand like other people. That he'd never forget that, as long as he lived.

At this point, Dylan wept and dad did, too. He'd pulled the car up in a lay-by and they wept together; two old hippie guys whose gentle, carefully constructed love-and-peace world had finally crashed and burned in the icy, excoriating light of the bright new century.

Dylan stayed with us for a few days; just sat and stared silently out of the big window, tears slowly trickling down his withered cheeks. It broke my heart, let me tell you. Dad had to break the news about his 'van that Monday morning. I couldn't bear it, I couldn't. I was as jumpy as a cat, I had to go and stand in the kitchen until it was over. Dylan didn't make a sound, just bowed his head as if nothing mattered to him anymore, nothing.

Afterwards, dad said the saddest thing he'd ever seen in his life was watching Dylan pick through the desecrated ruin of his caravan. Dylan didn't cry anymore, he just found his passport where he'd kept it stashed with his bank book in an old tin cash box under the floor of the 'van and a crushed but intact picture of Maudie, Bora and himself taken when they were young and Bora just a baby. He put them in his ditty bag and turned his back on the rest. Dad said he looked a million years old; it was awful. I don't think dad ever really got over that, either. He always seemed a bit, well, different from then on. More melancholy, older. Mum just seemed to withdraw into herself, as if it were too much to cope with, as if the whole world was suddenly a strange, dark and dangerous place she didn't really understand anymore.

It made me realise they would get properly old, become frail, that mum would…I mean, I knew, what with the MS, she'd…But somehow, what happened to Dylan made me feel it. That loss, that absence, a life without her and dad.

Dylan stayed, just being quiet and empty, while we all tiptoed round him trying to give him little treats to eat – honeycomb, or his favourite muffins. He just said thank you, but never touched them. He wouldn't even share mum's evening pipe. There was nothing we could do for him. Git was best with him, oddly enough. She just sat on a cushion by his feet and watched telly with him, or at least, she watched while he gazed into space. She chattered about her favourite pop stars, or her school and Dylan seemed calmed by her being so normal.

Then one morning, he was gone. A note said he was selling the campsite and going to see Bora. We never saw him again, nor heard anything after a letter came from Canada a few months later saying it wasn't working with Bora – Bob – and he was going to India. After that, nothing ever again. The campsite sold immediately. A national company specialising in 'leisure breaks' bought it and put a hustling, snappy manager from Essex in for the rest of the season. He told everyone 'his' company was going to make the place smart and 'up-to-date' with a bar, entertainment suite and swimming pool. They renamed it 'Polwenna Leisure Park'. The villagers were very pleased with the thought of an increase in proper, non-hippie tourists and their money – and why not? They had their livings to make now the fishing was gone. I used to wish someone could have put a little plaque up in the place somewhere, you know, with an inscription: *This was Mordros. Dylan and Maudie the hippies lived here*, or something. I don't know.

Sometimes, I thought about Dylan. I liked to think of him wandering about the vastness of India. I wanted to see him walking the dusty ochre hill roads, staff in hand, while the thick rose-and-saffron light of dusk warmed the dreaming peaks of Makalu or Chomolungma, that bountiful Mother Goddess. I liked to think of him eating a simple meal in the flickering candlelight of Diwali, his food donated by devout housewives in green and red saris, who approved of the quiet, respectable foreign sadhu with his long, white beard, faraway gaze and gentle manner. Or I saw him resting in the rose-filled garden of a Kashmiri ashram, the pale, ineffable light of morning embroidered with blue threads of incense smoke. Just sipping his cha, listening to the sing-song drone of a holy man telling him peace would be his in the long, unbroken chain of life after life; that his sorrow would be rewarded; that he would meet his wife again in another, better time where they would hold each other and find perfect love at last.

When things got really tough, I thought of all that. Old Dylan vanishing into the great world like a raindrop into the sea. Into the vast, unknowable bosom of the ocean; one face amongst millions, submerged but never drowning. Finding peace, anonymous, and without ego, without desire.

Chapter 17

'OK, so, when d'you think you can come over? I mean, Dylan's gone now, there's...'

On the other end of the line, Beaker had sighed. He never actually said it, but I could tell he hadn't wanted to come to our house while Dylan was there. Maybe he just felt awkward; he never liked 'scenes' or people with what he called 'mental problems' like depression. Or maybe dad had been right, the shadow over Dylan, and us, lingered.

'Look, I meant to tell you an' everythin' but – Don's made me assistant manager...'

'Beaker, that's fantastic! Congratulations! Oh, you deserve it, you really do and...'

He cut across me. 'Yeah, thanks – but see, it means a lot of extra work, late nights, to catch up, get the hang of things. You know.'

'Yeah.'

There was a long silence, then, full of unsayable things. It had been one thing being all cool at the gig about the way things were with us, it was another to be slithering about in the fast-disintegrating house of cards that was our relationship. I felt panicky now the crunch was here, and safety, which I'd so blithely wanted to chuck away, seemed very precious. I had a little mantra running round my head in those days: '*Oh God, let it all be how it was.*' Only I wasn't quite sure how far back 'was' was, if you get me. Last month, last year or when I was Smoky's age?

I tried again. 'So, what about rehearsals? I mean...'

'Yeah, well – we've decided to give it a rest, actually. I won't 'ave a lot of time to be messin' about an' Terry's thinkin' of singing for 'is cousin's band, that does covers up at the Lobster Pot. It's a good whack, regular, 'e'll need it if he's goin' to get married next year.'

'Oh – I'm sorry, Beaks, I...'

'Astra, I meant to say this before, but d'you think you could call me Tony? I mean, that Beaker thing, it's school stuff. I'd like, prefer it if people called me by my real name – I doan mean ter be funny, it's just what with bein' assistant manager, it won't look good people callin' me Beaker, see what I mean? I gotta think about stuff like that now. '

I squeezed my eyes shut. He was right, of course, it was childish. I had a sudden vision of his dad, Len, pottering in his neat-as-a-pin hankie-sized garden, humming to himself as he took cuttings from his geraniums or whatever. Len had been a jazz freak, that was where Beak – *Tony* had got his love of music. They were nice people, Tony's parents, good people. Quiet, homely, sweet. If Len had ever wanted to be more than just the drummer in the local jazz combo, if he'd wanted to 'go pro', leave Cornwall, play with Acker Bilk, then that desire had long, long since burned out. Like father, like son, they say, don't they? Oh, Beaker.

'Oh, yeah – sure, of course – sorry, I mean you're right, Be – Tony. No problem, I'll tell my lot, too, and Con. You're right, it's a good thing, yeah. So, when d'you think you could come over, then? How about coming for dinner?'

I sounded anxious, clingy, even to myself; but I couldn't seem to stop.

'Er, I doan know, maybe Sunday...'

'Right, fine, Sunday then. T-Tony, we've got to talk, you know.' There, I'd said it. It fell into the phone like a stone down a well.

There was a long pause again. 'Yeah, I know. I just doan want to get into it all on the phone, see what I mean? I'm at home, see? Everyone's 'ere. Look, I know – I ain't mad at you nor nothin', Astra, I ain't. It's – it's – I'll see yer Sunday, OK? Doan be upset, eh? I'll see yer.'

I hung on to the phone lamely. 'Love you.'

'Yeah, I know. I love you too. I'm sorry, Astra.'

I put the phone down and stared at it for some time, as if it would magically give me all the answers I needed. Oddly enough, it didn't, so I went to bed early with an American thriller I got from the library van about some depressed New Orleans ex-Vietnam vet detective with a drink problem and a severe tendency to batter anything that moved. I thought I should feel like that, too, should want to smack the shit out of something, be angry, hysterical, *anything* – but I just felt numb, washed-out. It was as if I was behind a thick pane of glass, greenish, cold glass, the sort with little flaws and bubbles in that distorts things seen through it. Everything seemed very far away through the glass and I had no energy to break through and do anything.

The detective relived his awful war experiences as I fell asleep. I didn't dream.

The next day, Angel returned from her life of sin with Richie-poo. By the look on her face it hadn't resulted in him leaving his wife and begging her to be his. In fact, it was the nearest to un-groomed I'd ever seen her and her pale (but still luminous, naturally, like the consumptive heroine of one of those tragic operas) complexion and suspiciously red nostrils rather gave the game away. Or it did if you were me and Cookie, but not, it seemed, if you were Con. Before crashing, Angel did manage to fill us in on Richie's mate's house over a full English and double latte.

It was none of your woodchip-and-rising-damp holiday 'cottages', oh no. It had been designed and was owned by none other than Harrison Mackay, that architect who built the Lemnco Tower in London that they made all the fuss about – the one Prince Charles said was a blight on the landscape of London or something. Mr Mackay's Cornish hideaway had cost hundreds of thousands to build and was set in its own, security-walled grounds. It came complete with private beach, and the house itself (with permanent staff in the form of a housekeeper/cook and handyman couple) was set into the hillside in a blaze of tinted glass, slate and teak, with layered decks and landscaped gardens – if you could call imported Thai driftwood, polished granite boulders, Perspex water features and aluminium lighting ensembles 'gardens' – down to the cliff edge. And the interior design! My dear, to *die* for. None of your got-it-cheap-at-Trago-Mills shite there, thank you. Well, saying that, of course Angel didn't know what the housekeeper's cottage was like, naturally. I bet that was a tad more down-market.

If you went down the steps to the beach (which had also been landscaped, nothing untidy or natural allowed), halfway down there was Harrison's 'Pod'; a tiny little fully outfitted bedsittery thing built into a cave in the cliff. Harrison meditated there, apparently, and gazed at the sunsets over the sea for inspiration. Angel said it was his homage to the troglodyte dwellings of southern Spain, apparently. Harrison was full of things like that. Little gems. Personally, I thought Harrison was just full of it, but I kept my mouth shut and looked for an opening in Angel's non-stop chatter in order to give her what-for about Git.

But there was no pause long enough. Richie was thinking of buying the Retreat, as it was called, off Harrison-baby and had rented it for the whole summer while Harrison was wowing them in Tokyo with his plans for some art gallery. Every weekend was going to be a party to die for, the crème de la crème of the London music and arts scenes would be there. Next week, Sucka were coming to chill before going into studio – God, just too fantastic, the singer, Floyd was gorgeous! And last night, in the Pod, Richie had almost, like really almost *proposed*. We refrained from mentioning his wife at this point, details like that were obviously irrelevant. I toyed with the idea of telling the Bodmin Beasts where all the coke would be this summer, but my better nature prevailed. Just.

Then, daintily wiping bean-sauce from her rosy lips, Angel glided upstairs to 'nap'. Cookie, Dot and I just looked at each other. Words were unnecessary.

So when the flow of customers diminished somewhat, we revived the other talking point in our little café society, Tim Norris. In the time Angel had been gone, he had revved up his 'courtship' something chronic. He sent inch-thick letters, left a number of those horrible over-size teddy-bear 'I love you because' cards in the café for his 'fiancée', stuck Post-it notes to Con's door with messages like *call me anytime, my angel – Tim X X X* on them and left five bunches of flowers. The roses kept coming, too, even though Con stopped the florist's delivery bloke and told him not to bring any more. Oh no – more than his job was worth not to, apparently. Paid for, see – the client would have to cancel, not the recipient. Anyways, he argued, nice to get flowers, eh? Someone must be in love.

For the best part of the day, Tim was – well, it's hard to describe. He was sort of *camped* outside the café on the beach. Public land, you see. He could sit there all day if he liked; there was nothing anyone could do about it as long as he didn't sleep there at night. He didn't need to. He slept in his car, parked opposite Con's door in the carpark. Or he did until Mr Eddy caught him and read him the riot act. He said Tim just looked at him as if he was mad and muttered something about 'Someone's got to look after her, for God's sake.' Mr Eddy said it were his opinion, the fella had a bad case o' lovesickness, but with a pretty liddle thing like that Angel, well – if he were twenty year younger, why…Yeah, right, Mr E, we all said, lovesickness. Sure.

It was really unnerving, Tim sitting out there, on a folding chair, a newspaper and a flask by his side, his watery, red-rimmed eyes fixed on the café, hour after hour. The tourists left a big space around him even though it was prime beach. Just left him sitting there in his chair, staring. Some of them commented when they came in for their teas – 'What's up with him?/God, nutters, they're everywhere these days, country's gone to the dogs/Is he safe, I mean, he's not dangerous is he? My kids, you see and…'

Apart from sincerely wishing he'd piss off, in our kinder moments we wondered about his job – even allowing he was self-employed he was out there for hours, what about his clients? He never went running anymore either; his routine was shot to bits. I don't have to tell you the whole thing drove Con crackers, but it seemed there was nothing she could do. He hadn't broken any laws by sitting on the beach, or sending Angel 'nice' presents. I said she ought to talk to the police about it anyway – and in view of Dylan, I wasn't that keen to get in touch with our local Plod, but still…I got shouted down by everyone about that idea. What could Con tell them? That her beautiful, sexy sister had so entranced a solid local citizen with a good, white-collar job that he was determined to marry her? I mean, you know, marry

– not kidnap, not abuse, but marry. In a church, with his aged mum in attendance. What terrible, violent things could she say he'd done to frighten her and Angel? Sent flowers and perfume. Written love letters. Sat outside on the public beach waiting for a glimpse of his beloved. OK, he'd lost it that night on the phone, but it was Con's and my word against his regarding what had been said. He'd just say he'd been upset, mad with worry. Sorry. Won't ever, ever do it again, officer. We'd look like hysterical fools.

I could see their point. That was my problem, I could always see everyone's point. I'd been brought up with that bloody hippie maxim about walking in another's moccasins before you judge them. Right. I could see what it was doing to Con, too – but then, so could everyone else, customers included. Tim really got to her. She used to walk out on to the veranda and stare back at him with folded arms, real Bradford, head-wobble and all. 'Motor's runnin',' Jim and Joey snickered after she did it one time. Tim just kind of looked round her, as if she was hiding Angel from him. She even went out to the beach and tried reasoning with him, but he wouldn't speak to her; just waited until she left in disgust. God, he looked so bonkers. Mad. Mad for love. It was like a Victorian melodrama. My whole life was turning into something by the sodding Brontë sisters, complete with love-crazed swains, desiccated village spinsters (duh, *me*) and brooding, cloud-filled skies.

Then Angel came home, delivered her tales of glory, slept and buggered off again early, taking the GTI, sneaking out the back door while Tim was staking out the front of the café. She thought his vigil was hilarious. A real hoot. She came back the next evening with her feet in a pair of silver-and-turquoise-tipped cowboy boots I hadn't seen before, denim Daisy Duke shorts, a skinny western-style sleeveless shirt and a carefully battered straw Stetson in her hand.

'Oh, yee-haw, ride 'em cowboy,' I said in a deliberately bored voice. I was pissed off good-style with darling Ange, what with Git and Luke and now this coming and going without a word to Con, who worried herself ragged. I'd have been pissed off at her about Tim, too, but somehow, I didn't think that was entirely her fault. Not entirely. Cookie heard me and sniggered audibly.

Angel looked faintly surprised at my lack of enthusiasm. 'Went shoppin' in Exeter. Gotta 'ave summat new for the weekend – what's up wi' you?'

I couldn't begin to begin, as the song sort of goes. She furrowed her spotless brow at me, then the irritation passed as swiftly as a cloud in a bright sunny sky. Angel had it in her mind I just loved her to bits and we were bestest mates, and nothing I did would shift that, I knew it. I expect she thought it was my period, if she thought at all. Actually, she was sort of right: I'd just finished and was in my usual post-menstrual, pre-ovulationary slough. But that was immaterial. It was.

'An' fer that matter, what *is* the matter wi' dickhead out *there*? I mean, has he been out there all the time I've bin gone? He has? Mad bastard. Mebbe I'll go tell 'im to sod off, what d'you think? That'd give him summat to chew on, eh?' She giggled like a five-year-old planning mischief.

I was about to seriously fill her in on her beau's activities when Con came down and saw her errant sister in all her Western finery. Her face lit up like a beacon. It was quite hard to see all that naked love shine out of her face. It should have been private.

'Angel, love! Where on earth have you...'

She didn't get any further because the sandy, shambling figure of Tim scuttled through the door.

'Oh, my God, my darling, my love, what have they done to you? Where have you been? I've been out of my mind...' He gabbled at top speed, his chapped lips writhing like worms drying in the sun, his eyes popping out of his head as he staggered towards her, his arms outstretched like a bloody mummy.

Con spun like a mother lion whose cub was threatened by hyenas.

'Out. Out. Get out, get out, you mad – get out of my café NOW!'

We all froze; everything seemed to go into slow motion – honest, it was like a film or something. For a terrible moment I – we all thought he was going to knock Con aside and grab Angel. The customers were staring, cups or forks paused at their lips. I dropped my tea-towel and took a step forward but Tim stopped. He stopped dead and his eyes slid from Angel to Con.

'You old bitch. You old *bitch*. Get out of my way. She's mine now, mine. Not yours, not…*Get out of my way…*'

Con reached over and slapped him hard, really hard, across the face, with a noise like a gunshot. He staggered back, knocking a cup of tea all over a fat customer in a shorty wetsuit. The bloke struggled up complaining as Tim smashed into the doorframe and careered out on to the beach like a rogue pinball.

There was a deathly hush for a few seconds, only broken by a child sobbing, 'Mummy, mummy, I'm frightened…'

Then all hell broke loose.

Everyone was shouting at once; the fat customer was brushing cake and tea off himself; there were children howling; parents complaining furiously; and Con just stood there, looking at her hand with its bright red palm.

'Angel – Angel! Get her upstairs, get her out of this! I'll sort things – Angel!' I gave her a little push towards Con.

'Don't shove, Astra, I'm – honest, what *is* goin' on? Con, Connie love, come on, come wi' me.' And she hustled Con upstairs.

It took ages to get everyone calm again. I couldn't think of anything worse that could have happened for the café, for our trade. I was half furious and half deadly worried. Most of the tourists left. One set of parents were going to complain, but who to they never made clear, another set stormed out without paying for the four meals they'd eaten, and a hideous Yah-woman gave me a lecture on 'riff-raff' and 'types' until I nearly did a Con on her. In the end, the café was virtually empty except for the fat customer in the wetsuit who turned out to be a pleasant enough bloke from Birmingham who was really decent about Tim knocking tea all over him.

'Look, sir, I'm so sorry about all this – it's – I think Tim – that man – I think he's kind of lost it and – can we get you another tea, or coffee, some more cake? On the house, of course…'

'Well, that'd be nice, ah. Thanks. Look here, miss, I don't mean to be nosey, but that chap, is he botherin' that girl, the one dressed up Country and Western? Only…'

I was about to deny everything automatically, but he seemed a decent bloke, with his cute accent and round red face. I sort of surrendered.

'Well…'

'Ah. I thought so, like. I seen him, sittin' there, every day; I thought, ey up, somethin' going on. You see, miss, it happened to a friend of me ex-wife's. Years ago now, like, but…Chap got stuck on her, see. Wouldn't leave her alone. Wouldn't take no for an answer. Sat outside her house in his car all hours, sent letters, cards, phoned her up non-stop. We all tried talking to him an' I, well, you know, I lost me rag with him – but it were no good. He was crackers, used to ring up her work, and say her mum was ill at the hospital, stuff like that, just so she'd leave an' he could see her. That chap reminded me of it, the way he was. I suppose I'm a bit sensitive to it now, like.' He wrinkled his salt-peeling snub nose and nodded meaningfully.

'Oh, God – that's *just* what Tim's like. How did your – your ex-wife's friend get rid of him?'

'Oh, she didn't, miss. He tried to kill her an' got put away; she moved, emigrated, akchully. New Zealand.' And he took a sip of his tea, thoughtfully.

'*What!*'

'Oh yes. He nearly did for 'er, an' all. Serious. He like, waylaid her as she walked out her front door on the way to work. Tried to strangle her, hurt her terrible bad; she were in hospital fer ages. He'd bin there all night, see, watchin' in case she 'ad another chap. Mad jealous, he were. Said if he couldn't have her, like, no one could. It was a neighbour what saved her, got the coppers an' everythin'. This fella, like, he got put away as I said, but – only for a few years. Judge said he were wotsit – unbalanced by his love for Tina. A cream passional. That sort of thing. Couldn't help himself. It were a bad do, no mistake. Her family – I needn't tell a nice girl like yourself – you can imagine. So you see, miss, I'd be careful if I were you, like. Tell your friend to be careful, 'cos yer never know, do yer? Stalkers, they call 'em now.

Chaps like that. Stalkers. You should call the coppers, they'm clued up on stuff like that these days. Better safe than sorry, eh? Specially with a pretty little wench like that, ah. Thanks fer the tea – it's me last day today, pity the weather's been so on and off, isn't it?'

And having dropped his bombshell, he waddled off, his over-stretched wetsuit creaking, presumably for one last body-board session before home-time.

I stood and stared at his rotund, retreating figure, my mouth open. Nearly killed her? I mean, *strangled* her? Jesus. What was all *that* about? And stalkers? That sort of thing only happened to celebs, didn't it? Didn't it? I was still standing gawping in shock when Luke came in.

'Hi, Astra. Are you closing early? It's really empty. Is…?'

'Yes, she is. No, don't – we've had some trouble. We – look, Luke, Tim – Tim Norris, you know, he's…'

'Yeah, he's been sitting outside on the beach every day, hasn't he? I mean what's his…'

'Let me finish, please – he saw Angel when she came in and – and he went a bit crackers. There was a scene. Con – Con hit him. All the customers left, only this bloke – oh, never mind. I'd leave it for a bit, I would. Just leave it. Ring her or something. E-mail her, I don't know.'

Luke's square jaw got suddenly squarer and his big, knuckly fists clenched. For someone that out there, he looked well pissed off – angry, even. His sea-blue eyes glazed in a peculiar way I'd never seen in him before. Then I recognised it, Lance looked like that before a punch-up. Testosterone. Oh, Christ, not Luke too. Not Luke, the epitome of laid-back, going all hold-me-back-lads-I'll-kill-him over Angel. That girl was a bloody, sodding liability and no mistake.

'Did he hurt her, what…' His normally quiet, rather upper-upper voice was thick with anger.

'Oh, Luke, you're too late, mate. No – no he didn't get near her, she's fine, just cross. Luke – Luke, stop it. Calm down. It won't help you getting in a state, too – look at us, we're all in a state, just be – be cool, eh? Dot – set the kettle on, eh?'

Luke relaxed, his body slumping back into its usual hands-in-pockets slouch. 'Sorry – sorry. I – you know. God, if anything happened to her because of that bastard, I'd...'

I pushed the images conjured up by the Brummie guy firmly away. 'Nothing's going to happen, it won't. Tim's just neurotic and stupid and Con's under a lot of stress, OK?' I didn't add Con was stressed-out because of Angel and her goings-on. There would have been no point: Luke had his dreamy Angel-face on again.

We all had tea and some yesterday's scones, then Dot and Cooks, who was obviously dying to talk to me, went out back for a fag. Luke sat in silence then eventually he spoke, not looking at me but at one of Con's beautiful sea-pictures on the opposite wall.

'Er, thanks for the tea. Look, I thought – I thought you'd be pleased to know the weather's changing – there'll be some surf. That will help with the café, won't it?'

'Well, yeah, sure. Will you do a bit then?' I said, casually. Will you go back to being King, Luke? Will you see off this young pretender who's saying you've lost it to anyone who'll listen? Will you be my hero again, Luke? Yeah, I thought all that, but I didn't say it. No, I didn't breathe a dicky-bird.

'Mmm, yeah. Prob'ly. Keep my hand in, you know. Look, if she comes down, will you tell her I asked after her? Tell her I'll – oh, OK, I know. I'll phone, yeah?' He smiled his sweet smile at me and left. I watched him as he scuffed across the beach, squinting up at the sky, which, to me, showed no particular change.

Surf's up, then, I thought. Oh good. That'll make everything AO-fucking-K, won't it?

Chapter 18

That evening, after locking up, I looked in on Con and Angel before going home. I wanted to tell them what the fat customer had said, to warn them and to try again to get Con to go to the police. I knew it was pointless trying to persuade Angel to do anything like that – she was incapable of taking any man, however barking, seriously. More than that, she knew no fear. Really, she was quite fearless. I don't think it was actual bravery, so much as she couldn't imagine anything shit actually happening to her. But anyway, my attempts to interest either of them in the horrific story or the possibility that Tim was actually a stalker were hopeless.

Con was in a terrible state of nerves, blindly going over and over what she'd done, literally wringing her hands and pacing while she said over and over, 'Why did I do that? Why? What's the matter with me?' Obviously, as far as I was concerned, the reason was sitting on the sofa obliviously cuddling Piglit with her clingfilm-wrapped hair covered in goo and a blue face-pack on. I tried to tell Con what was on my mind, but she was so distracted it was hopeless. I decided to try again another, more propitious time. That would at least give me a chance to prepare a good case.

I left them and ran up home, feeling flustered and a bit shaky myself, as if Con's nerves had been catching. I felt as if I'd failed to reach her, and as I trotted through the cut, bathed in the thick balsamic scent from the escallonia bushes that lined it, I had the strangest feeling that Angel had somehow prevented me from talking, even though she hadn't said more than two words. I couldn't shake the feeling that she disliked hassle so much, she'd risk Con's – well, her sanity almost, just for a quiet life. She'd sacrifice, if that wasn't too strong a word, her own sister without a second thought. It made me shiver. Against my will, Gwen's narrow, colourless face rose up in front of my eyes. Jeez, was I as bad as Angel in my way?

Consequently, with all this pondering twizzling round my brain, I was knocked sideways when I got home and found mum had cooked dinner. More than mere dinner, at that. It was a bit of a feast, actually. There was a clear Thai-style hot and sour soup, followed by goat's cheese and spinach filo pastry parcels, rosemary-and-garlic roast potatoes, then sticky toffee pudding with organic vanilla ice-cream. Mum was un-vegan at that point because her holistic energy field-twiddler bloke at High Tor had said she was in danger of osteoporosis so it was minimum dairy. Mum could cook when she wanted to, but it had been literally years since she'd done a three-course dinner.

We had nearly a full family, too; everyone except Gwen, naturally. It was lovely to sit round the big old kitchen table, candles lit, and eat properly instead of snacking off a tray.

'Wow, mum, this is fantastic, gorgeous,' I mumbled through a mouthful of sticky toffee. Dear God, I love food.

She made a 'modest' face and smiled. 'Oh, Gita helped me, didn't you love? She did all the hard work, I just directed. I suppose we should confess the pudding's bought…'

'I don't care, it's all delicious! Git – well done, you!' Git blushed scarlet and oh-mum'd. Ever since the gig and then Dylan, she'd retreated back into childhood a bit, like a baby turtle not sure of the terrain. A bit clingy and wobbly. If it had been one thing or the other I think she'd have been all right, but both together had given her a bit of a shock.

Mum beamed at her. 'Oh, you know, I just thought, with all the terrible things that have happened – I just thought it would be nice to have a proper dinner. The family.'

I was just about to agree with her when I felt Lance grab my hand under the table. He hadn't done that for years, since he was a kid and had been about to confess a bit of wrongdoing. His enormous paw was hot and sweaty and he was almost breaking my bones.

'Lance – what is it?' I hissed. He looked at me and I saw he was deathly white. Oh no, what now?

'Mum, Dad – everyone.'

We all looked at him in shock. Lance, speaking? I half expected a formation of pigs to swoop past the window.

'Er, I gotta bit of news, see. Um, fact is – er, well, see – oh, fuckit, mum, dad, girls, Poppy's pregnant. I'm goin' to be a daddy. You're goin' to be granparents. Aunties. There.'

I was stunned and I could see everyone else was too. Dad had his wineglass stuck halfway to his mouth. Our Lance, a daddy? Our Lance? Beam me up, Scotty. I heard mum snuffling and got up – was she going to cry? Was she angry, what? It was so unexpected.

'Oh, Lancelot, oh, love – oh, oh, that's so…That's so wonderful. I'm so happy, it's oh…'

'Doan cry, mum, you're supposed ter be pleased an'…'

'I am, I am, it's tears of joy! A granny – I'm going to be a granny – when, when, Lancelot?'

'She says five months. I'm goin' ter move in with 'er proper, look after 'er and the boy. It's a bit cramped but the council might get us a proper house what with us bein' regular together an' having the two kids. We hope it's gonna be a liddle girl, but it doan matter which, long as it's healthy, do it?'

'Son.' Dad got up and so did Lance. They shook hands solemnly, like a pair of grizzly bears, then dad pulled Lance into a hug and slapped him on the back, raising dust from his Harley sweatshirt. Dad was beaming, speechless. I half expected him to hand out cigars or something.

What can I say? It was so unexpected, so bloody unlikely, even. I suppose I still half thought of Lance as a kid, when, of course, he was a grown man and physically at least, had been so since he was fourteen. He was the boy who couldn't fit into his school desk, had to shave twice a day and on one famous occasion, nearly ran the headmistress over on his old Kawasaki. Every school's got a lad like him. I kept looking at him as if he'd grown another head but at the same time, I was so proud of him and I loved him so much. It just took something like this to bring it out in the open. OK, maybe he wasn't a great achiever in life like some, but he had a good, kind heart under that luridly tattooed chest and he was obviously bursting with pride and love for his girlfriend, her boy and his soon-to-be child.

We had a fantastic night. Mum insisted on phoning Poppy – who we'd hardly ever spoken to, just seen clinging like a skinny little limpet to the back of Lance's bike as he roared up the hill – and telling her how thrilled we all were and inviting her and her son to tea. Later mum said the poor girl had been pathetically grateful that we weren't 'mad at her' and agreed to come over the next weekend with her boy, Kieran.

Git was ecstatic at the idea of being an auntie, and ragged Lance to bits, her old liveliness returned. Mum insisted on digging out the dreadful home-made hippie baby clothes in insane colour combos we'd all worn in turn from the blanket boxes, and our childhood photos were pored over and giggled at by 'granny and granddad'. We all had a celebratory glass of wine – even mum – and got horribly sentimental. Totally fab. What a boy, my bro – a daddy. Way to go, Lance.

I woke up the next morning full of beans. I could hardly wait to tell Con. She'd be made up like she always was when someone fell pregnant and babies were in the offing. It would cheer her up no end. Especially since it would be Lance's child – she had a soft spot for Lance and was always feeding him. I ran to the front door and nearly fell over a fully loaded rucksack complete with bedroll lying on the hall floor. I was about to drag it out of the way when I heard Gwen's voice.

'Don't touch it. The taxi will be here in a minute.'

I looked up, and there she stood. What weird trip was she on this time? She was wearing a bizarre camouflage-type outfit way too big for her stick-thin frame – loudly patterned combat trousers, boots, a matching military-style jacket and a hideous orange T-shirt that drained every vestige of colour from her face. It was all brand new, stiff and box fresh. A very large crudely made wooden cross on a thong hung round her neck like a placard.

'What are you got up as, for fuck's sake?' I could have bitten my tongue, but at the same time, I couldn't help it. She always got to me, always jerked my chain.

She looked at me, her eyes full of contempt. 'I'm leaving, Astra. Kathy and I have joined God's Militia. We're going to the Good News HQ to become missionaries. Pastor Elms approves and that's all I care about. I'm not spending another night in this Godless house. It was bad enough you all harboured that child-molester – I mean, do you *know* what they say in the village about you? Do you even care? I have prayed and prayed to understand God's plan in mortifying me like this, but I just can't. I only hope it will be revealed to me in time. Pastor Elms says it was designed to bring me further into faith and I hope he's right. But it's too much, it is – and now that *pig* bringing more unbaptised bastard children into the world. I mean, who knows what those filthy bikers get up to? Satanic rituals, devil worship – that child and its slut of a mother are damned. They'll all go straight to Hell. I've failed here, I know, but Pastor Elms has forgiven me and I accept Our Lord's will and…'

'What the fuck are you on about, you mad bitch?' I couldn't help it; she drove me nuts, standing there ranting on, pouring out her cruel drivel as if she was some sort of twisted home-grown Joan of Arc.

She turned her face away from me for a moment, eyes closed. The swearing, probably. She was supposed to shut out profanity so she wouldn't be corrupted. She was sweating, perspiration beading her white forehead and darkening the stiff wisps of hair that escaped from her tight pony-tail. Yeah, right on, Gwen, you pass by on the other side, you fucking Pharisee.

'I'm going to the Good News HQ.' She repeated this information slowly, as if I was appallingly dense. 'It's in the Midlands. It's residential. I'm not coming back. I'm dedicating myself to Our Lord Jesus and the fight against Satan. I'm leaving, Astra. For good. I'm sorry, but that's how it is, and I won't be dragged down with you. I've had the Call, and I'm going. Kathy and I will do some good in the world, unlike you.'

'For fu — What about mum and dad, Gwen? Have you thought about them? Where is this place? What's the address? You can't just…'

'I can and I will. You've said yourself on many occasions I'm not part of this *family*.' She faltered, and took hold of the big cross round her neck, gripping it so hard her knuckles went white. 'As to mum and dad – oh, tell them whatever lies and slander you want. You will anyway; you always hated me, just because I didn't want to be dirty-minded and man-mad like you. Because I wanted to live a decent life. When mum started this nonsense about being ill, you were so happy, weren't you, Astra? So happy. You could just be a big bully and shove everyone around and be oh-so-wonderful Astra, the…I'm not putting up with it anymore. I've got my own life to lead. Get out of the way, the taxi's here. Get out of the way, Astra. I'll pray for you, all of you, but it won't do any good.'

And, dragging the rucksack, she stumbled out of the door, the back of her silly jacket embroidered with 'God's Militia' in big orange letters for all the world like Lance's 'Bodmin Beasts' colours. I ran to the door, but she didn't look back. She just sat in the car as it drove away and you'd have had to look quite closely to see she was crying.

I told mum and dad she'd gone to a Bible college. That she said she'd write as soon as she got settled. I said it had been a rushed, last-minute opportunity thing and she'd had to make a quick decision. I told them Kathy had gone too, which made them feel a bit better, because Kathy lived with her parents, wore navy pinafore dresses and white blouses and in mum and dad's eyes, was very straight and respectable. They had no idea Kathy's parents were the mainstay of the Holy Roller brigade and would have sacrificed Kathy like Abraham did Isaac without a second thought and never mind any of that nonsense about substituting a ram at the last minute. They probably bought her the Militia uniform and packed her bag for her, the poor little cow.

Of course, mum and dad weren't wildly happy about Gwen going off 'without a word', but to be honest, Gwen had hardly ever been in the house recently and when she was she didn't speak to anyone. They were so made up with Lance's news I think they just let it slide. I expect, from what I'd said, they thought she'd gone off to do a sort of summer course in advanced Christianity; a Holy Ghost A-Level kind of thing and that she'd be back come winter. That's what I'd wanted them to think.

OK, so it was a pack of lies, but what would you have done? Told your sick mother and big soft dad that their child, whom they had loved and nurtured to the best of their ability, was a screaming religious fanatic who was deserting them and never intending to see or communicate with them or the rest of her family ever again because she thought they were disgusting, perverted heathen sinners who were damned for all eternity to burn in hellfire? I couldn't. I couldn't. Damn Gwen. I couldn't tell them the truth. So she won. She made me into a liar and a hypocrite. Into what she'd always thought I was. Me 0, Gwen 1.

But it rankled, all that stuff about me loving it when mum got sick so I could be a bully and a control freak and have everyone think how wonderful I was. It bugged me because I couldn't help seeing a tiny, eensy grain of truth there. Not how she'd meant it quite, but it was there. That Hanged Man stuff, the deadly lure of self-sacrifice. Same as I'd been with Beaker and his gig, rushing around saving the world, thinking he couldn't manage without me, without Astra the Wonder Woman.

It was awful. I could see the black, ragged stitch of victimhood through my life and I wanted to pull it out because it's not good, oh no, not a bit. Like when I went with mum to High Tor, to the 'workshops' and the 'seminars': all those silly, New-Ager women with that bloody gloopy look of saintliness on their faces and that God-awful self-righteous whine about how men had been horrid to them, and how the unfeeling world had crushed their sensitive spirits. How they vied with each other to be the most hard done to, the most martyred. God, I didn't want to be like that. I'd vowed not to be like that when I started looking after mum and Git, but it wriggles and squirms its way into your life.

It starts with someone saying 'Oh, I do admire you for what you're doing with your mum and all' and the tiny little thrill of being *admired* tingles at the outer edge of your resolve, creeping further and further in until it becomes the core of your existence. The saccharine kick of being thought wonderful, it's addictive. First you can handle it; it's simply rather nice that someone's noticed your devotion and hard work. Then little by little, you start milking it, sucking up the praise, because you can't get enough and even though you can see the glazed, bored looks on people's faces, you can't stop. Then you run out of people and start going to therapy groups, one after another.

It's all about being loved, and being needed. It's normal enough, everyone likes to feel needed, useful – unless you've got nothing else but that and then it becomes a big, roaring hole that will never be filled. Old people's homes are full of unwanted, unloved girls working as carers, being *needed* by those poor old folks. They couldn't run the fucking places without that pool of damaged children.

Oh yeah, I knew how you got led along by the nose to those sick pleasures. No, no, *noooooo*. I had to escape. Apart from anything else, I wouldn't give my holy sadist of a sister the satisfaction. I needed to plan an escape route, one that wouldn't hurt mum, dad and Git, but that would save me from – from myself.

Not, I have to say, that everyone was fooled by my explanation of Gwen's disappearance. Lance, of all people, got me when I was cleaning out her bedroom in what I thought was a discreet way.

'She's fucked off for good, ain't she?'

'Jesus! Lance! You nearly gave me a coronary!'

'Sorry. She has, though, ain't she?'

'Oh, well, yeah. Yeah, I think so. She's joined some fucking stupid Christian thing called "God's Militia". I couldn't stop her; she had it all worked out, done and dusted. I don't know, I just couldn't tell mum and dad – I mean, the things she said, Lance…'

'Yeah. I 'eard the kind of thing. I knows them Militia an' all. They come up Bodmin, all paradin' around dressed up like fuckin' survivalists. Fuckin' tossers. I dunno, people go on about us bein' a gang but I don't see them's any different. They come round the Mucky Duck goin' on about how we was all possessed by demons an' shit. Crap. She'll be 'appy with that lot, though, Gwen will. Safe. Lots of rules an' regs. She likes that.'

He sounded bitter. I looked at him, leaning against the pink wall, half a beard on and his long curly black hair scragged into a pony-tail. Just like mine. Just like dad's. Our half of the family gene-pool.

'Lance – do you, I mean, Gwen, what…'

'What do I think? I think she's better off away from us. It's what she wants, what she's always wanted. Only she ain't bright like you, she ain't the university type. So she couldn't get out that way. Like me, eh? I know people go on about twins an' that bein' all connected, an' maybe it's right with identicals but not me an' Gwen. You know what I think? I think we was made out of opposites in the womb. I mean, look at us. I'm like you an' dad, she's like mum an' Git. 'Cept Git's more a sort of mix of us all, but you get what I mean. Me, I'm all fer the easy life, 'er – nothin' but nag, nag, fight, fight.' He stuck his lower lip out like a kid and stared at the day-glo 'Jesus Lives!' poster on the opposite wall.

'Lance…You don't have to answer this, but – but when she left, Gwen said, she said I'd enjoyed being a bully, bossing everyone since mum got ill. I mean, I don't want to think that was true – but what if it was and I hadn't realised and…'

He levered himself off the wall and put his big arm around me in a bone-cracking hug. He smelt of healthy-fella sweat and motor oil and, very faintly, of coal-tar soap. It was comforting. They ought to bottle it for lonely women, it'd do a bomb. Essence of Nice Bloke. Parfum 'Homme Agréable', par Chanel. I sighed heavily.

'Ah, doan mind 'er. She always knew how to get to people; always been spiteful, Gwen, spiteful an' stuck-up. It ain't true. But you do get in a state, you do, *that's* true. Like you is now. I can tell. You and Beaker's off then? I thought so. I 'spect it's best. You need someone with a bit more go, you do. Like me.'

I blinked at this new, sensitive, talking Lance, as he gazed at me benignly. I couldn't picture skinny little Poppy – not of course that I knew her, but even so – as having 'go'. Still, you never knew. Still waters, and all that. Golly.

'What you need is a change; 'ere, Danny Quintrell's still got a thing fer you, you know. Doan make that face, 'e 'as and 'e's all right, is Danny. 'E's growed up a lot since you went out with 'im. Want me ter mention to 'im that you ain't tied no more…?'

'*Lance.* No, I do not. No – I – honestly, *Lance.*'

'Never mind. 'Spect Cookie'll do that anyhows.'

'God, the gossips round here, it's…'

His face darkened and he let go of me, then pulled me round to face him, grasping my upper arms with his big hands.

'Astra, you wanna be careful what you say. It's right, they do gossip, but they ain't "they". I mean, it ain't you versus them, you versus the village. We live 'ere now. You still thinks like an incomer, an' it ain't good. I know you don't see yerself as Cornish, and true, you ain't, but I am now. But see, that sort of thinking, that sort of not knowin' where you belong is what fucked up Gwen, fucked her head up. You wanna settle your head here, you do. Doan be sayin' "they", and that. OK, OK, I know it's bad what the lads did to Dylan's but it's over, they ain't proud of it, believe me. Downright ashamed, some of 'em, an' they doan like talkin' about it on account of that. But it ain't just the village what gossips, Astra. Oh no. An' you wanna be careful what you say an' who you say it to.'

'What d'you mean? I don't…'

'I mean, doan be snobby about the village. They're good folks, generally. Think like they do. Watch out who you're mates with. Look, I bin meanin' ter say something to yer but – you know. I ain't one fer talking usually. No, hang on, let me – I'll be straight with you, right. That Angel, she's trouble. She's bad news – she's the one…Aw, look, just be careful. Doan get mixed up in all that business with 'er and that Tim. Oh, yeah. I knows all about that, we all do – did you think we didn't'? Or that Luke fuckin' Skywalker, fer that matter, neither. Just try an' chill out, yeah and doan get so worried about stuff. Doan get in a state about Gwen, neither, it was 'er choice. I won't tell mum and dad, they won't hear nothin' from me. Lighten up, 'ave some fun, you deserve it, girl.' He rubbed my head roughly and planted a smacking kiss on my forehead. 'I'll tell Danny you says hello…'

And smiling broadly, he sauntered off, leaving me in a state of complete astonishment. Mostly because I hadn't had a conversation with him in years, ever since, well, ever since he and Gwen had become teenagers properly and Gwen had started going on at him endlessly. Oh, God, how stupid was I? I hadn't realised before how her constant griping and cruel insults about him being stupid and ugly and disgusting must have really hurt him and caused him to withdraw. To be monosyllabic, Neanderthal Lance – only, he wasn't really like that at all. She made him like that and I'd – we'd all gone along with that image of him because, well, that's how some lads are, isn't it? If you don't bother to look further than the surface, that is. He must feel a burden had been lifted off him now she was gone. I mean, who likes being judged and found wanting all the time? Especially by someone you shared a *womb* with, for God's sake. I'd been so busy with mum and Git, it hadn't just been Gwen I'd let slip.

But he was free now. He could relax a bit and so could I. I felt that, all right, I might have lost a sister but I'd regained my brother and his fledgling family. And he was right, the big lump, I did get in silly states. I should get out and have a bit of fun. Even mum and dad said that, and now Git was older and mum seemed reasonably stable it would be possible. I was puzzled by him being so down on Angel all of a sudden, but I reasoned he hadn't liked her getting Git into trouble like she had – he was very protective of his 'womenfolk'. It reminded me I had to have a word in Angel's shell-like about that whole business. I had a lot to organise.

Danny Quintrell; no. Really, no. I couldn't. Could I?

Chapter 19

While I forged ahead blithely with my plans and sent off for prospectuses from all the universities in the south-west, summer courses, day schools, literature weekends and everything I could think of, things at Spindrift were not going too well.

After Con's outbreak, she was snappier and more stressed than ever. I think she was deeply ashamed of herself; it had been bad enough bawling out those Yah-lads for insulting Angel that time, but actually smacking someone in full view of the whole café – that was something else. Loss of control, big style. Not a Con thing, not at all. It ate away at her, undermining her sense of herself.

And I needed her. I needed her advice and support as a friend. Lance had been all too right. I'd had my 'talk' with Beaker and it had gone pretty much how I'd known it would. He'd been miserable and silent, then pleaded increased workload and the fact he'd started an evening course in business studies at the college, so he wouldn't be able to get over so much, if at all, for a while. I'd meant to be calm and mature, but had come across as weepy and clingy. We both said how much we cared for the other but that perhaps we needed some time apart. We agreed to be friends – of course. The whole dialogue was straight out of a woman's magazine. Clichés, platitudes we used to cover the fact we didn't know what to say – because saying 'That's it, it's over, see yer' seemed too cruel and harsh.

But it was over and we both knew it. It would dwindle from the odd phone call to the Christmas card to nothing. We weren't the sort of people who would hang on like grim death to a dead relationship and have reunions and more break-ups and 'accidentally' meet each other in the pub and have scenes. Or try to pretend we were still jolly good mates but get all weird when the ex found a new squeeze. We weren't like that. It was – over. I daresay I might bump into him sometimes over the years if I was shopping in Crossford, but that was it. What do they call it? Closure. We had closure. I think it's better that way. It was hard and it hurt but I couldn't see any other way working and I knew he wanted to get his new life sorted. Only sometimes, in the night, when I rolled over and his sweet, familiar, lanky, bony self wasn't there, loss and regret corkscrewed through me like – oh, you know. Everyone knows how it feels.

I wanted to tell Con. I needed to talk to her about it, as I had about every major thing that had happened to me for years. We'd drink tea and eat something carbohydratey and go over and over it until it was faded and soft; until it was bearable and I could fold it away. I wanted to hear her flat Bradford voice being sensible. But she was so wrapped up with Angel and the whole Tim-business that I didn't feel able to butt in. The brief revival of our former intimacy had, in the face of Tim's insanity, sputtered out. The idea of us going on a winter holiday seemed remote, to say the least. But I kept thinking Angel wouldn't be here for ever, not for much longer in fact if her heavy hints about returning to London any time were more than hot air designed to torture Luke and keep Con on her toes. When she went, after a while, Con would be her old self again, I knew it; she'd settle down again. It was just a matter of waiting. I suppose it was just one of those unfortunate family things – you know, so-and-so's a perfectly nice guy until he gets with his brother and they just rub each other up the wrong way and always have. Like Lance and Gwen. Only, in this case, Angel didn't so much rub Con up as reduce her to a quivering bundle of stressed-out bone and sinew.

It was Cookie I confided in, eventually. As Con seemed more and more distant, I took a lot of comfort in Cookie's company. She had the same calmness and cool good sense that the 'old' Con had. The pre-Angel Con. I felt bad about thinking like that, but I couldn't help it. The Con I'd known so long appeared to have gone, replaced by a nervous, worried, desperately anxious Con I hardly recognised. But Cookie – she was the sort of woman I admired and I felt – I hoped – she enjoyed having a friend, too. We'd just talk idly during breaks, taking Smoky out to play on the beach as she smoked and we watched the tourists enjoying themselves, rather in the same way we watched *Wildlife on One*. And after work, sometimes, she'd bring Smoky back to ours for a while, to mum's delight, and we'd make popcorn and watch TV before I borrowed the car and ran her home. Cookie was like a drink of still, pure water; you never had to try with her, or to be anything you weren't because there was no hidden agenda with Cooks. No deep, dark personal secrets; her life was the proverbial open book. I asked her about it once.

She shrugged. 'No point in 'aving secrets. They always git found out and where are yer? Fucked. Better not to 'ave 'em. Better to take the flak straight off than hope yer won't be found out, 'cause you will. It's like that singer, wossername – Teena B – 'er that says she were only twenty-one and turns out she's more like thirty-one and with a kid she farmed out so as it wouldn't get in 'er way. She 'ad that anorexia and said she'd got thin doin' yoga and then had plastic surgery an' new busums an' everythin' cos 'ers 'ad gone flat from not eatin' and she tried to hide it, but it all come out. It were all in the *Sun*. Made 'er look a right vain cow an' stupid with it. Better she hadn't lied ter start off with, know what I mean? All right, she's a famous person with the newspapers digging around an' that, but it's the same fer everyone. When I was pregnant, one of the girls I worked with said I should either 'ave an abortion and never tell no one or 'ave Smoky an' then 'ave 'im adopted straight off and tell no one. So I wouldn't ruin me life, she said. Well, no thanks. I likes things where I can see 'em. If you don't 'ave no secrets, then no one can get a 'old over you, see? What you sees is what you gets.' She paused and looked at me thoughtfully. 'Secrets fuck you up, Astra, they do. You end up carryin' stuff what gets heavier an' heavier as time goes on till you can't stand it no more an' boom. It all comes out at the wrong time an' in the wrong place. Look at them emmets you see havin' stand-up rows on the beach and that – they goes on 'oliday, relaxes and wallop, it all comes out, the stuff they been carryin' all that time back 'ome. Secrets – they ain't worth it.'

I knew what she meant, not that I had anything to hide, myself. My life was an open book, too. Or more like an open pamphlet since I'd never done that much of interest. I felt positively dull. I was pondering that as I wandered home and wondering whether a secret passion for triple-layer digestive biscuit and butter sandwiches counted as the stuff of blackmail when I got nabbed by Mrs Liddicoate and Beauty, her mangy old terrier.

'Coo-ee! 'Ello, my dear! My goodness, how are you then, I 'aven't had a chat to you fer ages. Get down, Beauty, you bad girl, doan go muckin' up Astra's nice trousers! Now, how's that poor mum of yours? An' your dad? I must say, 'e did my bridgework lovely, 'e did; very sensitive 'ands for such a big chap, ain't 'e?'

'Ah, oh, yes, er, mum's not too bad, thank you, Mrs L, and dad's fine, I must...'

'Oh, I won't keep you, dear. Off out with your chum, are you? I see 'er comin' an' goin' and all the boys mad about 'er! That nice Timmy from up New Polwenna, 'e's mighty struck, ain't 'e – do I hear weddin' bells? You young girls! Still, I was the same when I was young – oh, I was, you know! And such a lovely girl, that Angel – what a pretty liddle thing! You must be pleased to 'ave a friend down 'ere from up your way, nice to 'ave a bit o' company.'

'Oh, yes. But really, it's Con who's my...'

'Beauty! Stop it now! Doan mind 'er, dear, she's all excited on account of goin' out! She's a 'andful, even at 'er age – mind you that's what I says to Angel when I met 'er out with that beautiful puppy of 'ers – now ain't 'e the sweetest liddle thing? Yes, that's how we got talking, mind you, terrible all that, just terrible...Of course, I still says she was right to say what she seen. Now some would say – you know how people are round 'ere, dear, terrible gossips – that she ought to 'ave minded 'er own business, but I says, she may 'ave said it first, but see, Jeanie saw that poor kiddie brought back in that black thing so it weren't just...'

'I'm sorry, Mrs L, you've lost me, I...'

''Twas that Angel, dear, as told me about what Dylan up at Mordros done to that liddle summer boy. She was walking 'er puppy, see, up across the site – meanin' to come out at the back lane an' then down along through the village – an' she saw it all. As she said to me, Mrs Liddicoate, she says – she's such a nice polite girl, always has a smile, and...'

I heard a discordant cawing and fluttering and it felt as if the sky had darkened overhead; shivering involuntarily, I looked up. A black wing of crows had taken off from their roost in the old pine on the hillside above us. I watched them intently as they swirled across the misty sunset towards the golf course because I didn't want to hear any more. I didn't want to hear silly old Mrs Liddicoate, in her bobbled beige crimplene leisure suit, her bouncy blued curls tied up in a chiffon scarf and her yappy bastard of a dog tell me any more. I looked away from the crows and Mrs Liddicoate's face seemed to bulge grotesquely and her voice came from far away. I wanted to put my hands over my ears and go 'La la la, can't hear you', like we did at school.

'Are you all right, dear? You look a bit tired, I must say...Anyways, Mrs Liddicoate she says, it's terrible what goes on these days, why, I wouldn't let a child of mine go runnin' about like some folk do. An' then she says how she saw that Dylan take the liddle summer boy into 'is caravan and take all 'is clothes off an' 'im so bold 'e never even shut the door so she could see everythin' – well, you know. Now I just happened to mention it to Jeanie, you know Jeanie, dear, she cleans the caravans up at Mordros – or Polwenna Caravan and Leisure as we should say now! So Jeanie says how she was cleaning the caravan next to that family's and she saw with 'er own eyes that Dylan bring the child back wrapped frum neck to ankles in a black cloth covered in that Satan writing, an' skulls an' who knows what and...Why, you're white as a sheet! I hope you're not sickening like your poor mum! Now I heard of a girl as looked after 'er mum for nigh on thirty year then passed away just days after 'er mum did. You want to be...'

Her voice, and the snuffling yap of her dog faded as I ran up the cut. I didn't go in the house but stumbled further on, to the old half-hidden bench at the turn in the cliff path where I used to sit and wish

I was back in Bradford in my Goth days. I was shaking in all my limbs and it was all I could do to keep still.

I'd wondered who the girl with the dog had been. But I hadn't wondered hard or long because somewhere in my heart I'd had a bloody good suspicion. Now it was confirmed and I couldn't ignore it any more. Oh God, oh God – how could she have? It was just like Cookie said, she opened her mouth and out popped whatever was on her mind. We'd been talking about that Internet paedophile ring, she'd gone past Dylan and the kid and when she stopped to chat to Mrs Liddicoate – out it came. Out it fucking well came, without let or hindrance. Out of that beautiful, empty, idiot head.

And what now? What? *What?* Go and scream at her? Shake her – hit her? She deserved it, and more. But it wasn't just her, was it? It was Con. If I went and gave Angel what for, and it all came out that the terrible thing that had destroyed Dylan's life and caused so much pain and upset was Angel's fault, who would bear the brunt? Not Angel, she'd just pout, pack her stuff and either go back to London or stay with Richie Lomas at the Retreat. She wouldn't understand what she'd done, not really understand; she'd just think I was mad at her for gossiping. Nothing I could say to her would make her see what she'd done. I knew that, I knew her that well.

But Con would know. Con would feel it like a knife in her heart. She'd defend Angel but it would destroy her. She wouldn't be able to live here any more, she wouldn't be able to bear that. There was nothing she hated more than injustice, and to have her own flesh and blood be the cause of such an awful thing…But she'd never turn against her sister, never. She'd move away and her dream of living in her own bit of paradise would be ruined for ever. She'd carry Angel's burden like she'd always done. Oh, it was so cruel. So unjust.

I felt a hot, convulsive pain shoot through me and I put my head on my knees, my eyes congested with unshed tears. How flip I'd been about having no secrets – how 'amusing' about my dull, dull life. Now I'd lied about Gwen to my folks and kept that a secret and here I had another secret, not my own, but someone else's. Angel. Angel. Lance had tried to tell me but he couldn't. If he knew, all the village knew.

Cookie must know – no wonder she'd talked about the power of secrets so earnestly.

I could never tell. Never mention it. That's what happened with things like this. They just weren't spoken of. Cookie would never say it straight out, Lance wouldn't – and I wouldn't. I wouldn't, I knew that. Because – what was that old proverb? 'The word is like a sped arrow, it cannot be recalled.' None of us wanted to hurt Con, who'd always been good to us, had helped Cookie when no one else would and been kind and affectionate to Lance when everyone else treated him like a big, brainless yobbo. We *respected* her. We – I wouldn't do it to Con, even though if it ever came out, which it well might, one day, with the likes of Mrs Liddicoate around, she'd hate me for not telling her everything. For keeping her in the dark. But I couldn't tell her. Some things were just too hurtful to say out loud, if you cared about someone. Like those arguments where you say nastier and nastier things until only the really bad thing remains, the thing that will kill your relationship stone dead, and it hovers behind your lips begging to be set free. So you either spit it out, or you don't. Either way, you're fucked but at least if you don't say it, you buy some time. Sometimes you buy a lifetime.

Perhaps if I bought enough time, Angel would be gone and it would fade away, bleach out in the salt and the sun, until even Mrs Liddicoate forgot. Con would be safe. But to have that work successfully, until Angel left I'd have to be as nice as pie to her, as if nothing had happened. I'd have to behave as if everything were fine and the only way to do that was to put this damned thing away, fold it away like I did with my anger, stash it deep so that I could ignore it. Like Cookie had done. Like Lance had done – and how many others? Dot? Mr Eddy? Well, if they could do it, so could I. It was a kind of conspiracy of silence, only we would all be silent about it with each other, too.

I slowly got up and dragged myself back home.

Why did you come, Angel? Who sent you to mess up our lives this way? What terrible thing did we all do to deserve you?

Book 4

Roll on, thou deep and dark blue Ocean – roll!
Ten thousand fleets sweep over thee in vain:
Man marks the earth with ruin – his control
Stops with the shore…

—Lord Byron

Chapter 20

It was coming high season and the beach was pretty full even on weekdays, though not, as everyone pointed out at every opportunity, as full as it should be. That was due mainly to the weather, which continued cloudy and humid with a resulting pancake-surf scenario. It was fine round Newquay way, though. Angel never hesitated to give us all the details when she swanned back from her weekends at the Retreat. Sunny, it was there. Fresh. Surf? Oh, who cared about that when the likes of Bradford's own superstars Ultimate Angel dropped in after their mega sell-out Euro-tour – and Angel could have a nice homey gossip with Franco; he's *so* much nicer than folk say, you know…And the Sucka lads and that gorgeous Floyd popped in, taking a break from recording – back again! Honest, you'd think Floyd had another reason (giggle giggle) for coming other than to chill, not that Angel was suggesting anything (giggle). He'd said only yesterday that the Retreat was so, so restful and energising after the rush of London…And it was rumoured that a certain tiny little Aussie songstress was coming to the big barbie party Richie had planned – now, if she came, why it was pretty certain you-know-who would come with her and…

Every so often she'd say I really ought to come over to one of the big parties, I really should, it'd be such fun – but times and dates and specifics were never forthcoming and nothing would have induced me to beg for an invite. I had some pride.

Goodness, we were all riveted by these tales. Actually, in a horrid sort of way, we were. There wasn't much buzz, what with the surfless surf and the weather. The only excitement was weaver fish victims and the scarlet, blistered tourists who thought you couldn't get sunburn through clouds. Plus the flat, thick stink of the decaying seaweed coming from the next little cove up just got worse with every incoming tide that dumped more stuff up on the shoreline to rot. And the bloody crows, shuffling like massed undertakers on every available ledge or tree branch, peering at us all, beaks agape and giving a good impression of laughing. So we stood and sweated or chugged cold Cokes while Angel regaled us with showbiz gossip.

Most of the time I could look her in the face reasonably easily. Only sometimes, if it was really hot and airless, or I was really tired…Then I'd have to go and wipe tables, or tidy up the veranda.

At home, Git was back to her old self and naturally, hung on Angel's every breath with eyes like saucers, her face luminous with fake tan and her mouth a sticky sugar pink (courtesy of a Lancôme Juicy Tube – an Angel cast-off) O of worship. Marnie and her other chums had been ditched yet again and were occasionally seen adolescently seething round the back of the lifeguard's hut where in days gone by, they'd all sat for hours talking about little-lass stuff and making name-bead bracelets. Now Git bounced around regurgitating Angel's chatter or suggesting to mum that she should think about blusher, because no woman should leave the *house* without blusher. She *never* did anymore and Angel hadn't since she was *twelve*. She tried it with me once, but I must have had what our nan used to call 'speaking eyes'.

Mum didn't like it, but there was nothing she could do, bar forbid Git to speak to Angel, and to be honest, that would have been like trying to catch water in a sieve. I watched mum struggle to make contact with Git, who just rolled her big clumpily mascara'd eyes and sighed heavily. Mum had long serious talks with me about how worried she was that she and Gita were 'drifting apart'; I didn't have the heart to tell her you had to have been together in the first place to drift apart. Actually, we were a bit worried about mum, as her muscles were wasting quicker than we'd hoped, despite the belly-dancing, as she said, wistfully. There was a new thing at the big hospital in Plymouth, though, a sort oxygen treatment in a decompression chamber affair, like divers used when they had the bends, which had had some success with MS patients. I didn't fully understand it but our doc was making arrangements for mum to have a go. She was a bit unwilling at first, with her anti-establishment medicine attitude, but a High Tor person had said oxygen therapies were the cutting edge of healing techniques these days. Or something like that, anyway. So mum got it into her head that the NHS were trumpeting about a therapy the cognoscenti of the alternative medicine world had long known about, which she thought was hilarious.

'Oh, they might try and dress it up in all that medical mumbo-jumbo, you know, try and say they invented it, but honestly, they're fooling no one! The alternative therapy community have known about it for years, but it's so typical *science* wants to take all the credit. Still, I suppose I must be sensible – if the poor old NHS wants to pay for me to have it and say it's all brand new, well, who am I to refuse? Just wait till I get there – no, don't worry, I won't say anything, I'm not stupid, Astra, whatever Gita may think. Oh, it does make me laugh, though, the way they go on as if no one but them *ever* has a good idea and…'

I bet the High Tor Organic Juice Bar was buzzing with it. People boldly quaffing their carrot and Bramley cocktails and chortling over the wilful blindness of the patriarchally oppressive medicos with their starched whites and pitiful linear minds. Oh well, if it gave mum a laugh and more importantly, if it did her good, who was I to carp?

I didn't much care about anything, myself, to be honest. I felt like shit: no energy and my brain had gone to porridge. I couldn't even be bothered to read – I was halfway through *To Kill A Mockingbird* for the umpteenth time and even my favourite bit where Atticus shoots the mad dog failed to cheer me up. Maybe I should have got a new book from the library van, but I couldn't seem to summon up the will-power. Nothing seemed to matter. Cookie had started telling me to buck up because she thought I had developed a very un-Cookie-world tendency to slorm about 'lollygagging', as she put it. She wasn't wrong. The stuffy heat got me down but more than that, it was the whole Angel thing; it was like she was a black hole, just sucking everyone in. In my darkest moods, I thought she was like a sort of psychic vampire, feeding on other people's energies. Our very own Carmilla, the beautiful un-dead, scarfing up everyone's life force and becoming more glittering, more incandescent with every passing day. Yeah, yeah, OK, a tad melodramatic, but I suppose that's what comes from an unhealthy preoccupation with nineteenth-century literature.

But it wasn't just me, sloping around gormlessly. Luke was a bloody misery. Sometimes I just got a coffee and sat at his table silently while he watched Angel fluttering round the café like a silky-bright butterfly, her voile sarongs and tiny sparkly bikinis the envy of the Top Shop-clad tourist girls and a magnet to their boyfriends, brothers, uncles, dads, grandads and second bloody cousins twice removed. Luke and I watched Angel as if she were a video game: *Lara Croft – The Beach Holiday*. How many tourists can our feisty adventuress slay with knock-out glances from her super-power ultra-violet eyes? Ka-fucking-boom.

Luke was a mess. He should have been off where the surf was instead of slouching round Polwenna taking pics of interesting seaweed or whatever he did with the digital camera he always had with him now. It was as if the sea was punishing him for forsaking her by refusing to give him the big surf he loved, the surf he kept saying would arrive any day, but never did. Sometimes he went snorkelling, but there was a limit to how many times you could look at the same old crabs in the same old hidey-holes in a flat sea that resembled three-day-old minestrone. Mostly, he hung round the café, or drove Angel places if she let him. Sometimes he was allowed to drop her off at the Retreat, but he was never allowed to stay. I couldn't understand it; it seemed like the worst kind of masochism. The only time I broached it with him, he just blanked me and said – nicely, but he still said it – that it was his business. Which of course, properly speaking, it was. I expect it had only been a twinge in the bruised place that had been my long crush on him that made me bother asking him in the first place. Maybe that day his eyes had been the particular shade of watered-silk turquoise I'd loved so much – or was it the way he looked up and out at the sea, out at the Big Blue like a man looks at the loving wife he abandoned for a worthless whore? I don't know. It was funny that, now he was enslaved by Angel like I'd once been blindly besotted by him, we got on. We were almost mates, those days. Like the two drunks in that famous picture, *Absinthe*, by Degas; we'd sit staring at Angel, him loving her in a dull, hopeless way, me hating her equally dully and hopelessly, and never a word spoken. How sweet.

He'd lost weight, too – he and Con looked like Anorexics Anonymous. Me, I ate like a pig in that constantly snacking way. Grazing. I snaffled up leftovers, bits of broken pie, old scones, anything. I supposed I was getting fatter, but I still fit my clothes more or less so I put off dealing with it. I needed the comfort. I wanted comforting. I wanted to be wrapped up in a big pink fleecy blanket and fussed over, with people looking rather worried and bringing me little treats to eat like we'd tried to do for poor old Dylan. Only unlike Dylan, I'd have eaten them and enquired if there happened to be any more going.

So yeah, it was the weather; it was Angel; it was Luke. But more than anything else it was the shadow of Tim Norris – always hovering, a wraith just glimpsed out of the corner of your eye – that bugged me. He seemed to sum up all the crap that Angel had brought with her, trailing in her wake like the debris that is a comet's tail. He was a living symbol of every mindlessly destructive thing she did to people. It wasn't her *fault* – of course, no one deserved to be hassled by some nutter – but none the less. Yet again, Angel smiled her lovely smile, raised her perfectly plucked eyebrow and the karmic balance of the universe went bing-bang-bong and wobbled off its axis.

It was the old what-if; what if Angel had never come visiting, would Tim still be tedious old Timster the running man? It was obvious he'd always been a bit off centre, what with his rigidity and rituals and his sad, pathetic life with his mum; we just hadn't been bothered to notice as long as he kept it to himself and stayed in his persona as boring Tim the accountant. We could ignore him then. Not now, though. I wondered if Angel hadn't come, whether he'd have eventually cracked up anyhow and fixated on someone else – like, a Yah-chick, or Lisa, or me – or God forbid – Git? We'd never know, would we? Not that it mattered in the real world because no amount of worthy pondering altered the fact of Tim.

He was always, always around; even if he wasn't there physically, there were the constant letters and gifts, the flowers and the Post-it love-notes stuck to the café windows and Con's door. Every time I went to the café, I felt like he was watching me – silly, I know, but there you are. And the more 'research' I did on guys like him, the more magazine articles and newspaper stories and 'true crime' things I read, the more he unnerved me. Only, *I* was the only one who seemed to think he might be dangerous. That night in the car park after Beaker's gig, I'd seen the pure, no-holds-barred rage in him, a rage that ran through him like boiling lava. The sort of rage that could drive you to do anything, anything at all.

But it was no use me going on about it, no one else except Luke, who hadn't really taken it in, had seen Tim like that. They just saw the pathetic, love-sick fool. To everyone else he was either a source of irritation or juicy gossip fodder. Oh yeah, Crazy Tim, as he was now known universally, provided the biggest source of interest in our cosy little circle.

Jesus, Jesus – poor old Tim. I mean, not that he was old, or indeed, poor – but watching him beat himself bloody against the amused indifference of Angel was hard to take. Sure, I found him scary, but even so, underneath the bonkers behaviour you could glimpse the raw flesh of his sanity being eroded daily. I mean, in the books, blokes like him were always these cold, calculating evil monsters, who took cruel delight in the harassment and harm they did. But Tim wasn't like that at all. It was like he'd blindly stepped over some hidden line and his mind had turned into a twitching, itchy mess of pain and that awful anger; he certainly didn't seem to be coolly *planning* things, the opposite in fact. It was more like he couldn't help it and went on churning out those mad letters and trawling the Net for presents, totally unable to stop himself anymore.

I thought it was like when you're jealous of your boyfriend; you're so sure (for no good reason) that he's playing away. You know it's stupid, that you're blowing things all out of proportion but you can't stop dwelling on it. It starts as a niggly spot in your mind then as you pick and pick at it, it spreads like impetigo: thick, oozing and raw.

Then one dreadful night, you find yourself in the shrubbery across from his house, watching, because he said he couldn't see you on account of the lads coming over to play poker, eat pizza and watch *Goodfellas* on the vid. But you didn't believe him – at least until a froth of drunken blokes pour out of his front door at two in the morning. And you're crouching there, shivering and crying, and feeling like shit and the worst thing is – you're *still* jealous. You *still* suspect him. And you know it's all fucked up but you can't stop, you just can't stop and everything is winding up faster and faster to the big blow-out row that will end things irretrievably and for ever. But you can't control yourself anymore, you can't *stop*.

Watching Crazy Tim was like that; it was horrible, he was like a kind of wonky scarecrow automaton, its clockwork gone haywire, just clunking and chuntering round in circles doing the same idiot, repetitive actions over and over and over again.

He just never let up; it was ceaseless. Angel said her e-mail was yards long and Con's answerphone was jammed with his pleading and his increasing vitriol against Con, me, Luke, Jim, Joey, Cookie, Dot, anyone, everyone; except of course, Angel. We all stood in his way, we all prevented them from being together, especially Con, who was, according to the Crazy Tim world view, a vindictive and jealous old woman trying to ruin her sister's chance of happiness. I thought he'd single Luke out as his rival, or something, but he never did – he didn't seem to see that Luke and Angel were an item, or perhaps he couldn't admit it to himself, because that would mean she'd lied to him, betrayed him and of course, that wasn't possible. She was blameless, pure. He just lumped Luke in with the rest of us; we were *all* scum.

He still hung around outside the café all the time, but he seemed to have become preternaturally good at predicting when Angel was due to go off up to the Retreat. Usually, either Luke was allowed to run her, or she got a taxi. More infrequently, she borrowed the GTI but not often, as Con needed it. As soon as she set foot outside the door on her Retreat days, Tim would be there. He'd hang around the car park, as close to the flat door as possible without actually stepping on Con's property and wait, literally wringing his hands, his sunken eyes red-rimmed from lack of sleep. As soon as Angel appeared he'd start pleading with her; begging her 'not to do this to herself'. Sometimes Mr Eddy or Jim or Joey would 'escort' Angel to her vehicle if Luke wasn't there, never touching Tim, but trying to shield Angel from his torrent of beseeching. Sometimes, as the car left, Tim would actually sink on his knees, weeping. It was awful to watch, but at the same time like those fly-on-the-wall docudramas, it was compulsive. When she left, her knights in shining armour would come in for a free coffee and wiping their brows, blow out huge breaths and shake their heads, saying things about how sad it was he'd lost his marbles and how something ought to be done – only, no one quite knew what.

Personally, as I said, I was still with the fat customer's assessment that Tim had become a stalker; only, no one else agreed with me. In their opinion (*much they bloody knew*, I'd think righteously) stalkers went after famous people, not someone's sister, no matter how glam she might be. I was being dramatic, apparently. I took to cutting the things out of the papers and magazines I read and trying to present them as evidence in support of my theories but no one was interested. The general consensus was still that it was pointless involving the coppers because he wasn't violent in any way, just crackers, and that in time, he'd get the message, be very embarrassed at his behaviour and stop. Maybe even move away or something. It was probably some sort of male menopause thing, like when guys get to forty and buy a flash sports car or turn up in yellow flares and a tank top. There were endless stories of blokes someone knew, or their mate knew, who'd gone bonkers at forty-two and run off with a barmaid young enough to be their daughter, or done a Gauguin and sold the semi, dumped the wife then fucked off to Oz (this came from Jim and Joey) to have a last taste of beach-life and chill during their declining years.

But a stalker, no. Tim wasn't that sort. He wasn't a stranger – we all *knew* him. He was respectable, a businessman, or had been before all this. He was in the bloody Rotarians, for God's sake. He was normal, not some psychotic tramp or bull-necked thug who'd drifted into our village and was running amok. Tim was an *accountant*. It was just unfortunate his particularly extreme mid-life crisis had settled on

Angel the unattainable goddess, instead of him growing his hair and sporting a kaftan. My articles and clippings were brushed aside and the subtext was, I was suffering from too much reading. Intellectuals. You know, always coming up with some mad idea.

Angel didn't help, either. She thought it was all absolutely hilarious. She baited Tim and for a while, played to the gallery by appearing with a headscarf (Versace) wrapped Audrey Hepburn-style round her head and over-sized black shades when making her Retreat dash. Giggling, she'd wave ta-ta to Crazy Tim as he practically grovelled in the dust, and blow him a kiss. In fact, at one point she said that she hoped he *was* a 'proper' stalker because it was the chic thing to be stalked – like a real celeb. At the Retreat, apparently, anyone who was anyone had a *stalker*. It meant you were famous enough to be noticed; celebs *sans* stalker fed the media fibs about crazed fans on their trail to boost their profile. The sight of some poor little pop-chick, or soap star, her face carefully painted to the correct pallor, her snub nose tinted pink, clutching a hankie on the front cover of *Whoops!* magazine under the banner headline 'My Stalker Hell' was guaranteed to boost record sales and ratings. When I said I thought that was beyond crap, and what about the real victims and how awful…Angel laughed and shook her lovely head as if to say I had my wires totally crossed. Obviously, I was sweetly naïve to Angel, a loveable bleeding heart who was hopelessly old-fashioned.

It just didn't touch her; she didn't feel sorry for Crazy Tim, and she wasn't frightened a bit.

Con was. Con was stressed out of her mind. Where Angel got the flowers, the presents and the inch-thick love notes, saying she was a pure, perfect, adorable dream-girl, a living saint, whose tiniest tootsie was worthy of Tim's undying worship, Con got the abuse and the spite. Con wasn't scared for herself – she'd never been scared for herself in her whole life. But for Angel – in case anything should harm a hair on Angel's head – Con was eating herself up alive. I kept on trying to persuade her to get help. It was useless. She thought she could deal with it herself if it got any worse. How, she couldn't say. It drove me crackers.

'Con, Con, please. You've *got* to go to the police – just tell them how worried you are, I mean, they…'

'Astra, we've bin ovver this. I don't think there's owt they can do. Anyhow, I don't want us showin' up like that, makin' out we're hysterical females because some bloke's mad for our lass. We don't run off to the bobbies at the drop of a hat in my family, unlike some. I'm not airin' our dirty linen in public…'

'But Con, that's mad. Everyone round here knows what's going on. Jesus, they watch it like it was a fuc – like it was some sort of soap. It's too late to worry about dirty linen now, I mean…'

'No, I won't go to the police and that's an end of it. I won't – what could I say to 'em?'

'Say he's a bloody pain and he frightens you – he does, Con, I can see it. Look at yourself, you're so skinny! You're making yourself ill…'

She dropped her eyes and put her bony hand over them, her shoulders drooping. I put my arm round her; she felt like a bird, hot and terribly thin.

'I'm sorry, Astra, I am. I don't mean ter make you fret over us. You've got enough on yer plate.' She sighed heavily and rubbed her sunken temples with her thumb and forefinger. 'The fact is, right, I *can't* go to the police, she won't have it. I promised her I wouldn't. Says it's nonsense, all this Tim business. Says it'd put Richie off, any hassle like that. Real hassle, you know. She says a bit of a joke about stalkers and such at that place is one thing, but a hint of the law…If they thought there were, like, an *actual* problem, a proper mess…For a lass like her, on the edge, not really one of them – they'd close ranks against her. They don't like real-life trouble, folks like that, they like everythin' easy – you know. Oh, Astra, I wish to *God* she'd give it up with this Richie fella, it's not right, he's still married even if they are separated – least, that's what he says – but she won't. She's that stubborn. Says he'll get her everything she wants, that he's offered her to make a record and everything. She could be rich and famous, like she's always wanted but she has to go slow. Make like she int bothered. Refuse a couple of times so it looks like it's all his doin'. Treat 'em mean, keep 'em keen, like mam used to say. But this Tim – he's not right – the things he says to me on the bloody answerphone and the *looks*...But she thinks he's a joke and – I'm at my wits' end, I am that. Why can't she have took up proper with that Luke boy?'

I winced inwardly. 'I thought you didn't think much of him?'

'Oh, he's nice enough. Always polite, you know. And good-looking, more of a match for her. They look well together – I know I were down on him for bein' a waster but God, in comparison to that Richie fella, he's perfect. Oh, Astra love, I just want her to be *safe*...'

'I know, I know, pet. Look, um, I'm sure it'll be all right, we'll keep an eye on things and if it gets worse...Tim'll pack it in eventually, I know he will. He can't keep it up much longer; no one could.'

Chapter 21

'Oh, poor Smoky, 'as Mrs Cow lost her leggie, then – never mind, love, Auntie'll sew it back on again…Cookie, 'ave you got Mrs Cow's leg? Stop giggling, you nasty lot, it's serious when you're 'is age…'

While Cookie retrieved Mrs Cow's leg from Piglit, who was worrying it to death under a table, and took it gingerly over to the sinks to wash the slaver off it, we all settled back to our coffees and moaned companionably about the lowering skies outside. Jim and Joey drifted in, the bright scarlet and luminous yellow of their lifeguard shorts and jacket kit positively shocking against the dull grey of the early morning light.

'Mornin' Aas,' they choroused. Would I never get them to stop with the bloody 'Aas' thing? Joey smiled at me winningly and sat next to me, his red bulk radiating blokiness and what he fondly considered his irresistible charm. He'd suddenly noticed me as an actual woman since Beak – Tony – and I had split, and was totally puzzled that the fatal attraction he exerted on the tourist babes had so far not worked on me. I had thought about it; he was good-looking in a blond, slightly lumpy jock kind of way and he certainly had a great body – but I couldn't. It would have been incestuous. He was a mate. It wouldn't be decent. This was a man from whose back I had regularly and shriekingly peeled long strips of dead, sunburnt skin. I knew him too well. But that didn't stop him gazing at me with his salt-blond eyelashed eyes full of hormones. I didn't mind – OK, I liked it. Wouldn't you, in my place? I subtly squashed up my cleavage – not that subtly, though, as Dot caught me and raised a pencilled eyebrow. Men you could always fool, the Dots of this world, never.

My little moment of carefree happiness wilted as Angel swung out of the flat door, a sheaf of unopened letters in her hand, and plonked down opposite me. Con brought her over a double cappuccino and a big, fresh, hot blueberry muffin, buttered in the American way. I looked at it, steaming fragrantly and oozing sweet, golden farmhouse butter, and sighed. Angel never dieted or did any exercise other than walking Pigsie but she never put weight on. Genetics, I suppose – she stayed thin, I had great teeth. There you are.

Angel tutted furiously. 'Oh, God – look at this, another pile of crap from bloody Crazy Tim – the sneaky git posted it, I thought it were a real letter. What the…Jesus, he's mental – look…'

We looked. It was one of his usual rambling diatribes, but this time, included five or six samples of wedding invitations. Angel handed me the letter with another big sigh and a roll of her violet eyes. I scanned it as Dot and Cookie looked at the invites and commented on them, to Angel's disgust.

'Honest, you two – pack it in; I'm not marryin' him really, you know…no, pink's bloody awful for invites in my opinion; God no, I wouldn't – when I get wed I'll 'ave…'

'What is it, Angel love?' said Con anxiously as she recognised Tim's familiar scrawl.

'I dunno. Just 'is usual rubbish – int it, Astra…'

I made a face. 'Well, actually – er – according to this, I think he's actually booked St Morwenna's for September 15th. For the wedding. I mean…'

Con snatched the letter from my hand. 'He's done *what*?'

'Booked the church. He says Angel can stay with him and his mum and everything, so no one can stop him and her getting wed. I suppose he means us – Con, just ignore it, don't let it upset you, he's…'

'Fuckin' mental', supplied Jim gloomily.

'Well, yeah. Look, I'll ring the vicar for you, explain he's a stalk…'

Con shot me a look. 'No thanks, love. I'll do it. It's my business.'

I cringed inwardly. Bossy-boots Astra, trying to organise everyone's lives again. As I perspired, Angel was opening the other letters.

''Ere, Con, this un's for you – look at this – I don't get it – it's from some solicitors or summat…'

Con took it absently, and, squinting tiredly, read it. She seemed to freeze, then her face drained of colour and she handed it to me. At first I was reluctant, what with not wanting to interfere again, but as I got the gist, I forgot all that. This was serious. Tim had really done it this time.

It was from some solicitors in Plymouth – Landry and Kinver – and was absolutely unbelievable. I remember the best bits; I'd never read anything like it.

> '...*instructed by Timothy Norris, an individual who is highly respected and who holds a position as a prominent member of Polwenna's professional and business community...the afternoon of...entered the business premises owned by you and known, we are instructed, as the 'Spindrift Café' Polwenna...not only to interview his fiancée, Miss Angela Starbuck (your sister) but to take refreshment...Our client has instructed us that upon entering the said premises, enquiring of you as to the whereabouts of Angela Starbuck and her availability for interview...your response was to approach our client from behind the counter...you struck our client across the face...upon the blow landing, such was our client's shock at the violence and force of this vicious and unprovoked attack...we are instructed that unless, within seven days of the date of this letter you do admit liability in writing...we are to institute proceedings against you without further notice...yours faithfully, Landry and Kinver, Solicitors and Commissioners for Oaths, Plymouth.'*

I gawped like a landed cod and looked at Con, whose face was a silent scream.

'Jesus, Con – he's – I don't fucking believe it – he's taking you to court for slapping him...It's – it's – I don't know what to say...'

There was an uproar then, everyone wanting the details, and as I supplied them, I saw Con, out of the corner of my eye, staring fixedly out at the beach. She looked like death.

Angel was shrill in her denunciation of Crazy Tim; what she'd do to him next time he dared show his face again didn't bear repeating. He was really insane, he was certifiable, this was nonsense, he couldn't...

Over the babble of outraged voices I only just caught Dot saying '...o' course, 'e's done it afore, that's why...'

I waved everyone shush. 'Dot, what d'you mean, he's done it before?'

Everyone goggled at Dot, who bridled in a gratified way and patted her back hair.

'What I says. 'E's done it afore. That's why 'im an' 'is mum moved here – to get away from what 'e done.'

'*Dot!*' I hissed piercingly, 'how do you know – why didn't you say anything before?'

'No one arsked me. I ain't no gossip, not like some,' she said smugly.

I waited. So did she. I gave up. 'Dot, *please...*'

'Oh, all right. It's Pat as told me, see. She used to do a bit of home-help work, you know, an' when they first moved down 'ere, Pat done for that Tim's mam. She ain't strong, see, an' she never goes out. Can't, she's one o' them aggryphobics. An' she drinks. It were when she an' Pat were 'avin' a nip of sherry one arfternoon, when it all comes out. About how 'er boy had gone all crazy over a young girl as worked in the same office as 'im. How 'e'd wanted to wed 'er but she'd laughed in 'is face. 'E'd started followin' this girl around an' botherin' her, and then 'er dad beat 'im up – quite bad, it seems. But it dint stop 'im, 'e just said as how it were the dad as was standin' between 'im an' the girl, an' how she really wanted ter wed 'im but was frightened of 'er family. So one evenin' after work, 'e tries to get 'er to go with 'im in 'is car, to run off with 'im, but she goes mad, this girl, an' starts screamin' an' yellin' and then some o' them security guards come and then the police and, well, Tim ends up sacked and 'as a nervous breakdown. Gets put in the bin fer a bit. Terrible hard on 'is mam, see...' Dot nodded sagely.

'Wha...' I stuttered. Everyone else just sat there, Angel included, looking at Dot as if she were a space alien.

'Oh yes. Terrible do. That's when 'is mam took to 'er bed – and to drink – she says. Mind, I doan believe it, Pat says she drank like a fish; steady, but all day an' night. Takes practice, that. So anyways, they moved down here when 'e got out, a fresh start, you know. Dint do Pat no good, mind you, she got the sack when 'e come home an' found 'er an' 'is mam an' the bottle an' 'is mam cryin' an' goin' on. Never had no one else in to see to 'er so I 'spect 'e does fer 'em both 'isself. All alone in that bungalow together; it ain't right, to my mind. No wonder 'e's bonkers.'

I stared at her – and so did everyone else – in utter disbelief, 'Je – sus, Dot! Why didn't you say...'

'Dot, you shoulda said somethin', I mean...' Cookie cut in, a frown crinkling her pale forehead.

'Oh, right, thanks a lot, Dot. Thanks fer not tellin' me he's a registered header, really...' Angel glared at Dot, who started to look uncomfortable instead of smug.

'There's no need ter get funny with me, I was only tryin' to help...' Dot went into her outraged stork impression, her eyebrows arcing out of control and her orange fringe bristling.

'Stop it. Just stop it. That's enough. Come on, it's past opening time and you're all sitting around callin' like a bunch of old women. Let's get to work, forget this nonsense. Angel, take Piglit for his walk or something, eh?' Con was all business, sharp and brisk; but I looked at her face and under the work-Con, another mask strained and twisted. A ragged, twitchy Con, looking ten years older than her age, whose navy-blue eyes were dark pools of tension in which something frightened struggled and struggled.

'Callin'?' said Joey, puzzled.

'Oh – Joe – gossiping, it means gossiping up where we live – lived. Like two old biddies gossiping over a garden fence – Con, wait!'

But she was gone upstairs and already a stream of tourists were queuing for their tea-scone-pasty-beans-muffin-soup-Coke-ice-cream-cappuccino-sandwich-apple-pie-fruit-cake morning snacks, their children running riot and their flip-flops, newly bought from the Tiki Surf Shop, rubbing blisters between their toes and flipping sand everywhere.

It was a hectic day; everyone and their auntie seemed to have come to the beach and we were rushed off our feet. Even Angel helped by clearing plates and flirting and so of course, Git did too – though personally, I could have done without watching her practise her fledgling charms on lads older than Lance. In the end, I couldn't stand it and shoo'd her off out to go do whatever it was she did when she wasn't limpeting Angel. I decided I had to have a word with that person, too – so in the five minutes I had for a break, I called her out back.

After flapping my hands ineffectually at a dense knot of crows, who lazily took off into the grey like an unravelling skein of black embroidery silk, their harsh cries echoing round the yard, I folded my arms and turned to Angel, who lit a fag and leaned against the wall, smiling.

The reason I folded my arms was because my hands were shaking. I had studiously avoided any direct talk with Angel because I didn't fully trust myself not to blow up at her about Dylan and ruin my plan to save Con. Now, as she stood there, playing at blowing smoke-rings, the silvery threads in her lilac tankini and matching sarong glinting in the dull light, her icy hair almost luminous, her smooth brown belly stitched neatly with a blue topaz-set belly-bar through her navel piercing, I felt the old sense of impotence, of my inability to crack that burnished, smiling exterior creep over me. As always, I felt scruffy and blowsy beside her, which undermined what confidence I had. I scolded myself that I was ten times brighter than she was and that I was an adult woman with every right to be concerned about my little sister and Angel was an airhead who should be told the truth.

'I don't like Git flirting and carrying on like she does when she's with you. It's not right, she's only...'

Angel blew smoke. 'Yeah. I know. Only thirteen. Well, she's gotta practise somewhere – better she does it where you can see, int it? I wouldn't like to think of her sneakin' off to the beach at night gettin' up to who knows what like some of 'em round 'ere. My God, that beach is a right Lover's Lane at night, fairly heavin' wi' kids snogging an' just about everythin' else, as I've heard. Dint your other lass go handin' out leaflets about it, with them Jesus freaks?'

'Yes – no – I – Angel, my family doesn't like the way Git's…'

'Oh, don't worry, she's *fine*. I think of her as a little sis, meself; I wouldn't let any 'arm come to her…'

Yeah, right, I thought, *like you abandoned her at Jangles – what if I hadn't been there, what would you have done then, you…*

'So I've just sent him this, like, really, really hard e-mail, you know, tellin' the sick bastard where to get off. I'll not 'ave all this takin' Con to court business, I really will not. I mean, what if it got out and Richie heard about it? My sis in court for thumping some bloke? It don't exactly look good, does it? An' he's – Richie, I mean – he's bin talkin' about 'avin' me make a record again, too, and this time I'll say I will, I think, 'cos he's got it in his head it's his big idea so if it goes bang I can be all pathetic an' he'll blame 'imself not me so…'

Lagging behind again; I mentally ran to catch up with her. 'Who have you e-mailed?'

She stopped and looked bemused. 'What? Oh – Crazy Tim. Told him to fuck off and no messin'. Well, I can't 'ave him goin' on like he does, it's past a joke.'

'Angel, it never was a joke.'

'Oh, Astra, you know what I mean. Come on, love, don't get so wound up. Chill a bit. You int responsible for the whole wide world, y'know. Lighten up. Look, I know how you worry about stuff, we're mates, int we? Tell you what, I know I've bin dead busy recently, but let's 'ave a girls' night out soon, eh? Just us, go fer a drink, 'ave some fun. I'll do yer hair and yer nails and everythin'. You'll look fantastic, honest. And don't fret about Git, I'll look after her, I promise; just like she was my own. Happy?'

And with that she tweaked one of my curls, threw her fag down and ground it out, then sauntered inside.

I unclenched my teeth with some difficulty. Chill. Lighten up.

Chapter 22

'He is – he's bloody waiting out there again – Jesus! I don't believe it, I really don't – how does he know…' Angel glared furiously through a crack in the back door.

I'd been thinking about Tim's psychic ability to predict when Angel would be leaving the café, then I'd read a thing about cyber-stalking in the *Guardian Weekly*. It didn't take a great brain to put two and two together.

'Angel – do you e-mail Richie and Luke and everyone about when you'll be going somewhere and all that?'

She tore her gaze from the slit of light and the lurking stick-man that was Tim. 'What? Oh – yeah. 'Course. I can't do texts like normal what with the bloody signal being so crap round here – Jesus, sometimes it works sometimes it don't. Drives me mad, don't know how you stick it. Anyhow, it saves ringing Richie an' all because he – well, it int good to be ringing him, see. E-mail's dead private. Same as Luke and me mates. It's just easier. Why?'

'Who set up your Internet account? Tim, wasn't it?'

'Yeah. It's a Zapmail one. Zapmail, I'm Brightangel@zapmail.com. He thought up that name. I thought he were just bein' nice…'

'And you have to have a password for that sort of account, don't you?'

'Course – it's – oh my God! I see what yer gettin' at! Jesus, why dint I think of that! He knows my bloody password, he helped me think it up – it's 'Mollydolly', the name of me favourite doll when I were little – he can…'

'He can read your mail any time he likes,' I said. 'No wonder he always knows what you're up to.'

'God, Astra, you're that sharp, you! Like a bloody new pin!

How'd you work all this out – I thought you dint know owt about computers?'

'Read a thing in the paper – about something similar. Then it just clicked – you know.'

Angel gazed at me reverently. 'Oh, honest, you an' your readin'. Well, you come up trumps this time, love. What a pal you are – 'ere, I'll 'ave to get Luke to help me change all me Internet stuff now. What a bastard that Tim is – God, he'll have read all me messages to Richie an'…Oh, I could, I could – I don't rightly know. Swing for the bastard, probably. Not that it did our lass any good, goin' on like that. The rotten *bastard*.'

'Yeah. So where you off to anyway? Not the Retreat?'

'No, Luke's takin' me to the flicks in Crossford. God, I'm bored of the pictures, I'd give my eye-teeth ter go to a club, summat decent. But there's nowt round here I'd bother with. I don't know how you manage, I don't. I'd go barmy if I lived here all the time. So it's the pics or nowt. I fancy that new thing about a surfer who gets involved wi' the CIA or something on account of him seein' this horrible murder by accident at a surf competition he's at, and it was a copper who done it, and there's a lass who he fancies but she's really a sort of whatchermacallit – a witch or something and if he don't rescue her from these devil-worshipper types the copper was in with and wed her in a special ritual there'll be an earthquake and then the end of the world will happen – oh, you know – the usual sort of stuff. Still, it might cheer Lukey-boy up to see some proper big waves, eh?'

'Angel, Luke ought to be…'

'Oh – Luke. Yeah. I forgot you was gone on him…'

'I'm not, it's just he ought to be off where there's some proper surf, he'll lose…'

'You are too gone on him. I don't know why you get so funny about it, now you're single. Shame about that nice Beaker, he were right steady. 'Ere, I saw him the other night, in Crossford an' you'll never guess who he were with…'

'Cookie. I know. They're just mates, Angel. Not everyone is a walking shag-fest, you know.'

Angel looked aggrieved. 'OK, OK. No need to get huffy. 'Ere, you go out an' tell Luke to go up the hill a bit an' wait by the dairy, I'll go out the front way an' meet him. That'll nobble old Crazy Tim.'

'I don't...' But she was gone.

Unwillingly, I went out, and walked towards Luke's VW camper. Tim leaped up as I opened the door, then crouched back on the bench, staring at the door. I thought about saying something to him, trying to tell him – I don't know what. His sandy, terrier's face was peeling and red from sunburn and his wiry hair stuck up stiffly as if he hadn't brushed it for a month. Gossip had it he'd lost nearly all his carefully built-up clients, and I believed it looking at him. He looked ghastly. His eyes flicked to me as I walked past and I thought I heard him mutter something under his breath. I didn't bother demanding to know what it was – I knew. He always said the same thing about me. 'Fat Bitch.' That was his name for me in the letters he sent. 'That Fat Bitch. That jealous Fat Bitch. Trying to keep us apart because she hasn't got a man to adore her as I adore you, my darling, my love, my...'

Charming. I felt a hit of anger and adrenalin knot in my stomach and I walked quickly on. I mean, sure – half of me loathed the mad fuck, but the other half couldn't help feeling sorry for him. As long as he stayed at a distance, that is.

Luke saw me and waved. I went to his window and he leaned out, almost smiling. He smelled good: salt, sun, ozone. Hot skin. I felt the anger turn to – nothing. Nothing. *Nothing.*

'Hi. Er, look, she's gone out round the front because of *him*. She says she'll meet you up at the dairy and...'

He'd already started the engine before I finished, 'Wait, Luke – hang on – he's been reading her e-mails, that's how he knows where she'll be all the time, he set up her account so – so you'd better help her change all her Internet stuff, get her a new account or whatever...'

He paused and stared at Tim, who was oblivious. 'My God. He's mad. I mean, really mad...Someone ought to...'

'What? Beat him up? It wouldn't do any good – and anyhow, who? You? Look, I don't mean to be rude but it's not really your style, is it?'

He looked somewhat sheepish. 'Yeah. You're right, I suppose.

You're often right, aren't you, Star? Thanks for – you know, telling me. About her e-mail. I'll sort it all out.' He smiled at me, but it was a shadow of his old careless grin. 'Thanks. Really – you're a good friend to her, the best. It's nice to know someone like you cares about her.'

And he drove off in a blossom of sandy dust. Tim looked round sourly, then returned to his vigil. I didn't feel like running the Fat Bitch gauntlet again so I trudged round to the road and then back on to the beach and in the front. Don't think I wasn't upset by Tim, by the way; I was. It upset me just looking at him and every time I had to smell his sour stink or listen to his raw voice muttering insults at me, my fists clenched and a hot shiver of adrenalin ran through me. But this time, my mind was somewhat preoccupied.

Luke's parting words rolled like thunder inside my skull. Angel, Angel, bloody Angel. A good friend to her, he said. Someone like me. What, someone with 'sucker' written in big red letters on their fucking head? Or was I misreading it – maybe it said 'doormat'. And worse than that – it was a huge lie, all of it. I wasn't her friend – if anything, I was her enemy. But a secret enemy, a big fat hypocritical liar. Oh why couldn't she just fuck off? Leave us alone, leave us to our jog-along village life untroubled by celebs, stalkers, general lunatics and her appalling, disruptive self. I didn't think I could keep up this façade much longer and I knew that she'd say something trivial and I'd blow my stack good stylee.

That night I fell into the house exhausted. It had been a long, hard day and I was almost too knackered to shower, but the smell of food and sweat was too ghastly to bear. After a brief swipe at myself with a sponge full of cranberry and kiwi shower gel I slumped on to the sofa, reeking of fruit. The telly was on without the sound and mum was ensconced in the armchair doing what looked suspiciously like crochet.

'Is that *crochet*? Are you *crocheting* something, mother?' I intoned dramatically as she pushed her reading specs back up her whiffly little nose for the umpteenth time.

'Yes – I used to be so good at this but now – I think I've lost my touch what with my silly arm not doing what it's told. Botheration, I'm so out of practice.'

'Just as well. Crochet, dear God. It'll be macramé and batik next...'

'Aha, much you know, then, madam. As a matter of fact it's a rather nice disco bag for your sister. With fringing. And – oh, bugger, get through there, you silly thing – beads. They're all the rage again, though I don't think they call them disco bags anymore. It's called BoHo apparently, Hippie Chic. She showed me in one of her magazines. The clothes were quite pretty, I must say, but the bags – they were charging the earth! A fortune! So I said I'd make her one. If it...' she paused and grunted as she pulled a thread tight 'if it turns out nicely, I could go into business. Handmade bags. I could – oh, do go where I put you – I could make some extra money. What do you think of that then, Miss Know-It-All?'

I laughed and pretended to throw a cushion at her. She was in a good mood tonight. It was lovely to see her so calm and happy.

'Where's dad? And Git – Gita?'

'Astra, don't call your sister "Git", it upsets her aura, as well you know. She's gone for a walk, Marnie called her. I must say I hope they make it up, or whatever. They've gone for an ice-cream. Roy's mucking around with the computer, with the accounts. The language – awful. I'm glad Gita's not around to hear it.'

'Ah.' I didn't like to voice my suspicions that two thirteen-year-olds out for a 'walk' on a summer's evening by the seaside with a clutch of new tourist boys to giggle over wouldn't have ice-cream on their minds.

'You look tired, dear. I know we were pleased about you working for Con, but I don't like you wearing yourself out like this – it was only meant to be part-time.'

'It is, mum, it is – it's just that one of the girls let us down and – Con's not feeling all that well...'

Mum nodded, her specs slipping again. 'Well, yes. I can see why. That sister of hers. Is that man still bothering her?'

'Yes. He's – I don't think he's well, you know. But look, never mind that – has your oxygen appointment come through?'

'Well – oh, you devil, just go tight, will you – it has! I heard today, I was about to tell you. A week on Friday...Oh, there – pass me those scissors, will you, love? Thank you – yes, your dad and I have a plan.' She stopped hooking, pursed her lips and narrowed her eyes in a comic-cunning way. I played along.

'Ooh-er, a plan – nay, mother, hecky thump. Go on, then, tell, don't keep me in suspenders.'

She giggled. 'Silly. No, your dad and I thought, with it nearly being Gita's birthday, we could go up to Plymouth the night before, the Thursday, and stay at a nice veggie B&B your dad's found, then while I'm being done, he and Gita could go to the shops with her birthday money. It'll be a good opportunity to get closer to Gita, as parents, as a family, you know? I hope you don't mind not going, love, but I thought if I feel stronger after these treatments we could all go to the Eden Project together – Euan has got a job there and can get staff discount, apparently. I must say, it sounds lovely and Lancelot and Poppy could come too – I only wish Guinevere...But probably we'll have heard from her by then, she must be so busy with her studies... Anyhow, your dad says the shops in Plymouth are terrific, especially for a girl Gita's age and it's so good of him to offer to take her. Most men wouldn't want to bother but Roy – well, he's not most men, is he?' She sighed and a dreamy expression of devotion floated across her face.

'Oh, please. Mum, yuk. Spare me the soppy bits, do.'

She sighed and rolled her eyes. 'I would have thought you'd be pleased your parents still loved each other.'

'I am. I am. Honest. No, come on, it is a good idea. Great in fact and yes, dad is fab. Totally. No, I mean it. Don't you – don't you dare throw that cush – oh, right, that's *it*. You've done it now, you have.' And I tickled her gently until she gave in, pink with laughter.

As I made tea in the kitchen, half listening to dad swear inventively at the Inland Revenue from the office nook under the stairs, I thought, yes, clever dad. He knew that nothing would thrill Git more than going to Claire's Accessories or Top Shop or wherever and buying all sorts of unsuitable goodies that mum would have niggled her about. Left alone, mum and Git would probably have ended up having a huge row, but dad was the man who'd let Git go to school in a tiara and sparkly nail polish so he'd be a pushover when it came to psychedelic hot pants or God knows what all else Git could wangle. Not daft, my dad. As to the parent–child bonding thing – well, OK. Maybe it'd happen. I doubted it, but there you go, you can never tell.

I didn't mind not going at all. In fact, I looked forward to being alone – I so seldom was it was something of a treat. It was my day off, too – a whole day for me myself alone. Fantastic. Not that I'd do much, just chill, maybe pop down to Con's in the evening with a vid, get pizza, hang out. Perhaps I could persuade her to go to the police about Crazy Tim if we were alone together like the old days – and Angel wasn't there.

So, you know, no plans.

Chapter 23

'Astra, it's Con – look, love, I know it's your day off, but – can you come down? No, it's not work, it's – just come, it's – please…'

'Yeah, sure, no probs – Con, what is it? You sound…'

'Oh Astra – you were right all along, love, you were – I've got to go, the police are here…'

'*What?*'

But the phone had gone dead. I put it down and stared at it as if it might do something crazy by itself, then putting my brain in gear, flung on my jeans and a T and ran down the cut to the café.

Breathless, I skidded to a horrified halt, nearly knocking over a knot of gawping tourists, laden with windbreaks and beach bags. I could hear them talking as I stared in disbelief at the front of our beautiful café.

'Ooh, nasty, that, isn't it? I thought it was a supposed to be a nice, quiet place here…'

'Well, you expect that sort of thing in the inner city, frankly, but…'

'Mum, mum, I want some chips, I want some *chips*…'

This was a nightmare. I could hardly believe my eyes. I pushed through the little crowd, hearing them muttering behind me, and stepped gingerly through the open door. I had to be careful, because someone had nailed a dead seagull, wings drooping brokenly, to one of the double doors. Crows had eaten its eyes and its broken neck lolled elastically in a tattered ruff of crushed grey feathers. There was something written in big red sprayed letters across both doors, too. Although it was now cut in half, I didn't have to struggle to realise it said 'bitch'.

Bitch.

Crazy Tim. It had to be. Jesus – which one of us was the bitch? Who did he mean? Surely not Angel…

I rushed over and sat next to Con, who was talking exhaustedly to a concerned-looking constable taking notes in his traditional copper's notebook.

'Oh, thank God you're 'ere, love – this is Astra Sharp, my – my friend. And employee, I suppose, though really…I've told the officer everything I can think of about – about Tim Norris, I mean, I can only think it's…'

'Well, madam, it's a pretty mess an' no mistake. Nasty. Now, Miss…Sharp, Miss Starbuck here says you're close with her sister… Angela…'

'Well, yes, I suppose so…But he can't mean her – that bitch thing, he worships Angel. It must be – I mean, one of us, the other women – Con. He hates me and Con, he thinks we're preventing him from marrying Angel. I – it's mad, she hates him, but he…Look, can you arrest him or something? He's not right in the head, this is…'

He folded his notebook away in his breast pocket and sighed. 'Well, Miss, I wish it were that easy. But see, where's the proof it were the chap you say it is? But now – don't get me wrong – we take this kind of harassment very serious these days, and I'm going to send our security expert over here a.s.a.p. to look the place over, make some plans for your ladies' safety – I wish you'd saved these letters you told me about, Miss Starbuck, I do. You will in future, won't you? And you'll keep a diary of anything he does or says, phone calls and the like? And think about calling BT, they have ways of helping with nuisance calls…Anything, anything at all he does that bothers you – just ring, we'll deal with him. Nasty, this. A chap like that…Just ring us, anytime day or night. Now, I expect your friend here will look after you, Miss Starbuck, so I'll have to be off and make out a report…'

'Yes – yes. Er, thank you – thank you.' Tears trickled down Con's face and she wiped them away angrily as the policeman left, shoo'ing the crowd away as he plodded gamely across the beach to his car.

I put my arm around her and leaned my head against hers. 'Oh,

Con – Con. The bastard – the fucking bastard. Where's Dot and Cookie? Where's...'

'I sent 'em home. I couldn't bear it. I – I sent Cookie and the boy off in a taxi – says she'll drop Smoky off at her mam's and come straight back in it. I said she dint 'ave to but you know how she is. Thank *God* Angel's at the Retreat – I never thought I'd say that but honestly...Oh, the dirty, filthy, rotten...The mess, Astra, that dead thing and – Jim and Joey saw it first, and Mr Eddy. They were so upset, bless them; I nearly threw up, I did, my stomach turned. Bitch? Bitch? Why, Astra? Why? I mean, I know with that lawyer's letter and everything, but this – it's disgusting, disgusting.'

I made her some tea and tried to settle her down, but it was useless. You could see her tearing herself apart in fear for her sister, and horror at the horrible thing Tim had done. That dead bird – Jesus, I had to get it off the fucking door somehow. Believe me, I didn't want to, my stomach was churning too. I was only glad that Git and the parents had gone off so early; there was no way I wanted Git in this.

I put some rubber gloves on and picked up some old cloths and a disinfectant spray. Steeling myself, I went outside. I was standing there, my guts heaving, when Cookie came up the steps.

'Give them gloves here. And that spray. Go on, Astra, give 'em here. Now go get a bin bag, quick. Go on! You look after Con, I'll do this.'

There was no point arguing, and anyhow, I was extremely grateful I didn't have to do it. When I got back with the bin bag, the bird hung limp in her hand like a broken doll. She threw it in the bag, and, taking it from me, knotted it tightly at the neck, her face screwed up with disgust. Bloody, feather-ticked nails protruded wonkily from the door panel. Only two nails, mind you. Only two. Can you imagine driving two nails – even *one* nail – through a dead creature? How it must feel? And the smell and the – Jesus. He'd sprayed the word after he'd nailed up the gull; there'd been some paint on its feathers, luminous red like new blood on its grey pinions. God, did he kill it specially? Or did he find it dead and save it so he could – I saw Cookie looking at me worriedly.

'Stop thinkin', Astra, stop it. It won't do no good. It's done an' now we 'ave to clear up. Christ! I'll 'ave that bastard meself if I ever sees 'im near 'ere again – Smoky saw it, see. Before I could – he saw. Got that upset – I told 'im it were a puppet, you know, like on telly. But how much do they believe you? Little 'uns – you doan know, do yer? Dot's not 'appy either, I can tell you. Says she won't come back to work – but she will, it's just 'er letting off steam. Feels guilty, I expect, for not tellin' us about 'im before. Oh, the fuckin' barsterd; the fuckin' stupid barsterd.'

We couldn't get the paint off. Mr Eddy saw us struggling and came over, saying he could get some graffiti remover from the council, but it'd take a few days. The worst thing was the tourists, either gawking like milk-calves or complaining that they couldn't get their snacks. I sent them to the dairy – they did take-out teas and stuff. But Jesus, you'd have thought I'd told them to walk to Crossford, not a step up the hill. Oh, some were nice and offered their sympathies but on the whole, no. Not happy campers. And worse when I said I didn't know if the café would reopen tomorrow.

Cookie saw my face and collared me as I went out to the bins with the dirty cloths.

'Doan brood about it, Astra. Doan worry an' get upset – there's nothin' you can do, y'know. Nothin'. Con's made 'er bed with Angel an' now she 'as ter lie on it. It ain't your family, you done all you could an' more. That bloody Angel, I could wring 'er neck bringin' all this trouble on us an' not a care in the world.'

'But Cookie – Angel, well, she's not exactly my fave rave but – she didn't do this, it was... You know. She didn't...'

'She led 'im on. She took stuff off 'im an' made like it was her dues. She laughed at the poor fucker an', Astra, she never even thought 'e was a man, with a man's feelin's. She thought 'e was just a pathetic joke an' now look. I tell yer...' She stuck out her puggy little jaw and her green eyes darkened. 'If you think o'people as less than human, if you wotsit, underestimate 'em, cause you think you're better'n them, you're a great fool an' no mistake. 'Cause they'll find a way to make you see 'em an' it won't be a nice way, it never is. I know.'

She folded her arms across her chest and looked hard at me, her face a white mask under her stiffly curled hair.

'What – like how, Cookie, what…'

'Never you mind. I just know, is all. I ain't had life served up on a silver platter fer me like some I could mention, that's all I'll say – you knows that, Astra.'

'Sorry, Cooks. I mean, I know…'

'Yeah, well. Doan worry. It'll all come out in the wash, as they says.'

And she reached out and patted my arm. It was the first time she'd ever done anything like that – touched me. I had a flashback to when Luke had patted my arm all that time ago at the start of all this. How I'd resented it, felt patronised. Whereas now I felt, not to put it too strongly – *honoured*.

We spent the next hour taping newspaper over the damage until someone could get some paint or the special stuff Mr Eddy had suggested. Everyone and their auntie wandered up, offering advice, commiseration and comments. It was the talk of the village – and the tourists. Cookie and I were desperate. They say all publicity is good publicity, don't they? Well, it might be for the likes of Angel's mates at the Retreat, but for us, it would be disastrous. Who'd want to eat at a place that was the focus of some headcase's vendetta? We were at our wits' end. We were worried stiff about Con and though she didn't say anything, I knew Cooks must be wondering about her job.

Eventually, after we'd done what we could, we said a tired goodbye to Con, who locked up after us and exhaustedly went back to doing busy-work upstairs. I felt like I wanted to shake her, get her to open her eyes and pull herself together. If she didn't, she'd lose everything she slaved for all those years. She'd lose her dream.

But I didn't; there didn't seem any place to start. She was all locked up in herself and I didn't have the key. I trailed up to home dispiritedly.

Christ, some day off.

Chapter 24

I wandered about in the house for a bit then did the housework and laundry on autopilot while I tried to think of ways to wake Con up to what was happening. Eventually, around three, I realised I was starving hungry and made myself a plate of toast and jam and some tea. I tried reading for a while, but the print jumped and niggled and I couldn't concentrate. The last thing I remember was thinking I'd just close my eyes for a minute…

I woke up at gone six, drugged and raggled with sleep, the cold tea on the table in front of me, my cheek marked deeply with the mirror embroidery of the cushion I'd been lying on. I really hate sleeping in the day; I knew I'd never get to sleep later and then my whole sleep-pattern would be fucked up for days.

I scrounged into the kitchen, made some fresh tea and scarfed down a wodge of bread and honey. What to do now? The day was mine, all mine – only now, it was practically over because I'd crashed.

I wandered into the bathroom in the strangely empty, echoing house that felt faintly weird and haunted, as if the ghost-images of my family were still moving invisibly through their old familiar grooves around me. It was an odd sensation, being alone; I couldn't remember the last time I'd been here on my own. Not since I was about sixteen, probably.

I stared moodily into the mirror, wondering if I'd scarred myself for life with the cushion and whether facial branding was hip these days; ha ha. Anything not to think about that fucking dead bird and the café. About Angel and her bloody crazed swains. I was so, so sick of it all.

Turning on the shower, I stepped out of my kit and scrubbed myself from head to toe; then covered in suds, debated whether to bother shaving my legs and armpits. That's not as frivolous as it sounds – I'd got to the stage where personal grooming was a leaden chore. I could not be bothered. It's not as if I was mad keen to don a string bikini and loll about on the beach semi-naked; and now Beaks was gone too, so, like, who cared? I'd really nearly convinced myself to let my body hair grow wild and free when insecurity toppled my nice construct and I had a flash vision of myself, depressed, podgy and hairy, with greasy elf-locks and a mono-eyebrow like Lance. Hmmm.

I shaved. Actually, it was quite satisfying even though I nicked my ankle bone and nearly bled to death. Then in a kind of reaction to my slackness, I went mad with the vanilla-and-coconut body butter and did my eyebrows. I was a vision of loveliness, even if I did smell like a Bounty.

I sauntered back into the living room in what I fondly considered a glamorous manner, and went out on to the deck in my dressing gown. The air was fresher than it had been and a breeze was teasing up the surf into almost reasonable waves, the rushing breath of the sea so familiar I hardly heard it. The wind had lured out the bloody kite-flyers and the beach was criss-crossed with grumpy dads snapping at their tearful kids and trying to untangle strings; I could hear the whistling whine of the successfully airborne oversized stunters even where I was. Annoying gits, most kiters; they covered the beach with their painstakingly assembled yards of twine and got purple in the face with rage if you accidentally trod on any of it. I could see why the Chinese had kite-wars; as a hobby kiting certainly didn't seem to bring the best out in anyone.

Pulling my hair back off my face, I squinted down the hill. Someone – a bloke in white bib-and-brace overalls – was painting the front of the café. Jeez, was that Bill Hocken? By the looks of the enormous flaming ginger sideburns and ancient, paint-spattered red baseball cap, it certainly was. Bloody hell, Con must have called him out to cover up – that word. Must have cost her an arm and a leg, even if Bill was gone on her ever since he'd done the café that first winter. She'd be giving him his dinner as well as a fat wedge of cash without doubt. Oh well, that was my pizza-and-chat evening out.

It didn't look like the place was actually open for business, though – another day lost. Not good, not good at all. I really would have to have a proper, serious talk with Con; all this hassle was one thing, but if she let it destroy her business, that was plain stupid.

Flopping back on the sofa, I zapped the telly. The local news was on, presented in the endearingly naff way only south-west telly can really pull off. Hand-knitted TV. I stayed with it for the weather only to learn that a windy night was expected, but the long-term forecast was for more of the same flat humidity and cloud cover we'd had for the whole summer. I gormlessly stared at the box while my mind churned in a useless and annoying way.

But I couldn't stick the plastic stupidity of the national TV telly-folk, so I un-zapped and stared out of the window. I felt restless, I just couldn't settle. Out there, in the world, women my age were either looking after their kids, doing the dinner, being generally domestic and useful, or getting ready to go out for the evening, meeting friends, going to a bar or the pub. Maybe a club or a gig. The cinema, the theatre – a bloody full on toga-toga Roman-style orgy, for God's sake. Anything. They couldn't all be staring out of their windows clad in a disgusting old dressing gown with nothing to look forward to except a Charles Bronson film on the box and a pasta bows and cheese dinner. If they could be bothered to make it, that is and didn't just have a triple decker digestive biscuit and butter sandwich.

I thought about Gwen, out proselytising, her narrow white face blank and insectile with religious zeal. At least she was doing something even if it was barking mad. Angel – off up at the Retreat manoeuvring Richie-poo towards the altar and her life as a pop diva. Or Con, poor Con, picking at the lovely tea she'd have made for Bill, nodding and smiling while he burbled and munched, her mind turning and turning like a rat in a trap as she worried about her sister. Or Cookie, singing Smoky a lullaby in her tuneless monotone as she put him to bed, her family cursing and shouting downstairs, her olive-green eyes tender, her sharp cheekbones flushed a little with love and perhaps the memory of her boy's father seen in his son's smile.

I thought of all the girls I'd known in the village: Sue and Andrea and Shel – how I'd wanted to be mates but how we'd drifted apart. I should have made more effort, I should have made the time. I'd seen Shel the other day, with her new baby; I hadn't even known she was pregnant. She'd told me Andi had moved to Exeter with a new job and…Her voice had been polite, but distant.

I got up and with my arms wrapped tightly around me, paced around the room as I had that night Git had been ill and dad had said I needed 'you-time'. I stopped abruptly, my eyes full of tears, a big painful lump in my throat – Beaker – Tony. Maybe I hadn't made enough effort with him, either, just let him slip away. If he were here now he'd shake his head at me in mock despair and go put the kettle on.

Jeez-us. If I went on like this I'd be blubbing like a kid. I had to get out, go for a walk or something. It was a reasonably nice evening, I could just stroll around a bit. I couldn't stay in this empty house, though, I just couldn't. I'd thought it would be great having the house to myself but it wasn't. It was unnerving. It cast up too many questions that I'd spent years avoiding. I didn't want to answer that clamour now, or ever. What could I do? I could – I could – go to the Chy for a drink. Why not? This wasn't the nineteenth bloody century; I could go into a pub by myself if I wanted. Women did it all the time these days, if the magazines were to be believed. Strong, independent, free-spirited single gals – like me. Like I wanted to be. Yes. I could. There'd be sure to be someone I knew there, amongst the tourists. Loads, probably. I – I – oh for God's *sake*.

I got dressed. Clean, if rather aged and greyish undies. My purple sarong with the starfish pattern, the lilac scoop-neck T I'd worn to Beak's – Tony's – gig. It had been washed in with something dark and was now what my nana would have called 'ashes-of-violets'. Mauvey-grey, in fact and a bit misshapen. That's the trouble with cheap clothes, they don't last. I must stop getting stuff from the catalogue. My pink flippies. I paused in front of the bathroom mirror and fluffed my curls then strained round to see my hair was nearly down to bra-level and getting pretty raggy. Another thing to do – get a hair cut. I nicked some of Git's pink lip-gloss, and, spotting a pot of iridescent hair glitter, patted a bit on. Why not? Go mad. It looked rather nice, I thought. Cheerful, pretty. As I put it down I noticed the blue topaz earrings Angel had given me furred in that strange whitish bathroom dust that gathers no matter what you do – I must, must, must give her them back.

At the door, I paused. A sudden thought struck me out of nowhere like a cold chill. What if Crazy Tim was watching what I was doing through binoculars, or something? What if he – I don't know – tried to…For the first time, I actually felt a bit frightened, for myself. I mean, he *had* sprayed 'bitch' on the door and he always called me – no. It was stupid. It wasn't me he was interested in, I was just an annoyance to him. A minor player. But still…

· But still – what? I shouldn't go out in case he jumped out of the bushes at me? I should stay in the house like a sort of self-condemned prisoner 'in case'? Bollocks. This was my place, I lived here – had lived here longer than him, come to that. He wasn't going to stop me doing – whatever it was I was going to do. I shut the door and locked it firmly. Fuck you, Timmy. Sorry you're a nutter and everything, but fuck you.

On the beach, which was still heaving with blissed-out trippers soaking up every last possible atom of seasideness, I paused to take my flip-flops off and annoyed a kiter by stepping over his lines; boo hoo. Take up Tae Kwan Do or something, mate, get rid of some of that aggression. The sand was warm and soft at the top of the beach, my feet sinking in slightly as I walked carefully, trying to avoid the day's building projects and ankle-snapping pits that the children had created so lovingly and were now a definite hazard to traffic. As I walked nearer the sea and crossed towards the steps up the cliff side to the road, I felt the sand change underfoot to hard, damp salt-rimed ripples. There was a tangled rim of black-bronze bladderwrack, wet feathers, dismembered crabs and more human detritus like marge cartons and the ubiquitous pink rubber glove that always turns up on beaches everywhere at the water's edge – and lots of jelly fish, their purple and crimson veins making them look like popped eyeballs. Yuk. I stopped and picked up a particularly beautiful crab shell; it was worn so thin by the sea it looked like a little articulated white glass toy or a piece of modernistic jewellery. I moved its legs about a bit and marvelled at its engineering, then let it fall back on to the sand. I stretched and took a deep breath of the ozone-rich air. It was a nice evening, nicer than it had been for ages. The breeze was pleasant and fresh, the sky was a gentle, periwinkle blue, the clouds fluffy and white like clouds should be. I refused to wonder if Tim was watching me as I climbed the steps to the road, the sounds of the beach washing round me and fading away like a boat's wake as I walked.

At the top, I stopped and put my flippies back on. I could see the Chy, the small front patio area full of people sitting at the tables under parasols drinking and laughing. They all seemed to be in groups or couples. What had I been thinking? I couldn't go in there and…Yes, I could. I could. No one would look at me twice, no one would notice me – and if they did, so what? It was none of their business. I walked on, trying to look cool and collected, scolding myself for being silly under my breath. Then I stopped in case anyone noticed and thought I was a schizophrenic. The voices made me do it, they made me go for a drink on my own – oh, *stop*.

I was so busy arguing with myself, I didn't notice Luke sitting on a bench by the door until he spoke; I nearly fell up the step with surprise. I'd expected to meet someone I knew – but not *him*.

'Hi, Star. Nice evening.'

'God, you give me a start! What are you doin' here?'

He smiled. 'I could ask the same of you.'

'Touché. Sorry. You're right. I'm – I thought I'd – I'm just out for a walk, really. You? It's just you don't – I don't – I mean, you, I didn't think you went to pubs, to – here – drank…I'll just shut up, shall I?'

'Hmm.' He budged up on the bench. 'Have a seat – sorry, unless you're meeting someone…'

'Meeting – no, no one, I was just out for a walk like I said and I thought…'

'Me too. Restless, you know? Look, you want a drink – no, let me, I was off to the bar anyway – a Bacardi Breezer – any particular flavour? No? OK – you stay here, save our seats.'

A Bacardi Breezer? An alco-pop, for God's sake? Why ever did I say that? I'd never drunk anything like that in my life; I used to be a double-vodka-and-fuckit girl. But the tousle-haired lass in the pretty slip dress laughing with her boyfriend at the table over there was drinking one, out of the bottle like folk did now. It looked – young. I wanted that. I wondered what it tasted like.

It tasted like fizzy pop, innocuous and sugary, and the hefty amount of booze in it hit my empty stomach like neat Polish spirit. My cheeks felt red hot and that numb feeling was making my mouth feel peculiar – not that it stopped me talking. Oh no.

'I mean, look, Luke, why *are* you here?' I waved my bottle expansively. 'OK, it's got a nice view of the sea, it's live – lively, but you! I mean, you – not your usual…'

'I just couldn't stay in on my own; normally I don't mind but…'

'You – oh. I see – no, I do, I really do. So did I, I did. I mean, I couldn't either. Stay in, that is, not that I'm ever usually alone, and I thought it would be great but – it wasn't so I…Why didn't you want to be alone, then? If you don't mind me asking, that is.'

'Oh, I suppose I'm a bit fed up.' He looked up at me through his fringe and half smiled. My heart did not, repeat not, in any way lurch. It was just the booze giving me palpitations. I'd got over Luke Skywalker ages ago.

I looked back at him with a suitably stern expression which demonstrated admirably how I was merely concerned as a friend. 'Fed up…?'

'Yeah, just a bit. I don't know – I took her to that place last night – Angel. I took her to the Retreat. Hideous place. Ugly, it should be in London, not here. Anyway, I took her, she asked me – worried about that nutter Tim following her – you know. Still, I don't like – I mean, I know it's all for her career, but I'm not made of stone. I hate the thought of her with that sort of crowd – she's not like that. You know her, you're her friend. Sometimes I think: thank God she's got a friend like you. Someone solid.'

He took a swig of his drink and sighed. So did I, but inwardly, 'solid', eh?

'Luke – can I ask you a personal question? OK, I don't want to be – it's just that, you an' Angel, she doesn't seem like she'd be your type…'

'Yeah. It's weird, I know. Her being from the city and me – it's just, oh, underneath that urban thing, she's so unspoiled, you know? So natural, so into the same stuff I am. The sea, the mountains…' He looked wistful.

I hadn't actually realised Angel was a child of nature until then; I would have thought more a child of shopping. Obviously, I'd been missing something. 'Er, yeah. Sure. But still – I remember when you first saw her, it was – well, a bit dramatic…'

He looked away for a moment, out to sea, then back at me, pushing his fringe off his face. His turquoise eyes were full of hurt; proper hurt, not kid stuff. He looked like a person who was carrying a big black bruise deep inside somewhere, the kind of bruise that never goes away and you get used to it, used to the dull pain, until you knock it again and it hurts really badly. That was what was in his eyes. I didn't want to be the cause of that hurt. Also, I felt rotten for being superficial and bitchy, even inwardly. I waited, barely breathing, just listening.

'You see, well, a long time ago, when I was – I had a cousin, a second cousin. We're a big family. Annalise. That was her name. It's a family name. We called her Annie, though. We grew up together, came here, all us kids together, you can imagine. Went skiing in winter together – she was a brilliant skier, everyone said she was Olympic quality. I – loved her. She loved me. When we were eighteen we realised it was more than just – it was real. We thought, marriage, kids maybe, the family was really happy, everyone was happy…'

'Luke, you don't have to…'

'No, it's OK. I – I haven't told many people…' He smiled at me again, that sweet sad smile. 'I know you'll understand, you're so – kind-hearted, that's it, really. Kind-hearted. Well, she – Annie – there was a boating accident, Lake Lucerne. They never found her body. I guess that's why I got so involved with the surfing, with the mountains. I didn't want – anything like that again. But when I saw Angel, I thought for a moment…She's so like her. Maybe not totally, but…And when I spent time with her, I realised how like Annie she was in herself, you know? So – so at one with the world, so – well, pure, really. Gentle. Strong. Spiritual, almost. I mean the way she is with animals, nature, just like Annie was. And so beautiful, so generous. She thinks the world of you, you know…'

'Funny, she said that about you – thinking the world of me, that is…' I stopped short, suddenly embarrassed.

'Don't worry. She's right. I do – I do think a lot of you, you've been so kind to us…'

'Look, I'm so sorry about – Annie. Sorry for your loss. It must have been awful.'

'I don't have to pretend with you, do I? Yeah, it was. But time, you know? It's OK, really. And now there's Angel…As soon as she gets sorted with this record company guy, gets a contract like she wants, everything will be cool. I said to her the other day – she's bound to be a success and then she can use her position to really get some good messages across. Stuff about the environment, that kind of thing. People listen to musicians, stars. I could tell that really got to her, that idea, she was so happy about it, smiling; she said she couldn't believe the way I thought. Really dry, you know, like you Northern guys are. Yeah, I shouldn't get so – you know. I should just trust her, shouldn't I? She knows what she's doing – better than me, probably. I don't have a clue about how to deal with guys like that. Look, another drink? Hang on…back in a minute.'

I was speechless. What should I do? Enlighten him before he got his heart smashed to bits again? I'd tried that the night of Element's fiasco, and it had been water off a duck's back. But I couldn't just let him walk into another tragedy because he was too unworldly to see Angel for what she really was. Messages about the environment – dear God, no wonder she'd smiled. It was amazing she hadn't laughed out loud in his face. And that tragedy with his fiancée. Poor bastard, no wonder he'd been so distant with people; no wonder he hadn't wanted to engage with the world. Oh, Luke.

While I tried to think of some way of saving him from certain doom, we talked about everything under the sun. I told him about mum, and he was very sympathetic; I told him how I loved reading, and about my university days, and how I'd flunked the OU because of technical incompetence, which made him laugh and own up that it took him years to learn how to set a video even though he was quite good with computers. He told me about his family – how his parents had split shortly after Annie had died and how his mother was a potter and lived in an old villa place in Tuscany with his kid sister Livvy, but he hardly ever saw them because his stepmother, Patti, made such a fuss about it. She was the American who hated Polwenna.

'Not that I can blame her, really – Lanterns was all mother's and my father's, all our family's. Patti wanted a clean break; she doesn't trust mother, she thinks she's crazy, living out there in the hills messing around with lumps of clay and Livvy going to the local school and speaking less and less English. Patti's a bit of a culture vulture; it's all high art and couture shows and galleries for her. She's very beautiful, you know; she was a model when she met dad. I suppose she likes the high life, she's used to it and well, she's quite a bit younger than dad so I suppose he doesn't want her to get bored. She thinks it's primitive here – but not in a good way. The plumbing, it gets to her. Poor Patti, she wants me to be more "civilised", be a proper son and heir.' He nodded out to sea, where the breeze was whipping into a proper little wind and frothing up the breakers. 'She thinks surfers are all good-for-nothing bums with no sense of responsibility. Well, she's right in a way, I suppose...'

He was much nicer than I'd pegged him for, really. Maybe not an Oscar Wilde but certainly pleasant company and God, so good-looking; I could see other lasses checking him out, and a glow of pride that he was being so attentive to me, was with me, crept warmly round my heart. Just pure friendliness, of course. Nothing more. Because like I said, I was so over him.

A mini-flock of crows descended, squabbling raucously on an overflowing rubbish bin by the cliff. I gestured with my nearly empty bottle.'God, look at all them bloody crows, down there, by that red car; after the picnic remains, I should think.'

'Jackdaws. They're jackdaws. See, they're grey round the head and they've got silver eyes...'

'Oh, I thought they were crows, I thought...'

'What?'

'No, I feel stupid now...'

'No, go on, you thought...'

'Well, I thought they were – old crows. Grey-haired, well, feathered, crows...You're laughing at me!'

'No, I'm not – honestly. Old crows?'

I slapped his arm as he laughed. 'I wish I hadn't said that now. But honest, there are loads more – jackdaws – and crows than usual. And gulls and...'

'More jelly fish and more weaver fish and magpies. Yeah. Something's out of kilter. I mean, it does happen – like if there's a new motorway you get more scavengers because there's more road kill, that sort of thing. But there's no particular reason I can see...It's like the weather, it's not quite...It shouldn't be...'

'Right. Yeah. I know. Like it's just here and nowhere else. Maybe we've done something wrong. Annoyed the gods. You know.' Now, that just popped out. But after I said it, I thought, *I've been thinking that for weeks, but I had no one to tell*...Until now, that is. I felt a strange thickening of the air between us and I looked at him to find he was looking at me and our eyes locked, my blood quickened and the hair rose on my neck. If he shrugs this off, I'll just make a joke, make like I didn't mean it, I'll...

'Yes, I do know. I know exactly what you mean. It *is* like that, I thought that myself. Like we've been cur...'

At that moment, a bunch of A-class Yahs stumbled on to the patio, making a noise not unlike the crows – sorry, jackdaws – had. One of them barged past me and nearly trod on my foot, which I whipped away in the nick of time. He didn't apologise.

'Bloody Yahs.' It came out before I could stop it. I could have bitten my tongue off. Luke looked quizzical.

'Yahs?'

'Oh, er – it's what we, some of us who live here, call the, well, the upper-upper summer people types. Because they always say "oh, yah…" The horrible ones, I mean,' I added hastily. 'You know, the snotty ones – not the er, nice ones, because, you know, obviously, they're not all…'

'Am I a Yah?'

'You! God – no, I – of course not, God…' I spluttered.

He looked thoughtful. 'I suppose I try not to be. I still do it though, sometimes, without thinking. I say something, or make a judgement about someone…Then I think, shit; but it's too late. It's that inbred sense of superiority, I suppose; we were all brought up to think we were somehow better than anyone else. At my school, the others…They just seemed to accept the idea that we're the decent, right-thinking ones and the rest – are just, well, peasants. It's a sort of gentleman's club, the old boy's network, that sort of thing. It stinks, it really does. Yahs. Well, you're right. Mother hates it, hates all that, that's why she moved to Tuscany, took Livvy away. She wanted to be free of all that stuff, be an artist. Make sure Livs didn't grow up like those awful girls from London you see round here all summer. That's another thing that drives Patti mad. *She* thinks it's all great. Perfectly natural. Feudalism. Keep the peasants in their place, tugging their forelocks. Sees herself as a lady of the manor – if dad would buy her a manor, that is. She loves all that stuff – so English, she says. Tradition, fox-hunting, being, well, being Yah, I suppose. You know, most people won't even talk about it – it's a taboo subject – but you're not most people, are you, Star?'

'I'm sorry, Luke, I didn't mean to be rude, it's just a silly joke, a…'

'No, it's OK. They are crap, some of them. Unthinking. I don't want to be like that. I need to think about things, it's just that…I spend too much time avoiding thinking. Look, would you like to come back to the flat? It's getting a bit crowded here and…'

I opened my mouth to say, no, sorry, I couldn't. 'Yes, why not? Thanks.'

We got up, and, feeling faintly dizzy, I walked with him along the cliff road to Lanterns.

Chapter 25

There are times in your life, if you admit it and don't try to justify it out of existence, when you find yourself doing something that you know to be wrong, *inappropriate* and downright foolish, but you just can't stop yourself. It's like, you live your life how you've chosen to live it, dum-ti-dum-ti-dah, just plodding along, trying to get by, trying to be safe until suddenly, you just can't stand it anymore. For no particular reason, it's like you run amok. You can't help yourself and you do something really dumb. Like say something stupid and insulting to your boss at the office party, or spend a fortune you haven't got on a frock you'll never wear instead of paying your share of the rent, or get pissed and go off with someone else's boyfriend because you always fancied them and by chance and fate you're both in the wrong place at the wrong time.

And the Devil sees you do it and, man, he *smiles*.

Luke and I sauntered companionably along the cliff towards Lanterns, the great grey house on the spit that his family had owned for three generations. It was a hunched, brooding place, very romantic, very Daphne du Maurier with its mullioned windows, ornate chimneys and lichen-splashed slate roof. It was certainly the best and most coveted house in the village, if not the whole area, and what it would cost to buy now didn't bear thinking about. It was definitely imposing, but secretly, I liked our house better. Lanterns was a cold place, to me, a bit forbidding. Still, people round here admired it tremendously and spoke about it almost in hushed tones. I mean, legend had it royalty had stayed there, and certainly various aristos had parked their Rollers and Bentleys in the enormous garages that were now probably full of nothing more interesting than decaying polystyrene body-boards, old bikes, spiders' webs and incomplete croquet sets. Apparently the house once had well-manicured gardens running down to the cliff-edge, and certainly, the little slate-laid courtyard facing out to the sea still boasted giant stone urns and weathered stone benches. But the gardens were now just rough turf and the urns were empty, like the garages. It was a summer let, inhabited by strangers who paid through the nose for the privilege of boasting they were 'off to Lanterns for the summer, my dear'.

Luke's flat was over the garages; once upon a time it had been the chauffeur's, in the days when staff lived in. Now, redone for the son of the house, it was a self-contained unit, separate from the house. I staggered giggling up the wooden outside staircase and stood panting under the porch on the veranda, watching the sun set in a molten ball of orange fire into the 'sea of a thousand creases, like the infinitely pleated tunic of the god in the hands of the women of the sanctuary' as that French poet, Perse says. I've always liked that quote. It seemed very apt as I dizzily watched the ocean crinkling into the horizon.

'My God, this is brilliant – what a view! And you can hear the surf, Jesus, you can practically taste it, it's that close – we're right on the cliff-edge really, aren't we? And you could sit and have your breakfast here – well, you do probably, don't you, what *am* I saying, and…'

He unlocked the French doors and I stepped across the threshold.

As Luke fiddled with the door catch, complaining how knackered it was, I looked around – the inner sanctum, at last. The place only the privileged few got to see. The Skywalker's sanctuary. It was all wooden beams and floor, just the one big room with a vaulted, windowed ceiling like an attic, kitchen and bathroomey things at one end, the sleeping area down one side, the other side a mass of wetsuits, boards, a desk with at least two computers, a big TV and video set up, stereo stuff, clothes, cameras, old sheepskin surfie boots, snowboard things, all sorts of equipment, hundreds of pounds worth of gear, all in tangled heaps.

And on every spare bit of wall, photographs of Angel.

I knew he'd taken them because this was the Angel he'd talked about. Angel windswept and laughing, wrapped in a big old jumper, sitting on the sand. Angel cuddling Piglit, her violet eyes soft and her expression wistful. Angel in a form-fitting wetsuit (not hers, surely?), droplets of seawater glinting on her golden, tanned face. Angel in her no-waistband faded jeans, a tight white T-shirt and hiking boots (Con's?), a daysack (I could see it laid on the floor in the corner) on her back out on the moors looking like a model doing 'sporty'.

Angel the sea-maid, the country-girl, the mountain-lass. The images were as far removed from the Angel I knew as was humanly possible. The pictures shifted and layered across my vision, and drunk as I was, I felt the beginnings of a realisation irk and twiddle at the edges of my mind. This could explain something about her tremendous power, I knew it could, if only my brain would stop whirling long enough to catch hold of it.

'This is Annie.' Luke handed me a framed photo reverentially. I blinked to clear my vision and took it carefully.

A slim, pretty blonde girl, bearing a remarkable family resemblance to Luke, her hair caught carelessly into a pony-tail, goggles pushed back on her head, stood balancing easily on her skis, ski poles stuck into the snow, laughing at the camera. I looked closer and I suppose there was a kind of Angel look about her, but not, to me at least, a marked one. They were both slim, well-made blondes, but very different to a woman's eyes. Annie's cheeks were rosy – but it wasn't blusher. Her hair was very fair – and it wasn't bleach. Her physique was certainly stunning in her old, unadorned snow-suit but it was the body of a sportswoman, her thighs and calves muscular and defined, her shoulders wide, her hands large and square; it wasn't Angel's smooth, groomed perfection. Annie was everything that Luke had made Angel into in his photographs, only, where Angel was all artifice, Annie was all natural.

And Annie was dead. But as I stared at the picture, I realised with an awful clarity, that it didn't matter, because in dying, Annie's power over Luke was crystallised into a timeless, unbreakable, and unholy passion. A love that had crushed and blighted his emotions, that had stopped his boy's heart like a broken clock on the day he heard the terrible news that his childhood sweetheart was dead. Now no living woman could ever surpass his Annie, because in death, she was perfect and immutable, a marble goddess on a plinth, to be worshipped and adored. She would never grow old, demanding, ugly. She would never disappoint him, or embarrass or shame him. She would never, ever let him down or run off with his best friend or get whiny or worst of all – boring. She was like a rose in one of those glass paperweights, preserved at the peak of her glory for all eternity. The terrible hold the dead sometimes have over the living poured out of that photograph like a curse. I put it down, quickly. It was too unbearable to look at.

'You see – they're so alike, aren't they? It's amazing. Angel says she knows she and Annie could have been the best of friends, like sisters; but that's Angel, isn't it? I've never met anyone with so much, so much intuition, understanding…' He gazed blissfully at the wall of pictures.

Then it finally clicked in my mind.

Tim and Luke and God alone knew how many others were fascinated with Angel *because she was a blank canvas.* How often had I seen her looking expressionless and faintly bored while some bloke went crazy over her, how often had I wondered what they were seeing in her great, disinterested amethyst eyes?

They were seeing everything they wanted to see. Luke saw his Annie reincarnated, Tim saw – what? The perfect lady, the genteel sex-bomb? I'd pay money to see Tim's photos of Angel; I'd bet they showed her as demure, charming, the well-bred filly, leggy and soignée in pastel cashmere. Everything that went with his carefully cultivated, painfully wide of the mark, tweedy, sporty, wannabe-county self-image.

Angel was a beautiful gleaming silver screen on which they projected their ideal woman. I don't think she herself cared a bit what they thought as long as they were nice and adoring and gave her pretty things, jobs, lifts in their cars, or took her to fancy parties where more men could see her and want her and think she was their absolute perfect girl. She wasn't being nasty, or malicious, or grasping – she just *was.* She lived in the moment and the rest of us were simply shadows that flitted round her world, the centre of which was, naturally, herself. We had no more reality to her than dolls or puppets, that was why she said the things she said and did the things she did. That's why she wasn't frightened of Tim's insanity – it didn't mean anything to her. He was simply of no further use to her so he'd pinged out of existence, like a soap-bubble bursting. She didn't give him a second thought; he'd just gone wonky, blown a fuse. Oh dear, but so what? Some guys were like that – the jeweller from London, for example. And Luke, nice enough for a seaside fling, but a bit of a puppy-dog and really, summer's nearly over. Do not stop, go – straight on to Richie. And when she left her worshippers for another besotted, richer or more useful guy, they didn't hate her, they forgave her because she had never been real. Untouched by their desires, she didn't care enough to make scenes or weep or beg; she just left them with the image of her perfection and no other woman could ever live up to her.

It wasn't fair. It would kill Luke – oh, not physically, but inside – no, it wasn't right, it wasn't fair. But I could save him, I could. I could make him see, open his dreaming eyes. Hadn't he said I made him think about things? See things differently? I could fix this, I could. Oh, yeah, and what about Crazy Tim? Wasn't he worth 'saving'? Just because Luke was good-looking and sweet he was more worthy than poor, mad, hideous Tim? My conscience rose up to bite me, but I put my foot firmly on its head. I couldn't do anything for Tim, he was a lost soul. But Luke – I was here, wasn't I? He'd wanted me with him, he'd opened up to me, he obviously liked me, cared about me, even. I could rescue him.

I think, in that moment, in that place, I was quite crazy. I think I had lost the power to reason. Why? Maybe the culmination of years of stress, maybe the whole awful summer, maybe the unaccustomed alcohol, I don't know. Maybe I was sick of being sensible, practical; sick of being reliable old Astra. Sick of my life. I do know I felt a huge wave of exultation as the idea flooded through me: I could save Luke.

I could save my secret love. The man I'd watched and waited for years and years, who when we'd met again at the beginning of the summer had initially disappointed me, but who was now redeemed, was someone I could crusade for. Take care of. I could heal him, make him whole again.

It was an epiphany; I was blinded by the glorious light of our mutual salvation. Gwen would have been proud of me.

And, if I'd taken actual photos of Luke over the years, not just mental ones, what would they have portrayed him as? I wonder...

Oh, yes, make no mistake, I was off my head all right, and what happened next did not help at all.

'I made some coffee – I don't have anything to eat, sorry, I'm not good about food, I forget...And, could I ask a favour?'

I came to with a start. Luke was over by the TV holding out a plastic zip-lock baggie, whilst fiddling with the video with his other hand. Two mismatched mugs of coffee steamed on the floor by the bed platform – the only place to sit.

'Uh, sure – of course.'

'Could you roll us a spliff while I do this video – you'll love it, it's a documentary about big-wave guys in Hawaii, really fascinating – and then I think there's some bits from *Crystal Voyager*.'

I took the bag in a daze. Luke, smoking draw? *Luke?* This wasn't in the photo-fit. I wouldn't have been more surprised if he'd tied off and shot up in front of me.

'I didn't know – think – you smoked; I mean...'

'Well, yeah. It's pretty harmless, don't you think? I don't do anything else really. I've had a go at most things but I can't be bothered, too much hassle. But a bit of blow...I haven't tried this stuff, a guy in Cham gave it to me in exchange for a fleece I had spare, you know – but tonight...Why not? '

'Sure, OK – but d'you mean you brought this in with you from France?'

'Yeah.'

'Jesus, that was a risk – you in that old camper van. God, the customs must have been blind that day, you were lucky.'

'The camper – oh, no. When I go to Europe I take the Audi or the Range Rover – God, that camper, well, I love it but it wouldn't make a long trip. It's just for down here really. No, I leave it at the house in London and just blag one of the other cars.'

'Oh. I see. I suppose I thought…A house in London, er, that's nice.'

'It's OK. Dad's thinking of selling it quite soon, Patti says it's too small for all the entertaining they like to do. And it was my mother's place too; she decorated it, all that, so I suppose it's like Lanterns, Patti wants her own space. We've got a flat in Cham fortunately, so that saves a lot of trouble and of course, the cousins ski so they're often there. I'm not any place much these days, I like to keep moving, travel, and dad's mostly at his New York place at the moment – business, you know, boring, boring, boring.' He smiled, and drank some of his coffee.

Of course I'd known he was from a wealthy family, but somehow, I hadn't wanted to. I only ever saw him 'down here' after all; I had no idea what the rest of his life was like. Not that it mattered, of course. Not a bit. Money didn't mean a thing, didn't spoil you when you were a basically sound person, like my Luke.

I opened the baggie; it contained a good-sized lump of tarry black hash; it was unusual, and had a particular smell – sweet and bitter together when I burned it. A long time later, I asked dad about it, in a roundabout way. He said it sounded like zero-zero black opiated hash. Very strong, he said, very rare and expensive, for the connoisseur only and – why? I didn't tell him.

I rolled an old-fashioned three-paper spliff, biker style, and we smoked it as we talked and drank the ghastly instant coffee he'd brewed. Idly, I wandered over to the computer and looked at some print-outs of pictures.

'These are nice – those mountains look fantastic. I'm jealous, I've never been anywhere like that – did you take them?'

'Yeah – I was thinking of trying to sell them, maybe to a snow-boarding mag or something.'

Without thinking, I blurted out the first thing that came into my head. 'Luke – have you got a job – sorry, God, that sounds awful – I mean, how do you manage for money?'

'Money? Oh, er – well, I have an allowance of course, and then, the revenue from the house and…'

'The what from the house?'

'Lanterns. It's mine. Dad gave it to me after he and mother split; kind of a consolation prize, I suppose. Anyway, it's managed by this agency and I get the money from people who rent it.'

'So you're like, the landlord, then?'

'God, yeah – I guess I am. I hadn't thought about it that way before – a landlord, wow. There you are, you're making me think about stuff already.'

A thought occurred. 'Luke, have you told Angel about owning the house here and having the London place and the flat in France and the cars and stuff?'

'I don't think so. Why? I mean, she's not into that sort of thing, is she? Material things. Oh, I see – d'you think she'd be put off, think less of me for it, for being…'

'Rich?' I took a deep toke. 'Well, you know Angel. Perhaps you should play it down. Break it to her gently.'

I never said I was perfect, did I?

We smoked in silence for a bit then Luke zapped the video and we watched the documentary about the big-wave riders; the 'watermen' from Hawaii. I'm no surf-freak, but even I (all right, I was smashed) was fixated watching them bump down the sheer faces of building-sized waves that curled like Neptune's fists into glassy cerulean tubes. Then they showed them riding on the new hydrofoil boards that actually rose up what seemed like a couple of feet above the swell and made them appear to skim over the water like swooping birds. It was beautiful to see; it made me shiver, as if they'd momentarily become something more than human. Had broken the shackles of gravity. For the first time, I genuinely wished I could do that, be like them, be that physically free and at one with the ocean. Luke talked about going there and surfing with the guys on the film because they were the real deal, the true authentic, no-bullshit sea-lords – but I saw thick-set, older American men, family men, strong as bulls beside which Luke's slim Englishness seemed delicate and adolescent. Amateur, even. I quickly pushed that thought away. Luke was the best, after all, everyone knew that.

In fact, in my stoned haze, I pushed all the new, disquieting thoughts about Luke away; they didn't fit with the dream of him I'd cherished. My Luke was a gentle, beach-bum surfer, not interested in anything except his date with God and the Big Blue; unworldly, innocent even. Not a rich, spoiled dilettante…No, he was a – what? What was he, actually? Oh, let it go, let it go. It didn't matter, nothing mattered except I was here with him, it was my old dream come true and it was cool. Everything was cool. My photos were in place, untouchable.

The hash rolled through me, warm as the Pacific sun that lit those jade-green waves the hydrofoil surfers rode like kings; I felt that druggie boneless lassitude and physical heat as if I'd gradually been massaged from the inside out. I rolled another one and we watched the great old surf-trip movie *Crystal Voyager*, the soundtrack by Pink Floyd wooshing in and out of phase as I smoked, laid on the bed, Luke's bed, propped up against the wall on a heap of fleeces and old, musty-smelling cushions. He lay next to me, we touched down the length of our sides, his hip against mine, his brown, bare foot against my instep; I could feel the warmth of him, wick and alive against me. He smelled of fresh air and salt. He was talking about the days when his family was still together and Annie was alive and Lanterns was a family place, safe and beloved. I could feel him rearranging the memories in his mind like a devotee tidying the shrine.

'…so, I used to see you, years ago, when you used to go round all dressed in black – no, we did! Annie saw you too, she used to be scared of you; well, I was, too, you looked so angry all the time and you had that purple hair…But I wanted to speak to you, I did, you looked so interesting, but I didn't and then, you weren't there and – hmm, thanks – ah, then when I saw you again I wasn't sure it was you…' He smiled and handed me back the spliff.

'You were scared of me? God, I was scared of you, you know; kids like you lot up here were so – so sure of yourselves, so – such a unit, you know?'

'But you were, I mean I thought you looked so nice, when I saw you again, like a gypsy girl, so brown and strong and – like – oh, you know, I mean, seriously, if I hadn't met Angel, if...'

His face was two inches from mine as he leaned on his elbow, talking. I could smell the sweet, animal smell of his breath mixed with the bitter hash and tobacco. Two inches.

He picked up a strand of my hair and looked at it, twisting the black curl round his finger.

In the dim light from the flickering TV, the rolling images of the sea spread like skeins of shattered crystal across his strange, familiar, unknown face. I knew what was going to happen before he even thought it.

'Your hair, it's so pretty, it's all sparkly, like sea spray...'

I put my face up to his and he kissed me. His mouth bloomed on mine like hot, wet silk and I felt myself responding in a way I never had with anyone else. It was as if I didn't care about anything but this, the feeling, the desire; it was like a spell.

Then he pulled back, confused. 'I – I – we shouldn't, it's – I...'

'It's OK, it is, it's cool, these things just...Chill, Luke, it's OK, love, really, it's...'

Hadn't I known? Hadn't I known all along this would happen? Oh, yeah, hey, it *was* cool. It was fate, kismet. This was dreamtime and everything was OK. He sighed and kissed me again and I put the spliff out with one hand while he kissed my throat and took off his faded T-shirt and I felt his beautiful warm body against mine, his flesh sweet and smooth. Then it was way, way too late for reason and I fumbled with the knot of my sarong and the music from the film soared like a paean to unreason and he touched me, pushed up my T-shirt and bra and kissed my breasts, sucking, biting; I was dizzy with it and sweating with the drug that made a simmering fever of everything... And then he was inside me; hard and fast in a heated rush like a young and inexperienced boy, not a man. He trembled, hesitant and unsure, so I held him and moved for him and gave him what he needed while his blind face strained to make sense of his fall from grace.

Then it seemed to me I looked over his shoulder and the room yawed like a boat in a storm, the doors to the veranda swung open and the sea came in; the old god entered, roaring in the sound of the surf from the Atlantic below. The deeps crashed into the room, washing round the walls in a ghost-image of breaking waves and pearly, translucent foam pulsing with the beat of my blood, and everything was thick with brine, filled with salt-water; the air was heavy and humid with the primeval stink of seaweed and the fecund thickness of the far oceans. The sweat that dripped from his corded neck on to my face was salt, the wild water broke over us and I lost myself, my real self, in the churning wash of the Big Blue that filled the wooden room arced above with beams like an upturned hull. Then he convulsed and his weight fell on me and I bore it gladly while he put his hot, congested face to my cheek and as I kissed him I heard his voice like a tired child's on the verge of sleep sigh…

'Angel.'

And then there was no sea. There were no Atlantic-breathing deeps in that salt-soaked room, just the fiery burning pain that broke like lava in my heart. I was filled with it, and shame, and fury; and everything in me that was to do with pride and what my father used to call 'our Spanish blood' told me to get out before I tried to hurt him, this sleeping *boy*, as he'd hurt me so profoundly and so unforgivably.

As I'd hurt myself. As I'd let myself be hurt. Because I'd known all along, deep inside, that the whole thing, from meeting him in the Chy to staggering pissed into his flat was a tangled nails-down-a-blackboard exercise in gross stupidity. That I should have left well alone, left Luke in my fantasy, where it was safe. But no; I had had my moment of bloody unreason all right, and look where it had got me. And all my silly game-playing and clever-clever remarks, all my flitty little ideas about being bright and modern were consumed in a hot, primitive desire to hit him in the face as he lay sleeping with his arm flung across me, to hit him hard and see blood run and see him *hurt*.

A long shudder ran through me and I rolled out from under his arm. He didn't wake. I fumbled around in a kind of horrid frenzy for my clothes and dressed. Then grabbing my bag, I stumbled out. At the door, I paused and looked back. He was still dead to the world, his face and the fleece he was laid on sparkling with the cheap hair glitter that had rubbed off on everything. Now it didn't seem pretty and light-hearted, it seemed tacky and childish. Fake.

Fake. It had all been fake. I'd made it all up – loving him, saving him, being with him in a perfect world for ever – like a silly adolescent dreaming of a film star on a poster in her room. And Luke, Jesus. I could see it all now; all the thoughts I'd tried to push away came flooding back and stuck their ugly, grimacing mugs in my face and cackled. Luke – weak, emotionally stunted, in love with a ghost so he'd never have to engage with a real woman – my God, I'd thought he was so bloody marvellous and he was nothing, *nothing*. Just another bloody Yah summer person like all the others, only I'd been fooled by his looks, his careless diffidence and his casual good manners into thinking he was different from the others. But he wasn't. He wasn't. He'd just gone to better fucking schools.

I shuddered as I looked at those pictures of Angel, her great, blank eyes gazing at me from the photos on his walls. Then it hit me. What was the difference between Crazy Tim and Luke? What? Oh, yeah, one was nice-looking, well bred and polite, the other…But they were brothers under the skin, all right, they were both *obsessed*. Luke just presented it more acceptably, didn't he? He wasn't ugly, *Crazy* Luke, oh no, he was handsome, *Romantic* Luke, the stuff of thousands of love stories, films and plays. Tim and Luke. Both singing the same fucking song. I felt sick with fury, sick of all the hypocrisy and cant that people churned out about love and sex; I felt sick of myself and how I'd justified my behaviour, the silly, narcissistic delusions I'd cherished.

And worst of all, the thing that made me cringe with guiltiness: I'd cheated on Beaker with Luke in my head for years; cheated kind, decent Beaker of the respect and loyalty he deserved because of this flimsy chimera. How could I have been so cruel and stupid? No wonder Beaker had drifted away – he must have sensed he wasn't exactly top of my priorities, only he'd assumed it was my family that had stopped him ever really getting close to me. But it wasn't, was it? It was bloody Luke.

Why hadn't I had the strength of character to stop Luke when he kissed me? I'd known, I'd *known* it was disastrous, but that hadn't stopped me, no, not a bit. Why? I wasn't – I'm not – a stupid person, so why?

Because I was as bad as him. As bad as Tim. I'd been obsessed, too. It wasn't just a bloke thing, oh no. Nothing that easy. No wonder the Devil had smiled.

I felt nauseous with revulsion. I felt cheap, pathetic and grubby. All my idiot airy-fairy dreams lay ripped into tawdry shreds in the muck and tangle of Luke's precious little hideaway. I knew, knew in my aching bones he'd be mortified with embarrassment tomorrow, that he'd want to erase the whole thing from his memory so he wouldn't have to deal with it, like he always erased things he didn't want to think about. And he'd be scared shitless I'd make a fuss, a scene – tell his beloved Angel. God, that was a laugh! *She'd* told *me* to sleep with him in the first place – how would he like that if he knew? But there was no use telling him because he wouldn't believe me. He'd never believe anyone but Angel, that was part of her power; the ideal girl was incorruptible. It was silly bitches like me who ran around screeching and crying, who were wrong, mad, messy. Real.

The doors were open and I went out into the night.

It was still again, still and clingingly warm; the wind had died and the air was dense and heavy; it was like being wrapped in a wet woollen blanket and my lungs heaved with panic and lack of oxygen. The darkness seemed to crouch, waiting, like a great black cat about to pounce; it was like the whole earth had stopped breathing and was suspended, watching. I had to get away, get away from this mess. I was so hot, my face was burning and I felt itchy all over, fever churning through me, making my eyes unfocus.

I staggered out of the driveway and along the cliff road, my mind whirling, my breath catching like fish-hooks in my chest. It hurt to breathe. It hurt to walk: my joints were aching and my head pounding. I wanted to cry, but my throat was so swollen I felt like I'd swallowed a tennis ball and no tears would come. I almost ran down the cliff steps, nearly taking a header in the dark as my feet slid sideways out of my flip-flops, catching hold of the railing just in time and wrenching my shoulder nearly out of its socket.

In the dark, the pale wet sand glowed with a pallid phosphorescence, reflecting the few lights still on at this hour. The houses on the opposite cliff looked like those little ceramic model buildings you put tea-lights in as children's night-lights. Only they didn't comfort me, they made my chest ache with unshed tears. I looked out to sea and up at the full moon which hung livid white in the sombre sky; purplish clouds drifted across its face and disturbed the shining path of light it laid in the flat, inky, metallic sea.

I stopped at the water's edge, staring at that path of light. In my heart, I'd always been frightened of the sea – sure, I loved it, admired its untamed beauty and I'd learned to swim in it, even go out of my depth and dive down. But still I was an inlander, and deep inside, it scared me. That was one reason I'd admired Luke: he was so at ease riding on the vast, terrible chaos of the ocean that lapped so gently now at my feet. I had admired him for that, thought it made him heroic and that I was inadequate because I lacked his physical courage. I kicked my flip-flops off and walked further in, the cool water braceleting my ankles. But he wasn't brave, because he hadn't been afraid in the first place. Being brave was overcoming fear and difficulty. He'd never done that; he'd just run away into the place he'd known intimately since he was a child, into the wave's familiar embrace. I felt the sea pull at my sarong, the fabric lifting away from my knees, the water tugging at me.

I was so hot, so hot; sweat beaded on my forehead. The sea was up to my thighs now but I couldn't feel it, though I knew it must be cold. I felt a knot of emotions expanding in my head; I don't know what they were. I wanted to laugh, cry, shout and scream all at the same time, I wanted to tear the night apart and dance like a whirling dervish, tranced out with some kind of mad ecstasy. I waded further out along the moon's path, the sea moving round me slowly, with a low, dragging swell. Hadn't someone once told me it was dangerous to do this, that you got caught in the light and couldn't turn back, swimming and swimming until you drowned? Out into infinity, out into the horizon, into nothingness. Good. *Good*. Why not? Like poor, poor Dylan. Merging into nothingness, one drop of water amongst billions. Well, it didn't matter, nothing mattered anymore and in that moment of letting go I felt a fiery wave of energy surge through me and the whole of creation unfold like a rose, a crow-black rose, its dark velvet petals unrolling around me. For a split second I felt completely at one with the world, felt my place in the order of things, felt the terrible, beautiful power immanent in everything. As I held my arms up to the moon, my mouth stretched in a silent howl and that great rose bloomed in my heart and filled the night.

The sea was up to my waist, I could feel the pull of it but I kept walking, though it was harder and harder and my sarong wrapped like weed around my legs. I kept walking out along the shining path.

This was courage, Luke, I thought fiercely. Not your abdication from real life, your plaintive fantasies, your…This was real, the world was real, not a tottering construct ragged up out of shreds and tatters that you could hide in until the storm came to blow it all down, leaving you shivering and naked under the savage sky. *I* could face my fear; *I* was a fighter. I was strong, brave, I could do anything, I could…The water rolled up over my breasts making me gasp as I suddenly felt the cold and a prickle of panic sparked in my brain; this was silly, I shouldn't be here, I had to turn back, get out…And then, terrifyingly, a great wave reared up out of the black; I hadn't seen it rising in the distance, I hadn't been paying attention and that's what the sea waits for. Before I could do anything, before I even fully realised my situation, the wall of water gathered up and fell on me, and tangled in my sarong, I couldn't…Cold, cold, cold it surged over my head, in my eyes, I couldn't see, couldn't breathe, everything was grey and there was no up, no down, just this drenching grey – I couldn't – oh God, it was freezing…The water hit my fever-hot body like a sledgehammer, knocking me down, and then it was in my mouth, choking me, in my nose and…I felt it enter me, like icy fingers pushing into my body and my whole self revolted at the invasion but I couldn't…

And it was deathly chill; like a dead man's hand grasping my face the surf pushed me down again as I struggled to right myself, and

I fell, knocked over by the water's force, flailing and thrashing, my backpack turning and unbalancing me. All my childhood terrors of the sea clamoured in my panicked brain as I struggled madly against the weight of the ocean. All the monsters of legend I'd read about filled my mind with terror; slimy, unnatural creatures that writhed and tore at you until your blood bloomed red in the water like a signal flag. Mottled, fantastical fish with poisonous spines whose venom killed in an instant and huge moray eels that ripped your flesh with rows of tiny, cruel teeth; the kraken wrapping its giant tentacles round your legs and…Blind, bloated, blotched things with leprous masks that crawl up from the unknown deeps and grab you and pull you under…And the terrible sea itself; brutal rips and currents that swept you helplessly out of your depth and smashed your body on the razor-sharp rocks like a madman playing with a broken doll, tossing you around until you were a shattered, unrecognisable dead thing and fish ate out your eyes…I couldn't breathe, I couldn't…The sea boiled around me, the foam silver in the livid moonlight.

Another, bigger wave hit me, pushing me under; wipe-out, the surfers call it, the sea that rolled you off your board and held you down, filling your lungs with salt and fire until they burst – God – help, help me, so stupid – I couldn't get up and it was so cold, so cold, my brain wouldn't…

I felt sand under my hands and I clawed my way up to the shallows, the weight of my clothes dragging at me like the drowning; I threw myself forward, my legs like lead, coughing and gasping until I collapsed on the wet, hard-packed beach.

Jesus, Jesus, what had I been thinking? I looked around me at the empty strand; I could have fucking died – there was no Jim or Joey to save me from my own idiot behaviour at this time of night. What had I been doing? What? I was shaking uncontrollably, my legs trembling in long, racking spasms and I retched feebly, spitting the brine out of my mouth while strings of snot tracked down my face. I wiped the muck away angrily with a gritty hand. What the *fuck* had I been doing?

I had to get home. I had to get home. This was all a fucking nightmare; I retched again, my belly heaving. I had to get home.

Half crawling, I got myself out of reach of the sea and managed to stand up. Still shaking violently, I staggered crazily up the beach and the cut, then with useless frozen fingers I fumbled the key out of my soaking bag and fell into the kitchen, collapsing on the rug.

I was shaking in long uncontrollable waves; my teeth chattering even when I clenched my jaw hard. My feet and legs were numb up past my knees. There was no one to call for, no one to help me. I had to get warm; this wasn't a normal chill, this was bone-deep. How could I have been so stupid? I must have been mad. A small, still voice in my mind whispered, 'yes, crazy, and now you'll pay...'

I ripped my things off and got in the shower, the needles of red-hot water bouncing off my body until I yelped with pain as the feeling came back. Finally, I fell out of the cubicle, rubbed myself dry, my flesh scarlet, and crawled into bed, a damp towel round my head. My face felt raw and swollen and my hands stiff and claw-like, my legs cramping painfully. I wriggled under the quilt, rubbing my calves, trying to ease the pain, then against my will, I felt hot tears seep from my eyes and a throat-tightening ache oozed through my chest. Heartbreak; yeah, I felt broken-hearted. It wasn't rational, but then, when had I been rational or reasonable the whole night? It wasn't like Luke and I had ever gone out together, or lived together, or even actually dated; it had been a one-night stand, nothing more. *Nothing more.*

I struggled to remember that, but the layers and layers of Luke fantasies I'd lived with rose up like tattered butterflies and tangled round me, choking and confusing me. All those years of unrequited love, of what might have been if only Angel hadn't come and...Stop it. I had to stop it. I had to get real or I'd end up like Crazy bloody Tim, chittering round in ever-decreasing circles, victim of my pathetic obsession with a guy I never really knew.

But oh, it hurt, it really hurt, that brutal, crude ache of loss, even if it wasn't real; and I felt so guilty, too. I hadn't felt this bad when Beaker and I – oh, I'd been very upset, very – but I hadn't felt pain like this. And I should have, I should – Beaks was worth ten, twenty of that, that pathetic...

I fell into sleep without realising it; and that night I dreamed the recurrent nightmare that still returns even now. I dreamed I was drowning, sinking through the pale translucence of the upper waters, towards a mass of tentacled monsters that writhed and uncoiled way below in the freezing depths, their blind eyes white as dead pearls, their octopus beaks opening for me while I drifted down, down, my hands held out to my friends and family – mum, dad, Git, Lance, Cookie, Con; even Jim and Joey and Dot and Mr Eddy, everyone – who floated above me, leaning out over the sides of an old blue wooden rowing boat. They were looking for me; I could see their worried, frightened faces. They were calling for me; I could see their mouths open in silent shouts, but they couldn't see me and I couldn't call out to them, because if I did, the icy water, which was growing darker and darker, from aqua to sapphire to indigo, would finally fill my lungs, my body and I'd die.

I woke up thrashing and choking in the silent house. I clutched myself, weeping with fear. I wouldn't sleep again, I wouldn't…

Chapter 26

'Astra, Astra, love, if you're there, pick up the phone, it's Con. Astra? Oh, bugger – look, love, it's mayhem down 'ere, if you've slept in…OK, look, now I'm worried; if you're poorly, ring me as soon as you can, eh? Sorry to be snappy, it's that bloody Tim Norris, he's been on the phone all day an' night an' he's – there's been another of his letters, only this one…Never mind, I'll tell you later. Oh and if you see Piglit, can you bring him home? I must have left the kitchen door open last night after I fed him, he's gone an' got out, the silly devil, I can't find him anywhere, our lass will 'ave kittens…You ring me, love, eh? Bye-bye.'

I lay in bed listening to Con's jumpy, stressed-out voice on the answerphone. I didn't even try to get up and talk to her, I felt too bloody miserable. I'd been awake for hours, since just after dawn, turning everything over and over in my mind until it was stringy and white with handling. After the initial bout of weepy self-pity, other fears crept in with stomach-tightening horror: AIDS, VD generally, hepatitis – he'd said he'd tried all sorts of drugs, what if he'd used a dirty spike? I could have anything, I hadn't even thought of protection. Crabs. Herpes. At least I was near my period which meant pregnancy was unlikely; Jesus, *unlikely*.

I never did things like this, never, never. I was always scolding myself for being too cautious if anything. Too careful. I was the responsible one, the one in control – now I'd had my moment of bloody madness and did I feel liberated, free? Did I fuck. I felt like topping myself. If only there was someone I could talk to – someone sympathetic who'd understand. For a crazy second I thought about ringing the Samaritans, but I cut that train of thought off sharpish – what could I say, after all? 'Oh, I had a one-night stand with my friend's, no, with my, oh with someone I know's fella and now I feel like shit?' They had really fucked-up folk to deal with, never mind some silly cow chuntering on about her love-life. Once upon a time I'd have run to Con unhesitatingly. Once upon a time I'd been so close to Con I wouldn't have thought twice about telling her anything. But under the circumstances, I couldn't exactly do that, could I? I felt childish, worn out, petulant.

It made me laugh in a sour, unfunny way. More secrets. Once upon a time I'd thought I was so dull, and now I was stuffed to breaking point with secrets. I felt like my head would explode with it all and a heavy, persistent ache throbbed at the base of my skull, tightening my neck and hunching my shoulders. And it wasn't a hangover, either.

In the light of day, I knew why I'd felt so shit and been so crazy. Embarrassing though it might be to the likes of me, I'd smoked too much of that strong dope. I'd overdosed; the fever, the dizziness, the paranoia, it was typical of a hash overload. I know people say dope's 'just herbal', and you couldn't possibly OD, but that's a crock. You can get sick from too much vitamin C, for God's sake, so why not hash? Face it, it had been too much, too strong and on top of the alcohol, bingo. My only consolation was that no one had been around while I'd had my howling at the moon, druggie, near-death experience.

I crawled up and stuck my salt-water wrecked clothes, and even my backpack, into the washer. I didn't want anyone asking awkward questions. I'd lost my nice flip-flops. Just as I was making a cup of tea the family came back and I told them I was feeling flu-ey, one of those twenty-four hour things no doubt, but not to worry, I was already on the mend and after much petting and sympathising about the waste of my day off and having to look after myself, the rest of the afternoon was spent discussing mum's oxygen therapy and watching Git do fashion parades in her new kit. Personally, I liked the pink skinny-rib vest with 'This Is What GORGEOUS Looks Like' on the front in loopy glitter writing that shed sparkles everywhere if you even breathed on it. I might borrow that one. If I could get my chest into it.

Dad was the one who sussed all was not as it seemed, and he got me alone on the deck after dinner and quizzed me, but I fobbed him off with a story about missing Beaker and flu.

He sat watching me burble, his hand wrapped round his jaw. He looked so – so dad-like, I wanted to tell him everything, to have him go and sort that bastard Luke out – even though he hadn't actually done anything, I mean, nothing that I hadn't – oh, sod it. I just wanted dad to shout at him or something, defend me, but even I knew how irrational that was. I didn't say anything. Anyway, he'd never have done anything like that, it wasn't how he dealt with the world. He'd have talked seriously about karma, and forgiving myself, and allowing myself to heal. I couldn't bear it, though I knew under the hippie-speak what he really meant and he was right. But I didn't want 'right'. I wanted vengeance, which is pointless, so I wrapped my humiliation and shame up and stuck it away with my anger. I couldn't do anything else. That was life. Put up and shut up. Other people had bigger problems. Get a grip.

I nearly blew it when he hugged me, though, and mum gave me the biography of Colette she'd bought me as an unbirthday gift. I had to go to the bathroom and blow my nose loudly so they wouldn't know I'd been in there crying. They did though, they're not stupid. But they didn't say anything, just looked at me like tribal elders, waiting. If I wanted to tell, they'd listen. If not, that was OK, too. Mum and dad, mum and dad; I don't know. Love is inexplicable.

Around eight, I phoned Con. I couldn't not. I gave her the flu routine and she didn't question me, in fact, it was like she barely took it in. She sounded so awful, so distracted and miserable, I told her I'd come down and talk, rather than do it on the phone. She mumbled 'Yes, yes, OK', like she hardly heard me. I put on a thick, long-sleeved T-shirt and my dungarees and told mum and dad where I was off to.

'All right, kitten, but not for long, hmm? I don't want to, like, play the heavy father here but you're not well and…'

Joolz Denby

'Astra love, do you have to go? It's getting late and dad's right, flu can be nasty...'

They looked so sweet and concerned and I could tell they'd have loved to forbid me to go and make me have a cup of Black & Green's cocoa and straight off to beddy-byes, but they couldn't. I was too old and they were hippies.

'I won't be long, honest. She sounded so stressed out, I don't know...I'll just check up on her, see she's all right, then I promise I'll be right back.'

Con looked terrible. At least ten years older, her face drawn and pinched. She let me in, glancing round in a nervous way before locking up and hustling me up to the flat. She didn't ask me how I was, or where I'd been or anything, just went to the window and twitched the curtains together more closely and started pacing up and down.

'Did you see if he was out there?'

'Who?'

'Oh, Tim of course. That sod Tim Norris. He's been at it again, standin' out there starin' and talkin' to himself. Worse than ever. And the phone calls! You wouldn't credit the language, the threats. I've 'ad to talk to the police again. 'Ere. Look at this.'

Another Crazy Tim letter, even more deranged than usual, if that were possible. Pages of crap about Angel, and marriage and their eternal love, and how we were all in a conspiracy against them. Sentences would start and then stop for no reason, there was hardly any punctuation and he went over and over the same things like a stuck CD.

Towards the end of it he rambled on about death and how he wasn't afraid of anything and nothing would keep them apart; at first I felt a surge of concern at that, but as I reread it more calmly, the death bit didn't seem like an actual threat, more like it was on his mind, something he was picking at.

I said as much to Con. She was not impressed. 'Oh aye? Goin' on about death an' dyin' and how they'll never be parted? Sounds pretty damn threatenin' to me. You want to get your priorities sorted out, love, not be takin' his side.'

'Con, that's not fair, I'm not takin' his side, I wouldn't. You know

I wouldn't. Don't be like that, Con, please.' I was near to wishing I hadn't come. She was so upset she was lashing out at whoever was near and it wasn't like her.

She stuck her jaw out and eyed me furiously, then suddenly, she dropped on to the easy chair opposite and put her head in her hands.

'I'm sorry, I'm sorry, love. I am, I really am. I don't know what's up with me these days, I feel like...I don't know. I'm all at sixes and sevens with this devil and his goin's on. An' now I have ter get another answering machine fer this number here and get another number ex-directory for family and friends only, an' 'ave a CCTV camera an' more locks an' keep a ruddy diary of everythin' he does... The coppers say there's not much they can do unless I actually catch 'im vandalising stuff; they've helped me wi' security and they're nice about it but it's like, they know there's nowt they can do unless he does summat drastic an' I catch 'im at it. I said I'd get a restraining order, like in that mag you showed me, but they said best not, in case it meks 'im worse, annoys 'im. Annoys *him*! Oh, love, it isn't fair, it isn't. It's him as is doin' wrong, not me an' I'm the one who's payin'. I'm at me wits' end, I am. I'm that worried about our lass I...'

'Where is she, she ought to be here with you.'

'Nay, I don't want her here wi' all this goin' off. She's up at the Retreat, there's a big do, a barbecue party or somethin' this weekend, lots of celebs comin'. She's helpin' Richie, bein' a hostess, like. An' that silly bloody puppy's still missin', I can't find hide nor hair of him. Smoky's dead upset. I'm goin' to put posters up round the village, a reward an' that. I don't know, I just left the door open for a second.'

She was like an overwound watch spring. One more thing and she'd snap.

'Con, Angel – well, Angel's a big lass now, she can look after herself, in fact she ought to be looking after you a bit...'

'You don't understand, I 'ave to look after her, I 'ave to.'

'Yeah, look, I know how you feel, an' yeah, she's your sis, but...'

'No, you don't understand. She's special.'

'Well, yeah, of course she is, sisters are special...'

'No, it int that, not that. It's...I told you, when she was born, there was a – a problem. She's different than other lasses, I 'ave to protect 'er, I...'

'You mean she's still poorly – does she know? I mean, is it something she doesn't know about and...'

'Oh, she doesn't know, no one knows but me, no one.' She bowed her head as if its weight was too much for her to bear. Her neck was terribly thin and pale, and her little pony-tail stuck out in a dull, unbrushed jut, like it had been broken off short. I could hear her breathing, harsh and ragged. Then she spoke again, her voice trembling. Again, it wasn't like her at all; usually she was so steady, so calm no matter what.

'Astra love, I – you won't – you'll keep this between ourselves, like? Only if owt happens ter me, ever, you're her friend, her only... You'll look out for her, won't you?'

Everything in me said no way, no fucking way; me, look after Angel, the person who'd been the cause of so much trouble, so much disruption? But I couldn't say no, could I? I couldn't be anything except Angel's best pal, because of all those *fucking* secrets. I stuck my hands down between my thighs and clenched my fists where Con couldn't see.

'Uh, I'll do my best...'

'Good lass. You're a good lass, I knew I could depend on you, love.' She took a deep breath and looked around the little room. 'See, when she were born, as she were bein' born, she – God, she, well, she died. In the canal, comin' out, she died. She were born dead. It had been a hard birth, very hard, a long labour an' she died. The doctors were fantastic, they got her goin' again, got her breathin', resuscitated her.'

'Oh, that's awful, Con, but...' She didn't hear me.

'It were after, in the ward. There were this young lass, a new mum, Ukrainian or summat, a nice lass... We were talkin', her mum were there, this old woman all in black, traditional, old country, like. I told the girl about Angel, an' she translated to her mum an'... The old woman, her face changes, she grabs my arm and mutters at me dead fierce, an' meks the sign of the cross ovver me an'... I dint know what ter think, an' the girl is dead angry with her mum, jabberin' away in their language. I was upset an' I asked her what it were, what were wrong. She dint want ter tell me, but I made her. I wish to God I hadn't.'

'Your baby has no soul, my mother says your baby has no soul. God took your baby's soul back when she died and now she is empty and the Devil will claim her if you are not very careful. Watch her, watch over her always, she is...I am sorry, very sorry, it is all superstition, rubbish, I am very sorry.'

'Oh, Astra, Astra, I couldn't forget it, I couldn't. It preyed on my mind. My perfect baby, my Angel, my beautiful, beautiful – I couldn't forget the old woman's face and...'

It took me a moment to understand what I had heard. Oh, not the bit about Angel having no soul, though God knows that was creepy enough. It was the other thing. It sort of uncreased and unfolded in my mind like a newly hatched butterfly drying its wings; those blindingly bright wings opened and I understood. My heart thumped and a shiver ran over me. I couldn't believe I hadn't twigged before, it was so obvious – when you knew.

It was the bit where Con said 'my perfect baby'. Her baby. Her...

'Con, Angel's not your sister, is she?'

Con froze. Her face went grey with shock. I reached out and took her cold hands in mine. If it was true, if it was, then so much would be explained. Tears leaked thickly out of her wide-open blue eyes. She took a deep, shuddering breath.

'No, she int. She int. She's mine, my baby, Angel is my daughter. Oh God, oh God, oh God, no one were ever supposed ter know, I...You won't tell, you promise me, swear to me, swear you won't...'

'Of course, love, of course I won't tell. Never, I swear, I do. Oh, Con, love, oh love...'

She was weeping now, her thin shoulders shaking.

'I were so young, so young – there were a lad, you know. We – we went too far. We thought we were in love, we *were* in love but we were so young. I didn't think of getting caught out, it never crossed my mind. When I found out, it were...There was nowt to do but go on. He wanted to wed me but his parents went mad, packed him off ter relatives in Australia. He should 'ave told 'em ter go ter Hell, he should 'ave stuck by me…But he were only a lad, only young. They got 'im about as far away from me as they could, like I were a Jezebel or somethin'. But it weren't like that, it were love, an' my baby were a proper love-child. It broke my heart, him goin'. I never – I never got ovver it. Not even now. So we – mam and dad and I – we agreed that Angel should be brought up as my sister. That no one but his family an' mine should ever know. His lot were very happy to go along wi' that, very. Saved no end of scandal. An' my family – you know how our mam was. Keep everythin' in the family. Keep it contained, like. I were sent away, to a Home, it were awful, awful. The family said I was working away, at the seaside in a hotel. Mam made like she were expecting towards the end, came over to the Home, came back with a baby. Put it about it had been very unexpected, at her age, she'd thought she was puttin' on a bit of extra weight an' then oh, here's the bab. A sister for Connie. No one said owt, at least, not to us. They wouldn't have dared cross mam. But oh, Astra, oh it hurt so much, so much, ter see her grow so beautiful, so lovely an' never to be able ter be anythin' but her sister, never be her mother. So you see, I got to, got to protect her. Look after her. After what that old woman said and everythin' else…I've got to protect her…'

'Con, that – that superstition, it's not true, it's rubbish, you know that. It just stuck in your mind because of the – because you were so upset; Con, it's rubbish, it is – you poor thing, oh, Con, I feel so sorry for you, I do, love.'

We were both crying now. Proper hard sobbing, and I knelt by her chair and hugged her. She was so skinny, so burnt out, it was terrible.

Secrets. Like Cookie said, they ate you up alive. Poor Con, my poor friend. I couldn't let her down, I couldn't betray her.

So I took that secret too, and put it away with the others. They made quite a set, webbed, layered, crushed together like a fossil, living things turned to stone, dense and unyielding under pressure.

Now I could never tell Con about Angel; never. The door to that room was locked and bolted for ever. Done. Finished. Over.

I'd never felt so shit in my whole fucking life.

Chapter 27

'So that were that, done and bloody dusted. Oh, I could – I don't know what. Honestly, I dint know what to say, I were that mad. Leadin' me on all summer, makin' out like he were dead keen – ter give me a contract, that is, of course, you understand – then blowin' me out like I were nowt. So I called my Lukey here an' says, come get me now 'cos I int stayin' where I int wanted, no way. I want ter be with my friends, my real friends.'

Angel bridled furiously, her head doing that Bradford wobble, her violet eyes huge with crossness. Luke didn't take his gaze off her and nodded slightly in agreement, especially at the 'friends' bit. Irritably I wondered if he'd agree with her should she decide to set fire to the café and run naked in the streets. Probably.

He hadn't looked me in the face since they'd got in. It had been a long, tiring day in the café; one of the part-timers had gone home early because a customer had given her so much grief she'd burst into tears at the till, so the last couple of hours had been desperate. We were nearing the end of the season and believe me, tempers were shortening daily. We'd finally shut up shop and were legged out having a last coffee with Jim and Joey in attendance scarfing up the remaining buns (anything for free food) and gossiping languidly until Angel strode in and plonked herself down, demanding a double cappuccino with a shot. When I saw Luke, looking tired and sickly-pale, my stomach had turned over and I'd felt like someone had stuck a blunt knife in my heart and wiggled it around. I'd felt my hands trembling. Not good, not good at all. I'd quickly picked up a half-empty garbage bag and taken it out to the bins, where I'd stood and shook. Then I'd given myself a short, hard lecture on being stupid, and having some bloody sense, and controlling myself in front of everyone, pinched the back of my hand with enough force to make me wince, taken a deep breath and gone back in with absolutely no expression on my face.

I had so little expression Cookie stared at me and frowned, so I quickly stuck a slight smile on, like putting a sticky plaster over a graze. Being very far from dense, she still frowned, but then Smoky burbled in his playpen and chucked Mrs Cow across the room, followed by his furry stuffed lobster and some of his soft building bricks, so Cooks was distracted. I gazed at Smoky gratefully through the mesh of his playpen as he gurgled, kicked and smacked his hands. My hero.

Con had been torn between joy and worry at seeing Angel tromp into the café, trailed by Luke carrying her bags. It was so weird, seeing Con and Angel – Con and her daughter – together now I knew the truth. But also, now I did know, it seemed entirely natural; in fact, the remembrance of them together as 'sisters' seemed *un*natural; I thought of all the times Con's attitude to Angel had gone way past sisterhood and I'd thought it odd. Now I couldn't believe I hadn't sussed the truth before; it wasn't an uncommon story, after all. But there you are, sometimes you can't see the wood for the trees. I pondered on what Angel would do if she knew the sister she used and abused so blithely was in fact her mother. I'd liked to have thought she'd fall on Con's neck and weep tears of joy, but maybe it would be too much of a shock, make her feel she'd been deceived all her life, that she'd been living a lie and she'd hate Con for not telling her. That pulled me up short – was that why Con was so afraid of telling her? Was she terrified her adored Angel would reject her, despise her?

Locked in that unsettling thought, I found myself staring blankly at Luke. I looked away quickly. I didn't care what he thought of me now the first shock of seeing him was fading but I didn't want him to think I was yearning over him or anything. I glanced back and saw he looked embarrassed and slightly desperate, pleading almost. I knew that more than anything in the world at that moment he wanted me not to say or do anything; not to exist, if at all possible. I felt my jaw harden and a trickle of nastiness creep into my blood; *go on,* it said, *go on. Make a big scene. Ruin the spoilt rich kid's day. Don't let him get away with it. Fuck him up.* I opened my mouth and – nothing came out. I couldn't do it, it just wasn't me.

Anyway, a scene would accomplish nothing more than a momentary revenge trip and it would upset Con and everyone else. Worse, it would mean everyone would know I'd dropped my knickers for Angel's property. Second-hand goods. And what would I shout and bawl at him? 'You called her name when you came, you bastard.' Very nice, I'd look very nice then, eh? I searched around in my heart to hate him, to feel a good, clean blast of unalloyed hatred, but I couldn't. If anything, I pitied him, because whatever few seconds of discomfort I could cause him in order to alleviate the pain of my crushed pride would be as nothing to what Angel was going to do to him at some point.

He looked up and caught me staring; I didn't drop my gaze this time and it was his turn to look away. Something tiny glinted near his eyebrow, by his temple. Blue hair glitter. I bet that stuff had taken some getting rid of.

Disgusted with myself, I threw my dishcloth to Cookie, who caught it neatly and put it in the laundry bin. Her back was as stiff as a board and it didn't take a clairvoyant to see how much she liked Angel's return to the fold. Con had taken Smoky out of his playpen and dandled him lovingly on her knee, smelling the top of his head, inhaling that incredible perfume of healthy baby. She and Luke were united in the gaze-at-and-adore-Angel club. At least she had good reason; well, sort of. I mean, under the circumstances I was more willing to forgive Con.

Git, who'd come down to 'get me' as she put it, or in fact to scrounge a treat, slurped her banana and vanilla smoothie and bounced in her seat rapturously, her ringletty high bunches jiggling, and so excited she nearly knocked over Dot's coffee.

''Ere, easy does it, dear,' complained Dot mildly, as Jim and Joey snickered and slurped their lattes.

'Git – Gita, careful, please.' I sounded more annoyed than I actually felt and Git's face momentarily clouded. But not for long, she was too ecstatic.

'Mega-soz, Dottsie, but Angel, Angel – what about your record, what about Richie? What about the barbie? Did Kylie...'

Angel leaned back and looked somewhat smug. 'Well, like I always say, it don't pay ter put all yer eggs in one basket, know what I mean? Mr Big Shot Richie Lomas might think running off back ter London just because Grandma's gone and died is goin' ter put the mockers on my plans, but that just shows how wrong he is, don't it?'

She smirked triumphantly. I stared at her, aghast. 'Angel! You mean, his mum's died? You can't...'

'Oh, not *his* mum, I int that awful. *Her* mum. The wife's.' She looked at me in a mildly aggrieved way, as if I foolishly thought badly of her. Only the wife's mother. The children's nana. Oh, *that's* OK, then.

'See, now she's all ovver the phone carryin' on about how upset she is an' how the kiddies are missin' daddy – all of a sudden. Not that she give a toss before, like. So, now – 'ere Astra, you'll remember this fella – Naz Singh, he were at that gig, your Beaker's gig...'

'Tony. He's called Tony now.' Cookie and I exchanged glances.

'Whatever. But you remember Naz – hair to here,' she indicated her shoulders with the side of her hand. 'All in black rubber – dead skinny...'

For a minute I didn't have the faintest clue who she was on about, then it clicked. She'd been talking to a bloke fitting that description at the fateful Element gig. It was typical of Angel that she wasn't in the least embarrassed at bringing all that up. Git had gone pink – with shame at the memory, I hoped severely; but it was excitement, more like. Her goddess had returned to her, ten times as fabulous as before.

'Er, yeah, I remem...'

'Thought you would. Very strikin' is our Naz. He's a Bradford lad y'know, from up Manningham way. Been in London for years though, o'course. Well, he owns Guava Groove, the club label? Put out Bloocreme's last thing, that chill track with Queen Janxie? Oh well, never mind...So, he goes, come see me when you're in Town and we'll do some demos! Yeah, it's true! He's dead keen, really up for it – I've got me contract!'

She beamed at us. The wattage of that smile could have illuminated a small country. Yet again, that weird thing happened and she seemed momentarily to absorb all the light in the café and glow with a golden incandescence.

'Oh, Angel, how fantastic! Oh, you're gonna be a big star an' be on telly, an' do videos an' go to clubs an'...' Git was beside herself.

'That's right, love. An' when I do, I'll let you come an' watch, how's that?' Angel looked at me and smiled, patting Git's flying cinnamon curls. I smiled back. Not, I hasten to add, that I believed a fucking word of what she said. The demos – oh, sure. How many pretty girls got offers to do demos for clubland? Hundreds, I bet. It sounded so great, but I knew from Beaker and his 'music industry' stuff exactly what demos meant – zilch. Record companies threw money around like water; what sounded like a huge sum to us plebs was peanuts to them. They'd send darling Ange into a studio for a couple of days and if they didn't like the resulting tapes, or thought she wasn't saleable they'd simply chuck it all in the bin and wave a fond ta-ta. I'd be more impressed when I saw her on 'Top of the Pops' – *if* I ever did. And as for taking Git to see her strut her stuff – well. I think not.

But I smiled. Not for her, for my little sister. So she wouldn't think her deity had feet of clay. And for Luke. I would rather have been dead in my grave than give him the satisfaction of seeing me upset. That's wrong, though, because he wasn't 'satisfied', he wasn't anything regarding me; since I hadn't, like, bitten him or anything directly I saw him, he'd relaxed, he thought he was safe. He was safe, but not for any of the reasons he must be thinking. I could see his face had smoothed over and that I barely existed anymore except as an accessory to his beloved – oh, whatever. I wouldn't let him see me upset, for my own reasons. I watched him curiously; didn't he hear what Angel was saying? Wasn't he upset about the way she talked about Richie, or this Naz fella, or her ambitions? His face was full of blind devotion. I didn't know what he was hearing but whatever it was, it didn't disturb his obsession one jot. I remembered his idea that Angel would be a force for good with her music career. Maybe that was what he was thinking of. Something that fitted with his vision of Angel, something comforting. God help him.

'Sorry about Piglit, Angel,' I said, looking at Smoky.

'Pigsie – oh, I know – what has he done wi' himself, I'd like ter know? Silly little devil, honest…'

'I seen them wanted posters you put up round the village, Connie dear,' interjected Dot comfortably. 'But it woan do no good, my dear. E's bin dognapped, 'e 'as, poor liddle beast. Gorn God alone knows where. Mrs Liddicoate says 'ow as there's a ring o' them dognappers at work round 'ere – pedigrees they'm after, see, sells 'em on the Continent. She's worried about 'er Beauty. Keeps 'er locked up at night on account of it.'

Helplessly, we all burst out laughing at the thought of fat, mangy old Beauty being white-slaved to foreign parts – all of us except Angel, that is, who never got a joke.

'It's no good you all laughin', you mark my words, you'll not see that liddle fellow again,' Dot huffed.

'Stop it now, you lot, you'll upset the boy. Aye, I do wonder – mebbe Dot's right, mebbe some tourists took 'im. I call fer 'im every night before I go to bed, but I don't know…Poor little dog, poor silly little pup, eh, Smoky? Never mind, precious, he'll come home soon,' Con said, bouncing Smoky and kissing the top of his head. 'If he don't, well, Santa might bring a good lad another little friend, eh? Eh? Oh, well – nay, it's all right, you go on, Cookie, get goin' now – have a nice day off.' Monday was Cookie's day off and I could see by her face she was looking forward to it.

Cooks picked up her stuff and settled Smoky, who was getting flushed and cranky from wanting his nap, into the pushchair. I walked out after her, casually, while the Angel fan-club talked excitedly about their heroine's upcoming life as a pop diva.

Outside, we did our now usual Crazy Tim check. He wasn't evident so we relaxed a bit.

'I reckon 'e's got them binocliers, I do,' said Cookie gloomily. It made me jump, hearing her voice my worry about Tim. 'I bet 'e's up there now, spyin'.' She pulled the tattered broderie anglaise sun canopy of the rickety pushchair further down to shade the sleepy boy's face. 'Well, if you're there, Mr Crazy Fella, this is fer you.' And she stuck her pointed pink tongue out in the general direction of the cliff.

'Cookie!'

'Well, I'm sick of 'im an' 'is goin's on, I am. About the same as I'm sick of 'er. Madam. Records indeed. Load o' rubbish. I doan believe a word.'

'Funny, I thought that. Well, she'll be off soon, very soon, I should think. Then we can forget it all, eh?'

'Not 'im.' She gestured at the cliff. ''E won't forget. Not that 'un. It's locked in 'is 'ead, it's 'is whole life. What'll 'e do when Madam goes, I wonder?'

She smiled her tiny, barely visible smile and stomped off across the beach for the bus with her son.

I was about to go back in and get my stuff when Angel ran out and grabbed my arm, then pulled me further down the beach conspiratorially.

'Ow – Angel – what...'

'Sorry. I don't want anyone listenin' in, get it? Right, look, Astra love, did you know how rich Lukey-boy is? Did yer?'

I did, but I didn't want her to know I did, so I made a non-committal shrug and looked innocent.

'Well, he's fuckin' loaded! I mean, I knew 'e were wealthy, he 'ad to be the way 'e lives, but I 'ad no idea...I thought 'e were just a rich-kid surfer, a bum, you know.' Her voice sank to a hushed whisper. ''Is dad's only a fuckin' millionaire, like, a real one, not a Lottery one. Prob'ly 'e's a multi-millionaire. A billionaire. More than that, even. Proper money. 'Is dad owns whole companies, all ovver the world. 'E told me on the way 'ere. Weird though, 'e seemed dead worried about it, like it were a crime or summat, like I'd be put off 'im on account of it, said he was sorry an' would I still like 'im – *like* 'im! Can yer credit that? Mind, I allus had a soft spot fer 'im, dint I? D'you remember our little chats about 'im, how gone on 'im I were – well, if we'd known! God, I wouldn't 'ave bothered wi' that ugly little sod Richie, not fer a second. We're off up to 'is London place – his London place mind! – so I can go see Naz straight off, strike while the iron's hot, like. I couldn't stop here much longer anyways – I don't know how you stick it, I don't. I mean, don't get me wrong, it's grand fer two weeks, if you like it quiet, but God, it's that borin'. Nowt ter do but stare at the bloody sea, eh? Still, you don't mind, you, with yer nose in a book all the time – 'ere, you'll come visit us, won't yer? We'll 'ave a real time, go out, get yer fixed up nice – yer will, won't yer? Promise?'

She nodded vigorously, her earrings sparking deep blue in the dying sun. Our little chats about Luke. How gone on him she'd been. Right. A tight feeling banded my chest and I could feel something hot and dark welling up in my throat…

Then it happened so quickly; I was so caught up in trying to control the bile that had risen in my craw I couldn't take it in. Out from behind the lifeguard's hut in a flurry of sand, Crazy Tim staggered across the beach towards us, a pair of binoculars bouncing against his bony chest. He looked like a caricature of himself, like a cruel cartoon. I saw him from the edge of my vision, like one of those floaters that crawl in your eyes and you see, but don't see.

Angel saw him at the same time I did, and with a gasp, she turned on her heel and ran into the café, slamming the door shut behind her.

I was too slow; my desire for vengeance had tripped me up. He thrust himself up to me and I recoiled instinctively; as I did, I saw a mass of seagulls blister up from behind the café where the bins were, and the air was filled with their screaming.

Tim looked like Hell; like someone in Hell. His face was shredded with sunburn, burning red and blotched with white dead skin; his hair was torched to stiff, desiccated straw. He was unshaven and a scrubby, greyish beard worked its way through his scoured pores. His clothes, the clothes he'd bought so proudly to impress Angel, were patinated with dirt and he stank of sour, unwashed body odour and a repulsive undersmell of old piss.

Hand to my mouth, I tried to side-step him and get to the café, but he blocked my way; I was about to shout for help but he stuck his face close to mine, his watery, red-rimmed eyes crusty with sand and pus from his burned and irritated conjunctiva. His breath was rank and my stomach turned as he hissed at me, his face like some terrible tribal mask; a ghost mask, a dust devil totem.

'What did you say, *what did you say to her?* What did you say to make her run away from me? What? What? You dirty bitch, you fat, dirty – you can't keep us apart anymore you know, you can't…'

'Get the fuck away from me, get – Tim, get out of my way…'

'Oh no, oh no, not until I know what filthy lies you've been…'

I knew then he was quite mad. It was in his face that writhed like a bowl of maggots; it was in his body, twisted into strange and unnatural angles by the stress of his insanity and obsession. I felt very afraid, genuinely afraid in a way that doesn't happen to you often in real life; my legs went jellyfied and a sickening quiver ran through my body. I knew in that moment that he was beyond all hope and reason and I tried again to dodge past him. I had an instinctive horror of him grabbing or even touching me. I just wanted to get away from him and I silently cursed Angel for running off and leaving me. I could see people on the beach around us turning away; gathering up their children. I knew why they were doing it: they didn't want to be infected by Tim's wrongness, didn't want to get involved, but it drove me frantic.

And then, he started weeping. Raw, pain-filled sobs wracked his emaciated frame and juddered through him. He covered his face with his ruined hands, the hands that had been so white and well cared for when he'd seemed to us to be an ordinary businessman with a good reputation, and tears leaked out from the bony cage of his fingers. A wet, tearing, gulping sound came from him and though I was still jumping with adrenalin and fear of him, I felt suddenly, desperately, horribly sorry for him as I had so often before. It was a nauseating, confusing mix of emotions, and my insides lurched.

'Tim, Tim, stop it, stop. Go home, Tim, go home – go on, it's no good, you know that really, don't you? It's got to stop, all this, it's…'

'NO NO NO NO NO NO – shutupshutupshutup you disgusting – you – shutupshutup – ohhhhh Angel, my Angel, my Angel, my love, my love, Angel…You! You – I'll – you – what did you say? *What did you say to make her go?* She loves me, she loves me, it's you filthy lot that's keeping us apart, you...'

It was a howl an animal would make, not a human; I stumbled back away from it, my pity gone, and I tried to run round him but he grabbed my arm, in just the same place Angel had. Despite the state of him, or maybe because of it, he was strong, his hand like a hook of steel wire. I yanked away from him, nearly falling, stumbling and tripping, desperate to get away from him.

He scrabbled to get me again and succeeded in catching hold of the hem of my T-shirt; I twisted and hauled at it, sweating and terrified.

'Let go! *Let go* – Tim, fuck – let fucking go! Jesus, Tim, Angel's going away anyhow, do you hear? She's off to London tomorrow, she's going, this is fucking stupid, let go, let go of me...'

He dropped his hands as if I were poison. His head twitched towards me as I stood, frozen by the hideous state of him.

'Liar.' He was unnaturally calm; his voice would have passed for normal if you hadn't had him in front of you. The screeching, manic sound of the gulls overhead seemed to fill every particle of air with noise. His sudden stillness threw me and we stared at each other, standing face to face in a bizarre second of silence.

'I'm – I'm not lying. I'm – she's going, Tim; Jesus, you – you've got to see the doctor, get some help, it's – it's all over now, Tim, you...'

He whirled round and stamped off across the beach, scattering tourists who tried not to look at him, yet stole covert glances at his arrhythmic, gaunt figure as he ploughed through the sand. He looked like a revenant, like crazy, clockwork death. I felt dizzy and sick and staggered slightly, just as Joey caught me against his chest.

'Jeez, Aas, Jeez, you all right? I saw – fuck, he's nuts, man – you all right? Here, I'll, lean on me, I'll take you to the café; come on, I've got you now, you're safe.'

I leaned into him, weak with gratitude. All the strength had gone out of me and he half carried me to the café, murmuring nothingey comfort things to me, as he would to a child he'd pulled out of the rip. Bless him, he was almost more upset than me. I realised the whole scene had taken less than a couple of minutes though I'd felt it had gone on for hours. I was exhausted. Numbly, through the open door, I watched the gulls landing on the sand like white ash from a bonfire drifts down to the floor.

'I've got her, it's OK – the mad bastard – here, sit down, Aas, you sit down – Angel said you was just comin' but next thing – we saw him grab you…Jeez, should we get the cops, Con? Should we – don't you worry, he can't hurt you now, he – should we ring the cops, Con? I mean…'

Everyone – except Angel, Luke and Con – was out of their seats, rushing round me and all talking at once, their faces incredulous and bug-eyed with horror. Dot shoved a cup of lukewarm tea at me with the blind instinct of her generation and Git flung her arms round me, nearly suffocating me, her soft, round child's face scarlet with concern and a fierce protectiveness.

'Astra, Astra, I'm here, I'm here, he won't, I won't let him – Astra, you all right? You all right? Promise? Promise? Oh, I hate him, I hate him, the pig monster bastard…'

'It's OK, Git, I'm OK, really, love, I'm fine now – go on, love, go on, pet, it's OK.'

'What about the coppers – oh, well, if you – are you sure?' Joey looked faintly cheated he couldn't summon the cavalry.

'No, Joey, no. I'm OK, I'm – don't worry. Thank you, thank you, mate; honest, I don't – thanks.' I kissed his cheek and he flushed like a girl – or at least his sunburn deepened a shade or two.

I looked over at Con. It was her voice I wanted to hear but she was grey and silent, her hands working together convulsively.

Angel stuck her jaw out and glared righteously at the beach, then back at me. 'Are you all right, love? Honest, I thought you was just behind me, I dint know 'e'd got yer. Mad bastard is right; thank God I'm out of it.'

As she went on about how pissed off she was, I glanced at Con again, then looked away. It was obvious Angel had told her she was off while I was being harangued by Tim; it would be why no one had come out to help me, and anyway, it had been so quick, really. Con looked – beaten. Despite feeling horribly wobbly, I felt a spurt of joy.

Angel gone, Luke gone. Result. Now Con and I could get back to how we were. She'd be all right, I'd look after her, get her right again. There was that winter holiday, too – well, we deserved it, God knows.

I came to and realised Angel was asking me something; next to her, I saw that Git was on the point of tears, her glossy pink mouth pouting, her eyes tragic. It struck me she must have just realised Angel was going away, probably for good. It hadn't registered in her living-in-the-moment teenage mind before. Jesus, she'd be heart-broken. It was all very well talking about exciting records and clubs but the fact was that it meant her adored Angel would actually have to leave Polwenna.

'Astra – Astra! I was sayin', thank God Joey saw yer, eh? What did that nutter say ter yer? Did yer tell 'im I were off, like? Good, I'm glad yer did. Bastard. That'll put a kink in his tail. But yer OK now, int yer, a big strong lass like you? No need fer coppers or owt, eh? No need fer hassle. Look, I'm goin' ter start packin' me stuff so – you'll be round tomorrow? We'll 'ave a nice natter before I go, eh?' She winked at me, then glanced at Luke, giving him the full force of her violet gaze, pouting a little 'secret' smile at him, her body language radiating sexuality, the light from the windows haloing her platinum hair, gilding her body. Obviously, he was in her good books nowadays. Oh, surprise, surprise. He looked like a believer at the gates of Heaven. Then she flipped some internal switch to 'off' and stood up, all business. 'Luke! Bring that bag up for us, will yer, love? See yer then, all!'

And she sashayed out, followed by Luke toting her bags again. I sighed and hung on to the thought that she was going; she was going and everything would go back to normal. I saw Git get up as if to follow them, but I put my hand on her arm to stop her. She tried to pull away but I held on. I could feel how upset she was, but I didn't want her snuffling round Angel, I wanted her to come home. Dot was bustling about with her things and Con still stood like a block of wood, radiating misery.

'Con, Con, are you all right? Con?' I wanted her to speak to me; I think more than anything, I wanted her to acknowledge the nastiness of what had just happened to me. But it was no use, she was locked into the groove of Angel's leaving.

She blinked and looked at me. 'Me? Yes, yes, of course I am. I'm sorry, sorry about…' She gestured wanly at the beach. 'It's not your – you shouldn't 'ave been involved like that. I'm sorry.'

'Oh, I…'

Joey cut in. 'D'you want me to take you guys up to yours?' He was hovering solicitously; obviously he thought his Sir Galahad impression had finally secured him an in to my affections. It had, but not in the way he hoped. I smiled at him tiredly, the moment of reaching out to Con gone. Tomorrow though; tomorrow I'd definitely have a proper chat with her, get things more sorted. I felt incredibly tired. Tomorrow. Yeah. Poor old Con, she must be so blue. I smiled at her, but she didn't see, she was a million miles away.

'Nah, thanks anyway, Joey – and thanks for, you know. Git, come on; no, come on now, let Con lock up. You can see Angel tomorrow; yeah, I know but…'

She broke away from me and rushed out of the door, slamming it behind her. I sighed. Fasten your seatbelts, we were in for a bumpy night.

'Oh dear,' said Dot, meaningfully. 'What a day, really. Thank goodness Cookie weren't 'ere, is all I can say – you'd a' seen fireworks then, I can tell yer. Well, see everyone termorrer, nighty-night.'

'Night, Dot, love. ' I picked up my bag. Con was still standing by the counter, silent. I went to her and took her hand in mine. It was cold, clammy almost; the knuckles reddened with the day's labour, the skin loose and getting crepy. She was growing older ten years to a minute with all this trouble; you could see it in that sad, worn hand. I tried one last time.

'Con, I…'

'Wha – oh, night, Astra love. Mind you get some rest,' she said mechanically and turned away, pulling her hand from mine. For a crazy split second, I wanted to grab it back, to hang on to her, but obviously, I was overtired, done in. What would she have thought of me? I let her go.

Sighing, I went out, trudging round and up the cut. I felt like death warmed over. Tim's gabbling, destroyed face kept rising up in my mind like a ghost; I could see his blistered mouth working, trying to speak to me, but I couldn't hear what he was saying and I didn't want to. I shuddered. Poor Crazy Tim. Ugh. There but for the grace of God go I, and all that. What on earth would become of him now his perfect love was leaving? Another nervous breakdown, probably, and off to the Bin. Poor bugger. Oh, I was tired, bone tired. Maybe I was worn out generally. I thought longingly about the winter holiday. Spain? The Canaries? Perhaps somewhere more exotic; I'd heard you could go to Cuba pretty reasonably these days on a package. Cuba! Now, that'd be something. I'd mention it to Con, get some brochures, get her interested again. It would give her a distraction, take her mind off Angel.

I stopped and took a deep breath – the escallonia smelt glorious. Home had never seemed so welcoming, even though I knew Git would be throwing wobblers all night and would have already delivered a highly coloured account of the day's happenings to mum and dad, which I'd have to smooth over. It didn't matter, though. Things were looking up, Angel was going and everything would be all right. Git would be upset for a while, but when school started again, and she had things to do, she'd eventually get over it. She was so young and kids that age are very resilient. I'd try extra hard with her, too, I would. Make it up to her, the little scrap.

Yeah, I could fix everything, as long as I was calm and steady. I always had fixed everything before, that was what I did. Organised stuff, sorted things out. It might not be exciting or romantic or sexy, but it was a kind of talent, or perhaps a minor virtue, like my reading. I liked helping, being useful, being needed. Nothing wrong with that. Despite everything, despite the shock of the thing with Tim, and seeing Luke and all the crap stuff that had happened, I felt happy as I walked between those high, scented bushes towards my home; quietly happy. It would be all right.

We'd come through, all of us. Everything was going to be OK.

Chapter 28

'Well, you girls are up extra bright and early. The sun is barely up and my daughters are out of their boudoirs bouncing around full of the joys of – well, summer. Normally – I say, *normally* – your poor old dad has to breakfast all alone these days. Wow, maybe the sky is falling, or pigs flying – shall I check, hmm?'

'Oh, poor old dad, so hard done to, honestly. I just couldn't sleep, that's all, it's too hot. God, I wish this weather'd break, don't you? I hate it, it's my worst type of hotness, so muggy. Anyway, we left the café in a right tip last night so I thought I'd get there early, start putting it in some kind of shape before we open, give Con a break, you know.'

'Well, that's a nice thought, but go easy, eh, kitten? You don't look like you're totally over that flu to me, don't take on too much. What's mum's plan today, do you know?'

'Belly dancing and then reiki – I've arranged to pop up and see her before she goes, check the taxi comes. He was nearly quarter of an hour late last time, she missed the start of her class and...'

'Astra, Astra, can I have...'

'You can have whatever you like, *Gita*, as long as you get it yourself.'

'Ooo, Mrs Grumpypants.' She got up with a flourish of her ringlets and fetched herself a bowl of Granola, her face smooth, clear and untouched by the early hour. I looked at her as she floated by, chattering about how she was going to spend the whole day with Angel, and how she was going to visit her in London and go shopping, and how Angel said some girls her age were already models working for *Vogue* and since she'd never had spots, unlike poor, poor Marnie, and her hair was a very fashionable colour these days, well...She could get some photos taken (Angel knew someone) and be a...

'Yeah, we know, a supermodel.'

'Well, why not? You look at of some of 'em an' they doan look no better'n me, they doan.'

'Not much of a life, though, kitten, modelling. Very superficial, being judged by your looks. Better to stick at your studies, eh? I would think there's more to it than just being photographed. I mean, long hours, very tiring; not healthy, like, mentally or physically.' Dad nodded sagely, like a vast Yoda.

'Da-*ad*. School? How yesterday is that? No one needs *school* anymore, please. There's computers now for *everythin'*. Angel left soon as she could, and look at 'er. School, yuk, stupid. Gross. Skanky, skanky schoo-*ul*.'

'Gita, enough now. Eat your cereal before it goes soggy – yes – and before you throw it away and get more – you do, come on, eat. Tea, dad?'

'Oh, yes, thank you, hon. Here, girls, look at this, they finally sent me the info – bond-on tooth jewellery, what d'you think of that? Gold stars and hearts, and Austrian crystals, the latest thing. Bonds to your tooth, no harm done, very trendy. Would you like some? You'd be doing me a favour, I need a couple of guinea pigs.'

'Oh, dad, dad, dadd-eeee, please, please! Astra, you too, oh, go on, you could have a star, look, a star – like Luke calls you! Oh dad, please!'

Like Luke calls me; not anymore, ha ha. I quickly supped my tea and fled discreetly to the bathroom, where I snuffled pathetically and self-pityingly for a moment, then washed my face and flung on my dungarees. As I wrenched the brush through my incipient dreadlocks, I noticed the topaz earrings, and, shaking the dust-fuzz off them, stuck them in my pocket. This time I'd definitely return them and if she wouldn't take them back, I'd give them to Oxfam; at least there they'd do some good. I went out, pecked dad on the head, and volunteered for a *trendy* gold tooth star. What the heck, why not?

'Astra, can I come with you? I wanna show Angel this tooth jewellery stuff, see if she thinks it's cool. Can I come? I'll help with the tidying, I will, honest.'

'Gita, she won't be up yet – she doesn't – oh, OK, don't pout like that, you're not a kid. Come on though, I want to get sorted before I come back up for mum; Git, come *on*.'

It was deadly humid outside; out to sea black thunderheads were massing, outlined in molten gold. The light had that overheated, unnatural look, making the colours dark and bright at the same time. Rays of sun, like God's pointing finger, shone through the clouds and the sea was flat calm, a dull greyish green shot with dirty turquoise; soupy-looking. There was no one on the beach this early, except an old couple strolling at the water's edge. Couldn't sleep probably, like me. No surfers – there was no surf, again. At least Con would be up; she was always up and doing by six, even on holidays. I'd have to break her of that habit when we went away, definitely. I wondered absently if she'd fancy America – maybe Florida or a fly-and-drive to California. Not that I'd turn my nose up at the Canaries, or even Spain – yeah, Spain would be great. Con and I could check out dad's family's area, in the mountains near Marbella, that'd be fun, maybe I'd find some relatives and...

My T-shirt was sticking to me before we got to the bottom of the cut and sweat beaded my hairline. I stopped to twist my pony-tail up higher, coiling my hair into a knot off my neck. Not a breath of wind stirred. If it was like this now, what on earth would it be like at noon? Perhaps the storm would break by then, give us some relief from this awful heaviness. I thought of the café and how hot it would be in the kitchen – phew, Jesus, I was not looking forward to it at all.

Git was chattering ten to the dozen, but lost in formless, drifting thoughts, I didn't really hear her; it was like that with kids sometimes, you umm'd and oh-yes'd in vaguely the right places but you didn't really listen. She was going on about her modelling career, which mostly seemed to consist of her lording it over Marnie and the gang and dressing up all day long. I looked at her as we crossed the sand: leggy, pretty, cute with her pink hipster short-shorts and sparkly 'GORGEOUS' vest, the one that made me smile. Her high bunches were held up by elastics adorned by fabric and feather-frond roses, and more fake flowers were on her flip-flops. Glitter twinkled on her pale, red-head's arms. The whiteness of her reminded me to get more total sun-block; you could still burn through this cloud, and Git could burn in January. We used gallons of it on her every year. I put it on my mental list along with spinach and milk.

She was still chattering as we got to the kitchen door of the café, scaring a contingent of scavenging gulls, who took flight and fluttered down again on the car park resentfully. I told Git to wait a minute outside until I saw Con, not to go tearing in yelling for Angel, who'd still be asleep, and annoying Con with her ruckus. Secretly, I didn't want Git's teenage tactlessness upsetting Con, who no doubt would be feeling miserable thinking of Angel's imminent departure. I wanted Git to take it easy, so I made her promise to be quiet and wait a minute, then help Con and me until Angel appeared, whatever time that might be and reluctantly, she agreed. She could make Dot's and the part-timers' morning coffees too, and as Cookie wasn't here today, help Con cook. Pouting again, she scuffed the toe of her flip-flop in the dust, looking hard done to, though actually I knew she loved playing with the Gaggia. I felt like the world's hardest cow, but I couldn't have her rushing about shrieking, as I knew she would left to herself.

I tried the door handle; it wasn't locked so Con must be up and about. I went in.

Now, I find it hard to exactly remember it all. I know the blinds were down and the sun through the orange fabric cast a thick, amber light on everything. I think it was the smell that hit me first; like dirty copper money, metallic, sickening – it wrapped itself round my face like a filthy cloth, it seemed to coat inside my nostrils.

There was blood all over the room, you see; all over. Sprays of blood spattered the walls as high as the ceiling; it hung in ropey congealed lumps from the handles of the units; it had dribbled and dried on the surfaces; and the floor…

The floor was one great pool of clotted, sticky, blackening blood, and I had walked into it, was standing in it.

And in that stinking, disgusting mess lay a lump of butchered meat so hacked and cut about, so mutilated and torn that only by the strands of coppery hair and the blood-soaked clothes did I recognise it as my friend. As Con. Con. *Con.* Her face was gone, her sweet tomboy face was gone into a raw mass of hacked flesh; her far-seeing blue eyes were slashed across over and over; the cuts layered so close together it looked like she'd been bandaged in blood and scored flesh. Blindfolded. She was blind now, her eyes destroyed so they couldn't see the man who had done this to her, who had cut and stabbed at her over and over as she tried to defend herself, who had stuck the knives he pulled from the knife-block into her so hard the broken blade of one glinted from her chest; who had nearly cut off her face in his frenzy.

The man who lay beside her, toppled over from a sitting position on to the floor. Tim Norris, a hole in the side of his neck, sliced into his neck like you'd cut into the Sunday joint. His face was away from me, but he lay there, with that obscene hole in him, like a yellowey wax doll, like a dummy, empty now and saturated in the glutinous clabber of blood that had drained out of him and spread over the floor to Con. Her blood and his, mingled, indissoluble; how she'd hate that, how she'd hate…

A kind of dazzling wave drenched me; dark and dazzling as when you look too long into the sun. It shorted through me, electric and deathly. I was ripped out of my paralysis by it, my mind wrenched into understanding, to comprehension of the thing I was seeing. I felt myself take a step back, out of the blood, out of the stench, I heard the drone of flies and saw them walking over the bodies on the floor, walking black and shiny into Con's pitiful, awful wounds. I felt my mouth stretch open of its own accord and my throat fill with screaming but before I…

'Is she up yet? Astra, is she up? Angel – An-*gel*!'

Too slow, too slow, caught in the terrible clinging web of shock, I tried to turn and block the door. I tried to stop her but she ran past me, bright and joyful, full of excitement, the sheaf of papers in her hand.

Git ran past me and into the middle of the kitchen. She tried to stop at the same instant I started towards her but momentum and that congealing, viscous pool on the floor caught her, and her feet in the flimsy flip-flops slipped and went out from under her. Before I could grab her she fell.

It was like a terrible piece of slow-motion from a film; I saw her bright hair fly up, I saw her arms flailing, the papers flying away, her eyes stretched open in horror as she twisted to catch hold of the units and failed, as she fell on to the body of the man on the floor, her face a centimetre from that dreadful gaping hole in its neck; then as I staggered to her I saw her roll and scrabble away from it, pushing at the lifeless thing that groaned aloud when she shoved at it, air escaping from its dead lungs in a horrifying imitation of life that made my whole body leap in terror, and my heart pound wildly out of control, my pulse deafening. I saw Gita's mind tear across like a ripped leaf at that unliving moan, the noise that issued from her mouth was like a curdled animal bleat: '*mummummummyohmummyastrahelpmehelpm eeeeeee*'. It wasn't a scream, it was nothing like a scream, it was a dense, garbled prayer to the ruin of her childhood, her innocence, her spirit. I saw her frantic, frantic, as she turned and saw the other body, as she understood who it was; that the mangled thing was her beloved Auntie Con. Then I saw her finally stop, on her hands and knees, her mind gone, in that sump of blood gleaming with broken knives.

Her head was up. Her eyes were completely empty, the pupils expanded into calamitous, devouring darkness.

It was so slow, everything was so slow; it was like drowning, just like when I'd thought I was drowning, I couldn't move.

But I had to, I had to get my baby out of there, I had to. I felt the effort of will that powered my movement like a huge grinding of rusted gears; I had to *move*.

A roaring filled my brain, a sundering crash, and I reached across and grabbed her awkwardly by the arm, dragging her to me, holding her to me as I flung us both out into the daylight, slamming the door to that horror shut behind us. She was like the dead herself, her eyes still wide and filled with that awful nothing, her mouth open, her body in my arms rigid.

I didn't know what to do, I didn't know what to do. Nothing made any kind of sense, nothing fitted anymore, and the daylight seemed unreal and ridiculous, like a bad joke. I brushed her hair off her clammy forehead, tried to wipe her face, wipe the blood off her face as I'd so often wiped her face before, but the stuff just smeared and my hand was shaking so much. I know I called her name over and over, called her my love, my baby, my precious. She didn't hear me. She didn't hear anything, not Dot and the girls who had arrived for work and were screaming at the sight of us, not Mr Eddy shouting he'd called the police, not Jim and Joey sobbing like children and vomiting uncontrollably after they opened the door and looked inside. Not even the poor florist's delivery man, with the red rose trembling in his hand and his face as white as a sheet as he mumbled over and over 'What's goin' on? What's goin' on?'

She heard none of it, none. Gita, Gita – my sweetheart, my little girl; the flame of her hair clotted with reeking muck, her pure, child's face like a marble angel on a grave, sightless and filthy; my sister, cold and stiff as I held her closely to me, trying to give her the warmth of my body.

I should have stopped her, I should have yelled out for her to stay outside, to run over to Mr Eddy; I should have saved her. It was a hideous litany, squealing in my heart, over and over. I should have saved her from this horror and I didn't. I didn't. *I didn't.*

The police came very fast, I'm told; to me it seemed like hours. There were lots of them, surrounding the café, on the beach, keeping people back, looking strained and upset under their official, dutiful masks. With their arrival we could put ourselves away from it a little, give it over to them. I took Git to the veranda out front, sat her on the steps, Mr Eddy's old coat around her; the police were fetching dad, had radioed to have someone get him. Mum was at home; I stopped them going for her. I wanted dad to talk to her first and fetch the doctor for her. There was nothing for us to do but sit and wait.

Dot sat with us, white and shocked, holding Git's limp hand as she sat between us. Dot was so kind, just staying with us so we wouldn't be with strangers. I could see she was crying, but she didn't make a sound.

I felt a drifting lassitude creep over me: that irresistible fatigue again, only much, much more. I could have slept there on the step, I could have slid into unconsciousness if I hadn't had that hammering squeal chanting in my heart. The sky was black with thunderclouds, towering up like distant mountains, roiling, furious. Through the smudged inkyness, the sun kept breaking through in shafts of thick, molten gold as if it were struggling to free itself. I stared, transfixed. From the stand of twisted, wind-bent pines on the cliff near Lanterns, a dark mass of crows boiled up, dissolving into the obsidian clouds, black on black, their clanging, raucous calls echoing off the buildings and the dull, dead water of the sea.

I had just turned my head to look away for a moment, to will myself awake, when I heard Dot cry:

'Look, look there! It's 'er! She ain't upstairs, thank God! I'll go tell them police it's all right!'

Across the beach, caught in a fall of sunlight that streamed through a gap in the cloud, like a gilded mirage, unreal, like a fetch, all the heavy, yellow light drawn to her, bathing her in burnished red-gold, came Angel.

In the sombre storm dark, she seemed to burn, to blaze; she borrowed all the light around her and wove it into herself: unearthly, a glimmering dead man's lantern tied to the prow of a sinking ship. Fata Morgana. Walking fire.

Angel.

Looking puzzled, she waved at us.

I put my head down and wept.

Epilogue

Full fathom five thy father lies:
Of his bones are coral made:
Those are pearls that were his eyes:
Nothing of him that doth fade,
But doth suffer a sea-change
Into something rich and strange.

—William Shakespeare

Our lives were shattered, that's the only word that fits, for me. Shattered. Drop an old glass Christmas bauble on a stone floor and watch the shining pieces fly out. It only takes an instant and a family heirloom, one etched with happy memories, is destroyed irredeemably. That's how it was for us. Our old life was over, finished.

I don't remember much of the rest of that terrible day, or many days that followed. I know I heard Angel screaming shrilly and being restrained by the police from going into the café, then being taken to the hospital. 'Why? Why? Why did this 'appen to me? Con, Con – Oh God, oh God, why?' That's what she screamed. Fortunately, she didn't see what was in that room; if she had, she might have been silent like Gita and me.

Git was silent for a very long time. Curled in a foetal position on the sterile hospital bed, her thumb in her mouth, she was as silent as the grave. I sat by her for hours, days, watching the various doctors come and go, watching them shake their heads, watching the sweet little nurse who cleaned her up that first night try to hide her tears. I didn't cry myself, not after first seeing Angel crossing the beach. I felt too tired. Mostly that's what I felt, dead tired. I wanted to sleep for ever.

Cookie woke me up; she came every single day, talking about everyday things, nothing, just talking as if the terrible thing had never happened. She wouldn't give up. Day after day.

Then one afternoon, just as she was about to go, I cried. Once I did,

I couldn't stop. I cried and cried and cried while Cookie rubbed my back and hummed a tuneless lullaby. I cried until there was no salt in my body, all the sea in me gone. I cried for Con, for Git, for myself, for everyone.

After that, the mending had to start. Mum was very ill from it all, a relapse, and wanted to move away from Polwenna altogether. At first, we tried to dissuade her, thinking the move would be too much, but she was right. Though everyone in the village was lovely to us, really kind, we none of us could stay in that place. Dad sold the house, his practice, everything. It took a while, but he did it. Bought a house in a quaint little village near Exeter, convenient for the local hospital and for the group practice he went to. Lance stayed in Bodmin, an ex-Beast now, with Poppy, Kieran and little Brittany. We tried to contact Gwen, but it was hopeless. We left message after message at the Militia HQ, but she never got in touch. When it comes to it, you can't make someone come home if they don't want to, not in real life. Maybe in ten years or something. She'd like the new house, though, I know she would. It's got a very peaceful atmosphere and mum's happy there.

But in a way, for me personally at least, the most important thing that helped me recover was happening without me knowing it. Shortly before the move, I realised – or rather, Cookie realised – I was pregnant. More than five months gone. If she hadn't spotted it, I don't know what might have happened. You do read about women giving birth in the bath and God knows where else, because they hadn't realised they were pregnant. That could have been me, if not for Cookie's keen eyes. I'd had no idea I was carrying; God knows, under the circumstances some missed periods and mood swings were to be expected. I'd put that night with Luke – put Luke – away inside myself, deep inside myself, locked it up and thrown away the key along with all the other secrets, big and small. It hadn't been important anymore.

If I'd known earlier I could have had an abortion, I suppose. I do believe in a woman's right to choose and all that, but for me, it was way too late. I had a bout of furious claustrophobia about it, feeling trapped, hating it, wanting it not to be happening, but then I accepted it. Now I have my son, Matthew. My boy. I wanted a plain, simple, sturdy name for him, a name Con would have approved of. I know mum thinks it's dull, a boring name – I don't mind, he's Matty to me and his Auntie Cookie. Matty. Con would have loved him so much, doted on him. I love him more than I ever thought it was possible to love anybody, anything, ever. Sometimes I watch him sleeping after I've fed him and the whole world is centred in his perfect face and I cry, but from love this time. Pure love.

When he's grown, I'll tell him about his father. No secrets. Then if he wants to do something about it, it's his call. Until then, Luke won't hear of it from me. Matty's all mine; I think of him as the ocean's child, from that drowning night when the sea filled me. I always loved the sea, as much as I was frightened by it. Always. There's always that ambivalence, that attraction to its danger and the knowledge that it's greater than any puny human ever could be. It can hold you up, gentle as any loving mother while you float blissfully, or it can crush you out of existence in a second. Two sides of the same coin. Yes, Matty's the water's gift; my boy, he's all the beauty and wonder of the wild, dark blue ocean, the good things, the power, the ancient, untameable spirit, the flip side to my fears. He's my consolation. Silly maybe, but that's how I feel. I don't want to think about Luke, it unnerves me because sometimes if I do, I feel the old fantasies about him slipping back, sliding over the reality, softening it, erasing it. I have to fight against that.

Luke. Luke and Angel. He took her straight to a private clinic in London after they discharged her from the local hospital. His family took Angel in, made her one of their own and their lawyers dealt with everything for her. The specialist scene-of-crime cleaners and then the sale of the café, the will, the inquest, the funeral, everything. Cookie even had to ask Angel for Piglit via the law firm. Pigsie'd been found at Tim's house, tied up and starving; after taking him to the vet's he was put in an animal shelter. No one seemed to be interested in him or care what would become of him. So Cookie phoned the number we'd been given and after a while, the lawyers phoned back and said Ms Starbuck and her fiancé, Mr Scylur, planned to be travelling extensively for some time after their upcoming wedding, so a pet was out of the question. Also, Ms Starbuck felt the dog had too many painful memories for her so she was happy for Cookie to take him. They would pay any expenses he'd incurred, naturally. They thanked Cookie for drawing the matter to their attention.

Smoky was very happy.

Other things were found at Tim's, too. It all came out at the inquest and caused another flutter in the local press. In a bedroom they found the remains of Tim's mother, dead in her bed at least a fortnight; natural causes, he hadn't done it. She'd died and he'd sealed the room up and left her there. *Murderer Kept Body Of Dead Mum*, the papers said. Every possible wall space of the bungalow was covered in pictures of Angel, apparently. And there was a shrine-type thing with candles, mementoes of their outings, flowers, all arranged round a big framed portrait of Angel. I shuddered and my gorge rose when I heard about the photographs.

The inquest was a hard time for all of us, thinking of Con alone, fighting for her life, dying without a friend or a prayer. The police reckoned she must have gone down to the kitchen about midnight and opened the door – calling for Piglit one last time, probably – and Tim was there, coming for Angel. He must have pushed past her, shoved her out of the way and walked in, because the door wasn't damaged, like if he'd broken in. He didn't know Angel had decided to spend the night at Luke's. Then there was a struggle and…He'd tried to cut his wrists afterwards and failed, so he'd cut his neck open; severed the carotid artery. Bled out.

It sounded so cold, like that, the way the authorities say things; without emotion. I suppose they have to be like that, but for months my mind was filled with what must have happened; it all kept repeating and repeating like a horrible loop of film in my head. You see, I knew she wouldn't have been afraid when Tim pushed his way in, chuntering on about his darling, his precious girl. She'd have been livid, she'd have shouted at him to get out of her house, just *get out*. Con was fierce, she would have tried to shove him back outside, yelling at him, furious he'd dared to come into her home. She couldn't have known his mother had died and he was all alone in a world that despised and ridiculed him, that nothing earthly mattered to him anymore except his love, his obsession with Angel; that he was already dead inside his head, and only the deranged shell of himself was moving and breathing and he wanted his beloved to keep him company in Hell. Con's voice, the harsh voice of the 'bitch' who hated him, who wanted to keep him and his love apart, would have filled him with unbearable pain, that terrible shouting full of cruel words clanging like thunder in his aching head. He must have wanted her to shut up, shut up, shut up. The big razor-sharp Sabatier carving knife was on the counter next to the knife block and he picked it up and...Then there was nothing, except the slow, thick sound of blood dripping. Only silence and the overwhelming horror of what he'd done, and the passionate desire not to be living anymore.

People say to me they're amazed I don't hate him, that I can see it from his point of view. They seem to think if I don't hate him, I must have forgiven him. I nod, and don't speak; they think I'm agreeing with them. They're wrong. It is true I can see how he came to do it, put myself in his head because I've always done that, it's my curse. It makes my life so complicated: a thousand shades of grey, a million sides to every argument. But I can't help it, it's just how I am. It's also true I don't hate him. I don't hate anyone because to hate someone is as strong a bond as loving them and I don't want to be bound to anyone in hatred, in that deathly marriage. But forgive him? Forgive Tim Norris, mad as he was? Never, never, never. He murdered my dearest friend, *murdered* her. He hurt her, he hurt her and he took her away from me and nothing will ever be the same again. No air I breathe, no water I drink, no fire that burns to warm the winter night, no beautiful summer sunset, nothing; everything is different, everything is...I can't describe it, but it's like, there's nothing untainted by what he did.

But I don't say this, I just think it; I found out very quickly how uncomfortable the truth makes most people.

I'd wanted to talk to Angel, to somehow try and make contact with her, but the last time I saw her was at the funeral. There weren't many people at the ugly, grey concrete crematorium: a handful. Angel arrived in a sleek silver Audi with Luke. I hardly recognised him in his suit. He didn't speak to or look at me past the first polite nod; I had been successfully edited out. *She* looked as beautiful as ever, more so, even – or perhaps it was the shock of seeing her again. She was suitably pale, wearing big sunglasses, her hair longer and more golden, not so icy, not so funky, her black outfit understated and exquisite. She hugged me and said what a pal I'd been. How I must come up to London and see her, like we'd always planned. Her Bradford accent was noticeably less strong, more like Ilkley now. Fading every day, probably, I thought. Then she let a few tears fall gracefully from under her shades, dabbing at them with a wisp of black chiffon, and hugged me again. She smelled wonderful. The light from the modernistic stained-glass window shifted over her, staining her in jewel colours: sapphire, ruby, topaz. All the light going to her as ever in a lingering caress. Then she left, almost straightaway. There was no wake, no gathering afterwards. We had Con's ashes put under a nice silver birch in the grounds, marked with a small plaque on a stone; it had her name, dates and 'Beloved Friend, Rest In Peace'. The lawyers paid. I laid a white rose by it.

I didn't realise until hours later that Angel had never mentioned Con at the service. At first I was angry about her apparent lack of feeling but that passed. After all, I didn't know what she was like when she was alone, what she felt, how she mourned. She might have been devastated, privately. There's no point in judging Angel, none whatever. Like the sun or the storm, she just is. Moving on is her way of dealing with things; the past is the past, over, gone. She survives. It's a kind of strength, after all, and anyway, the truth is Con would have wanted her to survive more than anything, I know that. I just wonder: did Angel ever find out who her real birth mother had been? She'll never hear it from me, at any rate. A promise is a promise.

That was it, though; nothing more. I have no idea where she is, or with whom. Luke? Someone else? I never heard of her making a record like she'd planned, no 'Top of the Pops' appearance, no classy videos. I doubt if she needs to do that now. Is she in Monaco, Brazil or Timbuktu? I don't know. Maybe I'll never know. Wherever she is, you'll know her if you see her – all the light will have gone to her and you'll be watching her shimmer and glow from the shadows.

I still have the earrings she gave me, but I never wear them.

So, it's been over a year now, nearly two. I'm writing this in Bradford; it's autumn, the yellow leaves from the tree outside my window scudding away madly in the brisk wind, the skies iron grey in the northern cold. A faint tang of bonfires is filtering through from the garden and Matty is gurgling and playing with his feet in his cot beside me, gazing at the wooden painted fish mobile his Granny gave him. I came home to finish my degree at the Ridings, you see. I wasn't sure about doing it at first, but mum and dad insisted. They wanted me to have a life, as they put it. To move on. I didn't want to leave them, or Git, but they were determined. Fortunately, due to good care, Git's so much better, these days. She's putting some weight back on and she sleeps. My Gita – she's what I call a keychain kid now; all super-baggy low-slung jeans, studded wristbands, fat trainers, tight black T-shirts with skulls on them and masses of long keychains rattling as she bounces around to some howling New Metal band with her equally uniformed mates. No more baby-model glamour stuff for Git; I'm only sorry she cropped her lovely hair and dyed it green. I loved her hair. Still, it'll grow back, I suppose. Mine did all those years ago when I'd dyed it purple.

Yes, she's much better. But she won't talk about Con, or Angel. Won't mention their names. And if anyone does, she goes to her room and turns that music on as loud as she possibly can. I don't blame her. Not at all. She has that to distract her mind from it all and I have Matty.

I'm staying with Auntie Patsie and Uncle Kev again. It's nice to be with family and they adore my boy. I'm never in need of babysitters with them around. In fact, they've offered to care for him if I want to go travelling after I've finished uni. I know they'd like to adopt him, not that they ever say as much, but you can tell. Patsie is so happy looking after him; her whole being lights up and you can see the ache of her childlessness. I feel for her, I do, but I don't want to be without my sea-child, ever. Be a sister to my son? No. I'll go travelling and I'll take him with me. We'll go to all those places I read about, and more.

I'm pretty much OK now, really. Pretty much. I miss my lot, of course, and I miss Cookie. But we'll see each other again soon. I take it all a day at a time, I 'live in the Now' as dad says, bless him. I miss Polwenna, too; I thought it would be great to come home to Bradford and it's certainly a nicer place what with all the improvements and stuff. But it's not home, not like I'd thought it would be, like I'd always thought of it. I've been too long away. I don't really belong anymore. People say I've got a Cornish accent, but I can't hear it, and I know Cookie would hoot with laughter if I told her that. I can't go back to Polwenna, though, it's too full of ghosts: ghosts of the dead and the living – they swim under the surface, dimly, like great pale fish gliding through a green pond. I'd always see them, sense them.

I am OK, I am. Only, I still have that recurring sea-dream; and I have another one now, too.

I dream it's me in the boat, this time; leaning over the side, reaching out desperately. I strain every muscle, every fibre, and my voice is hoarse from shouting. I scream and rave, but it's just me in that wonky old blue row-boat, alone in a vast ocean, nothing else in view from horizon to horizon, the sun blazing like a great yellow wheel of fire in the cloudless sky. I'm becalmed, like the Ancient Mariner. I plunge my arms into the sea, the boat tilting dangerously, as I try to grasp the hand that's in the water, sinking fast away from me.

Con's hand. That work-reddened, knuckly hand, corded and long-fingered, the hand I know so well. And I see her, as she was, not as I saw her last, her hair fanning out like weed as she sinks through the water, her pale, oval face straining up to me as she dwindles down into the dark, cold depths, and I know, I know what's waiting for her, coiling and uncoiling, stirring from the uncharted deeps.

Down and down and down she goes, getting smaller and fainter as I frantically scream for help that I know can never come.

And I can't save her; I can't save her. And I love her so much, I miss her so much and I can't save her.

I watch her hand, the white palm gleaming, sink into the sea, into the dark, unfathomable Big Blue, the ocean so beautiful and so terrible; then she vanishes and I've lost her, I've lost her; my friend, I've lost my friend.

For ever.